I0631665

Suppression of Powers

Turn Six of the Hybrid Helix

JCM Berne

The Gnost House

Copyright © 2024 by JCM Berne All rights reserved.

The characters and events portrayed in this book are fictitious. Any similarity to real persons, living or dead, is coincidental and not intended by the author.

No portion of this book may be reproduced in any form without written permission from the publisher or author, except as permitted by U.S. copyright law.

No part of this book may be used or reproduced in any manner for the purpose of training artificial intelligence technologies or systems.

No part of this book has been produced with the assistance of any generative artificial intelligence technologies.

ISBN-13: 978-1-961805-06-4

Cover image and graphics by Jake Caleb

Acknowledgments:

I have more people to thank than I can easily count, starting with my wife, Moneeka, without whose support none of the rest of this would have happened.

My beta reading group: Jon, John (aka Kevin), Karl, and Vinay, who contributed immeasurably to early drafts.

My editor, Lauren Donovan of The Book Foundry, who (gently) pushed me to make changes that really needed to be made. My cover artist J Caleb who jumped in to help me out when I needed a cover sooner than my regular artist could manage it.

Jordan, Andrew (The Wizard), Craig, Boe, A.R., Kayla, Usman, Chris, HC, Esmay, Lezlie, and Sam, who brought me the thing I couldn't bring myself: more readers.

My sensitivity reader, acquired much too late in the process (entirely my fault, not his), Sridhar. Mistakes in early editions of previous books are not his fault.

My web and marketing guru, Marc Greenwald.

My online teachers: Brandon Sanderson, the cast of Writing Excuses, and Mur Lafferty, all of whom were there for me and asked for nothing in return (at least in part because they have no idea who I am).

The rest of my Twitter and Discord communities, who brought me so much encouragement and support.

Contents

Previously, In Arc One of The Hybrid Helix: Platinum

After ten years of committing atrocities for the il'Drach Empire, Rohan earned his freedom by ending the Hybrid Rebellion and retired to live as a tow chief on the sentient space station Wistful in Toth system.

He later:

Uncovered the secret behind what triggers the kaiju populating Toth 3 (anger).

Dated, lost, and reconnected with a space shuttle technician named Tamara, in the process gaining the enmity of her annoying ex-husband Lahnegarn and her father, the richest and most powerful man on Lukhor.

Returned to Earth to save it from giant sharks.

Defeated an ancient vampire and became the leader of the warrior class of the il'Sein, the original humanoid species (who have long since left the sector).

Rescued a man stitched together from people's memories of Hyperion, Earth's greatest hero, from a two-legged cephalopod supervillain, Dr. Kraken. Later (new) Hyperion declared war on the il'Drach and became Rohan's enemy (mostly by causing the deaths of a billion people on the planet Ohn).

Doomed, then saved, the il'Zkin, a species of feline humanoids of great Power, one of whom, Katya, has decided to be Rohan's bodyguard.

Found a home for Repentant, an ancient and unstable space station, and his son *Vyrhicant*, a baby warship.

In the process, Rohan has come to terms with the fact that if he's ever going to have a quiet, peaceful life, he's going to have to make some changes to the world around him.

He has inherited a magical technique from Spiral, his human martial arts instructor: a springlike helix made of esoteric (magical) Power that can absorb and return kinetic energy. Unfortunately, it doesn't work when he's angry, and when he's fighting his greatest enemies . . . that's often how he feels.

He has made a deal with the Assessors, the il'Drach who decide whether planets pose a danger to the sector: they will make him an Assessor; he will have the chance to save entire worlds from destruction, to change the Empire's callous approach to exterminating entire populations.

The price:

He has to kill Hyperion.

Rohan isn't strong enough to do that, unless he can master Spiral's technique and use Hyperion's strength against him.

Six months after that agreement was made . . .

1

Definitely Not a Terra-saur

Rohan blinked stinging tears of sweat out of his eyes as the bulky pterosaur leaned forward, the tip of its long, pointed snout just a meter from the Hybrid's face.

He swallowed and met the creature's predatory gaze. "Steady, boy. No eating your friendly neighborhood Hybrid. I might look tasty, but I'm sure my meat would be tough and gristly. Then again, I don't know what you normally eat. Maybe I'm a juicy morsel compared to that." He swallowed again. "I wish I hadn't said that."

The creature, tiny for a kaiju yet enormous and terrifying by any other standard, exhaled forcefully, filling the air with the smell of rotting meat and the bitter citrus of his acidic saliva.

Rohan inhaled carefully, willing his heart rate to slow, and took a tentative step to the side, his eyes remaining locked on the pterosaur's.

The kaiju's head swiveled, pinned to his movement.

"That's a good boy, Terry. Good boy. You stay put while your buddy Rohan circles around and answers that call coming over the comm. Okay, Terry?"

The comm pinged again, a high-pitched bell easy to make out over the background chirps of small insects.

The Hybrid flanked the pterosaur and was about to dash for his helmet when the creature sidestepped and blocked his path, leaning his head forward to butt at Rohan's chest.

The impact, equivalent to being hit square by a sledgehammer swung by a very large and very strong man, knocked him back several steps; he caught his balance and rubbed his chest, then waited for the pterosaur to charge. Or bite.

"Terry, cut it out!"

The reptile loomed over him; twice Rohan's height, with a ten-meter wingspan, he was built along the rough lines of a pterodactyl from Earth, if one had access to a bodybuilding gym, unlimited protein supplements, and a comprehensive suite of anabolic drugs.

And a mouth full of very sharp teeth.

I thought pterosaurs didn't have teeth. Then again, pterosaurs weren't three hundred kilograms, were they?

Terry opened his mouth and screeched, a roar loud enough to peel the paint off a shuttle, if any had been nearby.

Rohan's shoulders tightened. He had studied the kaiju's calls; this roar didn't contain the subsonic tones he used to call his kin, but it was still loud enough to leave a soft ringing in his ears.

Terry dropped his snout toward the Hybrid, who rolled away at the last moment. "Cut it out!"

Rohan spun onto his feet, brushing dirt from his shoulder.

I wish I could fly around this guy. I miss flying.

Toth's rays shone down on the meadow, heating it in an unpleasant contrast to Wistful's well-regulated atmospheric conditioning. The air smelled of the jungle: perfumes and pollen from ten thousand species of plant, fungus, and insect, all densely packed in, every remaining molecule of space taken up by the kind of stifling humidity more appropriate to gills than lungs.

"Steady, boy. Let me get to the comm."

The pterosaur huffed, blowing out air in an expression somewhere between a grunt and a laugh.

Can he laugh? I knew the kaiju were smart . . . do they have humor?

Rohan stepped to his right, waiting for the beast to step to intercept, then shifted to his left like a running back cutting to avoid a tackle.

The kaiju dug one massive fist into the ground, digging up a fat clump of dirt, and chased after him.

The Hybrid ran, careful to clear the ropes laid out close to the ground.

He'd placed them himself, sectioning the meadow off into labeled areas about three meters on a side, so he could easily record where he'd found any artifacts revealed while digging into the soft, mossy growth that covered the meadow.

He stepped over another rope when the pterosaur butted him again, on the shoulder this time, sending him sprawling through the site.

His leg swung out to catch him, and his foot slid through the moss, out to the side, over the lip of a meter-deep hole with square sides; freshly dug.

The Hybrid fell in, a hot breeze wafting over his back as the pterosaur sailed through the space he'd just vacated.

He landed on the bottom of the three-meter-square pit, grunting at the impact with the smooth metal he'd exposed just a few days before. Metal that had been buried under a layer of dirt and vegetation for four or five hundred centuries.

Rohan's jaw pressed against the metal, his cheek inside a fist-sized indent. He eyed the dial in its center, rimmed with hieroglyph-like characters, symbols of an unknown language.

He thought briefly about the five other indents, spaced a dozen centimeters apart.

Terry slid through the moss on the other side and spun to face the Hybrid.

Rohan felt a glimmer of fear as Terry let out a little roar; the creature's aura pressed down on the clearing, a torrent of Power that rivaled a Matron's.

If he were a different species, or had different training, that fear might have grown into a paralyzing terror. Instead, the Hybrid felt a burst of irritation, a little spark at the back of his mind, or perhaps his soul; a glimmer of defiance.

His curse, answering the call.

The esoteric construct he maintained, a twisted rod of spiritual energy with one end anchored to his right palm and the other to the base of his spine, flexed and shimmered.

Don't get angry.

Breathe. Let it go.

I must not fear. Fear is the mind-killer. Fear is the little-death that brings—Wait, isn't the little death a French term for orgasm? Is that what Frank Herbert was talking about? That makes no sense.

I am not good at this.

In my defense, it's hard not to be a little bit afraid when the creature attacking you could eat you in one bite and still have room in his mouth for dessert.

Rohan tried to roll to his feet but hit a crate of tools, knocking it over and scattering folding shovels, pails, brushes, and assorted other gardening equipment across the bottom of the hole.

Breathe. Don't get annoyed.

Get angry now and you lose the construct. Lose the construct and you've failed, and all of this work will have been for nothing.

Oh, don't think that last bit. That doesn't help.

The helmet pinged again, a touch louder, indicating the urgency of the call.

Rohan leapt clear of the pit.

Terry hopped over, somewhat awkward on the ground, the long last finger on each hand folded back against his arms, keeping the majority of each wing out of his way.

The pterosaur eyed the Hybrid with flat reptilian eyes and screeched again.

"Too loud, Terry! You're going to get me in trouble. Remember the first rule of digging on Toth: don't wake the decipedes."

Terry screeched again and leaned forward to butt at Rohan.

He rolled to the side, avoiding the strike, and scrambled back to his feet. *How many more times is that move going to work?*

Quick guess: not many.

His arm ached when he pushed against the ground, courtesy of the kaiju's earlier shove. The impact was sure to leave a horrific bruise. *I really hope he didn't break anything.*

"Gentle touch, Terry! Gentle touch!"

The monster tilted his head back and shrieked into the sky.

Rohan ran toward his helmet, tantalizingly close but still out of reach, but had to swerve to the side to avoid a swipe from one powerful reptilian arm.

He's not letting me answer the helmet.

I think he's playing with me.

He looked back at the kaiju, who shuffled to a spot directly between him and the helmet.

He is definitely playing with me.

Rohan exhaled, noting the soft butterflies in his stomach, a primal fear reaction to the menace of the kaiju in front of him.

He willed them away.

"You want to play? You want to play with *me*? You better watch out, Terry, or you're going to get what you want. You think you'll be happy after that?"

The kaiju glared at him and bobbed his head up and down.

Is he nodding? He can't be nodding.

"You think you can handle this? Do you have any idea what kind of person you're messing with?"

Terry leaned forward, extending his nose to butt Rohan in the chest again.

He's using his nose like a fist. Thrusting it at me like a man throwing a right straight.

The Hybrid grunted and ducked in for a takedown, stepping close to the pterosaur's body. He exhaled as he reached one hand up for the creature's throat, placing the other on a shoulder to stifle any attempts to swat him away.

He planted his feet and dug his fingertips into the soft leather of the animal's throat.

"Is that what you want? Is it?"

He scratched the pterosaur's skin, drawing lines from a collarbone as thick as his fist up to the base of the monster's jawline.

Terry froze and let out one long, shaky breath. Then he lifted his chin toward the sky and dropped to his knees, a heavy chest rumble vibrating through both of them.

"Is that what you wanted? You came here for scritches? What the hell kind of people-devouring monster are you, Terry?"

Terry leaned in, nearly knocking Rohan to the ground, and huffed as the Hybrid scratched up and down his neck.

"Terry, I have things to do. I can't spend all day rubbing your neck. Besides, what if the other kaiju see this? Won't they tease you? You don't want that, do you?"

The kaiju scooted his legs forward, ahead of his body, and planted his rear end in the moss-covered dirt. He lowered his chin, batting Rohan's arm toward his belly, and flopped onto his back.

Rohan sighed. "You're not going to let me get that call, are you? Fine." He ran his fingers down the creature's neck, over his chest, and onto his belly.

With both hands, the Hybrid scratched the softer flesh below the pterosaur's lowest ribs, shaking his head as the creature spread out, both arms outstretched, legs up in the air.

The kaiju's tail swished back and forth, flattening a three-meter arc of ground, scattering the dig tools far and wide with each stroke.

"You're making a huge mess, Terry. Why are you here bothering me? Isn't there anyone else you can go to for a belly rub? Anybody?"

He knew there weren't any other humanoids on the planet: Toth 3 was infested by monsters of all sizes that reacted to any feelings of anger or a desire to fight; there weren't any sentient species that could restrain those feelings well enough to risk spending any amount of time on the surface.

He could, but only because he'd been practicing.

A lot.

He continued scratching, pushing hard to dig his nails into Terry's skin but not coming close to breaking it.

The kaiju was tough.

The pings from the helmet stopped as Terry's tail continued to swish back and forth, its frequency slowing as he grew satisfied by the belly scratches.

"You had about enough, Terry? Is that good, boy? Can daddy answer his call now, or are you going to be a pain in my ass and knock me down again when I try?"

Terry flopped his head back and to the side, showing Rohan one flat eye closing in satisfaction.

The Hybrid gave one last set of double scratches and lifted his hands away. The kaiju wiggled, squirming his back into the ground, but didn't stand. His taloned feet dug ruts half a meter deep into the dirt.

Rohan pushed himself fully upright and walked around the spread-out form of the pterosaur. "Stay there, boy. I'll give you more scritches later. I really do need to take this call."

He stopped at the edge of the pit; looked down.

It had been two days since Rohan realized the discs turned. Were, to all appearances, like the dials on a stereo.

Or a vault.

He glanced over his shoulder at Terry, who rolled from shoulder to shoulder but stayed mostly prone. Then the Hybrid stepped around the excavated door and bent over to grab his helmet.

He looked into the facemask from the back without putting it on, tapping through the communication interface to see if his caller had left a message.

She hadn't.

He placed a return call; a familiar voice answered it almost as soon as it started to ring.

"Rohan."

He grunted. "Wei Li. Sorry I missed you, I was wrestling a kaiju. Business or pleasure?"

"You are well aware the call tone I used indicates a communication of some urgency, rendering your question moot, so I will assume that was a failed attempt on your part to provide an amusing conversation opener."

"Wow. It's like you're an empath or something, the way you can read my intentions like that."

Her snort was audible over the line, not quite a laugh but as close as he was likely to get from her in that situation. "I am short on time, Rohan." Sounds of activity were audible in the background: boots scraping along the ground, the rustling of clothes, an occasional heavy breath as if someone ran close by Wei Li's comm unit.

"Sorry, force of habit. Why the call, Wei Li?"

I can think of a dozen different possible emergencies that could be happening right now. Ironically, I came to Toth system to avoid that sort of thing.

"You wanted to know if we uncovered a central location for Boost dealers on the station. We have. I do not see the point in telling you this information, but I promised I would, and I am in the habit of keeping my promises."

He paused and thought.

"From the sounds in the background, you're planning to do something about it. Is that right?"

"Yes, Rohan. I am in the process of preparing to raid the warehouse."

"I'm confused. I thought Wistful didn't want you taking action against the Boost dealers, yet here you are talking about it on an open comm like it's fine."

Her voice came back softer, almost a whisper. "A group of Ohnian youth attempted to purchase a supply of the drug. I am not permitted to stop drug trafficking, but it is within my purview to make arrests on charges of corrupting a minor."

Rohan looked around the site, cataloging things he'd need to bring with him if he left in a hurry. Which he was strongly considering.

"How did you know about these Ohnians, Wei Li?"

"I might have been following them closely from the moment they boarded the station, having intercepted private communications indicating they would be trying to buy Boost on Wistful. Perhaps."

"You're adorable when you skirt the rules, Wei Li. You know that, don't you?"

"If you wish to sing the praises of my physical beauty, you will have to join the queue. Now, you have been informed, so I will go back to my preparations. Unless you want something further from me."

Terry shook, flinging bits of sand and clumps of moss around the meadow, then rolled to his feet, eyes seeking out the Hybrid.

"You're asking me if I want to come on the raid."

"Do you? Or do you wish to continue hiding on Toth 3?"

A fresh shower of irritation gathered in the back of his spine. "I'm not hiding, Wei Li. I'm training. To master an extremely complicated technique."

"Of course you are, Rohan. And it makes perfect sense that you are doing so. To practice somewhere with an abundance of skilled sparring partners, wise masters to guide your progress, and the most advanced training equipment available to facilitate."

"You're mocking me."

"I am. Because exactly none of those things are available on the planet, Rohan, yet that is where you have been spending your time. Perhaps 'hiding' was too aggressive an accusation."

He grunted.

Have I been hiding here? Have I been lying to myself?

Maybe I should go back to Wistful. If I really want to make this technique work, I have to test it in combat conditions.

Playing with Terry doesn't count. I can't get remotely serious with him or I'll become dino-food.

Rohan tightened his lips and made a decision. "I want in. Can you wait for me to come up there and join the raid?"

Wei Li paused. "I can, but are you sure that's wise, Rohan? Given your . . . situation?"

He grunted. "I'm not so incapacitated I can't take on some Boost dealers. They're not Hybrids, are they? Just your run-of-the-mill losers, right?"

"I would anticipate one or more of them being users of the drug, Rohan. Temporary as its effects may be, that makes them Powers. Minor Powers, but still."

"You think I can't handle myself?"

"My thoughts are irrelevant. What are yours?"

He grunted again. "I said I'm in. Will you wait for me?"

"I will wait, but do not tarry. The dealers will eventually realize they've been caught and vacate their location."

"I'll hurry. Thanks. Rohan out."

Terry straightened to his full height, putting his eyes almost three meters off the ground, and watched Rohan.

"Sorry, buddy. Daddy's got some work to do. I'll come back, okay? You go hunting or something. You're not eating enough."

The pterosaur screeched at him, his head bobbing up and down.

Rohan tapped at his helmet and opened a fresh channel. "*Void's Shadow*, you around?"

Terry approached him, less aggressively this time, and Rohan rewarded the reptile by scratching his neck with one hand while he waited for his ship's response.

The tiny kaiju had become a fixture in the camp over the previous week. Rohan wasn't sure how to get rid of him.

Toth lowered a couple of degrees in the sky while Rohan waited.

"Yes, Captain? You called?"

"Can you give me a lift to Wistful? Something's going on, and I need to be up there."

"I'll be right there, Captain."

"Sending coordinates now. Same place you dropped me off." The dig site was next to the area where Ben Stone's graduate assistants had landed to explore the planet's surface, two and a half years earlier.

Rohan scratched his beard, thinking about how quickly the time had passed.

I'd have made better progress on this dig if I had some help. But if I did, Terry would occasionally turn them into snacks. Hard to keep good help when that happens.

He shaded his eyes from the sun with one raised hand and waited for his ship to arrive.

2

Sometimes the Ram Batters You

Void's Shadow approached one of the small airlocks that dotted Wistful's long arms and extended an airtight umbilical tube. The tube struck the docking ring with a soft clang and locked into place.

In honor of Rohan's status as an officer-on-leave in Wistful's crew, she had granted permission for the ship to come close without a tow and to bypass the normal docks on the station's lower levels.

Rohan suspected that the station was really trying to save herself the effort required to catch his ship breaking normal protocols; *Void's Shadow* had the most advanced stealth technology in the sector and prided herself on her ability to sneak up on almost anything without being noticed.

"Captain, is your helmet sealed? Maybe you should put on a space suit, too? I have spares in the locker just aft of my anchor point. They're not exactly fashionable, but they're one size fits all, and they're up to Imperial safety standards."

He sighed. "The tube is pressurized, you know. So is the airlock. Why exactly do you think I need a helmet, let alone a full suit?"

"Come on, Captain. Accidents happen. I'd hate to see you explosively decompress. Or even decompress in a relaxed, nonexplosive way."

"I'm not that delicate, *Void's Shadow*. I'll be fine. Just open the lock and let me through."

"Yes, Captain." A soft whir accompanied the opening of the door.

Rohan rubbed his head, fingers still grabbing at the unfamiliar buzz of his close-cropped hair.

I thought I'd be used to having it short by now. I spent a decade with a crew cut, after all. But every time I touch my head, it's a little bit of a shock.

He held the rim of the airlock and pulled himself through, sliding through the narrow umbilical tube and into the person-sized chamber on the other side.

Three minutes later, the Hybrid mixed with Wistful's late-afternoon crowd of pedestrians: students heading home from school; businesspeople hurrying to work from a late lunch or an illicit afternoon rendezvous; tourists trying to find their hotels, distracted by the spectacular view of Toth 3, the green planet looming directly overhead, always visible through the single-facet diamond roof protecting the promenade from the cold harshness of space.

He bought a paper-wrapped block of sticky rice, heavily seasoned and laced with dried and minced meat, and bit into it as he walked.

The Hybrid avoided eye contact with passersby, but every so often someone would twitch as they passed and lift a hand as if to say hello, then turn away in confusion.

Ben and Marion told me I'd need to start wearing a mask if I wanted to remain anonymous. Or glasses. I told them nobody would recognize me if I cut my hair and stayed out of uniform. Looks like I was right. Mostly.

The crowd thinned quickly as he walked; he was headed toward an underpopulated section of station. The grassy walkway fifty meters across that separated two lines of ten-story structures was mowed but still wilder than elsewhere in the station; fewer benches and structures marred the surface, no gazebos or sectioned-off areas for sports or other activities.

Rohan approached an unmarked doorway and pulled his mask out of his hood, checking the directions Wei Li had sent him.

He was in the right place.

He opened the doorway and walked under weak yellow lights, past traces of trash and grime, down a hallway painted with tags and graffiti he couldn't make sense of.

A left, then a right, then another left and he heard evidence of activity ahead.

"Brother Rohan!"

Five hundred kilograms of warm, brown-furred bear bore down on the Hybrid, one eye full of humor, the other a shining red cybernetic light.

"Ang! Gentle, please!"

The Ursan ignored him and wrapped heavy arms around the Hybrid, lifting him off the ground in a massive hug.

I could say it's a bear hug.

"Brother Rohan, have been for missing you! Welcome back!"

The Ursan wore a Wistful security uniform: golden yellow with metallic purple accents, more of a vest than the jumpsuit-style most humanoids wore.

Rohan patted his friend's shoulder. "Put me down, Ang! Come on, I'm not a child."

Ang lowered the Hybrid to the floor gently. "You not for being a cub, Rohan. Cubs are for being cute and huggable. Still, was missing you."

"I missed you too, buddy. Is Katya around?" The il'Zkin, ostensibly Rohan's bodyguard after he'd saved her brother's life, hadn't been able to follow him to Toth 3's surface without inciting violence among the kaiju.

Ang's mouth hung open. "Why asking Ang this question, Rohan? For certainty others would be for knowing more than Ang."

Rohan laughed. The two had been inseparable for months. "Whatever you say, buddy. At least tell me if Wei Li got her involved in this raid."

Ang scratched the side of his furry head. "Hm. Maybe. Not remembering exactly. Perhaps if paying attention better . . ."

"Ang, you're a terrible liar. You and I both know you can smell her if she's within five hundred meters of this spot."

Ang's eyes widened, and he nodded furiously. "Yes, yes! Katya in the next room, Rohan, with Wei Li. Have been forgetting."

Rohan laughed and walked around the corner.

Wei Li stood in the center of an unfurnished apartment crowded with people and quietly addressed a group of uniformed security. Katya sat among them, her feline head and civilian clothes standing out.

Rohan waved and caught Wei Li's attention; she waved him over. Ang stepped in behind him, the heat from his massive body instantly warming the room.

"What's the plan?"

She sighed as Katya stepped between them and hugged the Hybrid. "Rohan! Ang has been very sad and missing you. And I had almost forgotten how ugly you are."

Rohan smiled. "Sorry for the reminder." He faced Wei Li. "When are you going in?"

Wei Li glanced at the tablet in her hand. "I'd like to move quickly, before they realize they've been found."

Rohan looked at her, then at the other security officers present. "I hear a 'but.' What's the 'but,' Wei Li?"

She pointed at one wall of the apartment. "The apartment next door is empty; the targets are in the following. I didn't realize before we got here, but five of them are regular users."

"Five?"

She nodded. "That is what I said."

Katya tugged at Rohan's arm. "There are five of what you call Powers! And we can fight them, for that is what the laws of this place say! I am very excited, Rohan, to fight five new people!"

He looked at Wei Li, noting the concern tightening the yellow skin at the corners of her eyes. The lines of red and green scales that marked her scalp bent slightly with the tension. "I'm sure we all appreciate your enthusiasm, Katya, but I'm not sure you should fight them all by yourself."

Ang huffed as he pushed his hands into a pair of battle gauntlets: metal vambraces reaching from claw to elbow, each trailing a set of heavy spiked chains.

"She is not for being by herself, Rohan."

Rohan rubbed his chest, remembering the wounds those chains had caused him when he'd first met the Ursan. "No, of course not. I didn't mean that. Not exactly."

Wei Li shook her head. "The five Powers are minor. Between Katya, the two Ursan officers, and myself, we are nearly a match for them. Nearly."

Rohan coughed. "I didn't hear my name on that list."

"No, you did not. Should you have? Are you able to fight?"

He rubbed his jaw; the rod of esoteric energy he held anchored to his palms and tailbone shook as his feelings stirred. "I can fight. I wouldn't want to face a clutch of Hybrids, but I can take out these drugged-up jokers."

She cocked her head, studying him with vertically slit pupils. "You are speaking with more confidence than you feel."

"Fake it 'til you make it. Isn't that what you're always telling me?"

"No. No, it is not."

I keep forgetting that faking it in front of an empath is basically useless.

Katya patted his shoulder. "I like this saying! It is very clever. I will say it to others on your behalf, Rohan. Can we fight now? I want to fight the new people."

Rohan looked at the floor. "Should we call in Wildeye?"

Wei Li shook her head, her eyes hardening. "She is working. It will antagonize Wistful to pull Wildeye away from her tow chief responsibilities. No, we can do this ourselves." She straightened her posture and projected her voice to fill the room. "Everybody not on the assault team, cover the exits. You know what to do: take positions on the floor above and below as well. Stay safe; Wistful doesn't want any casualties." The team responded with grunts and nods, then dispersed so rapidly Rohan blinked in disbelief.

Wei Li turned to him. "Last chance to back out."

"No. I'm doing this. I need this, Wei Li."

She nodded, a flash of satisfaction in her eyes. "Finally. That last bit was genuine. And truthful. Come on."

Rohan cracked his neck and followed his friend around the corner and into the neighboring apartment.

Ang and a second uniformed Ursan primed some explosive charges stuck to the wall and faced away from the blank metal, waiting for Wei Li's cue.

She gave it.

Ang tapped a control in his hand, and the wall evaporated in a bang of displaced air and shredding metal. Katya was gone before the sound died down, little lines scored in the floor where her claws scraped the metal clean in her haste to engage with the enemy.

The two Ursans followed, Ang bellowing a war cry as he spun his fists in the air, building momentum in the swinging chains.

Wei Li trailed them, Rohan bringing up the rear.

Feels weird: I'm used to being the first one in.

Guess the short hair isn't all I'm having trouble adjusting to.

He hurried after the security chief.

⊷ ⋯•⋯ ⊶

The dealer's lair resembled a gang den from a cheaply made martial arts movie. Cushions and repurposed couches, so filthy Rohan feared them more than the dealers themselves, were strewn about the space. Used food and alcohol containers stood in low piles against every vertical surface, as if propping up the walls.

The dealers themselves were reptilian, with pebbly orange scales broken up by dark-blue highlights. They had serpentine heads, hairless and triangular, and tasted the air with long, forked tongues as they moved.

Hm. Snake heads but humanoid bodies. No tail. Have I seen this species before?

The Hybrid nearly tripped over one of the dealers, stretched out across the entryway in a rapidly spreading pool of his own blood. The Ursans had another backed up against a far corner of the room; the man's limbs were tangled in Ang's chains while the other Ursan swung a short, heavy club into the reptile's head.

The dealer should have been crushed immediately, but he was blocking the club blows and matching Ang pull-for-pull, despite having at most one-fifth the mass of either Ursan.

Powers for sure.

Katya was a whirl of limbs and claws, her speed as impressive as ever as she fought the biggest dealer, a towering female with lines of scar tissue marring her face and head.

Surprisingly, she was holding her own against the cat-woman; blood leaked from Katya's mouth and chin.

Two of the dealers had yet to engage: a male and a female, dressed in more upscale clothing than the others. They backed away from the invading force, heading for a door in the opposite side of the apartment.

Wei Li motioned Rohan forward as she chased the pair. "We need those two."

Rohan grunted and followed Wei Li as she carved a path between the ongoing battles.

He sidestepped a wide swing from the big female fighting Katya, shuddering as the air whistled with the force of the blow.

The magical construct inside him shook, destabilizing slightly but holding.

Keep it together, Rohan. This is what you've been training for. It's all a waste if you can't maintain the spiral under stress.

I need a better name for this technique.

Spring of Reflection?

Something crunched in the other Ursan as the dealer landed a solid punch to his chest; Ang growled and leaned in, smothering the reptile with his mass and grinding the blades and hooks covering his gauntlets into its scales.

The two leaders disappeared through the doorway, Wei Li hot on their heels. Katya growled and attacked with a fresh frenzy, undisciplined and wild.

I should teach her how to actually fight, instead of just letting her get by on physical ability.

The il'Zkin swept her opponent's feet out from under her, sending her crashing to the ground with a room-shaking thud. The snake-headed female continued the motion, coming back to her feet, eyes narrow with caution as she faced the cat-woman.

Then again, raw physical ability is working pretty well for her.

He turned and followed Wei Li.

Shelves lined two walls of the next, smaller, room. Crates covered the shelves, clean and dust-free.

He pointed. "I bet that's the Boost supply."

Wei Li nodded and faced the two reptiles. "You are charged with corrupting a minor, selling Boost to underage buyers. Surrender and we can talk about ways to reduce your punishment."

The male sneered. "Surrender? I was about to say the same to you. You're outmatched."

The female's eyes pivoted to him. "You want them to surrender? What would we do with them? Do we have a jail cell set up somewhere? Idiot."

The male sighed. "Why do you always undermine me like that? All the time. I'm just saying, they're the ones in trouble, not us. They're not going to actually surrender. You're not really surrendering, are you?" He looked plaintively at Wei Li.

"We are not. However, I am willing to be lenient with you if you provide details regarding the identity and location of your supplier."

The man snorted. "That's not going to happen." He turned to the female. "Right, honey? It's not. Or are you going to disagree with me on that, too?"

She shook her head. "I don't disagree with everything you say, Reghis. Stop exaggerating everything. You just can't handle a female who's willing to tell you when you're wrong."

"That's not true! Oh, I'll grow a tail before I get you to treat me with the respect I deserve."

"If you had a tail, you might deserve some of my respect, Reghis. Let's take care of these two, then go help out Sirc. She seemed to have her jaws full."

Reghis cracked his knuckles. "Fine. Maybe a good fight will get you to finally relax. You've been tense all week."

The pair's auras intensified as they built up esoteric energy, their Power pushing at the walls, shaking the shelves hard enough to rattle the box lids.

Rohan swallowed. "Wei Li . . ."

"I told you they are Powers." She stepped forward in a combat stance: left foot forward, right fist covering her jaw, left fist by her navel.

Rohan took up a position to her right as she advanced.

The male rushed in first; he was fast, explosive like a striking snake.

Rohan remembered something about reptilians having better ability to move in intense bursts, but less endurance than mammals.

The way the dealers struck reinforced that belief.

Wei Li stepped back and pivoted away from the male's charge, flicking a jab into his face to slow him down.

The man's partner circled around and snapped a quick kick into Wei Li's side, launching her across the room.

I can't believe she didn't sense that coming. What's wrong with her?

The security chief landed in a heap, her limp body rolling until her back hit the far wall.

Rohan stepped between the pair and his friend, throwing a jab-cross combination that forced the male reptile to back up.

Need to keep them from going after Wei Li. I don't like the way she fell.

"What species are you, anyway?"

The male shrugged. "We're Takslee. You've never dealt with us before, have you, Hybrid? The speed of the Takslee is legendary."

Rohan grunted with relief as he saw Wei Li move, rolling to her side, then struggle to stand. "If you know I'm a Hybrid, then you know that speed won't be enough. You should really be taking Wei Li up on that offer of a surrender. The only reason you're still breathing is because I haven't really gotten angry yet."

The female laughed. "Oh, that's good. You're trying to bluff us. Not that I blame you."

"Bluff? What are you talking about?"

Reghis darted in, tossing a punch that the Hybrid barely slipped. Rohan made him pay by digging a short uppercut into the man's ribs.

A punch that seemed to have no effect.

The female continued. "We're not stupid. We follow Con-Conspiracy, watch all their vids. You don't have your Powers anymore. Look at you, it's so obvious. The real you would have come in here by yourself and taken us all out without breathing hard."

The male looked back at her. "That's not fair. I'm really strong. Even with his Powers, I could have given the Hybrid a chase for his eggs."

She shook her head. "Are you stupid, Reghis? No, don't answer that, I know already. The answer is yes and you absolutely would have stood no chance against any Hybrid with Powers, not even if you snorted every gram of Boost in this room. I swear, you're using too much of the product. It's getting to your head."

Rohan skipped forward and threw a kick into Reghis's knee, which the reptile avoided by pulling his leg back.

The male retaliated, using the same leg to kick Rohan in the chest.

The Hybrid caught it on his right palm.

The male looked confused for a moment; he followed up with another kick toward Rohan's head.

The Hybrid absorbed the impact from that one, too, using the same hand. The magical structure in his soul absorbed the energy like a compressing spring.

It's working. Don't lose it.

"Still think I lost my Powers? How is that even possible?"

The female smirked. "It's all over the net now, Hybrid. Hyperion released the footage of your fight. The mainstream doesn't want to believe it, but it's obvious to the analysts at Con-Conspiracy what happened.

"There's no way he could have beaten you like that if you still had Powers.

"You've been neutered."

"Neutered?" *What is she talking about?*

"I mean metaphorically. Why do you think we were willing to sell Boost here?

"Nobody's afraid of you anymore."

3

Who Said What Now?

Rohan's heart jumped a bit in his chest, filling him with a fluttery, hollow feeling.

"What are you talking about?" *I'm repeating myself. I should stop doing that.*

A thud reverberated through the floor, followed by Katya's voice from the other room. "I am almost finished with this one! Please remind me, are these aurochs or il'Zkin? I would very much like to eat this one when I am done."

A sibilant shout echoed after her. "I have five thousand credits that say you're not going to be the one doing the eating, mammal!"

Rohan cleared his throat. "Do not eat the Takslees, Katya. We don't eat sentient people. Remember the rule!"

A huff and another thud, then more growls from Ang.

"If they talk, I may eat them? Is that the rule, Rohan?"

A hiss of pain from the big Takslee fighting Katya.

"No, Katya. It's like the aurochs. If they talk, you most definitely may not eat them." He kept his hands up in a defensive posture and glanced over at Wei Li, who stood on shaky legs, her eyes pinched in pain.

The female Takslee tapped the male on the shoulder. "Finish them."

The male grunted and charged Rohan.

The Hybrid held his ground as the male reached back and swung a huge punch at his head.

Rohan absorbed it with his right palm.

The male's face twisted in confusion. He stepped back and repeated the motion, putting his entire body behind the punch.

Rohan caught it, the punch stopping dead against his hand, not moving him back even a centimeter.

The female coughed. "Stop playing with him, Reghis. We have to get out of here before more security comes."

"I'm trying, Keilee. He's blocking my punches."

Her laugh was more sardonic than humorous. "You're joking, right? He's not even a Power anymore. Hit him harder and he'll go away. Look what I did to the chief with one kick!"

"It's not . . . never mind." He reset his stance, glared at Rohan, and swung again.

Wei Li's eyes widened as she saw Rohan catch the punch.

The spring inside Rohan compressed further, storing more energy. *Almost ready.*

Katya's voice carried into the room. "Ang, I am coming! Hold him there, I'll finish him off. But Rohan said no eating."

Ang roared three times, Ursan laughter, like a bark, interrupted only by the hiccups of blows landing on his thick body.

Wei Li stepped toward Rohan and his opponent, but stumbled as her leg gave way, catching herself on the back of a lone piece of a sectional sofa.

Rohan shook his head. "You guys aren't going to win this one. Surrender now and we don't have to continue."

The male spat on the floor. "I don't know how you block those blows, Hybrid, but you can't keep it up. I felt your punch, you're not that strong. We'll finish you and then your friends."

Rohan settled deeper into his stance, right leg cocked to the side, left in front of him, then held his left hand up and waved the man forward. "Come on, then." *Too bad this guy hasn't been within a thousand light years of a Bruce Lee movie or he'd totally appreciate what I just did.*

The male took two steps forward, stabbing out a left jab, following rapidly with a right cross.

Rohan caught the jab; the cross caught *him* in the upper chest.

The Hybrid slid back three meters, muscles all through his core complaining at the effort needed to keep him upright.

He wiped the blood leaking out of his mouth with the back of his hand. "Not bad." *Note to self: stopping combinations is harder.*

The male nodded and closed again.

A trickle of anger called out to Rohan from the back of his soul; a wave from the deep well of rage that had been his closest companion for twenty years.

He exhaled slowly and pushed it away.

Wei Li made a noise, a cough mixed with a cry, as Rohan stopped the Takslee's jab again, shunting its power into the spring he still maintained.

The cross followed it, predictably, a sign of a powerful but poorly trained fighter.

Rohan leaned forward and put his left palm on the Takslee's chest, pushing his shoulder back to derail the punch.

At the same moment, he released the coil of energy he'd been keeping.

The combined kinetic energy of several punches and one kick blasted the Takslee back into a bare wall. The male slid down, eyes glazed over, leaving a body-shaped indentation in the metal.

Rohan looked at the female.

"Care to revise your opinion?"

She looked at him, then at Wei Li as the security chief hobbled to the center of the room.

The female held her hands up. "I surrender."

———•••———

An hour later, Rohan stretched out in the chair facing Wei Li's desk and sipped a mug of tea. "What do you mean she won't talk?"

Wei Li shrugged. "She claims to be more afraid of her supplier than she is of spending time in prison on Wistful."

"Oh, does she."

Wei Li nodded. "She does, and she is being truthful. I have leverage in this situation but not much."

Katya and Ang shared a loveseat across from Wei Li's desk. The il'Zkin growled softly. "I am sure she would tell you what you want to know if you let me eat just a little bit of her. Maybe an arm? Or a leg! Her leg looked meaty."

Ang patted her shoulder with a wide paw. "Your passion for justice is for being wonderful, my darling."

Katya nodded. "Yes. Justice. Also these Takslee look delicious. I am sad the big one snuck away."

Rohan rubbed his chest. The bruise from Reghis's punch was spreading and meshing with the ones left by Terry's swats. His torso was more damage than flesh. "Taking these guys out was a nice step, Wei Li, but we really need to get to someone further up the supply chain." He put the empty teacup on her desk.

She rubbed her heavily bandaged left arm, obviously in pain from where she'd been kicked. "I had heard there was a pathogen loose on the station, Rohan, causing an illness whose primary symptom was an uncontrollable compulsion to state obvious things. I am afraid you have been infected."

"Very funny."

"Because if you were not so afflicted, I am certain you would not be wasting my time and energy with such statements."

Katya reached out, lightning quick, and knocked the teacup to the ground. She flinched back as Rohan glared at her. "We talked about this."

She shrugged. "I am sorry. The cup wanted to be knocked down."

"What? Never mind. Don't do that again." He focused on Wei Li. "You're in a crabby mood. What's wrong? Other than the obvious?"

She paused, then turned to face the couch. "Would you two mind giving us a bit of privacy?"

Katya shook her head. "We are not stopping you. Go wherever you wish, we will stay and cuddle right here on this comfortable couch you have."

Ang coughed. "Darling, am for believing that Chief Wei Li, Ang's chief, is for requesting that we leave the office."

Katya nodded as she climbed to her feet. "Of course. I understood. I was only . . . checking to make sure you also understood. As a test."

Ang lumbered to his feet, wincing as he put weight on his right leg. "These Boost-selling peoples are for being stronger than they are looking, Chief. Am feeling have been in a real fight."

Wei Li sighed. "I am aware, Ang. I'm glad you're not more seriously hurt. Now, please. Take this as an opportunity to seek medical attention."

Ang led Katya out of the office; the door slid closed behind them. Rohan picked up his teacup and refilled it.

Wei Li looked at him. "You are not looking like yourself, Rohan."

"That's the whole point, isn't it? Cut the hair, trim the beard down to stubble, stop wearing the uniform. I'm in disguise. And it's working, for the most part. Though those Boost dealers figured out who I was pretty fast. I guess charging into action at your side gave away the game."

She closed her eyes and pinched the skin above her nose. "That is working, then? Your disguise?"

He frowned at her blatant display of distress. "It is. But I know that's not what you meant."

"No, it is not. I meant that, if I didn't know better, I'd suspect that the Takslee were correct in their assessment of your esoteric fitness."

Rohan waited for her to open her eyes, stretching his legs out in front of him, and nodded. "I'm fine."

"You don't seem fine. You've quit your job—"

"Leave of absence, Wei Li. Leave of absence. Nobody's quitting anything."

"If you say so. Yet you even left your apartment."

"It's part of the disguise. People knew where I lived. If they see me coming and going, well, you know. Look, you're going to have to trust me. I'm doing what I'm doing for a reason."

She studied him. "Very well, Rohan. I will extend my trust. For now."

"Great. Now, not to be silly, but I could say the same thing about you. I can't believe you got caught by that woman's kick. You should have seen it a kilometer away."

"Yes, I should have. I am currently impaired. If I thought the Takslee situation could have waited another day, or even several more hours, I would have postponed the operation."

Rohan sipped his tea and leaned forward. "What do you mean 'impaired'? What's wrong?"

"Nothing serious. I received some . . . disquieting news."

He nodded. "Anything you want to share?"

She rubbed her forehead again, fingers working on her yellow skin. "Some old acquaintances of mine are visiting Wistful."

"Trouble? You need some asses kicked? I can do that, you know. Maybe not as well as I could before, but I'm here for you."

"Not that sort of acquaintance. You should reconsider your habit of offering violence as a first response to every situation, Rohan."

"I wasn't . . . okay, fine, I was. You let me know if you need any help with these old friends. If they annoy you, I'll take them drinking with the Ursans. You won't see them again for a week, they'll be so hungover."

A smile flashed across her face. "That was a lovely suggestion, Rohan. I might even take you up on it. I could use some . . . moral support. These specific individuals are not supposed to be here, and I do not think their arrival is a good sign."

"I see. Well, no, I don't, that was super vague, but that's fine. You tell me when and if you need me and I'll be there. In the meantime, what are you going to do with the Takslees?"

"I can hold them for twenty-seven days. After that I have two choices: set them free or deport them."

Rohan sighed. "Those are Wistful's directives?"

"Yes. Excepting an immediate threat to the physical security of the station or its inhabitants, my hands are tied."

"They don't look—"

"Figuratively. Try to keep up. As I've confiscated their supply, I cannot really justify their presence as a threat, so the best I can do is send them on their way."

"And ban them from the station for life? Tell me you can do that, please?"

"Yes, that too. Which is not a significant enough threat to convince them to turn over their supplier. So we are at a dead end."

Fatigue washed through Rohan's back; he hadn't recovered from his encounter with Terry. "You really want those suppliers, don't you. That's why you risked the raid, even knowing you weren't at full strength."

"Boost creates Powers. Having more Powers on the station is not a recipe for stability."

"You're worried that it will be enough to force the il'Drach's hand? Make them attack or something?"

"Not really. I'm worried that it will lead to an unforeseen complication. When Powers are involved, problems simply become harder to deal with."

Rohan nodded slowly and finished his tea. "You mind if I talk to the Takslees?"

"Are you going to torture them?"

"No, just talk, I swear. I won't even threaten them. I have questions for them that have nothing to do with their supply chain."

"Be my guest."

———◆•••◆———

The prisoners were spread out among three holding cells, the apparent leaders of the group together in the first.

I'm not sure what's more impressive, that the big one went claw for claw with Katya and held her own or that she escaped the security gauntlet around the warehouse.

Rohan stood facing a single-facet diamond panel and watched them for several minutes. The male, Reghis, was swaddled in heavy bandages, a line running from the wall to his arm to dispense medication. The female, Keilee, sat near him, arms folded over her chest, her thin, scaly lips pressed together in a sneer.

The Hybrid flipped on the intercom.

"Hey."

Keilee stared daggers at him. "I told the other one, we're not turning over our supplier."

"I know. I'm not here for that . . . but maybe I am. I'm not allowed to torture or threaten you, but how about a bribe?"

Reghis's eyes opened.

Keilee studied Rohan. "What do you mean?"

"Two hundred thousand credits for the name and location of your supplier. Cash."

The Takslees locked eyes. Keilee coughed. "You can authorize that?"

Rohan shrugged. "I'm not offering you Wistful's money, I'm offering you mine. I'm rich, I can pay you."

She stared at him for a moment, shook her head, and laughed. "Nice try, Hybrid. I can't spend credits when I'm dead."

The male Takslee turned his head to her, eyes watering in agony as he stretched his damaged neck. "I don't know, Keilee . . . that's a lot of credits."

"Shut up, Reghis. What did I just say? About spending it when we're dead?"

"I know, but maybe . . . we could travel far away. Real far. Get away from . . ."

She snorted. "How far do you think we'd have to go to escape *her* reach?" She faced Rohan. "No deal, Tow Chief. Try your luck somewhere else."

Rohan looked at her, weighing her expression and body language. He nodded slowly. "I get it. And I'm not a tow chief anymore."

She waved her hand at him. "Whatever. Leave us alone. We'll do our time, right here, then be on our way. I don't plan to ever see you again after that."

"What's that supposed to mean? Do you have something against me?"

She sneered. "I don't like people born with Powers. Sue me."

Rohan exhaled and studied the pair for another minute. Reghis slowly brought his head back to neutral, obviously struggling to move with his neck stiffly braced.

"I guess I understand that, too. But let me ask you another question."

Keilee shook her head. "I'm not telling you where we get the Boost. I'm not giving up anyone in our organization. I'm not telling you how it works or how we sell it. Just move on, Hybrid, we're done here."

"It's not about Boost. I want to hear about the conspiracy thing."

Reghis's eyes flared wide as Keilee straightened in her chair. "Con-Conspiracy? What about it?"

"What is it? I have no idea. It's not a secret thing, is it?"

Reghis laughed, then grimaced in pain. Keilee shook her head. "It's on the net. Ohj and Vade, they're brilliant. They get the same news we do, you know, what the rich people and the il'Drach want you to think about everything, and they see right through it to the actual truth that lies underneath. If you're not watching Con-Conspiracy, you don't know what's really going on in the sector."

Rohan ran his hands over his short hair. "What does the name even mean? Con-Conspiracy?"

Reghis snorted and Keilee sighed. "That's the brilliance. They're not talking about the old conspiracy theories we've all been hearing about for hundreds of years. That all the humanoids were created by a single parent species, the fish that live in deep space, the il'Drach ships that supposedly wipe out entire species for some unknown reason, the hidden ringworld that monsters use to climb out of hell somehow."

"But all those things—"

"I know, I know! They're all false! Rumors spread by the il'Drach to distract us from what's really going on."

That's not what I was going to say. At all. Not even close.

"Okay. What *are* these guys saying?"

"All sorts of things. The truth *behind* those old-fashioned conspiracies. They saw right through Hyperion's video and told us what happened."

"What video?"

She laughed. "You don't know? I told you before. Hyperion released a video of him kicking your behind all over that jungle planet. A proper ass-kicking, that was."

"Really?" *Is it a real video or generated after-the-fact? I don't remember anyone filming. I guess it doesn't matter.* "I've been out of touch. I didn't know."

"He wants everyone to think he's some kind of super-Hybrid, beating you like that, and even Ohj thought so at first. But Vade pointed out what really happened."

"What really happened? As in, beyond Hyperion knocking me senseless?"

"Yeah. I mean, sure, he beat you up, but you'd clearly lost your Powers. We could tell you weren't flying right, weren't as tough as you used to be. You tell me why the Hybrid who faced down the entire Imperial Fleet two years ago gets put down with like three punches."

Rohan grunted. "Vade is telling people I lost my Powers. Even though that's not a thing that happens."

She nodded. "See, that's what they want us to think. That Hybrids don't lose their Powers. But if they can't, what happens to them? Don't tell me they all die in battle; Hybrids are tough as my mother's heart. Where are they all? We've never seen an old Hybrid. We hear about new ones all the time, we never hear about any of them dying in action, but the Empire is always short of the forces they need to do something or other. Well, people are starting to notice, and we're not believing the lies anymore."

Rohan cracked his knuckles, slowly, and chewed over what she was saying.

Is this another il'Drach thing? Confuse people who might otherwise figure some things out? Or just some morons latching onto a crazy idea to make a media career for themselves?

"So you think I've lost my Powers. How do you think I knocked your friend through the wall?"

She shrugged. "I don't know. Maybe you got some Boost for yourself. Maybe your Powers come and go. Like a light that's about to die, flickering a few final times before going dark. I'm not an expert. But people watched, and listened, and the ones who used to be afraid of you and this station are reconsidering."

"They're taking a big risk, don't you think? Putting so much stock into a video? How do they even know it's real?"

Reghis turned to look at her.

Keilee shook her head. "You can try to fool the others, but you won't fool me. Too many things add up for it to be fake or just a coincidence. When's the last time you towed a ship? I almost didn't recognize you with the haircut and the beard trimmed. You're never in uniform, never around. What else should we think but that you've lost your Powers?"

Rohan sighed. "Okay. Thanks for the info, I guess. I'll leave you to your perfect cube sentence and your exile. Don't sell Boost on my station."

Reghis grunted. "Huh?"

Keilee sighed. "Cube, idiot. Twenty-seven days. It's—"

Reghis groaned, the sound a person makes when they finally get a joke that they didn't get the first time and still isn't funny, and they both glared at Rohan.

He stood, straightened his loose-fitting black pants, and left.

The one good thing about all this is that it made me leave Toth 3 and come here, where I can see Tamara.

He checked the time to make sure his girlfriend would be awake and tapped a message to her as he walked out of the prison.

4

A Hybrid's Worst Fear

Tamaralinth Lastex took seven minutes to respond to Rohan's message with a quick note saying she was waking up and needed only a short time to get Rinth ready for school before seeing him.

He needed eight more to secure a spot at a quiet restaurant that served food suitable for both her breakfast and his dinner without using his real name.

Showering cost thirty minutes; longer than usual, but it was his first exposure to running water in weeks.

He called Katya as he finished changing into a clean uniform and gave her the evening's itinerary: better that than having her tear up the station looking for him while he was trying to eat.

Something he'd learned from experience.

Picking Tamara up took fifteen minutes; their meal another seventy-eight.

The walk back to his apartment afterward was six minutes, one minute longer than he would have managed if the urge to tickle her hadn't been quite so strong.

She tickled him back, adding two more minutes.

All of which added up to a far greater delay getting her into bed than he would have liked, a delay made palatable by the belief that the effort of cleaning up, arranging a meal, and picking her up himself made him a bit more like a gentleman and less like a horny twentysomething on a booty call.

Nothing in her expression gave him any reason to think his assessment was incorrect.

An hour later, Rohan was in his favorite place in the sector, spooning the naked green back of his partner in the middle of the king-sized bed he'd installed in his spacious apartment, tucked away from the promenade on Wistful's east arm.

He relaxed into her, pressing the entire front of his body into her warm skin, just slightly damp from their exertions but drying quickly in the conditioned air. He ran a hand along her side, watching as her skin rose in goose bumps, and she shivered and used her elbow to push his hand away.

"Too much?"

She shrugged and reached around to pat his hip. "You can touch, just don't tickle me."

He leaned his head down and touched his forehead to the back of her head, letting out a long breath and relaxing more fully, sinking with equal measure into her back and into the mattress.

She stroked his hip absentmindedly. "I missed you."

He sighed. "I'm sorry, I—"

She lightly slapped the crease right above his hipbone. "I am not asking for an apology. I know that if you are kept away, it is by important things."

He smiled even though she couldn't see it. "They are important. Not more important than you, though—"

"I said you do not have to do that. I'm not looking for assurances."

"Okay. Well, I won't say I'm sorry, but I will say that I really, really wish there weren't so many things drawing me away from you."

"That, I will accept. Speaking of those things, how is the dig site? I assume it is going well, as the monsters have not eaten you. Yet. Have you managed to uncover anything of interest?"

"Hm. Ben Stone's students said there were structures under the moss when they landed on the surface, what was it, two and a half years ago. I can confirm that they know what they're talking about."

"Structures? How old? Are they intact?"

"I'm not sure. Tens of thousands of years. Maybe older. I dug deep enough to find a . . . I don't know what it is. A surface. A ceiling, maybe?

Like the top of a building that's now buried underground. Except there's a door in the top, which isn't normal."

"A door? Did you open it?"

"I can't. It's locked."

"Tens of thousands of years and it's still locked? In a way too strong for a Hybrid to break through?"

"It's not like I can go and use Powers to tear through it. For a few reasons. And I'm not sure that would be a good idea. Maybe it's locked for a reason. Who knows what's inside? Could be another vampire. Or a self-destruct device. Or something that will decay and be destroyed instantly when exposed to air. Or a suite of viruses that would annihilate me and all other life on the planet."

She shivered lightly against him. "You have a very active imagination, my Rohan."

"Bad things keep happening; it's easier if I try to anticipate them instead of just throwing my hands up in surprise when the next catastrophe rolls through."

"My poor man, always at the forefront of the effort to stave off disaster."

"Are you mocking me? I think you are." He squeezed her waist, and she wiggled against him.

"Never."

"Never?"

She laughed, a soft, breathy exhale. "Almost never. Certainly not all the time."

"Well, all right, then. Fair enough."

They snuggled quietly for a while, basking in the light sound of water falling over stones.

Rohan grunted. "That reminds me."

"Yes?"

"Do you happen to know anything about the waterfall over there?"

"What waterfall?"

"Right there. Three meters from the foot of the bed. Covering the entire wall over there that definitely didn't have a waterfall a week ago."

"Ah, that waterfall. What about it?"

"Do you happen to know where it came from?"

"You mean the name of the manufacturer? Or are you asking where it was built? I believe it is from Lukhor. We make all the finest luxury items."

He gently poked her ribs. "You know what I mean. Was that from you? It looks expensive."

"It was!"

"I thought money was tight. Though you know I have plenty."

She breathed in and out before answering.

He watched her ribs move and didn't complain about the delay.

"My father has been attempting to mend our relationship. With extra vigor since I visited home six months ago."

"Your father. The guy who hired an interstellar hit squad to keep men he didn't approve of away from you. Including the father of your child."

"Yes, that 'guy,' as you say. Did you think I had more than one father? My species has only two sexes, and I believe we procreate in a way mathematically similar to yours."

"No, I know. I was being snide. What does your father have to do with my new waterfall?"

"My father has reinstated a significant portion of my inheritance in an attempt to find favor with me. And probably to convince me to return home."

"Oh."

"It is his way. As a consequence, I am quite wealthy. Again."

"I see. Does that mean—"

"That I'll be going home? Not at all. I did not come to Wistful because I was poor, Rohan. I came because I wanted to be here. And away from him. Money doesn't change any variable in that calculation."

"Oh. Good. I mean, I guess that's good. As long as it's good for you. I don't want to stand in your way or anything. If you want to, you know. Make amends. Even if it means you move."

"I know you would not stop me. But I am not planning to go anywhere."

"Still, money's nice. You can quit your job. Hey, I already quit my job. You'll be able to stay here with me all day long. Just . . . right here." He ran fingers along the side of her shoulder, down her bare upper arm.

"My sweet, hairy man, I am not quitting my job. First of all, I like my job. And I do not wish to depend on my father's generosity. It is his way of obtaining control. It is . . . unseemly."

"We wouldn't want that. No. We want to stay seemed. Very seemed."

She laughed. "Yes, we do. So I will keep my job and spend my father's money only on frivolities."

Rohan chuckled. "Like a waterfall for your boyfriend's bedroom?"

"Yes, exactly. Do you like it?"

"I do. It's nice."

"I was not . . . overstepping? Decorating your bedroom? I did more than place a plant or leave a toothbrush by your sink."

He contorted his neck and kissed the top of her shoulder blade. "I don't mind. Don't go and throw out all my clothes, though."

"I wouldn't dream of it! You would be forced to parade around the station exposed for all to see."

"I think I'd probably just stay in the room."

"Now you are trying to tempt me."

He laughed. "Not what I was going for. But seriously, I don't mind. I mean the waterfall."

They lay quietly for a while.

"Rohan." Tamara's tone was tenuous, almost shy, lacking the casual warmth it had held moments before.

Rohan's heart did a little flip-flop in his chest. "Yes?"

"I want to talk to you about something. No joking."

"Oh." He sighed as the flip-flops performed an encore. "Sure."

◆ ··· ◆

Tamara hesitated before continuing, to the point that Rohan began to wonder if something was seriously wrong. When she spoke, the bubble of tension around them popped so strongly Rohan half expected to hear it make a sound.

"Rohan, I think we should move in together."

He exhaled.

"What? I mean . . . what?"

She shifted her weight, leaning away from him, then pressing against him, never turning so he could see her face. "Move in together. It is a thing people do when they have separate accommodations, then decide to instead share their living space."

"I know what the words mean."

"I know, but I thought you would appreciate the humor as a way to bring levity to the conversation."

"That's my thing. You're doing my thing. You can't do my thing, then I'll have to do yours, and I'm pretty sure that involves high-level math and having children, and those are both things I am not good at."

"I asked you to be serious."

"And you're the one who started with the levity!"

She sighed. "You are right. I am sorry, I will be serious."

"You want me to move into your place? With you and Rinth?"

She shrugged. "Or we could move here. Rinth's school isn't so terribly far away. The station is safe for travel. This apartment is large, and I've already put in the waterfall."

Rohan looked around. He had three bedrooms, mostly because he'd bought the first apartment with a view he liked, not because he himself had needed that much space.

"But . . . why?"

Her voice hardened by two and a half tones. "Why do you think?"

"I mean . . . I'm away a lot. I don't see that changing. You'd be farther from your sister."

She let out a long breath. "I told you, I miss you. I understand that you will be away, but when you are here, I would like to be with you. For moments like this." She took his hand where it rested on her side and brought it to her lips, then gently kissed his knuckles.

"You know I have to go back down to Toth 3. And I have some . . . things coming up. That might be dangerous. I don't know what's going to happen to me."

"You still need to deal with Hyperion. And you have larger aims than that, beyond him. Other things you need to accomplish. Other things you need to protect."

"Yeah. I do. And having you move in with me doesn't change any of that. I have responsibilities."

"You've chosen those responsibilities."

"Sure. I chose them. But that's exactly it, it's past tense. I chose them. I've made promises, even if they're only to myself, about what I was going to do. I'm not going to break those promises."

"Rohan, I am not asking you to. I am not asking you to stay here when you need to be away. I am not even asking you *not* to risk your life, though I hope you have enough at stake to avoid throwing it away needlessly."

"You know I won't be doing that. I'm not suicidal." *Anymore.*

"I want to be with you when you are here. It is that simple. I am not trying to bind you to this place."

"Will I be able to see other people? Ohmei gave me a free order of biscuits this morning; I think she's sweet on me."

She playfully slapped his thigh. "Ohmei is transdimensional, so having any sort of relationship with her would shatter your mind. And we have already decided not to see other people, remember? Over dinner. It was very good, the meat of a small jumping mammal from Rogesh, sauteed and very spicy. Served with—"

"I remember the meal. I was . . . that time I wasn't being serious. Wow, I am really not good at staying on topic and avoiding jokes."

"You are not. It is endearing, though on occasion you do veer into the territory of annoying."

"You are not the first person to tell me that." He didn't know what else to say.

Tamara coughed. "You are thinking. Are you deciding how to say no, how to say yes, or which response you wish to give?"

"Yes. No. Wait. I'm not sure."

She waited for him to continue.

After a pair of breaths he did. "I have to think. It feels . . . I don't know."

"Does the idea not please you?"

"It really does. Yeah, I'd love to have you here when I come back from a fight or whatever so you could stitch me up or soothe my troubled brow or do whatever else women do for the men who live with them."

"Don't expect me to cook; that is still beyond me."

He laughed. "I'll tell you what, anytime you want to make dinner, you can make reservations."

"Now that most definitely is within my scope of practice."

"I know."

"You said the idea of living with me would please you, yet you have not said yes. What is holding you back?"

"Living with you is also a responsibility. I wouldn't feel right just having you here when I need you and not returning the favor. I'd need to make sure I'm doing right by you. And Rinth. This can't be a one-sided thing, that's not fair."

"You can have a second waterfall put in, just for me."

"Sure I could. I have the money for it. But I don't think that's enough. If I don't have the . . . mental space to commit to a relationship, it just seems wrong, somehow."

She kept his hand in hers, near her mouth, and stroked his arm. "I see. I think."

"I'm not saying no. I just need to think about it."

"You have not thought about this before?"

He exhaled. "Rudra save me, I haven't. I've been so preoccupied with Hyperion and the il'Drach and training that I guess I haven't been thinking about the things I should have been. I really am sorry."

"I understand. Perhaps I knew you were preoccupied. And perhaps I decided that it would behoove me to take the initiative to jolt you out of your preoccupation."

"You offered to move in with me to get me to think about our relationship? That's . . . I can't decide if that's a little manipulative or just smart."

Her hair rustled as she shook her head. "That is not exactly accurate. I asked because I *do* want to live with you. I might have also been aware of the probable side effect of asking, which is to motivate you to think about certain things that you have been avoiding."

"Not avoiding. Avoiding requires intent. Just . . . forgetting. No, missing. I'm sorry."

"No need. Think about it now, should you have a chance. That is all."

"I will. I promise." *She's everything I want in a partner, pretty much. Hot. Smart. Caring. Supportive. Hot.*

Why am I hesitating?

Did I mention hot?

"Good. For now, we can relax and enjoy the day."

"Don't you have a shift in . . . seven minutes ago?"

"I have some time off. You know I'm never late for things, I would have left if I had work."

"Right. Absolutely. You are good about that."

She got up to use the bathroom.

When she came back, Rohan stretched and watched her walk across the room.

"I hate to bring this up—"

"Then don't."

"—but I think I should. What about Lahnegarn?"

"What about him?"

"What would he have to say about . . . us? About his son living here?"

"He can say whatever he wants to say. Nobody has to listen to it. He has no rights over my child, not anymore."

"What about Rinth? What does he want?"

She paused. "I haven't discussed this with him at length. Doing so before you agreed seemed premature. I thought it would be confusing for him if you didn't want it."

"I get that."

"But I am his mother, and I know him well. He likes you, and I highly doubt he would object to living here."

"Ah. Good. I think."

"I'm not asking you to be his father, Rohan. Just his friend."

"Right. I'd be a terrible father. As nature has undoubtedly noticed."

"I disagree, but that isn't a debate we need to pursue. As I said, I'm not asking you to be his father. Just a presence in his life. Which, to be honest, you are already."

"Yeah. For better or for worse."

"Stop saying things like that, it's not right. And your self-deprecation is less endearing than you think it is."

"I'm still hung up on the idea that I could get killed and leave that kid in a bad place."

"So, try not to get killed. Or if you do, get killed in such a way that he can remember you with pride, and meaning, and so for him, the memory of you will be a blessing."

5

Sometimes Life's a Beach

One hour later.

Rohan leaned back on his soft plastic chair and sighed. "You know, I chose this building for a lot of reasons, but in the end it was only this one specific reason."

He sipped from a sweating glass containing ice and his latest attempt at perfecting a recipe for margaritas that didn't require real tequila, actual limes, or anything that could fairly be called Cointreau.

The only authentic ingredient in this is salt. Good old sodium chloride, available everywhere in the sector.

The drink was delicious, even if it didn't taste much like an actual margarita. Ang drank from his own glass from the next chair over. "For pool? Is good reason. Women like pool, though is mystery to Ang why anyone keeping so much water with no fish inside. Pool would be better with fish." The pool itself was about a quarter the size of an Olympic standard, and along with the artificial beach it took up more than half the top floor. It was the signature amenity of the luxury building.

Rohan took another sip. *Not too much. If you can't concentrate, you lose the spiral. There will be plenty of time to drink all you want . . . later. If you survive.*

"I'm not sure you're wrong, but maintaining fish in the pool would be a lot more complicated. You need food, some way to clear out the fish poop. And you wouldn't want to *not* maintain them, would you? Trust me, a layer of dead fish floating in here wouldn't make the swimming any more pleasant."

Ang nodded. "Good point. As good as this drink you are for making. Very sweet. Like dessert."

Rohan nodded and held still as flecks of cold water splashed onto his face.

Tamara laughed at his expression from where she stood in water that lapped her shoulder. "You were looking far too serious, my love. Time spent next to water is meant to be fun."

Rohan looked down at her and forced a smile. "I know, this is nice, it really is. I'm just . . ."

Tamara narrowed her eyes at him. "What? Concerned about what we discussed?"

Ang sat up straight. "What were you for discussing? Will you be having cubs now, War Chief?"

Rohan sighed. "No cubs, Ang. I can't, remember?"

Ang let his head hang. "Am forgetting. Sorry, War Chief. What else is for man and woman to be for discussing?"

"Really? That's all you think men and women can discuss? Cubs? Is that what you talk about with Katya?"

The il'Zkin pushed through the water to the edge of the pool and put her elbows onto the fake sand next to where Tamara waited. "What are we talking about?"

Ang laughed, hollowly. "No, Brother Rohan. Is too soon for that speaking. Perhaps talk also of the practicing for making of cubs."

Rohan looked from the five-hundred-kilogram bear to the sixty-five-kilogram cat-woman. "Dude, I'm not sure time is the only obstacle when it comes to you two having cubs."

Tamara shushed him. "Rohan, don't pry. That is between them. It may not be possible normally, but there are many alternative methods that can be used."

Katya leaned over and licked Tamara's shoulder. "What may not be possible? I can't hear, there is water in my ear. I am not sure my people are supposed to swim, but it is great fun."

Tamara rubbed the il'Zkin's upper back. "Don't worry, the men are being silly. Rohan, what's wrong? You're not having fun."

Rohan sighed. *No sense worrying people with the truth.*

"I miss Terry."

The others exchanged glances. Ang cleared his throat.

"Who is for being Terry, War Chief?"

Rohan shrugged. "My kaiju. I sort of adopted him, down on Toth 3. At the dig site. Well, maybe he adopted me. You'd like him, Ang; he can fly and he's about your size. You could wrestle him. Except he'd kill you and eat you."

Katya pushed herself up out of the water. "Is he for fighting? He sounds fun to fight. What is a kaiju again?"

Tamara shook her head. "Rohan, if you want a pet, we can get you a pet. I'm sure Rinth would love to help care for an animal. Perhaps a pseudodragon. I fondly remember my own, her name was Fiera."

Rohan swallowed while Ang rubbed at his ears.

Ang looked at the Lukhor. "What is pseudodragon? Ang is for thinking translation module is for malfunctioning."

Tamara held her hands about shoulder width apart. "A winged lizard, about this long. They are very smart but resist training of any kind. Unless they want to be trained."

Ang scratched his jaw. "That is not for resembling the Ursan word I heard."

Katya shook her head. "My people have no pets. Animals are for eating or for killing us, nothing else. What a wonderful galaxy you live in."

Rohan smiled. "Katya, maybe you can have one of your own. How much is a pseudodragon, anyway?"

Tamara shrugged. "If you want, I can buy her one."

"It will be for all of us. After all, I'm sure she'll insist on living with us, won't you, Katya?"

Katya nodded. "I cannot protect you if I live anywhere else, Father Rohan. I will stay by your side until my debt is paid."

Ang sighed. "Always for talking about her debts."

Rohan slapped his back. "Sorry, big guy. If I could convince her to forget the whole thing, I absolutely would. But she's stubborn."

Ang sighed. "Ang knowing."

Katya slapped at the water, splashing both men where they sat poolside. "Ang, come into the water and play. You can drink anytime, we only come to the pool once in a great while."

Ang lumbered to his feet. "For you, dear Katya, Ang will enter fishless water."

"Yay!"

Rohan smiled as the big bear slid off the side and splashed both women, letting out a gentle and very fake roar as he did so. "Ang is coming for you!" He grabbed Katya by the waist and tossed her up into the air.

Tamara fled, wading through the chest-deep water, shrieking as Ang chased her. Katya came down with a splash, then rose out of the water a few seconds later, sputtering and spitting.

"Ang!"

He turned to her. "What? Ang is for playing!"

"I will show you how to play!" She trudged through the water, heading for the Ursan, lifting her knees high with every step.

Ang's eyes opened wide as the slender cat-woman reached her hands into his armpits, leaned back, and tossed him overhead.

Rohan stood. "Not too hard! Don't break the roof, we don't want to have to pay to fix that! Also, there's vacuum on the other side!"

The Ursan landed with a tremendous splash, further soaking everybody, and Katya laughed. "I have been very good about not breaking things, Rohan. At least not the big things. See? I only threw him a little bit."

The waves splashed up and over the edges of the pool, quickly subsiding. Rohan looked down. "What happened to him?"

Tamara hopped out of the pool to get a better look. "Ang?"

Rohan stepped to the edge next to her, his toes digging into the polymer-ized sand. He examined the water, finally noticing a dark shape approach-ing Katya. He pointed.

"There!"

Katya looked at him. "Where?" She turned to follow the direction of his finger when the shadow hit her and sucked her under the surface.

A great deal of splashing ensued.

Tamara moved to Rohan and pressed her shoulder against his arm, then reached around and hugged his waist. "They're cute."

He nodded, watching to make sure nobody drowned in their exuber-ance. "They are. I'm glad for them. Katya hasn't been home in six months; she would be very lonely without him."

"She seems happy."

"Yeah."

"Unlike you, today. What's wrong? I don't think you're upset about me. Or are you?"

He sighed. *She's not letting me distract her from this question.* "No, I'm not."

"What, then?"

"Nothing to do with you, Tamara. There's a rumor going around that I have lost my Powers. I didn't think it would be this widespread."

"Ah. That. Well, you have left your job and disappeared from the public eye, for the most part."

"I know. I just hoped nobody would notice. Wildeye is towing ships, and I've been staying under the radar."

"Were people searching for you with radar, Rohan? How would that work?"

"It's an expression. Point is, I have enemies. If they sense weakness . . ."

She squeezed his arm. "Katya will handle them."

He laughed. "I don't really want Katya fighting my battles."

"Of course you don't. She, however, will be thrilled to do so. You should tell her, as soon as she comes up for air."

"I should. Tell her I've put our lives in chronic danger, and she's going to be elbow-deep in blood trying to keep me alive for the next . . . however long."

Her hair tickled his arm as she rested her head on his shoulder. "Perhaps things will not be so bad."

He shook his head like a dog come in from the rain. "Sorry, that was too much. Maybe I do actually miss Terry. I was getting used to having him around."

Tamara laughed. "I would say you should bring him to the station to stay with you, but something tells me that would not work out for the rest of Wistful's inhabitants."

"Oh, no. Definitely not. Bad idea." He shuddered at the image of the pterosaur flying down Wistful's promenade, casually eating any civilians annoyed by the wait at their favorite food cart.

"Perhaps we can get a pseudodragon after all."

"I guess. But this is all connected, you know?"

"I do not. What are you talking about?"

He scratched his beard. "If people are going to come after me, that affects our living situation. I don't want you put at risk. You or Rinth."

"We can take care of ourselves."

Rohan frowned. "You know I love you, and I think you're amazing, but you are not equipped to deal with the kind of problems I'm talking about. Angry Hybrids? Powers? If people figure out what I look like now and where I live, that would present a terrible risk."

She paused, as if preparing to argue with him, then shook her head softly. "I know, Rohan. You are not wrong. I cannot face down an angry Power seeking violence. And while I may not be afraid for my own safety, I do have a child."

"Exactly. I'd never forgive myself if anything happened to either of you because of your association with me."

Tamara poked his side. "Or Lahnegarn, right? We wouldn't want your connection to me to endanger his safety either."

"Oh, no, that would totally be fine. Hyperion can come along and squash Lonnie like a bug and I wouldn't lose a wink of sleep over it."

She poked him again. "I thought you might respond like that."

"Heck, give me Lonnie's address, and I'll put something on the net that says I'm sleeping on his couch. Let all the bad guys go knocking on his door, looking for me."

"Perhaps that would be going too far."

"Hey, he was very eager to brag about knowing me when it suited his purposes. Let him suffer the consequences."

Ang and Katya drifted to the edge of the pool, their playtime concluded, fur plastered flat to their bodies. Ang barked a laugh. "This fishless water is for being great fun! Now all I am for needing is more margarine."

Rohan shook his head. "Margarita. More margarita."

"That as well, War Chief."

Rohan stretched and looked up at Toth 3 through the diamond roof covering the pool area. "One minute." He walked away from the edge to the small table where he kept the pitcher of drinks and started to pour a fresh glass.

The doors to the pool area crashed open, startling everybody. Rohan spilled some of the drink as he spun to face the entrance.

Ursula strode through the doorway, her mouth open as she panted. The gray hairs on her muzzle seemed more prominent than usual.

"Rohan! War Chief!" She drew in a deep breath. "Am for having to warn you."

Three of the four people at the pool froze.

Ang launched himself clear of the pool and reached Ursula's side before Rohan could react. He grabbed her arm and put his shoulder underneath, taking some of her weight off shaky legs.

He growled in Ursan; Rohan understood only because of his fluency in Fire Speech, the meta-language that underlay all spoken communication.

"Are you hurt? What happened, Ursula?"

She growled back in the same tongue. "There are people looking for the war chief. Strong people."

"They hurt you?"

Ursula nodded, leaning harder on Ang and lifting her left leg off the ground; the male grunted with the strain, his own leg having been injured just hours earlier.

Ursula looked down. "Are you also hurt?"

He shrugged. "I've had much worse. I was hurt more than this on my wedding night, by my own wife."

Ursula laughed and looked over at Rohan, switching to Drachna. "War Chief, were you for hearing?"

Rohan ran over and was about to take Ursula's weight off Ang before he remembered that she might crush him. He waved Katya over. "Can you help her? Ang's hurt."

Katya muttered something under her breath as she rushed to Ursula's side, deftly replacing Ang as her crutch.

Rohan glanced toward the door, then to the former captain. "Ursula, what happened?"

"Some people for asking questions about War Chief. All denied knowing anything, but they were for persisting."

Tamara joined them. "What kind of men, Ursula?"

The Ursan faced the Lukhor. "Powers."

Rohan cleared his throat. "How many?"

The doors to the pool area slammed open, and a group of figures strode through the opening, their auras spilling out and into the room, pressing everyone back a step like a heavy wind.

The figure in the center spoke. "Five. We are a consortium of five, and we have come for The Griffin of Drachna. The Murderer of the Crucible. We are here to claim retribution."

6

Never Start a Naval Battle on Tolone'a

R ohan instantly recognized their species; even if he hadn't, he'd never forget the accent with which they spoke Drachna.

It was thick and clumsy, the diction belonging to lips and throats made to make sounds underwater, ill-suited to functioning in air. Warbly and slightly shrill, impacted by stray vibrations that were meant to be dampened by the sea.

Over it all was a tone of mockery. More than mockery—of disdain. As if the speaker had learned the language under duress, but couldn't respect it, couldn't enjoy it, and longed for an age when their descendants would be free of it forever.

He looked at the five and straightened. "The Griffin? You've got the wrong pool, guys. Nobody here by that name. But sit, have a margarita. Maybe we can help you look for him."

The speaker had a standard humanoid body, the skin bluish-gray and slick like a dolphin's. Small high breasts and wider hips marked her as female; she was also taller than the others and thicker through the shoulders and arms. "You can change your uniform and haircut and even the trim of the disgusting fur that covers your mouth, but we will know your face anywhere, Griffin. Your image has been seared into the memories of every Tolone'an alive today, and, finally, we have found you."

Her head was the furthest thing from humanoid, as if an octopus grew out of her neck, a curtain of heavy flesh hanging around the base like a kerchief, four meaty tentacles anchored to it, each half again as long as an arm.

Rohan swallowed and opened his Third Eye, looking for more information about their spirits.

He immediately wished he hadn't.

"Okay, you got me. I've heard of The Griffin. He was famous for a while, right? But he's not me, is he? Look at my aura. He's a Hybrid, right? Spirit oozing Power, I'm sure. Not mine. Just take a look."

The male next to the speaker tapped her shoulder. "Squeya, I'm not sure he's a Power, let alone a Hybrid. Something is wrong."

Squeya slapped his hand away. "We're not wrong, there must be an explanation. Perhaps he has a way to mask his Power. It doesn't matter; what matters is what he's done, and what our mission is."

The male nodded and took a step away. "As you say, Squeya."

Rohan shook his head. "Come on, you know all mammals look alike. There are a billion people like me on my home planet. Okay, half are women, give or take, but that's a lot of people who you couldn't tell apart from me without a DNA test. Why would you think I'm this Hippogriff guy?"

Squeya shook her head, tentacles swirling back and forth with the motion. "We would not have found you, Griffin, but for one man. And if we had found you, we would have had no chance to stand against you, no more than we did when you destroyed our religious caste, if not for one man. But that man came and changed everything. You will regret his actions for the rest of your short life."

Rohan felt a lead sinking in his belly. "One man? Oh, don't tell me. Please don't. It's not another Hybrid is it?" *Did Hyperion go to the Tolone'ans? That doesn't sound like him, but . . .*

Squeya shook her head, her eyes swiveling on their short stalks to take in the room. "No. I don't know who you mean."

Rohan snapped his fingers. "No, you're right, of course not. Not him. Let me guess . . . someone with a medical degree of dubious origins? Who claims to be a nurse or something but can't seem to provide a certificate from an accredited medical school no matter how many times we ask nicely?" *Dr. Kraken?*

"We are not here to talk, mammal." Squeya stepped forward, pointing her tentacles to the four other mammals in the room. "Kill them all."

Rohan felt a surge of anger as he held his hands up. "Hold on, hold on. Not cool." The esoteric spiral he had been maintaining shook and trembled as the loops tightened, his own energy no longer soft and flexible enough to easily maintain the shape. "Nobody's dying here. You guys are barking up the wrong tree. Or coral reef. Swimming across the wrong coral reef. Not many trees on Tolone'a, are there?"

Tamara looked at Rohan. "What's happening?"

Ang coughed. "War Chief for being in trouble. Ursans will protect him."

Squeya stepped forward, close enough to touch the Hybrid with her tentacles. "You are guilty of crimes against the people of Tolone'a, Griffin. Deception. Theft of civilian property. Theft of military property. Sabotage. Murder. Mass murder. And, finally, for the destruction of the religious caste, guilty of genocide."

"Do I get to defend myself? Offer a plea? An explanation? There were some extenuating circumstances, you know. Like an il'Drach fleet waiting and willing to sterilize the planet if I didn't end your rebellion."

Katya eased Ursula into an empty chair, her eyes on the Tolone'ans. Ang stood by Rohan's side, still clearly favoring his bad leg.

The male who'd spoken looked at Rohan. "What are you talking about?"

Squeya waved him down. "No. This is not a court, not a hearing, not a trial. You have been found guilty, Griffin. We are not your judge or jury. We are your executioners."

Rohan sighed. "Fine. Do what you have to do. Why harm these other people, though? What crime did they commit, Squeya? Is liking to swim a crime now, on Tolone'a?"

"They are guilty of association with The Murderer. They die today."

"You're not giving me a lot of options here."

Squeya nodded. "I had no intention of offering you anything, Griffin. Other than death."

Rohan surveyed his friends. Katya bounced lightly on her feet, preparing to charge the Tolone'ans. Ang stood, his leg sound enough to support his weight but not more than that. Ursula rose from her seat, obviously hurting but not immobile. Tamara's face was a washed-out green, as pale as he'd ever seen, her lips set and determined.

Fear licked at the back of Rohan's soul. *These are not good odds.*

His spiral shimmered; one of its coils loosened and sprang free.

"Ang, get Ursula and Tamara out of here. Whatever it takes."

"Rohan . . ."

"They're Powers, Ang. All of them. Not like the Takslee. Stronger. I'm counting on you."

Ang looked over the Tolone'ans, then at his friends, then to Rohan. "Ang is for counting on."

"Good." Rohan turned to Squeya. "I'm going to say this once and you should really listen.

"If you think I'm The Griffin, if you really believe it, then you believe, in your heart or hearts or whatever other organ you use to pump blood through that cephalopod body of yours, that I'm the guy who devastated your world. Fine. I get it. You want revenge.

"I'll fight you. I'll give you that satisfaction. But you let these other people go, because they had nothing to do with that.

"And if you don't, if you involve them when you don't have to, and if you're right about who I am, I will bring a tsunami of fresh hell to your planet that they will never forget.

"Because when The Griffin conquered your world, he didn't even want to do it. He didn't hate you, wasn't angry at you, had nothing against you at all. He was just a guy following orders trying to save as many of you as he could from a very unfortunate situation.

"But if you don't let these people walk away, you're going to see a whole new side of that same guy. The angry side. And you're not going to like what you've unleashed."

He cracked his neck and waited for Squeya to absorb his words.

Her second-in-command tapped her shoulder again. "Squeya, maybe—"

Again, she slapped him away. "No. We are not afraid, not cowed by this mammal. We are proud warriors of Tolone'a, and we will not compromise our mission. They all die."

Rohan swallowed. "It was worth a try."

Katya stepped between the five attackers and the Ursans. "I know they are speaking, Rohan, but may I eat them? Please? They look like a kind of fish, and I am quite hungry after all the swimming."

Rohan grunted. "Sure. We'll make an exception to the rule. Chomp away."

Katya nodded. "Thank you."

Squeya stepped in and threw a big overhand right punch at Rohan's head.

He stepped to meet her, catching the strike on his right palm, shunting the kinetic energy into the esoteric spring he'd been maintaining.

He felt a small surge of relief as the spring held its shape.

Good start.

Squeya's eyes widened, showing the perfect rectangular pupils, and she swung a left.

Rohan reached over with the same palm and absorbed it.

Katya leapt at the male who'd been talking and drop-kicked him across the room, letting out a little growl as she landed on her feet, then grabbed two tentacles of another Tolone'an and swung her into a third.

Ang, Ursula, and Tamara formed a little pack, all leaning on one another for support, and made a beeline for the exit.

Squeya whipped a tentacle across Rohan's jaw, too fast for him to catch. A small fireworks show went off behind his eyes.

Ouch. It's not even Canada Day.

Katya wheeled to face the last standing Tolone'an while Rohan struggled to keep his feet.

Squeya punched him again, settling for a faster jab instead of a big, telegraphed swing; he caught it, but barely, his spiral shimmering in his Third Eye as it lost some stability.

Keep it together, Rohan.

Katya slashed her claws across the Tolone'an's face, barely missing his eyes; he extended one hand and one tentacle toward the pool, and a wall of water emerged and slid between him and the il'Zkin.

Squeya threw another punch, which Rohan ducked; he stood and slapped her across the face, releasing his esoteric spring just as his flesh made contact with hers.

The combined energy of three of her punches pushed a shockwave through her fleshy head, spinning her completely around and sending her tumbling to the ground three meters away.

Rohan held his hand palm up and blew across it, as if putting out a fire. *Too much? Yeah, that was too much.*

The Tolone'ans that Katya had entangled finally separated and leapt to their feet, using a hand and two tentacles each to push themselves upright. Katya checked on Rohan, then snarled and charged the pair.

The Ursans hurried toward the exit, Tamara between them, half them shielding her from harm with their massive bodies and half her supporting them to the best of her ability, making up for some of the weakness in their damaged legs.

Rohan looked back toward Squeya just in time to see her moist fist rocket toward his face.

He slipped to the side; she lifted a knee, catching him with a glancing blow on his arm that threw him through the air.

He spun, long years of flight helping him orient himself without touching the ground, and stumbled to a stop, upright and waiting for Squeya to hit him again.

She didn't disappoint.

He absorbed the energy while watching through the corner of his eye as Katya opened the belly of one of the Tolone'ans with her claws.

An instant later, a stream of water struck her from the side, sending her sliding across the slick floor.

Red blood poured out of the disemboweled Tolone'an, while the female Katya had drop-kicked stood, shook off, and found herself in front of the Ursans.

She raised a hand to strike.

Rohan's heart jumped into his throat; Tamara stood trembling, sandwiched by the injured Ursans, a Powered punch heading toward the spot directly between her antennae.

"Ang!"

Squeya lifted an uppercut into his sternum; he pressed his thumb against his chest and absorbed most of the blow but the twisting rod of spiritual energy began to shudder.

He saw Ang spin the group, taking the blow on his thick back, wet fur absorbing much of the impact.

The three mammals still slid several meters across the floor.

Rohan grunted; the excess energy of the punch had *hurt*.

Katya closed on a Tolone'an while the one she'd clawed open sank to its knees.

The Tolone'an turned his head and called for help; the female who'd been menacing the Ursans abandoned them and ran to his side.

Ursula pushed Ang, shoving him and Tamara toward the exit as quickly as her injured legs could carry her.

Rohan coughed, blood flecking the back of his hand, as Squeya closed on him again.

Tamara turned back from her spot between the Ursans, her face pale, eyes wide with fear.

The Hybrid's stomach fell.

The esoteric spiral anchored to his palms shook and began to unravel.

He panted, air whistling through his mouth and nose, as Squeya snapped jabs toward his face; he watched her with one eye while the other was trained on the exit and Ang reaching out with one big hand to push open the door.

Keep it together, Rohan. Keep the spiral together.

These guys aren't important, this fight isn't important. You're not important. What matters is beating Hyperion, and to do that you need the spiral.

Leave the fear aside, leave your anger aside. Let it go.

Focus on the spiral.

Two Tolone'ans faced Katya while another knelt by their bleeding comrade and administered first aid.

She hissed as they closed slowly, each angled to flank her, tentacles outstretched to limit her mobility.

Rohan coughed and slipped punches, twisting maniacally to avoid more contact, dipping and ducking as Squeya tossed strikes with increasing speed and confidence.

I don't think I can do this.

The spiral shook again, the rod losing another twist as the shape slid away.

No, no, no. If I can't keep this going during a fight, this will all have been for nothing.

All this time.

All the work. All the hope.

He exhaled sharply as the big door swung shut behind the Ursans.

Good. Tamara's safe.

Squeya tapped his chest, her punch just barely hitting him as he leaned back and away from it, but the impact was enough to send him to the ground.

He exhaled, his breathing too fast, the spiral losing another loop.

Almost gone. Focus, Rohan. Focus.

He curled into a fetal position, then rolled to his knees and elbows, head down between his fists. He inhaled fast, then exhaled slowly, eyes shut, holding on to the remnants of his esoteric technique for all he was worth.

Keep the spiral, Rohan. That's all that matters.

A tentative impact on his side flipped him over; he rolled through it, coming up on his elbows again, eyes screwed tight the whole time.

Katya called out to him. "Rohan! Stand up!"

He heard impacts as she struck and was struck, grunts and exhalations.

Something hit him again, harder, right on the thigh. He slid across the floor, spinning, the world a dark, dizzy storm.

"Rohan! I can't fight them all myself!"

Squeya spoke as she tapped him with her shoe, badly bruising his ribs but not breaking them. "He's given up. He's not much of a fighter, is he?"

Her second-in-command cleared his throat. "I don't like it."

"Have faith, Squero. What is happening here is a victory for our entire species. Our entire genus."

Rohan kept his eyes shut and forced his breathing to slow. He slowly bent the rod again, adding a loop to the helix it formed inside his subtle body.

Katya growled. "I will dine on your entrails."

Squeya responded. "You're strong, but there are four of us."

A quick scuffle, a heavy thud, and the sound of crunching bones and torn cartilage. Katya spat. "Three."

She can't win three-on-one.

I need to stand up and fight with her.

He lost the loop he'd reconstructed.

I don't think I can.

Another bang as the doors swung open. Something hissed into the pool room, crossing the wet floor at astonishing speed.

A thud, then an exchange of blows.

Squeya shrieked. "What are you doing? You'd betray your own people?"

The answering voice spoke with a much subtler Tolone'an accent, the Drachna polished and smooth. "I won't let you kill him, Squeya. I told you already."

"You can't stop all of us."

"I really can. You, mammal. Take the Hybrid somewhere safe. I can hold off these three."

Katya answered. "What about you, then?"

"I'll be fine."

Squeya grunted. "No, you won't. We'll peel that armor from your body and send you back home in seven different boxes."

Rohan pressed his forehead into the cool tiles and focused on his helix.

Bend it. Create a loop. Keep the back anchored to the wellspring of your Power; keep the other end in your palm.

Katya coughed. "We will fight them together."

Squero interrupted. "Squeya, we can't stop Slokoda's bleeding and Dirigo isn't moving. They need medical attention. We can get the Hybrid another day."

"No! His life ends now."

"We don't have the resources. We'll come back better prepared. The Hybrid has nowhere to go."

Wet smacking sounds as Squeya slapped the floor with her tentacles. "Damnit! Gather up Dirigo and Slokoda. I know a medic who will help us."

The newcomer spoke. "You should give up your revenge. I'll protect the Hybrid. With my life if I have to."

"You'll have to."

The doors swung open again.

And shut.

7

Iron Squid Part 3: The Dripping Bucket

Ninety minutes later.

Rohan sat at the back of the booth, flanked by Katya and the Tolone'an, whose black armor with contrasting accents in gold did not fit the general atmosphere of the bar.

A waiter hurried over with bottles of Sein Ale for the booth.

Rohan nodded his thanks and took his bottle, actively scanning the room for trouble. Katya sipped from her own. The Tolone'an picked up his bottle, paused, set it down, then tapped to release the latches at his neck and lift his helmet high overhead, his tentacles pulling free with soft popping sounds.

"Garren. I can't say I'm not happy to see you. Surprised, though. What's going on?"

Garren held a napkin to his mouth and coughed, clearing air or phlegm that had accumulated inside his armor. "Rohan. It is good to see you."

Katya darted forward, licking Garren's forehead before he could do more than flinch back. She sat back in her seat. "Do not worry, I rarely kill and eat friends. And I like your clothes. They are strong and shiny. Can I have a set like it?"

Garren looked at Rohan with wide eyes, his rectangular pupils standing out, then laughed. "I'm afraid it wouldn't work for you . . . Katya?"

She nodded, and Rohan smiled. "Garren's a friend. He's a student of Marion Stone's."

Garren nodded. "Was. I haven't worked on my dissertation in two years."

"Well, you're wearing it. I'll vouch for you if Academy is willing to consider an honorary degree. You can be Dr. Garren."

Garren flinched. "Given recent circumstances, I don't think I'll be pursuing that particular title."

Katya leaned forward. "Have you fought Rohan? You seem very strong. I would like to fight you as well."

Garren looked at Rohan quizzically. The Hybrid shook his head. "She just likes to fight; she doesn't mean anything by it."

"Ah. I see. Perhaps another time, right now I think I need to stay sharp in case we run into The Consortium again."

Rohan nodded. "About them . . ."

Garren sipped from his bottle, slurping noises coming from under the curtain of flesh around the base of his head. "I will explain. Is this a good place? The service is good but . . ."

The Dripping Bucket was a bar of ill repute, owned by proprietors of ill repute, run by waitstaff of ill repute, and populated exclusively by customers of the lowest possible repute. It was known for bad service and worse food, but it was a good place for people who did not want others noticing their business.

Katya looked at Rohan. "They are bringing us drinks very quickly, but nobody else's."

Rohan chuckled. "Yeah. Ever since you and I came here and threatened to kill everybody in the place, they've been very accommodating."

Garren lowered his voice. "Really?"

Katya nodded. "He was very intimidating. Really." She patted Rohan's hand.

Garren looked at the Hybrid. "Why did you do that?"

"I needed something."

"Did you get it?"

Rohan sighed. "No. That's not the point. Look, it wasn't my proudest moment, okay? But I was trying to save lives. I didn't actually hurt anybody."

Garren held up his hands and two tentacles, palms and suckers forward. "I am not criticizing, just asking. Anyway, The Consortium." He took another long pull from the bottle. "You are aware of Dr. Kraken's activities."

Dr. Kraken, a villain who had terrorized Earth for hundreds of years, was of a humanoid-cephalopod species that predated the Tolone'ans.

Rohan swallowed. "I didn't know he was still alive."

"Oh, yes. Why wouldn't he be?"

"I beat him nearly to death about a year ago. I know, I know, another of my not-proudest moments."

"It would be better for us all if you had succeeded. Was it you who ruined one of his tentacles?"

"Guilty."

"Ah. That explains some things. He has relocated to Tolone'a and has been activating Powers as fast as he can. The same way he did for me."

Katya looked at Rohan. "What is he saying? Activate?"

Rohan waved the server over and signaled for three orders of the house fries. "A portion of Tolone'ans can become Powers. Usually the ones descended from the warrior caste, though modern Tolone'ans aren't divided along caste lines the way they were a thousand years ago."

Garren nodded. "A dark era of our history. We have become much more egalitarian."

"That, and the il'Drach don't want pureblooded warriors. Only the religious caste could activate Powers, and . . ."

Garren leaned forward. "They . . . were wiped out. In a war." He looked at Rohan, eye contact showing that he was willing to leave out the fact that it had been Rohan who had committed that particular act of genocide.

Rohan cleared his throat. "Yet another of my not-proudest moments. Katya can hear whatever you have to say, I trust her. No religious caste meant no more Tolone'an Powers, though apparently Dr. Kraken can do the same thing."

"He has many abilities lost to my people for millennia. He is creating Powers again, and because of this he has become very influential to a certain segment of the population."

Rohan tapped the table. "Let me guess. The angry segment."

"Yes. He greatly desires your death. I did not know why, before. I assumed he saw you as a general obstacle to whatever long-term plans he has."

Rohan exhaled. "That or good old-fashioned revenge. I'm not sure it matters, to be honest. It's not great news."

Garren lowered his voice to a barely audible level. "There is more to it. He believes you have lost your Powers. That is why The Consortium, his strongest disciples, came here, now, to kill you. Rohan, I hate to ask, but the way you fought . . . is it true? How?"

Rohan shook his head. "It's complicated. For now, just assume I'm having some . . . issues. What can you tell me about these guys? Are they going to give up? Something tells me they're not the type to run home with their tentacles over their eyes."

"I'm sorry, Rohan, but probably not."

Katya slapped her fist into her palm. "We will fight them, then."

Rohan took his helmet out of his hood and checked messages.

Nothing new from Ang; the Ursan had already told Rohan he was safe.

Tamara had sent another message reassuring him that she was fine, merely startled by the attack, and was safe. Her sister had agreed to take care of Rinth while she stayed out of sight.

He tabbed through settings screens on the mask, his finger hovering over the 'cancel connections' button.

I don't want to be out of contact with everybody, but I need to cut off every avenue The Consortium might be using to track me.

With a sigh, he pressed it.

The Hybrid rubbed his forehead. "I was right about that story of me losing my Powers causing trouble. I hate being right."

Katya shook her head and finished her ale. "That is not true; you are very smug and happy when you are right, even about bad things."

"Don't give away my secrets, Katya."

Garren chuckled. "You do like being right, Rohan. I should tell Katya about the time you saved Professor Stone's students—"

Rohan looked up. "Speak of the devil."

Katya followed his gaze. "Who is the devil? Ben is the devil? Why did no one tell me?"

Ben Stone, former child sidekick to Earth's greatest hero, Hyperion; active professor of exobiology at Academy; husband to Marion Stone, the sector's premier scientific mind; approached the table.

"Rohan. Katya. And . . . Garren? I wasn't expecting to see you!"

Rohan waved him forward. "Sit, please."

Katya half stood, took the hand Ben extended, and licked the back of it. He blushed slightly and shook his head, then sat at the head of the table. "What's happening?"

Rohan held out his helmet. "I have data for you. I wanted to hand it over before anything happened to me, and I'm not sure it's safe to transmit over the net."

Ben grunted and took the helmet, tapping the inside of the single-facet diamond facemask. "Let me guess. Folder called 'The Dig.'"

"That's it."

"You found something? Under the moss? Where we located those signs of ancient structures?"

"I did. I'm not sure what to make of it, but it's something."

Ben tapped some more, opening files and examining the images Rohan had taken. "That's a door."

"Looks like it." He finished his ale and placed the empty bottle on the table.

"With a combination lock. Six dials. Two, then one, then three."

"That's what I thought."

Katya patted Rohan's shoulder. "See, you are very smart, Rohan! You knew what the Professor knew! You didn't need his help after all."

Ben looked at him. "Did you decipher these symbols?"

"I can't. Yet again, I wish I knew written Fire Speech, I'd be able to read any text ever recorded. They look a little like, er, very old writing but that's just a wild guess." He held a hand to his ear. *Somebody might be listening. Don't want to mention the il'Sein out loud, the il'Drach don't like that.*

Ben nodded his understanding. "It's a good guess. This isn't the same old writing you're thinking of, but there's a resemblance. Also looks a bit like Sanskrit."

Katya swiped the bottle off the table. Rohan glared at her; she shrugged.

The Hybrid looked back at his friend. "My mom somehow neglected to teach me ancient Sanskrit when I was a kid. Might have come in handy."

Ben smiled. "I'll take these back to *Insatiable*, run them through some analytics. I'm very curious about what's behind that door. It's very well-preserved, considering how long it's been there."

Rohan nodded. "Long time. Regular materials would have degraded by now. Roots would have torn it apart, stuff like that."

"Yes. Has anybody else seen this?"

The Hybrid shook his head. "You're the first. I just got back. There's also some data on the kaiju you might not already have. Like where they like to be scratched."

Ben exhaled loudly. "What was that?"

Katya nodded. "Rohan has a friend kaiju. What is the word you use, a pet. He whines all the time how he misses it."

"Not all the time."

"Most of the time. It is very sad."

Ben shook his head. "I'll have to look at the data; that sounds fascinating. Is it tame enough for us to go down there safely?"

Rohan coughed gently. "I really doubt it. I think once someone nearby gets angry, all bets will be off. I was only safe because of some pretty intense meditative practices."

Ben handed back the mask, the data transfer complete. "Rohan, this dig is interesting, but staying on the surface is very risky. Even for you. Maybe especially for you, in a sense."

The Hybrid nodded. "I had to. It's complicated."

"Simplify it for me. We're worried about you. All of us. This behavior . . ."

"Don't. Please. I have to learn to stay calm, and I have to do it under pressure. The surface of Toth 3 seemed like a pretty good place to put that to the test."

Ben nodded and put his hands on the table, preparing to stand, when Rohan looked over his shoulder, eyes wide, and muttered, "Rudra save me. What is *he* doing here?"

—◆··◆—

The Lukhor approaching their table was on the tall side, his twin green antennae twitching and bobbing as he walked. He wore simple clothes, the uniform of a station maintenance worker, and had dots of grease on the backs of his hands and on his cheeks.

He approached the table, eyes focused on Rohan.

The Hybrid groaned. "Lahnegarn. What can I do for you?"

Tamara's ex-husband scanned the table. "Can we speak? In private?"

Ben finished standing and nodded to Rohan. "I was about to go anyway. Rohan, I'll let you know if I find out . . . anything. About any of this."

"Thanks, Ben."

The Professor looked at Garren. "You know, Marion would love to see you."

Garren cleared his throat. "I didn't have a chance before, I had to come directly here. But I'd like to see her as well. Pay my respects."

Rohan waved him away. "Go say hi. And say hi for me while you're at it."

Garren looked him over. "You two are on good terms now?"

Rohan shrugged. "No, but better than you'd think. It's fine, you can go, those five won't be coming for me until they have a chance to get patched up, thanks to the way you and Katya left them."

Garren nodded. "I will, then. But take care. For the reasons you already know."

"I appreciate the reminder."

Garren and Ben left. Katya studied the Lukhor.

"This one reminds me of your mate, Rohan. Is he her family?"

Rohan coughed. "Not exactly."

At the same time, the Lukhor responded, "Yes."

The two males locked eyes. Katya grinned as she studied them, reaching for a fresh bottle of Sein Ale to drink. "I believe this will be a very fun conversation."

Lahnegarn looked at her. "Does she have to be here?"

Rohan shrugged. "You can say whatever you have to say in front of her. Unless it's a threat, then you should really wait until she's somewhere else, otherwise she's likely to cut your throat for it."

The Lukhor nodded. "I'll remember that. Fine, she can hear what I have to say."

The waiter loomed behind the newcomer, standing tall to catch Rohan's eye while holding up a bottle.

The Hybrid shook his head. *No need to buy him a drink. It's not as if we're friends.*

Lahnegarn sat in the chair Ben had vacated and faced Katya. "Tamara is my wife."

Rohan coughed. "Ex-wife."

Lahnegarn waved his hand in dismissal. "And I'm Rinth's father." He looked sideways at Rohan, as if daring him to disagree.

Rohan nodded. "No argument there."

Katya sipped her drink. "The former mate of the current mate. Fascinating. Are you the type who remains jealous and upset that your mate has left you for another? Or did you leave her for another, and you commiserate with Rohan over his misfortune in being with her now?"

Lahnegarn blinked hard. "Are those the only choices?"

Rohan laughed. "Aren't they? Kind of? Maybe it's not *always* that simple. Look, Lahnegarn, what did you want to talk to me about? I doubt you're here to discuss what bet you want to place in the next Fight for the First Fist tournament."

"I wanted to talk to you about Tamara."

"Your ex-wife. I don't think we have anything to talk about there."

"And Rinth."

Rohan sighed and drained his beer. A server brought three bowls of salted fried sticks of a starch Rohan couldn't recognize, something like a purple sweet potato. The Hybrid motioned for a fresh bottle of ale. "Go on."

"He won't talk to me at all, Rohan. I can take him for the night, but he barely says a word. I don't like it, and it's your fault."

"Is it, though? Really? What is he now, eleven? You've been kind of a schmuck for a while, Lahnegarn. He was bound to notice sooner or later."

Lahnegarn looked confused, and Katya raised her hand. "Oh, I know! I know this word! It is Earth term for the male sexual organ! It is a very funny word."

Lahnegarn sighed. "You turned them against me, Rohan. You undermined me and made them see me as weak. Unfit. You caused this rift."

"You have no idea what you're talking about. I didn't undermine you. Actually, that was Tamara, making sure your plan to get on the good side of the rebels wouldn't work. A thing she did to save your life, I might add. Because she thought it was something worth saving. That wasn't my idea, I assure you."

"You mock me at every turn, Rohan. I see it. You think I'm stupid, but that's a grave mistake."

"I don't think you're stupid. You really overestimate me. I mock everybody. Almost everybody. Even people who are a lot smarter than me. It's a character flaw, don't take it personally. Well, try not to."

"It's more than that, and you know it. I'm not going to sit still and just watch you steal my family."

"You pushed them away yourself, big guy. Hey, have you been working out? You seem a lot more solid than the last time we spoke."

The Lukhor glanced down at his arms. "Yes. I've been . . . preparing."

Well, that sounded ominous. "Was that what you wanted to tell me? That you blame me for the bad decisions you made which led to the end of your relationship?"

"You took advantage of the situation to steal my wife. My family. I hoped there was something I could do about it, but it's not exactly a fair fight, is it?"

Rohan rubbed his forehead. "What are you talking about?"

"You're a Hybrid, and I'm . . . not. I can train and practice all I want; I'll never stand a chance against you."

"You mean like in a fight? Come on, Lonnie. That's crazy talk. Tamara isn't with me because I fight better than you. You threw away your chance with her. That had nothing to do with any kind of hypothetical fistfight with me."

Katya laughed. "You threw away Tamara? But she is so much more attractive than you! Why would you do such a thing? Are you one of those . . . what does Rohan say . . . the gays? Did you prefer a mate who also had a schmuck like yours?"

Lahnegarn's cheeks darkened. "That's not funny. You know what is funny, though? What happened to you is funny. I should know. When I watched that video, I laughed and laughed."

Rohan sighed. "You're sounding a little unhinged there, Lonnie. Why don't you go somewhere and calm down."

"I know, that's what people say. I bet I can predict what you'll say next. Ignore the video. It's not real. Hyperion faked it. Generated by computer or something. Except I know the truth, Rohan."

"Do you now?"

"I do. Because I'm the leading expert on video and surveillance in this system. Maybe this side of the sector. And I did a little digging. That video is raw footage. Untouched. You really lost to Hyperion. We all saw it.

"When you fought him, you could barely fly. It's like you weren't even a Hybrid anymore."

8

Ultimata

Katya grinned. "He says you have no Power anymore, Rohan! He is very interesting." She picked up a handful of fries and stuffed them into her face.

Rohan sighed. "Look, Lonnie, things are complicated. So far you've shared a few things that I'm not sure I care about. Was there a point to all this?"

"I'm giving you a chance, Rohan."

"To do what?"

"The right thing. I don't know exactly what happened, but you're weak now. Just a normal guy, kind of like me. Except with a lot of very strong enemies. And when they come after you, Tamara won't be safe. Rinth won't be safe."

Rohan swallowed. "What's your point? You think you can keep them safe?"

"I think the only way you can help them is to walk away from them. Leave Tamara. Walk away from Rinth. Go crawl into a hole somewhere and hope the bad guys don't come for you."

"You think I should just give up."

"I think it's the only responsible thing to do. Don't worry, once you're out of the picture, I'll make sure they're well cared for."

"Lonnie, I don't think that would go the way you think it will. I'm not the only thing preventing you two from having a happy relationship."

"Whatever. I know you tell yourself that. I don't care what you think; with you gone, she'll be with me again, and I'll get my son back. The only question is, will you walk away on your own or am I going to have to force you?"

"You and what army, Lonnie?"

Katya leaned forward. "I think that was a threat, Rohan. Was it? Can I kill him? I haven't killed anybody all day and my claws are itching."

"No, Katya. Tamara would be upset, and she's your friend."

"She is. She is my friend. I will let him live. For now. Besides, he doesn't seem like a fun fight. He is not strong enough."

Lahnegarn huffed. "I'm stronger than I used to be, Rohan. I won't let you endanger my family. Stay away from them or I'll make you stay away."

Rohan finished his beer and motioned for the check. He scratched his stubble. "I think we're done talking, Lonnie. Don't push me. You won't like the results."

"I know what will happen. I know everything that happens, remember? I'm the one with cameras everywhere. I know about your little excavation on the planet. I know about the pod of Tolone'ans who attacked you. I can make your life very difficult."

"One last time, Lonnie. Don't do it. It won't work out in your favor."

Lahnegarn stood. "I'll risk it if that's what it takes to keep my family safe."

"I almost respect that. Almost. Now go."

"See you around, Rohan." The Lukhor walked away and disappeared into the back room of the bar.

Katya looked at Rohan. "He seems unpleasant."

The Hybrid sighed. "He does. That doesn't make him wrong."

◆ ··◦·· ◆

Rohan sank back into the uncomfortable cushioned bench, ignoring the way a hard spot on the right dug into his side, and focused on the diminishing quantity of Sein Ale in his bottle.

Katya kneaded his shoulder and back with both hands, then leaned in and licked his cheek, her whiskers tickling his jaw. "Rohan, it is fine. I am sure your mate will not abandon you to return to her ex-mate. He is not funny at all and lacks something that you have."

"I know you're trying to comfort me, and on some level I appreciate it, but that's not what I'm worried about at all. For the sake of my curiosity, though, what is it that you think I have that he doesn't?"

"You never ended your relationship with Tamara, while he has. Women value that sort of consistency in a mate."

"Actually, I have broken it off with her. We just got back together after. It was before you met her."

"Well, then, I take it back, you *should* worry."

Rohan examined her face as she drank, looking for a sign of humor or sarcasm in her furry cheeks or cat eyes.

He ate some chips and sighed. "The problem is, he has a point. I thought I could keep Tamara safe. The way things are right now, though . . . I don't know."

"I will protect you both, Rohan. So I can repay my debt. I believe today's work has already gone some way toward that goal."

"That's great. What will you do then? You want to return to your people? Go back to Pilli 4? To your tribe?"

She sipped. "I do not know. I like it here. I have many new people to fight, many new foods to taste. I like Ang. Maybe I should stay regardless."

Rohan felt a little tension in his back ease off. *I'm glad her imagined debt to me isn't the only thing keeping her here.* "Whatever you want, Katya." He looked into his mask. No messages. *Of course, I just turned them off.*

Katya pointed at the screen. "Are you expecting something?"

"No. Yes. When I have moments of self-doubt like this, Wei Li always shows up with coffee or food and tells me exactly what I need to hear. That's kind of her job in this relationship. I'm surprised she isn't here to do it."

"Perhaps she has decided that you are a grown man who can manage his own emotions without her interference."

A laugh escaped his chest. "No, that's definitely not it. Come to think of it, she didn't warn me that five Powers were coming after me either. And hasn't checked up on us after the fight. I don't think she's very on top of things right now."

"Perhaps she has found a mate she fancies, and she is on top of *them* right now! Ha, Katya made a good joke!"

"Yes, fantastic. Maybe she is. But it's not like her to be unaware of a security situation. I would have thought she'd at least be monitoring the Tolone'ans. And she was out of sorts when we did the raid the other day."

"Out of sorts? Is she usually in sorts? What kind of sorts?"

"You know, distracted. She was distracted. Got knocked around by that one Boost user. Shouldn't have happened. Maybe we ought to check up on her."

Katya finished her bottle. "You should, Rohan. I will come with you, and we will make sure our friend Wei Li is well."

Rohan stood. "You don't want to visit Ang?"

She shrugged. "He is hurt. I suspect he will be whiny and perhaps a bit needy. I will visit Wei Li instead."

"You're a tough woman, Katya."

"That is why he likes me. Let us try her office first."

"Lead the way."

Rohan slipped some cash to the server as they left; they turned up the promenade and toward Wistful's center section. Ten minutes later, they approached Wei Li's office.

The security officers guarding the entrance recognized the pair and let them through without comment.

Is my disguise not working? Or is Katya that unique?

Should I shave the rest of the beard?

Nah. Have to maintain the brand.

The office door was open; Wei Li sat behind her desk, chin resting on steeplechased fingers.

She raised one line of scales, right where a mammal might have a right eyebrow, as they entered.

"Did I summon you and forget? Or did we have an appointment that is somehow missing from my calendar? Should I put in an urgent ticket for some software engineers to check my scheduling system for a heretofore-unnoticed bug?"

Rohan pointed at a small clock on the wall. "We're worried about you. It's almost midnight and you're in your office. I was going to say, in your office, working, but as far as I can tell, you're just staring at the wall. I'm not sure that qualifies. Unless it does, you're the chief."

Katya sat on Wei Li's desk and leaned over. "It is true, this is not normal behavior for you, my friend Wei Li. Please tell us what is wrong so that we may help."

Wei Li glared at the other woman, then sighed and slumped forward. "Perhaps I was harsh. You are my friends and your concern is, perhaps, warranted."

Rohan took the chair facing her. "You want to tell us what's going on? Or is this one of those things where you're sworn to secrecy? Or knowing the truth would put us all in grave danger?"

Wei Li focused on the Hybrid. "You are being melodramatic. I have a situation, and it is distracting me. That is all."

"What, an old boyfriend showed up? Got you all hot and flustered?"

"Yes."

Rohan's mouth dropped open; Katya's hand slid from where it supported her, and she crashed to the desk, her other hand flailing to catch her weight.

She recovered quickly, hopping off the desk to stand straight. "For reality? You?"

Wei Li sighed. "Why do you find this so hard to believe? I have told you that I am considered very attractive among my people. Did you think I was lying?"

Rohan waved both hands in front of him. "No, no, it's not that at all. I just didn't see you for the type to get so . . . disrupted by the appearance of an old flame, that's all. You seem too . . . practical."

Katya nodded. "Yes, practical. No-nonsense. Not flusterable. Is that a word? It seems like it should be."

Wei Li tapped her nails on the desk. "It is not simply the appearance of a former mate that has me distraught."

Rohan looked behind him; Wei Li took the cue and shut the door by tapping a control on her desk.

The Hybrid nodded. "You know we won't leave you alone until you tell us everything, so you might as well just start at the beginning and spill all the beans. Good and bad."

Katya grinned. "Yes, beans. For you, I will eat even plants, my dear Wei Li."

The security chief nodded and ran her palms over her head. "Before coming to Wistful, I was trained to use my abilities in a special school on my homeworld."

Rohan nodded. "Let me guess, your head teacher was the most powerful empath in the world, and he was bald and a paraplegic, so he rode around in a wheelchair all the time. And had inappropriate thoughts about at least one of his students despite her being a third his age."

"No. Well, yes, he was bald, because my entire species is hairless. As you well know. But the rest . . . what are you talking about, Rohan? Have you received fresh head trauma?"

"Sorry, I've been waiting to make a Professor X joke for almost three years. That was really just for me, I guess."

She sighed while Katya watched them, no comprehension showing in her eyes.

Wei Li tapped the desk again. "Do you want to hear what's wrong or make silly jokes nobody else appreciates?"

"Do I have to choose?"

"Yes."

"Fine. Go on."

"My . . . professor is here, on the station. No, perhaps that isn't the right word. My mentor? My master? The man who taught me everything I know. Gave me a purpose beyond myself."

Rohan nodded. "And he's your old boyfriend. Creepy, but not the first time it's happened."

"No! We never had a relationship of that sort. It would have been inappropriate, even if desired, due to his position of authority over me. I had a closer relationship with two of the students, who are now his primary disciples. They have come with him to Wistful."

Katya nodded. "Two? At the same time? You were a . . . what is the word? A throuple?"

Wei Li shrugged. "That term is as accurate as any. And yes, they are both here on this station."

Rohan swallowed. "So it's not about an ex. It's about two exes. Twice the drama."

Katya shook her head. "Why does everyone on this station make things so complicated? If you are with somebody and it doesn't work out, then it doesn't work out. You move on. Why do you obsess so much? None of my people do this."

Rohan nudged her shoulder. "We don't have our former lovers in our faces all the time, Katya. It's not like the rest of us live in a village with just a few hundred people, is it? You're forced to face your old lovers every day. We . . . aren't. So we get to hold on to feelings we shouldn't be holding on to."

Wei Li looked at the cat-woman. "Do your people never get jealous, then? Never feel hurt?"

Katya shrugged. "Perhaps some do, sometimes. But as Rohan said, they are forced to handle those feelings. I didn't think of it from your way of living."

Wei Li nodded. "Yes. Krai Wu and I did not leave things on good terms. I do not relish the notion of spending time with him. But I owe it to Master Turtle."

Rohan rubbed his eyes. "Okay. Krai Wu . . . is that a male or a female? Just so I can keep all this straight in my head."

"Krai Wu is male. Mai Si is female. She better understood why I left, and held it against me . . . less."

"Must be tough, being in a complicated relationship with another empath."

"Neither of them are empaths. That is my gift alone."

"But they were in the special school with you, right? Are they Powers of another kind?"

Wei Li leaned back in her chair and stretched her arms overhead. "The school was not for children with Powers. It was for members of a particular order. Some were Powers, if only minor ones, and there were several empaths like me."

Katya ran her claws gently over the desktop. "What does this mean? Order? I do not know this word." She looked at Rohan, who shrugged.

Wei Li tightened her lips. "Members of my family have been bound to a common purpose with other families for many generations."

Rohan swallowed. "Many? That is very vague. How many? Three? Thirty? Three hundred?"

"Perhaps more than that. Records from the earliest days of the order are sparse."

Rohan leaned forward, resting his elbows on his knees. "What kind of order, Wei Li? Religious? Don't tell me you worship something with tentacles. I mean, if you do, no judgment, but please don't tell me. I can't handle that today."

"Nothing quite like that. My ancestors were bound by an oath, that is all."

"You're bound by an oath sworn by your great-great—look, I'm not even going to try to say that three hundred times. That's crazy."

She shrugged, the hollows behind her collarbones deepening with the motion. "Nevertheless."

Katya cocked her head. "I don't understand."

Rohan rubbed his eyes. "Wei Li's family does things because their ancestors promised to, a very long time ago. And their kids still follow those instructions."

Katya nodded. "Ah, I see! They have a law."

Wei Li looked at her. "What?"

"My people obey the law in all things. All of us. Well, except when some do not, then they are killed. Usually. Unless Rohan interferes. You know the story. But almost always we follow the law, which was given to us many,

many generations ago. You do the same, but only some of your people follow your law."

Rohan's mouth dropped open again. "I can't even argue with that comparison. It *is* kind of the same thing."

Wei Li nodded. "Our oaths have been passed down for centuries. They have survived a dozen languages, transcontinental migrations, at least fifty wars, and countless changes in government. The chosen families have not wavered in our dedication to it."

Katya leaned forward and licked the reptilian woman's forehead. "That is most admirable, Wei Li. I approve."

Rohan sighed. "Is it, though? What exactly is this oath? What are you sworn to actually do, Wei Li? Are you just keeping the secret recipe for fried chicken? Or are you waiting for an order to assassinate somebody? Or start a war?"

Wei Li paused, blinking rapidly before speaking. "It is somewhat . . . complicated."

"Too many of us are saying that too often, and most of that is from me. I'm not letting you get away with it."

"Our oaths are to be kept secret from outsiders."

"Can you give me a hint? Are there any exceptions? Maybe, I don't know, for Hybrids?" *Fat chance of that.*

"Maybe yes."

Rohan's mouth dropped open again. *That's three times in just this one conversation. I was not ready for this.* "Wait, really?"

Wei Li shrugged. "As I said, it is complicated. The fact is that some of the details of our code may have been lost over the centuries."

"May have been. Maybe you could be a little more specific."

"Our oaths were recorded in a language that is no longer spoken. Records of that time have been transcribed many times, and it is possible, or even likely, that at various points in time they were kept in a purely oral form."

"Spoken. So there were writings, but they've been lost, and you can't really read them anyway, and at some point they were actually recreated from what somebody's grandma remembered of something she memorized as a kid?"

"The chain of evidence is not so convoluted as that. But let us say it is imperfect. Some in the order disagree regarding some of the details and their meaning."

Rohan sighed. "This is . . . you're serious? Or are you messing with me right now? Because it's starting to sound like you're messing with me."

Katya stared at him. "I don't see a mess."

Wei Li shook her head. "I am not."

Rohan waited for her to explain further; she didn't. He looked at her. "You disagree with your old boyfriend's interpretation, is that it? He thinks you should be doing something specific, and you're not sure, because you don't believe in the oath the same way he does. Am I on the right track?"

"You are."

"What does he want you to do? Let me guess. He's the top student at the school for gifted children, and you're the top female, and your creed says you're supposed to bear his children."

"No."

"What, then?"

"He wants me to kill our master."

9

Ask No Questions, Hear No Lies

Rohan stared at Wei Li. "That's metaphorical, right? Kill him metaphorically. Like, you'll become the master, and he'll be the disciple. Or kill him like he's Buddha and you found him on the road. You don't mean literally walk up to the guy who trained you and, like, murder him. Do you?"

The security chief shrugged. "It's complicated."

"I think you say that as a way to avoid answering the question."

"Yes."

"Did you learn that from me?"

"No, Rohan, you did not invent avoiding questions. People have been avoiding questions for as long as there have been uncomfortable questions. Which is probably about one day less than there has been language."

"Right."

Katya's eyes whipped back and forth as they spoke, tracking the speaker at all times, wide and curious. "After you kill him, will you eat him, Wei Li?"

Wei Li's jaw tightened. "In a manner of speaking."

Rohan threw his arms up. "I give up. This is insane."

"You asked me to explain, I am trying to explain."

"It's not really explaining if it doesn't make any sense! It's just . . . obfuscating. It's the opposite of explaining. You're giving me a headache."

Katya slid over to a spot next to him and began kneading his shoulder with both hands. "It is fine, Rohan. I am sure you will figure everything out eventually. You are much smarter than you look."

"I look perfectly . . . you're trying to distract me too. I think you're doing it on purpose."

Katya smiled, showing off long incisors, and turned to Wei Li. "Can we meet your friends? Before you kill any of them, I mean. I like new people, and perhaps one of them will enjoy fighting."

Wei Li looked at Rohan. "That's an interesting idea. Would you like to meet Krai Wu?"

"Why?"

She shrugged. "Why not? Is that not what people do? Introduce one another to old friends?"

"Sure. Yes. I think. I just . . . it's not something *you* do. You're acting weird."

"What do you mean?"

"You're acting weird by acting normal."

She tilted her head and glared at him through the corners of her eyes. "Rohan. You are not making sense. Perhaps it is you who are the source of your confusion."

"Okay. Okay, yes. I will meet your Krai Wu and Mai Si and this Turtle Master guy you're supposed to kill. When do we do it?"

"It is late, and I believe they acclimated to Wistful's circadian cycle during their trip, so we should wait for morning. We can have breakfast. Pop's?"

"I can't go to Pop's. People know me there, and I'm in hiding, remember?"

"Sorry, I do. Where, then?"

"I'll message you a place."

She nodded. "Good."

"But first, do you mind if I have a few minutes alone with that Takslee Boost dealer?"

"The leader? Keilee?"

"No. The male. Reghis. I think he'll give me something."

"Give me five minutes to make arrangements."

—■·•·■—

The snake-headed Takslee sat on a bare bench, leaning against a bare wall, resting his bare orange-scaled feet on the bare metal floor while he glared at his visitor.

"I'm not telling you anything."

"Of course, of course. I'm not keeping you up, am I? I know it's late. Almost midnight."

"I'm not a kid, Hybrid. I can stay up. Kind of have to, in my line of work. If you know what I mean."

"I do! Makes sense."

The Takslee glared at him with vertically slit pupils. "I don't know why you had me separated from Keilee. If you think she's the tough one, you're wrong. I'm plenty tough without her."

Rohan shook his head. "No, no. You misunderstand me. It's not that I don't think you're tough. It's that I think you're the smart one."

Reghis's head lifted. "What?"

"Yeah, I could tell before. Listening to you. While you were talking. Which, I think, isn't something you're used to, right? Having someone listen?"

"Well, I guess not. Sure. Keilee isn't much of a listener. More of a leader, I guess."

Rohan nodded and folded his arms across his chest. "I know that's what she thinks, and maybe that's what you think, but I'm not sure it's fair. Why is she the leader? You're just as powerful. I felt that fighting you guys. And she's the one who surrendered first. You're pretty smart, too. Why aren't *you* the leader?"

"That's just not how things work. In my species. The females are the leaders."

Rohan leaned forward, close enough to smell the faint musk from the reptilian's glands. "We're not on your home planet, Reghis. You don't have to always do things the regular way."

Reghis swallowed. "I know. That's not the point. What do you care, anyway? It's none of your business."

"No, it's not. Nothing to do with me. I just wanted to have a little talk with the brains of the outfit, and from where I was standing, that seemed to be you."

"Yeah?" He swallowed again. "Sure. Maybe. What do you want?"

"I just want to ask a few questions."

"What, more about Con-Conspiracy? I don't think I have anything more to tell you about it. You can just watch them on the net. They're all over."

"No, not that."

Reghis's eyes hardened. "What, then?"

"I was hoping you could tell me a little more about selling Boost on the station."

"I told you, I'm not going to—if you think getting me alone is going to get me to give up Granny, you have—"

"Wait, hold on. Granny?"

Reghis sighed. "All the Boost on Wistful goes through Granny. You didn't even know that? Oh boy, are you guys lost."

"Yeah. You're absolutely right, Reghis. We are. Lost. Who is this Granny person?"

The snake-man shrugged. "I'm not telling you that. Come on, we already explained. There's no point trying to get me to do something that's only going to get me killed. You said it yourself, I'm too smart to fall for that."

"Oh yeah. You definitely are. Too smart. But maybe you could give me something. Not, like, an address."

"Definitely not."

"But something more general. You already saw how clueless I am. Just help me understand things a little better. Like, right now, I wouldn't even be able to score any Boost for myself, even if I wanted to. Maybe you could help me with something like that."

"You want Boost? Why? You guys took our supply. That should last you for years."

Crap.

"Right. But what if I wanted something more than that? An opportunity."

"What kind of opportunity?"

"I don't know. Maybe we could work something out. I bet we could move a lot more Boost through Wistful if she was cooperating. Maybe security could be on Granny's side instead of fighting her."

"I don't know anything about that."

"Of course you don't. But Granny might be interested in that, wouldn't she? I'm still a Hybrid. Maybe I could help her in . . . other ways."

Reghis shifted in his seat, squirming his hips against the hard bench. "No, I can't. I don't even know where she is, to be honest. I can't help you."

"You might not know where she is exactly, but I'm sure you know how people get to meet her. There must be a way to arrange something. How would anyone go about setting that up?"

Reghis's forked tongue flicked the air. "It's not that easy. She has lieutenants. Four of them, one for each arm. They can contact her, but they're going to have an empath around to screen you. You can't just go up to them and lie about why you want to meet her. They'll sniff you out and—" He clapped his hands with a sharp slap. "That's the end of that."

"Who says anything about lying? I'm not afraid of an empath screening me. I have nothing to hide."

"Yeah? Okay, sure. Good luck to you, then. You're going to need it. Granny's no joke."

"I'm sure she isn't. How do I find one of these lieutenants? So I can set up a meeting?"

Reghis laughed. "That's the problem, see? I know where they *were*. At least a couple of them. But I'm sure they heard about what happened to us. Especially since Sirc escaped. They'll all be taking precautions now, moving to new spots."

Rohan sighed. "I guess that makes sense."

"Hey, I'd help you if I could. If you're serious, and you get past the empath, it could be a real coup for Granny. She'd owe me a favor, maybe. But I can't do anything, not from in here."

"And if I let you go?"

The reptile shrugged. "I'd like to say I'd be able to help, but the truth is I'd probably leave the station the millisecond I could catch a flight out. The others won't trust me after being captured."

"Right. Right. Okay, then." Rohan stood and straightened his pants and shirt. "Thanks for your help."

"I didn't help you. But whatever."

I could threaten him. Say that I'll spread rumors that he gave up all kinds of details about Granny.

Then have him cut loose and see what happens.

Nah, he's probably right. The other dealers will probably just stay away from the guy.

I know more than I did this morning, but this is still a dead end.

10

Who is the Master?

R ohan and Katya found another place to sleep: an unofficial flop-
house nestled in the back of a building in one of the poorer parts
of the southern arm, far from the promenade, accessible only through
openings cut through walls where no doors were supposed to be.

Rohan paid cash for the room, the hood of his red sweatshirt pulled low
over his face, his baggy black pants the furthest thing from his tow chief
uniform that he could have imagined.

Katya did her best to disguise herself, covering her face with the long
cowl attached to a cloak she'd bought herself in a shopping frenzy ignited
by her discovery of credit and instant-fabrication shops.

I wonder why these other people are staying here and not someplace nicer.

*I guess if they were willing to share their reasons, they wouldn't be staying
here to begin with.*

The sheets were clean, the mattresses comfortable, which was more than
Rohan had expected when paying for the room.

Katya spent half an hour talking to Ang over an encrypted line.

He missed her but was fine; other Ursans had bandaged his leg.

Tamara was staying with one of Ursula's cousins, where nobody would
think to look for her. Rinth was safe. The Consortium wouldn't have any
way to find either of them.

Ursula had made many friends, all over the station, especially since beginning her political career. She had activated that network; they were alert
and listening for any word of a group of Tolone'ans looking for a Lukhor.

Prepared to misdirect The Consortium away from the innocent.

Ursula's a good friend. That's as much as I could do to keep Tamara safe. More than.

That thought triggered a spike of loathing-tinged anger; the esoteric spiral in Rohan's soul trembled.

He exhaled, willing the anger to dissipate.

None of this matters. Not in the big picture.

Have to stay calm. That's the first step; keep the helix going. Figure that out and everything else will fall into place

He found a restaurant where he wouldn't be recognized; sent the address to Wei Li.

They slept.

Ten years of service in the il'Drach Fleet had given Rohan the ability to sleep under any level of stress or duress. Katya's ability was natural; her people could curl up and sleep anywhere, at any time, no matter the situation.

They woke to Rohan's helmet alarm.

Half an hour later, they were clean and waiting at a table in Wisdom House, an Ohnian eatery opened by some of the handful of refugees who hadn't left Wistful for their people's new home on Pilli 5.

Rohan secured a table for six; the furniture was well-polished wood, every piece showing the natural contours of the trees, not planed down to flat boards and right angles. Knots were stained and exposed, the grain emphasized, especially where it was uneven.

Katya purred and ran her hands over all the chairs, then over the table itself. "It's a little bit of nature, Rohan! Like home. Better than home."

He nodded. "It's not Ohnian, I don't think, but I'm not surprised this is the stuff they would gravitate toward. Oh, look, Wei Li is here."

He had never seen four people of Wei Li's race, the Vor'karei, together.

The males were tall, the younger a few centimeters taller than the older but both close to two meters. The younger male was trim and muscular, with a jawline like a cowcatcher on a train and an impossibly triangular torso, shoulders like barn doors and lean hips. The female was Wei Li's height but softer, carrying more fat than the lean security chief.

Each had a distinct pattern of red and green scales marking their yellow skin, the lines differing in number and placement.

Rohan stood involuntarily.

Something had struck him.

One of the group had an aura, an esoteric presence, a subtle body, completely different from the others.

A Power.

He swallowed and waved to catch Wei Li's eye. His friend led her little group to the table.

Rohan couldn't take his eyes off the older man.

While he was short, his presence was overwhelming. His skin was lined with age but still vital; his physique thick, as if a sack of boulders had been stuffed into his shirt. He walked with the easy rolling gate of a trained athlete: relaxed and calm but radiating the potential for explosive power.

Wei Li cleared her throat, drawing Rohan's gaze away from the man he presumed was her master.

"Rohan, this is Krai Wu, and this is Mai Si. This is Rohan."

Krai Wu put a hand to his chest and gave a shallow bow. "Tow Chief. It is an honor to meet you."

Rohan shook his head to clear it. "I'm not an active tow chief at the moment. Just Rohan is fine. It's a pleasure to meet you. Wei Li has told us so much about you, it's as if I know you already."

Krai Wu's scaled brows lifted. "Really?"

"No. She's very tight-lipped, actually."

Mai Si gave out the sort of sparkling laugh that would be heard throughout the restaurant and put all but the sourest patrons into a better mood. "Darling, you can't have forgotten how she is. How she always was."

Krai Wu lowered his head, his cheeks darkening slightly. "Of course. It's just been so long."

Wei Li nodded and moved to take the spot next to Rohan. Her master followed behind, a soft smile on his lips, his eyes clear but unfocused, taking in everything around him but settling on nothing.

Rohan elbowed his friend. "Aren't you going to introduce me to, er . . ."

Krai Wu cleared his throat. "The master is engaged in a meditative ritual. He can no longer speak or, we think, understand speech."

Katya walked around the table and stood close to the older man. He looked right through her.

She leaned forward and licked his cheek; Wei Li started forward, as if to pull her away, but the il'Zkin didn't continue.

The old man's smile never wavered.

Katya tapped her lips, a puzzled expression on her face, and returned to her spot.

Rohan swallowed. "I . . . it's a pleasure to meet all of you."

Wei Li put a small box on the table and tapped a button on top of it. "Privacy screen. We may all speak freely here."

Mai Si nodded as she took the seat next to Katya's. "We were eager to meet you, Rohan. You have performed great services for Wistful."

"Have I? Towed some ships, I guess. Not sure why you'd care, to be honest."

She looked at Wei Li. "He does not know."

Wei Li shook her head. "There has never been a reason to tell him."

Katya clapped her hands as a server put two trays on the table and lifted the woven cloth covering each. Steam escaped in a cloud, coming from two matching piles of fluffy buns.

"Those smell wonderful! Are these from plants, Rohan?"

"Yes, Katya. It's bread. You've had bread before. Wait, there was never a reason to tell me what? What haven't you told me?"

Krai Wu nudged their master, then pointed at the bread. The old man reached for a roll, picked it up, pulled off a piece, and put it into his mouth.

Wei Li watched him do it, her shoulders slumping.

Rohan shivered. "I don't need to be an empath to see that you think something is wrong here, Wei Li."

She shook her head. "It's not wrong. Not exactly. I just wasn't ready."

"Ready for what? Is this a prank? When are you going to actually tell me something about what's happening here? Maybe start with what's going on with him. Or what I haven't apparently been told because there wasn't a reason. I'm pretty curious about that."

Katya stroked his upper arm. "Relax, Rohan. I am sure they will tell you in good time. Be patient. Like me."

"You are never patient." He noticed how fast his heart was beating and laid his hands flat on the table, then exhaled slowly. Katya took a bun.

A calming aura washed over the table; something like the wave of aura that Ursula could project when she wanted to reduce tensions, but somehow cleaner, more sterile.

It came from the old man.

Rohan sighed. "How can he be so calm? I've never sensed anything like it."

Krai Wu tore a bun in half and smelled deeply of the interior. "You should have seen him before. He was the fiercest warrior on all of Plassek. His anger could be truly terrible. As could his love."

Wei Li nodded. "He was fierce, and bold, and strong. To see him like this . . ."

Mai Si reached across the table and put her hand on top of Wei Li's. "He wanted this. He thought it was time."

"Why now?"

The female cast a quick glance Rohan's way. "With The Guardian weakened or removed, Wistful needs protection. Master Turtle is too old, and not familiar with the station and the situation here."

Krai Wu shook his head. "It wasn't age. He thought Wei Li would be a better Shield. She's the strongest empath he ever trained, with the—"

Mai Si put a hand on his shoulder, gripping it tightly. "Do not speak as if we are home, my love."

He put a hand over hers and nodded. "Sorry, that was careless."

For a moment they froze: Mai Si's right hand on Wei Li's, her left on Krai Wu's, a delicate energy suffusing the scene.

Master Turtle finished the bread and belched.

An Ohnian, tall with a single large eye dominating the center of his face, came to the table to take their orders.

Katya ordered four entrees 'just to try.' The others picked from a variety of dishes, simple combinations of beds of cooked grain with fresh greens laid on top, dressed in one of the five primary sauces of Ohnian cuisine.

It wasn't Rohan's first Ohnian meal.

After the orders were taken, Mai Si looked at the Hybrid. "Our families have been sworn to certain responsibilities for a very long time, Rohan. We three were born into it, and we sometimes forget that others do not share that background. We are not trying to confuse or disorient you."

"Well then, I hope you don't decide to do it on purpose, because just by accident you're doing a hell of a job."

"I apologize for that. The first thing you should know is that—"

Wei Li interrupted. "Is this necessary?"

Krai Wu looked at her with cold reptilian eyes. "You brought him. You know it is."

The security chief glared back at him for a long breath, then broke contact and nodded while fidgeting with the bandages over her ribs.

Mai Si smiled. "The Lifters tasked our ancestors with certain responsibilities. One of them was keeping watch over Wistful."

Rohan swallowed. "Two sentences and there's already a lot to unpack. Lifters?"

Wei Li took a roll while Master ate a second. "Our species was uplifted from more primitive reptiles. The humanoid body type did not evolve on our world, it was created."

"Really? A whole planet of creationists?"

"It is not a theory, it is fact. It is true for most humanoid species through the sector. Some may have evolved, but most were designed. Some by their own predecessors."

"Okay. Why Wistful?"

Mai Si looked at the other two, who shook their heads. Then she turned to Rohan. "That is a matter for debate. I would say most of us think it has something to do with the wormholes."

"A debate because you lost the original orders, right?"

Krai Wu laughed sardonically. "All we have are fragments and scraps. The occasional relic. Nothing dating to the time the oaths were first sworn."

"Okay. You were supposed to watch the station. Did you?"

Mai Si nodded, her chin doubling briefly with the motion. "We have watched, in one way or another, for almost our entire history."

Krai Wu snorted. "Except for the three hundred years when we were cut off from star travel because of our internal squabbles."

Wei Li pointed a finger at him. "Even then, some were smuggled through space. They did what they could."

He shrugged and drank from his glass of water.

"Wei Li was sent here to be The Watcher."

"So, what, one of you people has been acting as security chief for three hundred generations? And it's been a secret? Wistful didn't realize?"

Wei Li shook her head. "Not always security chief. That was my idea, because of my abilities as an empath. I thought it was the way I would be able to do the most good."

He turned to her. "Does she know?"

Wei Li shrugged. "I have never told her. I have also never asked. It is possible she knows and has simply . . . never brought it up."

He scratched his beard. "Okay. That's it? You're supposed to watch her? There must be more, right? Something you're supposed to do."

Mai Si smiled. "That, too, is a subject for debate. At some point we are to protect her."

Krai Wu put his roll down half eaten and leaned forward. "We are to be her Shield."

Rohan nodded. "When?"

The younger male laughed. "That is the hard question. We don't have a specific date, only clues."

"Of course things couldn't have been easy." The Hybrid looked at Master, at his potent aura, calm and deep and serene like the ocean on a still day. "How are you supposed to protect her? Do you have a fleet of ships to fight with? More Powers?"

"The Lifters blessed us with both purpose and a weapon to be used."

"I hope it's a doozy of a weapon. Is it an axe? Axes are cool. Swords are passé, if you ask me. Been done to death."

The three younger Vor'karei looked at their master.

Mai Si cleared her throat. "It is neither sword nor axe. The weapon left us by the Lifters is a technique. I should say a set of techniques. Martial techniques."

Krai Wu shook his head. "It is more than a technique or a collection of techniques. In truth, our weapon is a soul."

11

The Cost of Beautification

Servers brought their food, heaped high on lacquered wooden bowls; chubby spoons the only utensils.

Katya sampled each of her dishes before picking one to devour completely.

Krai Wu and Wei Li helped Master Turtle eat, mostly by putting the spoon in his hand, pointing at his dish, and nudging his arm in the right direction.

"He's your weapon?"

Mai Si smiled. "The Lifters taught our families blood magic, Rohan. We can absorb the soul of another, and by so doing, add their ki to our own. Take in their strength."

The Hybrid scratched his beard. "That's . . . vampirism. And it's a problem because you absorb their personality as well, and if you do that too many times, all the conflicting character traits drive you insane. Which you already know. I shouldn't have to tell you this."

Wei Li swallowed. "They also taught us a way to scrub clean our soul before passing it on. Toward the end of life, each master of the order purifies their spirit, removing all personal traits, until all that is left is the desire to release that soul to a deserving recipient."

Katya squealed softly as she bit into something unusually tasty. "Rohan, eat. These are some of the best plants I have ever eaten! The only thing that could make this any better would be replacing them with meat."

"Ohnians don't eat meat. I'm glad you like it. Hold on, I'm still processing this." He looked at Master Turtle, then at Wei Li. "That's what he's doing, isn't it? Cleansing his soul so he can pass on all that accumulated Power to his disciple. That's why his aura is so strong. He's eaten three hundred generations of his ancestors, metaphysically speaking."

Wei Li nodded. "He has decided it is time to pass on the Eternity Ki."

Rohan rubbed his temples. "And to pass it on without driving his inheritor insane, he has to remove any traces of his own personality from it."

"Exactly."

Mai Si sighed. "He has to destroy every trace of himself. It is why he now appears as if a child."

"He's killing himself. In any meaningful sense of the word."

Krai Wu shrugged. "And in the normal sense of the word. He is destroying himself as a person, but once he passes on the Eternity Ki, his body will die as well. It is only a question of when."

Mai Si looked at Wei Li. "When, and *to whom* the weapon will be passed."

Wei Li shook her head. "I told him, and I told you, I don't want it."

Krai Wu snorted. "I told you she wouldn't change her mind. We should not have come here."

His partner glared at him. "What alternative did we have? Master Turtle insisted it be her. He did not want you to have it, my love. Should we have forced him? How? Do you want to be the one to try that?"

"We just had to wait, my dear. He will forget who Wei Li is soon enough, and then he will give it to anybody. In fact, that's exactly the problem. If we are here, that anybody could be someone outside the order. Or someone unworthy. Is that what you want to see?"

"Of course not." Her voice accrued a hard edge it hadn't contained before. "Your fight is not with me, darling. Nor should your anger be directed my way."

He held up a hand in peace.

Wei Li's cheeks were tight. "Why now, though? What is urgent? Was he ill? He seems healthy. Physically. There are still two closed wormholes, and there hasn't been any special activity recently."

Mai Si shook her head. "He wanted to come when the first wormhole opened, you know that. You convinced him to stay, that the station was already shielded, with the Hybrid here. There was no apparent threat."

Rohan raised a hand. "Me? I'm the Hybrid?"

Mai Si nodded. "We must form a Shield to protect Wistful. That much is known and is not in dispute. However, the question regarding when, exactly, we are to do so, that is another matter."

Krai Wu chuckled. "We all thought The Shield should be created when the first wormhole opened. Only Wei Li doubted. If it were anyone else, there would have been no discussion, but Master Turtle has always trusted her wisdom."

Wei Li glared daggers at him. "Given that he is your master, and that *he* trusted me, perhaps you should have done the same."

"I did! I bowed to his decision. As did we all. We waited. And another wormhole opened, and the station was put in great danger!"

"Danger against which we prevailed! In large part because Rohan was here!"

Rohan coughed. "Not that I don't appreciate the credit, but in large part because you were here too, though. Let's be fair."

"My point is, Wistful is safe, and her safety was secured without the Eternity Ki. No further intervention was required."

Katya swallowed the last bite of her first dish and reached for the second. "You don't need a shield here now either. I'm here, and so is Wildeye."

Wildeye is doing fine as a tow chief, but I'm not sure she's keeping anybody safe.

Mai Si shook her head. "Wildeye is not enough. Don't argue with me, Master Turtle said so. He read the reports."

Rohan swallowed. "Why are you all here now, exactly? Break it down for me."

"Master Turtle saw you defeated by Hyperion. This place is important. We have known that for hundreds of generations. It must be protected. It is our sworn duty to protect it.

"If you are unable, then our greatest weapon must pass on to Wei Li so she can be The Shield that guards this station from any who would interfere with her."

◆ ··•·· ◆

Rohan dug his spoon into his bowl, mixing the heavily seasoned vegetables into the rice-like grains at the bottom.

I guess that makes this my fault.

Wei Li shook her head. "You should not have come here. It isn't time. Wistful is safe; the prophecies don't say—"

Master Turtle's aura expanded and thickened, like mist forming out of humid air, covering the table, muffling sounds and sensory input.

The sounds of the other patrons muted and dulled. The view of the promenade through the front window blurred. Rohan could barely smell the roll in his hand; even the feeling of the smooth wood he sat on seemed to come from very far away, as if his body were disassociated from him somehow.

The old Vor'karei smiled, the calm and relaxed expression on his face draining the tension out of everyone at the table. Rohan sagged back into his chair, his spine a puddle, his hips turned to gel, his neck limp.

The aura lifted slowly, losing its intensity evenly.

The smile remained.

Master Turtle reached out and put one arm on Wei Li's shoulder. She faced him; they all faced him, all eyes on the old man.

He turned to Wei Li and gently squeezed her shoulder.

Tears leaked down her cheeks.

◆ ··•·· ◆

It took ten minutes for anyone to speak after that.

Katya began describing her third dish, significantly creamier and less spicy than her second, and offering tastes of it to the others. Mai Si took a bite, then Krai Wu, and soon all were making small, satisfied noises and passing dishes to try.

Wei Li's eyes remained haunted.

Krai Wu finished his meal, pushed his bowl away, and told the story of how the three of them had first become romantically entangled.

It involved a sporting event, excessive alcohol consumption, and both Krai Wu and Wei Li coming off bad breakups.

Mai Si told a story of the camping trip where they had first agreed to be exclusive. By the end of it, Wei Li's face began to relax.

Master Turtle watched them talk, no sign of comprehension in his eyes, his hand never leaving Wei Li's shoulder.

Katya told the others about her brother, her brother's best friend, and Rohan's part in their friendship.

The Vor'karei laughed at his errors. After a minute, he joined them.

Servers brought pots of tea, three different kinds, and several trays of tiny cookies topped with sugar and fruit preserves.

The group sat and chatted and sampled cookies for half an hour. Rohan told the story of meeting the Ursans for the first time and how his relationship with Tamara started.

Wei Li's comm pinged, calling her to work.

She gently removed Master Turtle's hand from her shoulder and stood. His smile never wavered, but his eyes didn't follow her movements.

"I must go, my people are expecting me."

Mai Si stood, came around the table, and hugged the security chief. "We will see you later, yes?"

Wei Li nodded. "I'll see you after the shift."

Krai Wu stood and hugged her as well, holding significantly more stiffness in his arms and back as he did it. "Don't take too long. He doesn't have much time."

Wei Li sighed. "I won't change my mind."

"You will. You'll just be stubborn about it. I pray you're not so stubborn that it becomes too late."

She nodded without responding and left.

The Vor'karei sat as Rohan finished his tea.

Krai Wu looked at the Hybrid. "I hear you lost your Powers. I did not think that within the realm of possibility for an il'Drach Hybrid."

Rohan shrugged. "It's complicated."

"Is it a result of the damage you sustained? Will they come back? Will you be able to protect Wistful?"

Mai Si patted his arm. "Do not interrogate our new friend. You are making him uncomfortable."

The man's eyes hardened. "If questions bother him so, then he is not fit to be The Shield."

Rohan nodded. "I agree."

Krai Wu's eyes widened. "You do?"

"Yeah. I was a tow chief, not a Shield. I never signed on for this. Today is the first time I'm even hearing about any of it."

Mai Si nodded and looked at him, concern filling her reptilian eyes. "You are going through a difficult time, Rohan. I sympathize. We might be able to help."

He stretched. "I don't think I was asking you for help, but what did you have in mind?"

She looked at Master Turtle, then at her mate, then back at Rohan. "If Wei Li will not accept the Eternity Ki, perhaps another might do so."

Rohan scratched his head. "What would that entail? What would you need me to do?"

Mai Si smiled. "You would have to accept the oath of our order, of course. To be The Shield protecting Wistful. And some other things. To agree to pass on the Eternity Ki to another heir in the order when it is time."

He shook his head. "Something tells me that this whole Shield business means putting Wistful's safety at the top of my priority list. Is that right?"

She nodded. "Of course. That is our purpose. That is the purpose for which the Eternity Ki has been purified and passed down through the generations."

"Look, I care about Wistful, and I'll work to keep her safe. I have worked to keep her safe. But she's not my top priority. I have a lot of other responsibilities."

Mai Si traded a look with her partner. "Are you sure? This could be a way to restore your abilities. You might not be able to protect everyone, but as you are now, you can protect no one. Surely our way is better?"

Rohan laughed. "First of all, don't underestimate my ability to take care of people. I might not be as helpless as you think. Second of all, I'm sort of famous for my unwillingness to walk a path just because it is the lesser of two evils. It's kind of my brand."

Krai Wu scratched under his lantern jaw. "I respect that attitude, but sometimes the world forces us to compromise."

"I'm still on team looking-for-a-third-option. That's the hill I'm ready to die on, to be honest. For . . . reasons."

"I see."

"Also, I'm not sure the purified soul inside that old man would play well inside a Hybrid. I'm half il'Drach. There's stuff in there that might reject the Eternity Ki. Or corrupt it. Make it angry. You don't really want to take that kind of a risk."

They looked at Master Turtle, who took a cookie from the tray and ate it.

Katya finished the last bowl of food and leaned back in her chair. "I have never eaten so much in my life. Why did you let me order four meals? What makes you think I should be eating four entire meals by myself? I am a tiny person. I am half your size."

Rohan grunted. "Was I supposed to stop you? I'm not your father."

She burped. "You might as well be. You are one of the Fathers, yes? And they are the same as the Lifters those two spoke of, are they not?"

Four reptilian eyes focused on Rohan. Mai Si spoke. "What does she mean?"

Rohan sighed. "There is a race of people who came before the il'Drach. We think they are responsible for spreading humanoids, at least mammalian humanoids, across the sector."

Krai Wu nodded. "And you believe these are the Lifters?"

He rubbed his eyes. "I don't know. Maybe. They built the wormholes. We think. Left weapons behind. Like the kaiju on Toth 3."

Katya nodded. "And Rohan is one of them! An honorary member, but still. He is leader of their soldiers. Their general. A general without an army, but still. He has an amulet and everything."

Mai Si sat up taller in her seat. "That is all the more reason to think you are worthy of inheriting the Eternity Ki! It was the Lifters who taught us to create it, who left us the technology. For it to be returned to them, and to their general."

Krai Wu shook his head softly. "He doesn't want it, though. You heard him. Wei Li doesn't want it; he doesn't want it. The greatest treasure in the galaxy and nobody wants it. Truly the universe is mocking us."

She put her arm around his shoulder. "Don't say that. There is still time. We will talk to her again. When open eyes become The Shield. She will hear it, if not today, then tomorrow."

Rohan's eyes tightened. "What was that?"

Krai Wu nodded. "That is the prophecy. When open eyes become The Shield."

Rohan mouthed the words. "That doesn't even make sense."

"We know. Something is missing. Perhaps a word was lost or some meaning was misplaced in translation. Mai Si keeps a notebook with the writings to study; you can look yourself."

Rohan looked at Katya, who shrugged. "I am no linguist, Rohan."

He eyed the pot of tea, considering, then gave in and poured some more into his cup. "I don't know what Wei Li will do. Or what he wants her to do." He tilted his head toward Master Turtle when he spoke, indicating who 'he' meant. "But I'll try to help you find a solution to the problem at hand. How much time do we have? Before he's . . . finished with his cleansing?"

Krai Wu sighed. "We do not know exactly. Days. Perhaps a week. At some point he will have lost so much of himself that he won't be able to control the transfer."

Katya looked at Rohan. "This was fun, but I want to check on Ang and the others."

Rohan finished the cup of tea. "You should, but I can't be seen around them. Too many people know we're friends. We can meet later."

"Back at the room where we slept?"

"Yeah. I might as well go there and . . . I don't know. Meditate."

Katya hugged the others goodbye, licking Master Turtle's face with an enthusiasm that he neither denied nor returned, and left.

"What will you guys do today?"

Krai Wu shrugged. "Watch over our master. Wait for Wei Li. Train."

Rohan tapped some instructions into his mask. "I'll talk to Wei Li, see if I can get her sorted out. But no promises."

Mai Si hugged him. "Thank you, Rohan. You have been a good friend, taking care of Wei Li for us. We will always be grateful to you."

"I think you have that backward, but it's my pleasure either way."

12

New Friends With Pets

R ohan sat at the table, drumming his fingers on the smooth wooden surface and sipping tea, and watched the Vor'karei file out, Mai Si taking the rear, subtle touches steering Master Turtle toward the exit.

Servers brought a fresh pot of tea; he paid with coins and stared at the far wall of the restaurant.

Twenty minutes passed while his mind churned through the things he'd learned.

I can't tell if they gave me more answers or more new questions to ponder. My head is spinning.

Wei Li is here on a holy mission to protect this station, and all this time I thought she was just a retired cop looking for an easy life.

This is turning out to be one of those days.

He drank tea until his bladder forced him to get up, then took care of things and left.

The Hybrid looked up and down the promenade, noting the crowds that could have concealed any number of angry Tolone'ans, Boost dealers, or other malcontents out to ruin his day.

He set his mask to push music through the comm that adhered to his skin, just behind his ear, and set it to his work playlist. With a grunt, he took the nearest staircase down to the transit level and waited for a two-person pod.

He hummed along to "Saiyaan Ji" as the pod whisked across the station.

When he got out, he took the stairs up to the promenade and looked for a foyer in the right place for the call he had to make: secluded but close enough to a certain ship's dock.

He found it, an enclosed lobby leading to offices that were all shut down for the weekend.

He took out his mask and dug deep into the settings to connect to an intranet by manual selection.

I used to know how—there it is.

"Hail, *Insatiable*."

"Oh, Captain Rohan! It's so nice to hear from you! I've been looking at the most interesting thing, you wouldn't believe how strange and wonderful it is. Do you remember those ruins on Toth 3 that Professor Stone's students found? That time they went to the surface and almost got eaten by a decipede but you swooped in and saved them? Even though in all honesty they probably didn't deserve it so I guess you were fighting evolution by doing it. Still—"

Rohan laughed despite himself. "I do! I do. I was there, *Insatiable*."

"Of course you were. I just said that, didn't I? Oh, you mean that since you were there, you remember those events and there's no need for me to repeat them, right? I forget sometimes what biologicals remember and what you don't. Professor Stone will forget to eat for two days, and I'm supposed to remind her to take breaks, you know. How could someone forget to eat?"

"I know it's confusing, but I'm in a bit of a hurry right now. I don't really have time to chat. Or explain. We'll catch up when I'm in less of a crisis, okay?"

"But, Captain, you're almost always in some sort of crisis. If you don't mind me saying so."

"I don't think that's true. There are calm moments between the more explosive times. We'll talk the next time things are a little calmer. I promise. And don't worry, I know all about the ruins, I'm the one who dug them out."

"I thought that might have been you! I was wondering who could manage to stay on the surface long enough to excavate some ancient buildings without getting turned into bug scat. Let me tell you, the list of people I thought of was very short, and you were definitely on it."

"Yeah, it was me. I had . . . it's complicated."

"You don't have to explain yourself to me, Captain. I'm sure there's a perfectly reasonable explanation for why you left your post as a tow chief and began a career of amateur archaeology. I'm learning to be more patient, so I can wait for you to explain it all to me! No hurry. Nope."

A mechanical hum arose behind her words that he hoped wasn't mounting tension.

"Look, *Insatiable*, can you give me an encrypted connection to Ben? There are some people on Wistful looking for me, and I don't want them to be able to locate me or listen in."

"I certainly can, as long as you're not going through Wistful's intranet. Which you aren't, I just checked. So yes. It's done. Should I put you through now?"

"Yes, thank you, *Insatiable*."

He watched passing foot traffic through the tinted glass of the lobby doors until he heard Ben's voice.

"Rohan?"

"Hey, Ben, how are things?"

"I can't complain. Well, I could, but nobody would listen to me."

"I'm sure somebody would listen."

Ben chuckled. "Maybe. You sound distracted. Are things escalating? Your life tends to work like that."

"I noticed. No new instances of violent attacks, but Wei Li dropped a few bombs on me."

"Really?"

"Not literal bombs. You ever hear of Lifters? Like, a group of people calling another group who engineered them or something?"

Ben was silent for a long minute.

"I might have. Short for Uplifters, I assume? Many species have myths about an unrelated, older species uplifting them from some simpler ancestor of theirs. In fact, I'd say almost half the humanoids tell a story like that."

"Huh. You know anything concrete? This is Wei Li's species. From Plassek."

"I don't. We have very little in the way of actual evidence. My best guess is that they're all talking about our old friends who built Repentant and Wistful. But the il'Drach have wiped clean almost all evidence of them, so it's hard to be sure. Is it important?"

Rohan sighed. "Wei Li thinks so. She and her friends are part of a group whose great-great-three-hundred-times-great grandparents swore some kind of oath to their Lifters."

"Really? Sounds apocryphal."

Rohan ducked away from the glass, into the shadowy interior of the lobby, as some people walked toward the doors. They checked the address printed on the glass and moved on. "What do you mean?"

"Occam's razor. Which one is the simpler explanation: that a group of people maintained a secret society like that across ten thousand years, longer than the recorded history of the human race, without interruption, or that somewhere along the line someone came up with this idea and convinced all the younger people that it had been going on for two hundred and ninety-five generations?"

"How would we know the difference?"

"If they had texts or artifacts from the time of the supposed oath-taking, we could date them in any number of ways. I assume they don't."

Rohan rubbed his forehead to put off the oncoming headache. "I don't think so. They admit there were some . . . breaches of continuity."

"I can't say for sure. Like I said, Occam's razor. Take the simplest explanation. But that doesn't mean the oath isn't very serious to Wei Li or her people."

"I guess it doesn't really matter. Did you make any progress on those characters I had you examine? I see you put *Insatiable* to work helping with them."

"I did, but it didn't make any difference. I think your guess was correct. Maybe. They are at least consistent with the writing we found on the planet under Repentant."

"In the tomb? Or prison cell, whatever. Where the vampire was. The ar'Tahul."

"Yes."

"What do you mean 'consistent'? Did they match?"

"They matched in the sense that if you grant hundreds or thousands of years of linguistic drift, then add in the fact that words are written with many different fonts and flourishes, they could belong to the same language."

"Not conclusive, then."

"No. And that doesn't help us translate the characters or figure out how to open the doors."

Rohan sighed. "Okay. Still, it's a start. If the writing were cephalopod, that would lead us to an entirely different set of conclusions."

"Correct. I did check it against cephalopod and megalodon writing, and those did not match."

"So the door wasn't built by giant octopi or sharks. Good to know."

"It never hurts to check."

"No. How's Marion doing? Did she see Garren?"

"Yes, they had a nice chat. He's walking the station right now, trying to find The Consortium."

"I would ask if he has any idea just how big Wistful is, but he probably knows better than me. What with all the physics knowledge he has."

Ben chuckled. "He knows how big she is, and I'm sure he knows how high the odds are stacked against him. I think he's doing anything he can to feel useful. He's quite upset about them and what they're trying to do. Sees it as a betrayal of true Tolone'an values."

Rohan watched a child bouncing a ball along the walkway at the edge of the promenade, pudgy hands slapping at the ball as it rose. "If enough of them let Dr. Kraken talk them into doing whatever he wants them to do, they're going to be in a lot of trouble with the il'Drach. But I can't spend too much time worrying about that right now."

"What do you mean?"

"Ben, there's a reason the il'Drach wanted to sterilize Tolone'a. If Kraken makes enough Powers and they rebel a second time? I can't go back in to squash the rebellion again. Which means the Fleet will nuke the planet into steam."

Ben grunted. "Let's hope it doesn't come to that."

"Let's get Garren home so he can make sure it doesn't."

"Will do. Anything else you needed me to look into? I think I'm at a dead end with those writing samples."

Rohan scratched his beard. "Yeah, one more thing. What can you tell me about Boost?"

"What do you mean?"

"Where's it from? How is it made? Is it something any high school chemistry teacher can cook up in the bathtub in his trailer? Does it require specialized manufacturing facilities? Is it grown? Extracted from something?"

Ben hesitated before answering. "I'm not an expert, but I might be able to find out. The il'Drach suppress legitimate information about it, though, so my research avenues are limited."

"Well, don't get them riled up about this. But if you can find out anything, I'd appreciate it. I still want to do something about the dealers on Wistful, and it would be easier if I had an idea of what their supply chain looks like."

"Meaning you want to know if they're importing it, and if so, from where. As opposed to synthesizing it themselves on the station."

"Exactly. Can you try to find out? Like I said, quietly, though. Don't get anyone wondering why you're asking questions."

"I can take care of myself, Rohan. I'll find something."

"Thanks, Ben. Say hi to Marion for me. I'll talk to you later."

"Later."

Rohan disconnected from *Insatiable*'s intranet and rubbed his eyes.

I'm going back to my room and back to bed. There's too much going on.

He pulled his hood low over his face and made his way to some stairs nearby. Two minutes later, he was on the transport level, reversing his earlier trip.

He played music and sat in the lotus position on the floor of the pod, focusing on the spiral of energy inside him.

Four loops. Bend the rod at the end, twist it further . . . further . . .

The pod came to a stop.

He climbed to the promenade level, hood over his face, scanning the crowds for anyone who seemed too interested in his appearance.

I should have done ninja training when I was on Earth. No, I said, I don't need to learn how to sneak around, I can fly. I'm bulletproof. What the hell did I know? I sure wish I knew how to turn invisible right about now. Or throw a smoke bomb. I don't even know where I'd get a smoke bomb to throw. Do ninjas make them? Order them online?

He ducked into the poorly maintained hallway that led to the off-the-books hotel and started thinking about lunch.

A turn, then another, and he passed the lobby where an inebriated Rogesh slept on the counter, his horn rising and falling with every loud snore.

Rohan turned down another corridor and entered a large square atrium that had doors to individual rooms lining its walls, eight to a side.

He took two strides into the room when he heard a happy bark.

A dog, its head as high as his knees, lean with short gray fur, ran up to Rohan, stopped directly in front of him, and nuzzled his knee.

The Hybrid looked around, seeing nobody taking responsibility for the animal, and knelt to pet it and check for tags.

"Hey there, boy. Are you lost? Are you looking for someone?" He reached down and scratched its neck.

The dog barked again, its tail wagging fiercely. Rohan touched a collar and began working his hands along its length to see if it had any kind of identifier for the dog's owner.

Then someone stepped out from behind a nearby plant and punched him squarely in the face.

◆ ⋯•⋯ ◆

Rohan had been punched many times before.

He'd been punched by Powers, by monsters, by gods and vampires and other Hybrids. He'd been hit by twenty-meter-tall cattle and by bugs bigger than a football field. He'd been struck by starships in the depths of space and whales the size of small cities in the deepest oceans.

In most of those cases, his own Powers had been active, and the telekinesis inherent to his esoteric abilities had blunted the impact of those traumatic events.

He'd also fought with his Powers suppressed, mostly sparring sessions with Wei Li but also on other occasions.

Rarely in those sessions had he felt those blows as much as he did that fist on that day.

The Hybrid tumbled to his backside, eyes still focused for some reason on the barking dog. He reached his left hand behind him to break his fall, the right outstretched in front in a vain attempt to fend off further attacks.

"What?"

Almost without thinking, he caught a punch in his palm, redirecting the impact to the esoteric spiral inside him.

Nice. All that practice is paying off.

He absorbed two more punches, each delivered with the force of a highly trained heavyweight boxer but not an actual Power, before he managed to push off the floor with his left and scramble to his feet.

The person attacking him was tall, over two meters, with four arms, two above and two below, and a full double set of muscles to support them: four heavy pecs straining at his black silk shirt, and two sets of capped shoulders pushing his upper arms up and out.

Must be hell to buy jackets.

Rohan caught another punch from the attacker's upper right arm, but the lower left dug deep into his belly, coming faster than the Hybrid expected.

"Ouch. Do you really have four arms or am I already concussed from that first shot?"

The attacker smiled, short tusks jutting up over his lips from his lower jaw. "I am Ruk. I am a Quattro." He attacked again.

The next five seconds were a disorienting whirlwind of punches delivered from odd angles, the one-two of a normal boxer replaced with a weird one-two-three-four rhythm: upper left, lower right, lower left, upper right.

Rohan absorbed about half the punches with the magic spring while the others pummeled him.

The dog barked.

He coughed, tasting blood in the back of his mouth.

"What do you want? Is it cash? I'll give you mine, hold on."

Ruk grinned again and threw another punch.

Rohan had figured out the pattern; he sidestepped the right straight aimed at his solar plexus and thrust his open left palm into the Quattro's sternum.

As he made contact, he released the energy stored in his esoteric spiral.

The Quattro absorbed the combined energy of a dozen of his own hardest punches, enough of a blow to toss him four meters through the air before landing hard on the metal floor and sliding another two, then coming to a rest.

Rohan stood, panting. The dog barked at him, tail still wagging.

"I'm glad you're having a good time." He coughed; tasted more blood. "Damnit."

Ruk grunted and rolled to his left, then his right, obviously in some amount of pain.

"I have no idea why you're messing with me, man, but you picked the wrong guy."

Ruk put his right hands on the floor and pushed up, caught his feet under himself and stood. He shook his head and spat on the floor next to him. "Not wrong guy. Tracker knows who you are."

"Tracker? The dog? Why the hell is that dog after me, then? I've never even seen him before. And dogs like me. I'm nice to dogs. This is ridiculous."

Ruk laughed. "Tracker is good boy. Never makes a mistake."

"I'm sure he's a very good boy. As to whether coming for me is a mistake . . . let's be fair, I have no idea. You have a problem with me? Is it personal, or did someone hire you?"

The Quattro shook out his arms, loosening his shoulders, and took a fighting stance again.

Rohan sighed and settled into his own stance: left foot forward, left fist on the right side of his belly, right fist up by his jaw. "Come on, then."

Ruk charged, quicker than was fair for a man his size, and led with a left jab that Rohan parried.

The right uppercut that followed whistled past Rohan's face; the Hybrid caught the straight from Ruk's left lower arm, then leaned back and out of the way of the vicious hook from Ruk's upper right.

Rohan felt a flicker of anxiety in his belly. *This guy is big and tough. I don't know if I can take him without—*

A kick whistled through the air at knee height.

The Hybrid leapt clear of it, landing a meter behind where he'd been. "Too slow—"

Four arms snaked around him from behind.

13

Sins of the Fathers

R uk closed on the Hybrid, feet covering distance fast, two fists up by his cheeks while he held the other two lower, ready to punch.

When he got close enough, Rohan kicked him in the groin.

The Quattro twisted his hips to save himself, but was too slow; the top of Rohan's foot caught him squarely in the genitals.

He collapsed upon impact.

If he has four arms, how many—

The Quattro behind him lifted him off the ground, torquing his body from side to side to stop him from getting any purchase. He struggled, but he didn't have the leverage to break the four-armed grip.

If these guys wanted me dead, there's no way they wouldn't have brought at least a knife or something to this fight. They're trying to capture me.

A third Quattro, nearly identical to Ruk, ran across the atrium, lips pulled back in a snarl, exposing tusks that matched Ruk's.

That's not good.

The new Quattro pulled up short, eyeing Rohan's feet warily, afraid to come too close. He looked down to the side and spoke in a language Rohan didn't recognize.

"You all right, brother?"

Ruk grunted and rolled to his feet. "I will be. He's tough."

"He's a Hybrid. How many Hybrids have you fought?"

Ruk held up a hand and started extending fingers to count. "Uh . . . none. I was looking forward to it, too."

"You want me to hit him?"

"Just tranq the guy. I'm not in the mood to fight anymore."

The Quattro holding Rohan growled. "Hurry up! He's squirmy. I can't hold him forever."

The Quattros slipped plugs into their noses. The third Quattro pulled a flask out of his hip pocket, opened it, and held it close to Rohan's face. "Just breathe. It's the least painful way for you to get through this."

Rohan held his breath. On principle.

Ruk pointed at the Quattro holding him. "Now."

The Quattro squeezed, compressing Rohan's belly and pushing some of the air out of him. He tensed.

Then Ruk punched him in the stomach.

Twice.

Rohan coughed, inhaling by reflex, and took in a lungful of gas.

I really hope I'm right about them not wanting me dead.

It was not the first time Rohan had experienced being slapped awake.

It was his least favorite way to wake up; the sharp smack of skin on his cheek, the little jolts of pain spreading across his face, smaller echoes straining at his neck and shoulders.

As he woke, his neck tensed, muscles catching the momentum of his head, and by instinct he tried to bring his hands up to protect himself.

They were, of course, strapped to his sides, so his effort was in vain.

He inhaled deeply and braced for another slap.

Instead, a man spoke.

"Enough."

Rohan exhaled slowly and opened his eyes, his focus directed entirely inward.

He *reached* down into the pool of spiritual energy behind his tailbone; pulled out a long rod of astral power; anchored one end to one palm, another end to his other palm, and the first end at the same time to that well of energy.

The geometry of the nonphysical space where his Power resided didn't quite line up with the real world's.

He twisted the rod, applying torque until it buckled and bulged, first curving, then forming something like a loop.

Except that the ends didn't quite meet; instead he turned them again, and a second loop formed.

The beginning of a spiral. Or a spring.

His eyes started to focus, and the blur in front of him resolved into a room. About twice the size of the space he'd shared with Katya, it contained two beds, a dresser, the chair he was strapped to, and not much else.

He strained against the wide straps digging into his sides; nothing moved.

He wasn't surprised.

The three Quattros stood facing him, arms folded across their chests, four forearms stacked in front of their bodies. They were identical to Rohan's eyes, the same two meters tall, the same muscular builds.

The pressure on his knee was a dog nuzzling him.

A fourth man stood directly in front of Rohan. A Lukhor, with green skin and a pair of short antennae jutting out of his forehead; he wore a simple tunic and pants, loose and flowy, made of a fabric that gave the impression of luxury by the way it draped from his shoulders.

He was short, fifteen centimeters shorter than Rohan, and slender, a hint of muscle showing through the tunic but not more than that. He was bald, with wrinkles around the corners of his eyes and a hard mouth that said he had no tolerance for fools without him having to say a word.

"You are Rohan of Earth. Formerly known as The Griffin. Interestingly, the Scourge of Zahad. Among other titles."

Rohan coughed, tasting blood. "I'm not really sure what my play is here. Can I deny it? After all, if I were really Rohan, could these jokers have managed to capture me? Surely The Griffin would have wiped the floor with these three. Not the dog, though, the dog's cute."

The man nodded. "There is no point. I know who you are and why you were captured."

"That's great, then. Can you tell me more about myself? I just got punched in the head a bunch of times, I think I might be forgetting some things."

"Do you recognize me?"

Rohan swallowed and slowed his breathing. His sides throbbed; his ribs were hurt, possibly broken. "Am I supposed to? Have we met before? Don't tell me we had an appointment I forgot. Are you upset about that? You didn't really need to hire these goons to rough me up, you know. I'm just criminally disorganized. It's not personal."

"I'm not offended. I'm harder to upset than that. Allow me to introduce myself, belated though it might be.

"I am Eldarinth Lastex.

"First Citizen of Lukhor and Tamaralinth's father."

Rohan looked over the older man. "I thought you'd be fatter." The Hybrid coughed, clearing fluid from his lungs, and took a slow breath. Two of the Quattros moved in to hit him, but the old man held up a hand to stop them.

"I understand. You've met other wealthy Lukhor."

"Yeah. On this station, actually. They tend to be morbidly obese."

"It is an odd affectation. The very rich on my world choose to flaunt their wealth by demonstrating that they can afford to be physically incapacitated."

"Then what about you?"

"I said the 'very' rich. I am well beyond that classification, Rohan. As you must be aware. I am far beyond the need for such posturing."

"I get it. That's cool. You're so rich you don't have to bother flaunting it. Everybody just knows."

"Exactly."

"Probably easier on your joints, anyway. Not carrying all that weight."

"I never saw the appeal in it, honestly."

Rohan coughed and squirmed a bit in his chair, trying and failing to find a comfortable position between the straps. "I guess you're not after me for diet tips. What can I do for you, Eldar? Can I call you Eldar? It's funny because it's a name in one of the Earth languages."

The old man examined Rohan for a moment, then nodded. "You can call me anything you like. Concern over such trivialities is base, and I rarely allow myself to be base."

"Great. Hey, Eldar, how about loosening these straps? This isn't comfortable at all. I'm sure you wouldn't want it to get out that you're treating your guests this way. What would people say about your hospitality, First Citizen of Lukhor, roughing up the people you invite over?"

Rohan looked past the Lukhor and noticed something on the bed. *Is that a plate? Were they eating?*

"In due time. I would like to have a conversation with you, and given your species and your penchant for pointlessly resisting events you wish to avoid, the straps are a . . . necessary evil."

Rohan smiled. "I don't like it, but I have to admit you have gotten a very solid scouting report on me, good sir. Pointless resistance is my middle name. My brand. My modus operandi. My trademark."

"As is idle chatter."

"Got it in two. Well, since you have me trapped, why not tell me what you're here to talk about? Unless you want me to guess? Do you? I'm a really good guesser. You looking for a tow chief? You have a station up in Lukhor that needs some ships towed?"

The old man studied the Hybrid for a long moment before answering. "I don't think you'd be a very good choice for the job right now, do you?"

Rohan laughed. "Touché. You definitely got the good scouting report. It hardly seems fair, you know so much about me and I know so little about you."

"I have people who tell me things, but I needed to see your current state with my own eyes. Which I just did. You are clearly not the man you once were."

"Ouch. That hurts. It really does."

"I was impressed by you at one time, Rohan. Not when I first heard you were dating my daughter. Most Hybrids are uncouth brutes; I didn't think it was possible you'd be good enough for her."

"A tough but fair assessment. Most Hybrids *are* brutes. It's not our fault, it's our upbringing. Nurture. Or lack of it."

"Regardless. I didn't think my daughter could be safe with you. Yet you surprised me. Proved me wrong."

"Jolly good for me."

"Yes, it was. As I said, you impressed me, Rohan. Scaring off the Shayjh without excessive force. I was disappointed that she wound up with that fool Lahnegarn after that."

"I promise you one thing, Mister First Citizen, you were nowhere near as disappointed as I was."

"I can imagine. She's a lovely girl, isn't she? My proudest achievement."

Rohan sighed. "Finally, some common ground. Now that we're getting along so well, how about you undo some of these straps?"

"Not just yet. The thing is, Rohan, you were never the man I would have chosen for Tamara. But I am an adult and I understand that even a person in my position cannot always get what I want."

"Very mature of you."

"Don't push too hard, Rohan. You are still strapped down, and I have a Quattro with sore genitals who would be more than happy to break some of your bones. Or all of your bones."

Rohan swallowed. "Noted."

The older man paced a tight circle in front of the Hybrid, gathering his thoughts. The Quattros waited patiently, as if having performed in that precise scene before. Tracker the dog moved to their left and sat, tongue hanging out of the side of his mouth, panting happily, tail wagging back and forth.

"I allowed Tamara her freedom, with regards to you, for quite a while. As I said, you are not the sort of person I would choose, but at least you kept her safe and reasonably happy."

"My pleasure."

"I'm sure. Then I began hearing things."

Rohan sighed. "You have no idea how hard it is for me to not make jokes about your auditory hallucinations. Even though I'm fully aware that's not what you meant."

"I don't. Have any idea. Still, thank you for showing restraint."

"Don't get used to it. But seriously, what things? Or should I say, which things?"

"I walk in rarefied circles at times. I heard whispers that you are becoming someone, or something, important."

Rohan laughed. "Important? To whom?"

"To the Empire. Your name is spoken, rarely, but spoken. In whispers. Some think you are becoming an influence on the Empire itself. As a whole."

"You've been talking to my dad. He's delusional; I'm nobody. He *wishes* I were important, that's all."

What is that thing on the bed? Were they eating before? They don't look like they were eating.

"I appreciate why you hesitate to admit the reality. You use anonymity as a shield. I'm not trying to expose you, Rohan. To do so would be to put my daughter in danger, and that is . . . perhaps the last thing I want."

"Great. I'm glad we're on the same page. Now stop asking me questions. Undo these straps and let me go."

"Not just yet. The thing is, Rohan, you impressed me. You were impressing me. You were going places, places worthy of a person who could be a companion to my daughter."

"I'm really not enjoying your use of the past tense, there. Are we having a conjugation problem? Why the past tense, Mister First Citizen?"

"Because something happened when you fought Hyperion, Rohan. You failed. He beat you. And ever since then, you have not seemed like the sort of person who could keep my daughter safe. Who would be worthy of standing by her side."

Rohan took a deep breath, then exhaled slowly. "If you think your daughter should only date people who can beat Hyperion in a fistfight, you're going to condemn her to a very lonely life, Eldar. That guy is no joke."

"I am aware of the threat Hyperion represents. I keep my eye on anything that could impact the sector-wide situation, and he is high on that list of things."

"So what are you saying?"

"I'm saying that you have a way of accumulating enemies. You have reached for high places, and others have noticed it. Which was fine, as long as you could back up your plays. But now . . ."

"You think I can't."

The old Lukhor stood straighter and backed up a step. "I know you can't. If you could, I'd be the one strapped to the chair, and my Quattros would be collecting flies. Ruk, Rak, and Kor beat you, and they were barely trying."

"Those are their names? Not very imaginative."

Eldar shrugged. "They are triplets. Highly trained Quattro assassins. They have been in my employ for many years."

"Okay. They aren't bad."

"They are trained to fight Powers. Together, they can handle a low-level Power, if they are lucky. They took you down without breaking a sweat."

"I think Ruk is sweating a little bit after that kick to the nuts."

"Please."

Rohan sighed. "Okay, fine. I'm not interested in debating you about my competence. What do you want?"

"I want you to stay away from my daughter. Not because you aren't good enough for her, though you aren't. No. I want you to see reason.

"If you love her as you claim to, you should stay away from her because your presence in her life endangers her, and you can no longer protect her from those dangers."

"Lonnie already gave me this speech."

"Lahnegarn is an idiot. But even idiots are right, occasionally. If you care about her, stay away."

Rohan sighed. "You're underestimating your daughter, Mister First Citizen."

"What do you mean?"

"You think she'll just let me walk away? You think she'll just accept that my presence in her life endangers her and say, oh, that's fine, just leave me alone? She's very stubborn. You should know that by now."

"Then convince her."

"Honestly, I'm not sure I can. She's very sweet, but she's not much of a listener. Sir."

The old man frowned at Rohan. "You're not taking me seriously. I didn't think you were this foolish."

"Then maybe your scouting report wasn't so great after all. I am exactly this foolish. Maybe more."

"I suppose I'm going to have to work harder to convince you."

Rohan squirmed a little inside the straps. "Having your goons hit me more isn't going to change anything. Not really. Tamara is going to do what she's going to do, and I'm not sure either you or I have as much control over that as you think we do."

"If she resists the separation, find a way. I don't know, you're supposed to be a problem solver. Cheat on her. Send her back to her husband. Tell her you don't want a child to care for."

Rohan snorted. "You want me to break up with her and blame it on Rinth? That's awful. What kind of parent are you?"

"I'm a parent who knows that five Powered Tolone'ans tried to kill his daughter yesterday and I wasn't around to save her."

"You had assets in place, though, didn't you? Close enough that you heard exactly what happened."

"I am too public a figure to leave her completely unprotected or un-watched. You should understand that much. I have enemies of my own."

"So that's it. You're not worried about the Tolone'ans. You're worried that your own enemies come after her."

"Those are not exclusive propositions. You drove the Shayjh away from her."

"They weren't keeping her safe, they were keeping her single. They pushed Lonnie away from her. I don't like the guy, but he wasn't exactly a danger to her, was he?"

"They did both. You made them abandon her, which I understand. As I said, at the time I thought you would present an adequate substitute for their protections. Now . . ."

"I keep telling you, you're talking to the wrong person. Go talk to your girl. Not like this, I mean, don't strap her down. Take her to lunch.

Breakfast. Sit and tell her what you're telling me. She's smart, really smart. She'll evaluate your points and do the right thing. You want a hint? Keep mentioning Rinth. Tell her that as long as I'm in their lives, he's in danger. That should work."

Rohan looked past the Lukhor and the Quattros. The disc on the bed kept drawing his attention.

It's not a plate.

Eldar stared at the Hybrid. "That's not bad advice. Are you trying to help me?"

Rohan shrugged. "I'm trying to get you to understand that I want what's best for your daughter. But I'm not going to let you force me to do something we're all going to regret."

Eldar tapped his chin and nodded slowly. "I like your plan, I really do. I'd be inclined to try it. Except that my daughter, for all her brilliance, has exceptionally poor judgment when it comes to men. I do not think your plan will work."

"No harm in trying."

"There is harm. Or at least could be. She is in danger, right now, because of you. I can't afford to wait and hope she sees reason. No, you are going to leave her, somehow. Better her heart be broken metaphorically than for it to be damaged in fact."

"That's not going to happen. I won't lie to her to get her to stay away from me."

"If you won't, I'll have to convince you. Ruk. Get the tongs. We'll start with his left eye. The colors don't match, it's distracting. He will be easier to look at if we pluck one out."

Rohan's heart beat faster. "Let's not be hasty. Plucking eyes? That's a little gory. Why don't we start smaller? I can be tortured in all sorts of ways. Did you know I'm ticklish? Very ticklish. Get some feathers out, you'll have me screaming for mercy in no time."

"Enough talk. We'll do this the hard way."

Ruk walked over to the bed, reached under it, and pulled out a suitcase. He put it on top of the comforter and unfolded it. "Tongs . . . no, that's a knife . . . torch . . ."

Rohan swallowed.

If they hurt me badly enough, if they maim me, I won't be able to stop Hyperion.

But if I cut loose now, if I lose control, then I also won't be able to stop him.

Billions of lives are at stake.

What do I do?

What would . . . no, that won't work.

Ruk reached for the disc on the bed, lying right next to the spot where he'd put the suitcase. He flicked it off the bed; the disc hit the floor and rolled toward the other Quattros.

As it got closer, Rohan recognized it.

I know what that is.

The door at the back of the room opened, and a green-skinned boy, all gangly limbs with the first hints of teenage muscle showing on his thin frame, stepped out of the closet and into the room.

It's a Frisbee.

"Grandpa, stop! Don't hurt him!"

Oh, Rinth, you really shouldn't be here.

14

Who's the Big Bad Wolf?

Eldar turned to the boy. "Rinth!" He spun back to Rohan. "What is he doing here?"

Rohan sighed and shrugged. "I have no idea. Why are you asking me?"

The older man turned back to his grandson. "Why are you here, Rinth? This is no place for a boy."

Rinth pointed at Rohan. "Grandpa, why is Rohan tied up? And why is his face all messed up? I think you should be helping him, not yelling at him. He needs, like a band-aid or something."

"Rinth, you're just a boy, you don't understand what's going on. I'm sorry you saw this, but you have to go back to your aunt; she'll watch you while I finish things up here. Kor will take you." He motioned for one of the Quattros to escort Rinth away.

Rinth ran across the room, the dog following him, then wrapped his arms around Rohan and shook his head. "I'll go, but Rohan has to come with me." He paused, his antennae wiggling as he concentrated. "I have something to tell him. You untie him and we'll both go."

Eldar sighed. "That's not going to happen, Rinth. Rohan and I are still talking."

"I was in the closet the whole time, Grandpa. That wasn't just talking. You were going to hurt Uncle Rohan."

"That's not true, Rinth. We were playing. Just having a little fun, right, Rohan?"

Rinth shook his head. "You were going to take his eye out, Grandpa. Rohan has a saying about fun and losing eyes, don't you, Rohan?"

Rohan laughed, just a chuckle at first, then harder, finally coughing painfully as his injured ribs complained. "It's all fun and games until someone loses an eye! I do say that! It's an Earth thing."

Rinth nodded. "See? That's not fun anymore, Grandpa. I think you should let Rohan go. Maybe you can visit Mom and Auntie, have some tea or whatever you guys do."

Eldar gritted his teeth and tried to stare down the boy, but Rinth didn't flinch.

Rohan chuckled again.

Eldar faced him. "You think this is funny? My grandson is in danger because of you."

Rohan shrugged. "That's a very weird interpretation of what happened. Hey, Rinth, how did you end up here? Don't you have school?"

"It's the weekend. You never remember. I went home to get a game to play when Grandpa broke in with the big guys and the dog. I heard them talking about you, so I followed them."

Rohan shook his head. "That dog really tracked me all the way here from your apartment? After I haven't set foot in there for two weeks? That's amazing."

Rinth nodded. "Oh yeah, Tracker's the best." The dog leaned against his side; Rinth freed one arm and began petting him.

Rohan looked up from his chair at Eldar. "He wouldn't be here if not for you. The only violence he's been exposed to was instigated by you and your goons. Blaming me for it isn't very logical. And I don't have a full scouting report on you, but I've heard that you're usually very logical."

Rak nodded. "He's right, you are, boss. Very true."

Eldar shook his head. "Shut up, Rak. Kor, take my grandson somewhere else. Don't hurt him."

The Quattro looked down at Rinth, shrugged apologetically, and stepped forward, arms outstretched, ready to grab the boy.

Rinth held up a hand. "Wait! I really don't think you want to do that."

Kor looked from the boy to Eldar. "Why not?"

Eldar sighed. "Don't be silly, boy. He's four times your size. And an adult. And he's spent his entire life training in the killing arts."

Rinth tightened his lips and looked at Rohan again, then back to his grandfather. "Because if you hurt Uncle Rohan, Mama will get real mad! And you don't want her mad!"

"I'll manage my daughter, Rinth. She's a shuttle tech on a station in the middle of nowhere, what do you think she can do? Now run along."

"Oh, Grandpa, I know what you're doing. There's a word for it. It's not lying, not exactly. Mom keeps telling me they're different things. Oh, I remember! You're bluffing!"

"I'm not bluffing. I'm going to do what's best for her, and for you, whether either of you appreciate it or not. Go with Kor, I promise you don't want to see what's going to happen in here."

Rinth's smile widened. "I don't think so, Grandpa. Because I'll tell Mama, and she'll get mad, and Mama is the only person in the sector who scares you."

Eldar paled slightly. "Who told you that?"

"You did, Grandpa. I mean, kind of. You weren't talking to me. I don't think you even knew I was in the room. I was hiding, you know, under the bed. I don't remember why. But you said Mama was the only person who scared you for real."

Eldar's eyes hardened. "No, I didn't."

"Yeah, you did. I asked Mama about it, too, a few days later. Because I didn't know why you would be scared of her. She's not *your* mom. She can't take away *your* games or make you go to bed when you're not ready or anything."

"That's right. I'm her father, not the reverse. I'm not scared of that child. I was there the day she was born."

"Right. That's what I thought! So I asked Mama, and she didn't really answer me, she just rubbed my head and told me I was cute. But I hate that, because it's not really an answer, so I asked Auntie."

Eldar frowned. "Did you."

"Oh yeah. And I was smart. I waited until the weekend and Auntie and Uncle had dinner and they were drinking wine. I kept refilling their glasses and being really helpful, because they like that, and they probably had more than they should have. Then I asked them about why Mama scares you. Uncle wouldn't say anything, but Auntie laughed and told me that the last time you tried to force Mama to do anything, she broke the stock market and cost you a billion credits."

Eldar grunted. "It wasn't a billion credits. And the word is crashed. She crashed the market."

Rohan coughed. "Tamaralinth?"

Eldar looked at him. "She never told you? Why I let her come to this forsaken place?"

"She . . . not with any detail. You wouldn't let her go?"

"No. It took her six months to break the Lukhor markets. Cost me ten billion credits. Took *me* five years to make it back."

The Hybrid laughed. "You're not the scary one, she is! I knew she was brilliant, I thought it was all math stuff. Configuring bootstrap drives."

"Oh, she's brilliant at math all right. But she has a knack for the psychology behind markets, too. It's why I wish she would come home and take my place in the business."

Rohan rolled his shoulders as far as he could inside the straps. "I know you're worried about her. I get it. And I know that you love her. The problem is that you don't trust her."

"You don't know what you're saying. I trust her with my life!"

"Sure, but you don't trust her with *hers*. You've convinced yourself that her bad taste in men is her fatal weakness, and the only way to save her from it is to act behind her back."

"History supports that narrative, Hybrid."

"Sure. Lonnie's a bit of a—cover your ears, Rinth—moron. But she knows that. She's not stupid, and she is capable of protecting herself."

Eldar sighed. "What do you suggest I do, Rohan?"

"Look, you want her safe? Ask her to keep some security around. Leave the Quattros here to watch out for her. But ask her first, make sure she's okay with it. Don't go behind her back. No more Shayjh manipulating her life behind the scenes."

Eldar looked at Rinth. The boy nodded. "You should listen to Rohan, Grandpa. He's smarter than he looks. That's what Mama always says. Don't let all the hair fool you."

"You talk back more than my other grandchildren."

Rinth nodded. "Mama says that's going to get me in trouble someday. But I'm not worried, I have her and Uncle Rohan to help me when I'm in trouble."

Eldar smiled grimly, his eyes still hard, and faced Rohan. "I can't argue with that. I didn't want Rinth involved in this. So I'll let you go. For now. But I'm not leaving the station unless you prove to me that you can protect my girl. And I'm not a patient man."

Rohan nodded. "I have no idea how to do that, but I'm sure I'll think of something."

"I like your confidence, warranted or not." He turned to the Quattros. "Cut him loose."

Rinth let go to make room for the henchmen to approach the chair. As they undid the straps holding him down, Rohan smiled reassurance at Rinth, whose face was still paler than normal. He turned to Eldar.

"Did she really cost you ten billion credits?"

Eldar hesitated, then shook his head. "It was closer to twenty."

Rohan shook his arms out as circulation returned. He stood, slowly, moving his head from side to side to test that all the parts moved the way they should.

Eldar looked up at him. "How does it feel to be The Griffin, a man whose name parents used to scare wayward children all over the sector, now saved by an eleven-year-old boy?"

Rohan shrugged. "I'm not the one he saved, Grandpa. Your biggest problem right now is that you don't understand that."

◆ ·· ◆· ◆

Rohan left the room, exited the boardinghouse, turned up a back alley, and slumped against a cold metal wall, breathing heavily.

Crap. I just got saved from certain mutilation by an eleven-year-old boy. This has not been a good day.

Yesterday was pretty good, though. I still have yesterday.

Wistful's promenade was fifty meters wide along most of the length of her four arms, rolling fifty meters below a single-facet diamond ceiling. Flanking the promenade were parallel structures, also fifty meters wide, just as high, filled with spaces where people of a thousand races lived, played, worked, and made things.

As was the case everywhere in known space, some parts of those buildings were more desirable than others. People clustered in the parts of the building closest to the promenade; the lower levels were highly utilized to a depth of twenty or thirty meters. Above that, deeper than that, the station had a lot of underutilized space.

Or so most people thought.

Those deep sections, the undesirable spaces, *were* inhabited. Over the millennia, people had colonized those spaces, far away from the promenade and the transit system. They had cut alleys and tunnels through the buildings, broken into abandoned warehouses and set up housing, greenhouses for growing food, offices, and even schools.

When people didn't want to be found, when they wanted to be off the official grid, as much as it was possible inside a living technological organism, they disappeared into the deep spaces.

The boardinghouse was in the center of that, stretching across structures that had belonged to four different buildings in the station's original plan. Rohan turned up an alley and climbed four flights, then turned again and headed up a corridor that reached a kilometer in either direction.

Hooded figures loitered in unlabeled doorways, watching for the lost or misguided. Painted tags on walls and especially intersections told people where they were, but nothing was spelled out in Drachna.

It was a place hostile to visitors and fiercely protective of its inhabitants.

Rohan didn't quite fit into either category.

He had spent time scouting those deep areas in the year and a half since learning of their existence, but that wasn't enough to give him more than a cursory understanding of the layout.

It had been enough for him to learn the informal rules of the station's depths: don't ask too many questions and don't look too closely at any faces. Don't bump into anybody.

Pay in cash.

He bought kebabs from a food cart without asking what animals the meat had come from. The spices stung his lips where they'd been split by Rak's fists.

He washed it down with a paper cup full of a tart, pulpy juice.

Walked half a kilometer before climbing to the top of the station and finding a public seating area, twenty meters square, where people could look out into space.

Sat, closed his eyes and checked on his spiral: four loops and holding.

Exhaled and reclined the chair so he could lay flat and look up at Toth 3, blue and white and hanging in the center of the view. Melted into the chair.

Sat up partway and slipped his mask out of his hood. He put it over his face and tapped the side, scrolling through menus until he found the setup for a tightbeam transmission.

Pinged *Void's Shadow*.

If she was somewhere in line of sight, there was a chance she'd detect the tachyon transmission.

Small but not zero chance she'll be in range.

He settled back in the chair and ticked through the events of the previous day in his head.

The mysterious door at the dig site doesn't open, but the letters on the combination lock look like Sein-na writing.

Tamara asked to move in together.

Lonnie threatened to take her back.

Eldar threatened to take me out if I stay with her.

The Consortium, five Tolone'an Powers of considerable strength, wants me dead, at the orders of Dr. Kraken. Garren, my old armored friend, is here to stop them.

Granny is running Boost through Wistful, and I can't find her to stop her.

The leader of Wei Li's sect wants her to inherit his Powers, which will kill him and herald something in their prophecy about this station.

Oh, yeah, also Wei Li belongs to a sect whose mission is to protect Wistful, and they're guided by ancient prophecies.

I can hold on to the spiral technique and use it in a fight, but only if I stay really, really calm. Unfortunately, when the fights are really important, when the stakes are really high, I can't stay calm. I get scared, then I get angry, then . . . poof. So I can only win when it doesn't matter.

He remembered Master Turtle's aura.

The man had an unnatural level of calm. Of serenity. Of peace. A thing Rohan had only sensed in small doses before.

Spiral's teacher had a bit of that. Sid. I only met him briefly, though.

How do I get some of that?

Do I have to wipe my personality? If I did, would I still even want to fight Hyperion? Would I even remember I had to?

"Captain?"

He stiffened, startled. "*Void's Shadow*?"

"Yes, Captain. You were calling me."

"Oh buddy, I'm sorry! I totally was! I kind of drifted off after I started the call. Are you okay?"

"Sure, Captain, I'm fine. Why do you ask?"

He sighed. "I don't know. Any signs of trouble?"

"What kind of trouble? Like Fleet showing up because they've decided to destroy Wistful? Or an Assessor coming to order the sterilization of Pilli 5? Or 4? Or another wormhole opening? Or Repentant or *Vyrhicant* losing the weak hold they have on sanity and coming through the wormhole on a rampage of destruction? Like that?"

"Yeah. Any of that?"

"Nope."

"Okay. Good. Great. Anything else going on?"

"Captain, are you lonely?"

"Huh. Am I?"

"You don't usually call me to talk about nothing."

"I should, though, shouldn't I? We're friends. We never just hang out."

"It's fine, Captain. We have different interests. I like swimming in methane lakes on the moons of outer planets, and you like . . . actually, I don't know what you like, I don't listen when you talk about personal stuff."

"I have never felt more like a parent than I do at this exact moment."

"Really? Is this how biological children relate to their parents?"

"I'm not sure. My relationship to my parents wasn't typical. Actually, I think my dad raised me a lot like the way a typical il'Drach would have raised you, if you'd stayed in Fleet. Which is kind of funny."

"I don't get it, Captain."

"It's not really funny. Sorry."

"It's okay, Captain. Most of your jokes aren't funny. I just laugh to make you feel better."

"Thank you. Should I be thanking you? I'm not sure anymore. I don't have the spare processing power to figure out the answer."

"Are you feeling overwhelmed, Captain?"

"Little bit. There's a lot going on all of a sudden."

"Is it really sudden?"

He sighed. "Maybe not. A lot of fallout from that fight with Hyperion."

"You mean the last fight. Where you lost."

"Yeah. People know about it. Which is causing a whole host of downstream issues that have nothing to do with Hyperion and everything to do with people thinking I can't defend myself."

"I see. Should I tell them that it's not true?"

"I don't think that would help. I wish it would. But I appreciate the thought. You just go on swimming in methane lakes and having fun."

"I will, Captain. Do you want me to come back to this spot so I can catch a transmission from you later on? Maybe tomorrow?"

"Yeah. If you don't mind. I'm going to try to find Katya or Garren, but all the places where we could meet are sort of compromised, and I don't want to use Wistful's intranet to communicate."

"The intranet isn't perfectly secure, but it's not exactly easy to hack into either. It should be fine."

He sighed. "They're going after Tamara and Rinth, not just me. I can't risk it."

"Oh. Well, good luck, Captain. Let me know if I can help."

"I will. Rohan out."

The line clicked off.

Rohan took off the mask and rubbed his eyes. He stared at the planet and settled his breathing, then swung his feet over the side of the chair, ready to stand.

He saw a snake-headed reptilian standing across from him. She was tall, with hulking shoulders stretching at the fabric of a green cloak. She surveyed the room from underneath a low-drawn hood much like his own; their eyes met.

He blinked.

I know those eyes.

The Takslee enforcer flinched, turned, and ran up the corridor away from the reading area.

15

Chasing Dreams

Rohan stood and followed the fleeing Boost dealer.

What was her name again? Search? Sirc?

It doesn't matter. I bet she knows who their supplier is.

First step, catch her. Second step, make her tell me.

Within eight steps, a throbbing pain in his side reminded him of the trauma his ribs had undergone over the previous twenty-four hours.

Not sure how I'm going to manage either of those things in the shape I'm in. Hopefully inspiration will strike.

She ran like a fullback; forward lean, arms up and ready to knock people out of the way with forearm shivers and the occasional well-timed stiff arm.

Rohan had no trouble following her trail, even if he found it physically difficult to match her pace.

He turned left where a delivery person crawled across the floor picking up spilled pastries, then took a long staircase four steps at a time.

The Hybrid coughed blood as he hit the landing too hard, then paused to take some breaths.

Yells came from the end of the hall as a half dozen other people muttered, rubbed at fresh bruises, or picked themselves up from where they'd been crumpled into heaps.

Rohan took off after her.

He turned a corner and saw a knot of students at the end of the hall, packed too tightly together to get out of the Takslee's way; they yelled and threw some punches as she tried to plow through them, but they simply had nowhere to go.

The enforcer turned, her vertically slit pupils focusing on him. Her hood fell back, exposing the orange scales covering her head and neck.

Rohan ran toward her, heart thundering in his chest.

She pointed at him. "You!"

He grinned.

Does the blood on my teeth make me look like a badass or like I'm about to fall over dead without her even touching me?

The students behind her fell into a hush as she took a traditional boxing stance, left foot forward, fists up by her jaw. "Where's your backup?"

"I won't need backup to deal with you." He coughed with the last word, ruining any possibility of intimidation.

"I think you're wrong. More than that, I'm willing to bet quite a bit on it."

He coughed again, then drew a ragged breath. "I have a problem with Boost dealers. It's a character flaw."

She nodded. "I have a flaw too. Mine means that I have debts to pay, and I'm going to have a really tough time doing that from prison."

She stepped in and threw a jab-straight combination.

He absorbed the jab with his spiral but wasn't quick enough to do more than slip past the straight.

He snapped out a quick kick into her thigh; she took the impact without flinching and sent two more punches his way.

The last one landed, too high on his ribs to knock the wind out of him but sending him stumbling up the hall.

"If you need money, you should try fighting professionally. That's a wicked cross you have."

"I did. You don't follow Takslee boxing, do you?"

He caught his balance and slid forward, eyeing the distance between them carefully. Three of the students had tablets out to film the fight.

"I did, during the Three Queens era, but then they retired, and who has time to keep up with everything? Plus there's no distribution rights here, so all I could get were bootleg copies of the actual fights."

She stood up tall and squinted at him. "You know the Three Queens era? You actually know something about our sport?"

He snapped out a jab, forcing her to lean back, and followed with a right to the belly. She swayed back again, but was off balance when he slapped his left hand across her jaw.

Releasing the impact of the three punches he'd absorbed in the previous minute.

Her head snapped to the side, and she stumbled to the wall. She leaned against it, shook her head, and glared at him.

He shrugged. "Not really. About two-thirds of combat sports has something like a 'three high ranking members of the nobility' era. Three Kings, Three Queens. The Three Marquis of Lukhor fencing. It was an even bet that your people had something similar."

"You're funny. And you have a hell of a left hook. You a Power?"

"Sometimes. Are you on Boost right now?"

"My stash is low, and I'm not sure when I'll get more. Something about my personal supplier getting locked up. You wouldn't know anything about that, would you?"

"I feel like I should apologize. But that stuff's terrible for you. Come on, you're an athlete. I can tell. Boost will kill you. Destroy everything you've built."

She snorted. "Like you care."

"I'm not saying I care. I am curious."

"You're a Power. You'll never understand. I trained harder than you could imagine, weighed every gram of food, counted every kilocalorie, trained six hours a day. I still couldn't go toe to toe with even a minor Power. And most of them are just born with it. Don't even try or train. It's . . ."

She stepped forward and hit him again.

He absorbed the jab and the cross that followed.

Just when he thought he was doing well, he realized the combination hadn't stopped; her left hook whisked past his nose, but she stepped in with an uppercut he didn't have time to escape. The world exploded in light as her fist caught the tip of his chin, snapping his teeth together.

He was looking at the ceiling, falling to his back, when he remembered where he was; his esoteric spiral was gone, dissipated into ether when his concentration broke.

The Hybrid twisted to the side, avoiding a pair of punches he hadn't even seen coming, and lurched across the corridor, stopping only when he hit the opposite wall.

The Takslee closed; he set his shoulder against the wall and landed a kick on her solid belly, stopping her forward momentum.

"Not bad. I actually felt that."

"That's what she said."

The Takslee's forehead bunched up. "What does that mean?"

"It means my jokes work better when I'm home and other people get all my cultural references. Out here, none of you have seen the shows I grew up with. It's sad. That was actually really funny."

She tapped the side of her head; an affectation of some sort. "Was it?"

"Probably not. My judgment is impaired. Someone keeps punching me in the head, and all the brain trauma makes my sense of humor a little weird."

"Now I think I should apologize."

Rohan stepped away from the wall on shaky legs, then slid back to it. "What you should do is surrender. I'll make sure they go easy on you. Give me the name of your supplier and you can walk away from all this."

She laughed. "That's not going to happen. Also, you can barely stand. Am I supposed to be afraid of you?"

Someone stepped up into the spot next to Rohan and spoke. "Yes."

Rohan looked at her. "Oh, Katya. Just in time."

◆ ··◆·· ◆

The students stared at the il'Zkin; they'd never seen her species before.

Katya sighed. "I would have met with you earlier, but you weren't where you were supposed to be. You should follow your schedule, Rohan."

"I tried. The room was compromised. They had a really good dog. The dog wasn't what compromised the room. I'm not making sense."

"This is the Takslee I fought before, yes? She is very tough."

"I noticed."

"She seems to be getting the better of you."

"I noticed that, too."

Sirc cleared her throat. "Are you both going to fight me or can we just call it a day?"

Rohan held up a fist. "As soon as the station stops spinning, I am going to finish this fight and make you rue the day you met me."

"I already rue that day. It was awful. I lost both my employers in one raid. I've been on the run since then. I slept on the promenade last night."

Rohan sighed. "That doesn't sound like fun. Unless it's camping and you're doing it on purpose, then it's fun." He stepped away from the wall again and stumbled.

Katya stepped in and propped him up with her shoulder. "Rohan, you are not well. Perhaps we can end this fight?"

"I'll end it, all right. I told you. As soon as Wistful stops spinning. Why is she doing that? It's very disconcerting. Can't be good for morale."

Sirc locked eyes with Katya. "Do you want to tell him or shall I?"

Katya shrugged her free shoulder. "Go ahead."

The Takslee nodded. "You are concussed. The station is not moving abnormally. You should let me go."

Katya nodded. "I agree. There is no point to fighting her right now. Even if we brought her to Security, she wouldn't tell us anything."

Rohan sighed and leaned harder on Katya. "Fine. Go and . . . find a new line of work. Don't work for Boost dealers. They're the worst."

Sirc laughed. "If you think those two are the worst, you haven't been around much. But I will go. Don't follow me."

"Oh, I won't. Because . . . I don't know. I was going somewhere punchy with that line but now I can't remember what I wanted to say."

Katya sighed. "I hope we can fight again, Sirc. We have not finished, so I do not yet know who is senior to whom."

Sirc shrugged. "I'm out of here." She turned and pushed her way through the students, who made extra efforts to get out of her way after watching her fight.

Katya leaned forward and licked Rohan's forehead. "No fever."

"I'll be fine. I just need a nap. A weeklong nap."

"Let's go back to the room." She half-directed, half-carried him up the hallway.

"We can't, they found me there."

"Who found you, Rohan?"

"Tamara's father. His goons beat me up. It was very embarrassing."

"Are they still after you?"

"No, but—"

"Then it will be fine. Come. I will message Garren to meet us. Wei Li told me your enemies probably won't be monitoring my comms. Because I'm new here."

"Oh. Okay. Good idea, then."

"Yes, I know. Come on, I shouldn't have to carry you."

"You could have taken her, you know."

"Who?"

"Sirc. She's no match for you right now. She wasn't on Boost."

"I could tell. That's why I didn't fight her."

"What?"

"There's no fun in fighting her when she's no match for me, Rohan. I will fight her again later, when she is stronger."

"Right. Perfect. Makes total sense. Wouldn't want to just take care of her now and save a whole bunch of people from Boost addiction and certain death."

"Hush. Focus on walking or I will pick you up and carry you like a cub, slung over my shoulder."

The pair made their way back to their room in Wistful's back corridors, stopping every hundred meters or so for Rohan to cough gently and probe his bruised ribs.

"I might be dying."

"You are not dying. Your cough already sounds better, and it's only been ten minutes. Why are you suddenly whining so much, Rohan?"

He sighed. "I'm not coping well with being useless."

"You are not useless. You are still good for a great many things."

"Like what, Katya?" They stopped and let a man walking four small animals on leashes pass them in the corridor.

"You have money, so you are good at paying for things that I can eat."

"So I'm just a credit card with legs to you."

"Not only that. Let me see. You attract a great deal of trouble, bringing people near for me to fight. That makes me very happy."

"I'm starting to wonder at your real motivation for this whole body-guarding thing. I think you saw me leaving Pilli 4 and realized I could get you in a whole lot more trouble than you'd ever get into at home, and that's why you attached to my leg."

She laughed. "Perhaps that was in the back of my mind. Along with other things. Look, we are almost there. Just up these next stairs."

Rohan grunted as he climbed, relieved to see that his legs and hips were working normally. "Even without Power helping, I still heal really fast."

Katya snorted. "Yes, Rohan. You are most remarkable. You have many positive traits that are yours by virtue of your birth. Oh, also, look at me, I should be valued because of the lovely quality of my fur and the regularity of my whiskers, because both those things are qualities I absolutely earned through good character and correct action."

He shrugged. "I'm just saying it's a good thing, considering how much I'm getting beaten up lately. Can't a guy look at the bright side without hearing any snide comebacks?"

She laughed and helped him through the front door of the makeshift hotel.

The Rogesh seated at the front counter was awake. He blinked at them through bloodshot eyes and waved the pair over.

Katya looked down at him. "Yes?"

"You get one warning. Another fight, and your friend there is banned for life."

Katya cocked her head. "But he was attacked. Shouldn't you be apologizing to him?"

The Rogesh shook his head, his half-meter horn swinging perilously close to Katya. "We guarantee discretion, not security. And not protection. Final warning."

Rohan touched her back. "It's fine. If we get attacked here again, we'll want to move on anyway."

Katya sighed and helped him to their room.

She let him wash up in peace, then placed him in his bed, propping pillows up around to support him. Then she stepped back and looked him over, surveying her handiwork.

She exhaled and placed her hands on her hips. "Rohan, you know that you are my friend."

"Oh, please don't start conversations that way. It's never good. You're about to lecture me or break up with me or something. And we aren't even dating. I can't tell if that makes it better or worse."

"You did not let me get to the 'but.' That's the important part."

"I know! I knew you were heading for a 'but'! That's why I interrupted you!"

"Let me finish."

He exhaled harshly. "Fine."

"You have been practicing your new technique very diligently for quite some time. Especially the past six months, but even before that."

"Yes. Yes, I have. Thanks for noticing. Not everyone appreciates how hard I work."

"Perhaps it is time to acknowledge that you have failed and move on to something else."

Rohan put both palms to his forehead and pressed. "You want me to give up?"

"It is not about what I do or do not want. It is a question of . . . how do I put this? Is the technique working? It does not seem to be. You are losing a great many fights lately, Rohan. That is not the man I remember coming to my planet."

"I know. It's hard."

"I understand hard. I have done hard things, Rohan. I wonder if this is a waste of your time. Were the men who beat you today very strong? As strong as Hybrids?"

"The Quattros? No. I mean, yes, they were plenty strong for non-Powers, but not compared to a Hybrid."

"Six months of dedicated training, and you lost to three normal people. How many more months before you can fight Hyperion? Sixty? Six hundred? Can you afford to spend fifty years training before stopping him?"

"I don't think it's going to be that long."

"Perhaps not, but the point remains."

He sighed and put his hands on his head, pushing to one side, then the other, until he heard crackling sounds from his neck. "I think it will work. I think it's my best chance to beat Hyperion. Maybe my only chance."

"Yet it isn't even your best chance to beat three non-Powered individuals. I know you have great respect for your teacher, this Spiral person from Earth, but you should also listen to your own thoughts sometimes."

"I do listen. I mean, it's not *just* respect for Spiral. And those non-Powered individuals were really tough. They had four arms each, so they were like six people. If you go by arm count."

"Then what do you need to make this technique work in a way that will give us all hope that you aren't wasting your time? You tried training here. You tried training on the surface."

He sighed. "I'm not sure. My anger gets in the way. The helix loses stability when I get emotional. Then I don't trust it, and it becomes even less stable. It's a cycle."

"I see. Is it possible that your temperament isn't suited for the technique?"

"Spiral thought it was. He handed it down to me when he gave me the soul gem that contains it. And he's usually pretty astute about that kind of thing."

Katya nodded slowly. "If you are the right person for this technique, then your training for it is clearly not the right training."

"I know. I can maintain it when I'm calm, but once the fighting starts . . ."

"You don't need to practice keeping the technique, you need to practice staying calm in the face of emotional challenges."

"Thank you very much, Professor Katya. I knew that already. How am I supposed to do that?"

She shrugged. "I am not sure. Who do you know who is very calm? Perhaps they can help you. Or you can emulate them."

He answered without thinking and without hesitation. "Master Turtle. Calmest, most tranquil dude I've ever been around."

"Then perhaps you should be spending more time with him."

Rohan took his mask out of his hood and tapped through the screens, looking for messages.

There were none, since it wasn't connected to Wistful's intranet. *I didn't notice how often I scroll through messages just to kill time until I turned them all off.*

He looked up at his bodyguard. "I think you're right. First let me rest a bit."

"Good. Then perhaps talk to Wei Li, who seems to need a friend more than usual."

"Great plan."

16

Prophecies Hard and Cold

R ohan woke up a few hours later with a light headache and lingering pain in his side. Katya snored from her own bed.

He sat up and walked gingerly to the small bathroom, his legs supporting him with more security than before.

Katya woke to the splashes of Rohan pouring a second glass of water.

She groaned and murmured wordlessly, and when he stepped back into the room, she was stretching and yawning wide, displaying sharp canines.

Are they called canines on a feline? I should look that up.

"You know, you're a bad influence on me. I never used to sleep this much."

She shrugged. "Your Powers protected you from many things, including fatigue."

"You're a Power too; what's your excuse for sleeping so much?"

She tilted her head and smiled. "I don't need to sleep this much, I simply enjoy it. And I don't need to give any excuse for doing something I enjoy. Not as long as it is within the law."

He drained the glass and poured a third.

"What time is it?"

"It is five, the end of the workday. A good time to visit Wei Li."

He hopped up and down, then swung his arms in wide circles, testing his joints. "Since your comm is still connected, can you contact Tamara? Make sure she's okay."

"I will. Hold on." The il'Zkin fumbled with her tablet, a small unit limited to basic comm and intranet functions. "I'll tell you when she answers."

"Thanks." They headed out; Rohan kept his hood up while Katya sauntered unconcerned in a yellow floral-print dress.

They navigated several blocks through the deep corridors before cutting over to the promenade, figuring that if they were recognized, it would be harder for anyone to trace their appearance back to the boardinghouse.

Katya relayed news from Tamara; she was safe, with the Ursans, working on a project and staying where the Tolone'ans couldn't find her.

Rohan sighed his relief and kept going.

The main avenue was crowded, typical for the end of the normal business day, packed with residents going home or leaving home for early drinks or dinner.

A short time later, they arrived at security; as before, they were waved through without question.

"I think we're spending too much time here. Those guys must think we're troublemakers."

Katya laughed. "We *are* troublemakers, Rohan. As far as security is concerned, at least!"

He shrugged as they entered Wei Li's office.

Rohan took a chair quickly; his legs were stable but weak, and they needed a rest. "This open door policy isn't a great idea, Wei Li. You could have all sorts of riffraff coming in and disturbing your workday."

She smiled, a barely perceptible twitch of her lips and cheeks. "The door, and my officers, remember the people who come here most often. If I knew a reliable algorithm to identify the riffraff consistently, I'd add it to the door's programming, and you'd probably have a harder time pestering me."

"Well, good thing you're an empath and a security chief and not a software engineer, then, right?"

A broader smile flashed across her face, gone almost before he noticed it. "What can I do for you? Are you here to discuss a fight that was unofficially reported by an unofficial business located in the unofficial back corridors of the southern arm?"

Rohan put on his best blankly innocent face and turned to Katya. "I don't know what she's talking about. What are you talking about, Wei Li?"

Katya shrugged. "I was not there for that fight. I did want you to know that we ran into the female who fought for the Boost dealers at the raid yesterday, but were unable to capture her."

Wei Li's face hardened. "Where did this happen, and how much collateral damage was caused during that altercation?"

"Near that spot on the southern arm I know nothing about, and very little."

"Very well. Is that really why you're here?"

Rohan cleared his throat. "Actually, I wanted to talk to you. About you."

"That is a surprise. Pleasant or unpleasant I am not yet sure, but definitely a surprise."

He sighed. "Come on, that's not fair. I'm worried about you, that's all."

She leaned back in her chair and looked at Katya, then back at Rohan. "I know you are. I'm an empath, remember?"

"You're going to make this hard for me, aren't you?"

Katya patted his shoulder. "This is what my people would call justice."

Wei Li nodded. "Mine call it giving the chef his own cooking. Rohan, you do not need to worry about me. I will manage."

"If you wanted to manage on your own, you wouldn't have invited me to breakfast this morning to hear all about this situation, right? You're looking for help."

"I will be fine, Rohan." She looked at the screen on her desk. "I am due to meet with the others for dinner. If you'll excuse me." She stood.

Rohan looked at Katya, who shrugged. He coughed; his lungs were feeling better. "Hey, Wei Li, can we join you? I don't mean to be rude, just inviting myself to tag along, but I really think spending more time around Master Turtle would help me with a problem of my own."

She froze. "Master Turtle? He can't even speak. How do you expect him to help you? He's already sacrificed almost everything he has to help others. Almost everything he *is*."

"No, I don't mean I want him to do something for me. I'm talking more along the lines of being an example. There's something about his aura that's so . . . so calm. It's like he's the opposite of my anger. He has all this Power, and it's not stormy. It feels like I could learn to emulate it, even if only a little bit, just by being near him."

She shook her head slowly. "I do not think you will get from him what you are hoping to get."

"Please? Let me try? You know what's happening, what I'm trying to do. Besides, what's the harm? I'll come to dinner. Sure, I'll make some bad jokes and Katya will lick somebody who doesn't want to be licked, but they'll all be fine, right?"

"I suppose. Very well, you may come. We are eating at the apartment I procured for them; I ordered catering."

Katya jumped and clapped her hands. "Catering! That sounds amazing. Is it fish? I love fish!"

Rohan shook his head. "It means food from a restaurant, but they bring it to your home."

Her eyes widened. "Restaurants can bring food to your house? Is this true? Why does anyone ever cook for themselves?"

Rohan shrugged. "At the moment, I have absolutely no idea. I'm sure I'll think of something."

Wei Li led them away.

<hr>

The apartment was the sort of three-bedroom place that businesses would use to house workers with families on temporary assignment. Commercial-grade furnishings that were stylish but highly damage-resistant; an adequate kitchen; less storage space than one would expect.

Rohan spent some time admiring the mass-produced artwork decorating the walls, then helped Mei Si set the table and put out the trays of food that had been delivered.

The Vor'karei drank tea before the meal and water with it; Rohan wasn't sure if he wished for something stronger or was better off without.

Katya sipped the tea, having learned to be wary of hot beverages the hard way, and asked questions about their lives training on their homeworld, Plassek.

Krai Wu talked at length about what it was like to grow up in what amounted to a monastic order.

"We woke at dawn every day, washed, and trained for an hour before eating. Breakfast was always simple: gruel with a bit of fish or milk."

Mai Si shook her head. "Except for the holidays. And the festivals. Of which we had many."

He nodded. "Yes, of course. Our order has roots going back through seven civilizations; we celebrate them all."

Mai Si nodded. "But none so much or so fervently as the holidays for each of the Twelve Who Began, who received the prophecies from the Lifters, one of whom we remember at the start of each month."

The Vor'karei dipped their heads when she said the number, touching their foreheads in a gesture reminiscent to Rohan of Catholics crossing themselves.

Rohan looked at Wei Li. "Are those the prophecies you . . .?"

She warned him to quiet with a glance.

Master Turtle sat at the head of the table, a warm and unwavering smile on his face. He sipped his tea, but only when prompted, Wei Li or Krai Wu putting the cup in his hands and pushing it toward his lips.

Rohan and Mai Si dished food out onto plates and brought them around: sliced fish, seared but raw in the center, drizzled with thin lines of a dark acidic sauce, next to a porridge of three grains cooked and lightly seasoned together.

Katya dug into hers first. She made happy noises while the others poked at their food.

Krai Wu looked at Rohan. "All Vor'karei honor the Twelve. They were the heroes who led the first generation of our sentient ancestors after the Lifters abandoned us. The prophecies are referred to as lost by most common people; only our order maintains them."

Rohan nodded. "That's amazing. My people, I mean my mother's side, can't agree on what things mean that were written two or three thousand years ago. Here you're still following text that's ten times as old."

The security chief snorted. "You're assuming we do, in fact, still understand the meaning of those prophecies. Not all agree." She shoveled a heaping spoonful of grains into her mouth as if trying to silence herself.

Krai Wu shook his head. "Come now, Wei Li. We understand well enough. We know what we have to do."

Mai Si put a restraining hand on his forearm. "Don't start."

"Start? What have I started? She denies the prophecies. Our entire reason for being. How much has been sacrificed, for how long, leading up to this very moment? She swore to uphold the edicts of our order, and now look what is happening." His hands trembled; the spoon he held bent under his grip.

"Calm yourself, my love. This is not the way you were trained."

Rohan felt a soothing, reassuring presence fill the room. He looked at Master Turtle, who gave no outward sign of so much as following the conversation.

Krai Wu put his utensils down and rubbed his hand. "I know. My temper. It is the reason Master Turtle has not given me the Eternity Ki. Why he wanted it to go to Wei Li. I have tried, by the Twelve—"

"Do not blaspheme, my love. Swear by the Nine or the Three but not on them all together. Please."

He let out a long breath. "I apologize. I should not let my feelings get the better of me."

"I understand. I think we all understand, even if we do not agree, yes? Wei Li?"

Wei Li, who had been staring at Master Turtle, shook her head and nodded. "I understand why you're upset. I just happen to disagree with what lies underneath it."

Krai Wu shook his head. "What is there to disagree *with*? When open eyes become The Shield. The eyes are opening already. Three of the wormholes have opened. Three! What are you waiting for?"

Rohan looked at Wei Li. "What becomes The Shield? The wormholes?"

Krai Wu answered for her. "The word has a double meaning. It means the wormholes, which open, and The Watcher, who watches. With eyes. Wei Li is one of the greatest Watchers the order has ever known. Her esoteric senses are unmatched. It is no coincidence that she is here, ready, during the time of the eyes opening. Ready to take the Eternity Ki and become The Shield."

Rohan took a bit of the food, enjoying the unfamiliar spices. The grains tasted of dark yellow, something like mustard. "I guess that makes sense."

Wei Li took her attention away from Master Turtle. "There are other prophecies, not all of which are understood. Did you forget that? Tell him why I'm reluctant. Go ahead."

The Vor'karei shrugged. "Finale when Shield and Watcher unite. That's the one you mean, isn't it?"

Rohan scratched his beard. "I don't get that one. 'Finale'?"

Mai Si swallowed. "And therein lies the problem. No, don't roll your eyes at me, my love, there is valid disagreement regarding the meaning of that word."

"It's 'finale.' It means the end, which means victory. To think it means anything else would be defeatist, and if we are going to lose in the end, there would have been no point in the work we have done for hundreds of generations! Why would we have been set on this course if the Lifters knew we would fail!"

Wei Li shook her head. "It means the end, not simply victory. The end of our order, perhaps. Perhaps the end of our mission. Or the end of Wistful. Or of the world. All of those are things that can end. The second prophecy might be a warning, that if The Shield and Watcher unite, all will be lost, not gained."

"Then answer the question I just posed, Watcher! If you think your understanding of the Lifter's words superior to mine, explain the rest of it! Why create the order if we're doomed to fail?"

"That's not what I said and you know it. It's a warning. That the Ki and Watcher should not unite, or only when it's absolutely necessary. Absolutely, *unequivocally* necessary. Because it will end the order. It's a final step—a finale! We can't go back from it, can't say, oh dear, we were premature in our actions, let us revert to the status quo."

"A final step to be taken when the eyes open! Which is happening!"

"Perhaps. But you can only claim to understand the first prophecy if you are certain that the word 'eyes' refers to both wormholes and Watchers. That is a possibility, but not a certainty. I am not willing to risk everything, hundreds of generations of sacrifice, until I am sure."

"What else could it mean?"

Wei Li opened her mouth wider, as if to yell, then looked at Master Turtle to her right. She deflated, slumping forward in her seat.

Katya pointed at Krai Wu's plate. "Are you going to finish that? Because I will eat it if you do not want to."

Mai Si stood. "Come, Katya, we will get you more. There is plenty in the kitchen."

"I like kitchens." She picked up her empty plate and followed the Vor'karei.

Rohan twirled his spoon in his food. "What's the plan, then? I'm hearing from Wei Li that she's not going to take the Eternity Ki. Not without some kind of . . . I don't know. Something more. Some guarantee."

Wei Li scoffed. "What kind of guarantee? What are you even talking about?"

"I don't know. Not exactly. I'm just saying, be fair, you can't rule anything out. Things have been really weird here lately. I mean over the past three years. I get that you don't know what the prophecy means, but how do you know the Lifters didn't anticipate this situation? Maybe they're about to come back in a big ship and actually clarify what they meant."

Krai Wu shook his head. "If they were able to do that, there would have been no need to leave the prophecies."

"You're thinking too narrowly. You don't know the whole situation. Maybe they planned to return and the prophecies were just a backup. A failsafe. Or their return is the failsafe, but they're on their way. Neither of you really know for sure what's going to happen. Maybe they're right behind the fourth wormhole with a giant Rosetta stone that will clarify everything."

Wei Li sighed. "I don't know what that is."

"Something that helped people translate some old writing. I think. You don't happen to have any audio recordings of the prophecies? As they were spoken?"

"So you could listen with Fire Speech? We do not."

"Damn. I really should have learned how to read in it." Krai Wu grunted; one by one, everyone at the table noticed that Master Turtle was watching Rohan.

Rohan swallowed.

Wei Li tapped her plate. "If the Lifters come back and give me clear instructions, I will follow them. If we receive a new source of information that I deem relevant and clarifying, I will act accordingly. However, for now, I refuse the Eternity Ki. The stakes are simply too high."

Krai Wu sighed. "I wish you'd change your mind."

Her voice softened. "I wish for a great many things. I have wished for many things for many years, Krai Wu."

He smiled, a genuine smile that crinkled the corners of his reptilian eyes, and rubbed a hand over his head. "We will have to find another recipient. I do not think Master Turtle would choose me. I have . . . some anger issues."

Rohan chuckled. "I know a little something about that. Why can't we just keep Master Turtle like this? He seems okay. A little weird, but we can keep feeding him and hose him down once in a while. Keep the bugs off. What's the rush?"

Mai Si spoke from the doorway. "If his condition progresses, he will die. He is stripping away everything that he is. Eventually, that will include the will to beat his heart, to draw breath. His time is finite."

"So what do you do? How do you find another . . . host? Carrier?"

Krai Wu grunted. "We had hoped Wei Li would reconsider."

Mai Si smiled at him. "You had hoped, my dear. I knew she wouldn't. You forget how stubborn she is when she thinks she is right."

"Fine. *I* had hoped."

Rohan looked at them. "Is there a plan B? Anything? Some kind of special gemstone you can stick it in? A pet?"

Krai Wu looked at his partner; she looked back, and they shared a long stare.

He maintained eye contact with her. "There is a plan in place. For a situation like this one."

Mai Si shook her head. "You cannot be serious."

"I am. I don't like it either, but what is the alternative? She won't take it. He won't simply give it to you or to me. There are no other members of the order on this station. He will not live through the return trip, not long enough for us to find a suitable host. What else is there?"

Rohan finished chewing. "I feel like you guys are talking about something specific, but I don't know what it is."

Mai Si sighed. "If there is nobody in the order available to receive the Eternity Ki, we must find an outsider to do so."

"Great. How do you do that? Wanted ad? Scour the temples looking for a suitably devout person? Or, don't tell me—"

Wei Li fixed her eyes on Master Turtle.

Mai Si shook her head softly. "Yes, Rohan."

Krai Wu folded his arms across his chest. "It is the only way. To find an outsider, there must be—"

Rohan half-stood from his chair, shaking his head. "No, you can't. That's a terrible idea."

Wei Li grabbed the old man's shoulder with her left hand. "Master Turtle. Rohan, it's Master Turtle."

Rohan turned. "What?"

"It's happening faster than it seemed. We don't have much time. He will be gone . . . soon."

Krai Wu nodded. "Then it's settled. What we have to do."

Mai Si sighed. "Only once before in three hundred generations . . ."

"I know. Yet the conditions align. He will not pass it to me, and Wei Li will not take it. We must find someone. We must hold—"

Rohan grunted. "Don't say it! This is a terrible idea. The worst idea."

Mai Si shook her head. "My love is correct. It is the only way."

Krai Wu held up a clenched fist. "A tournament."

17

Like Father, Like Son

The silence that followed Krai Wu's declaration was broken by a knock on the door.

Mai Si turned to face the door, startled, then turned back. "Did you order more food?"

Wei Li shook her head. "We got everything. If security needed me, they would call, not knock."

Krai Wu stood. "I will see who it is." He left the table, crossing paths with Katya as she returned.

Rohan looked at Mai Si. "You're really going to have a tournament? That seems . . . very much like something that happens in comic books."

"Comic books?"

"Er . . . stories with pictures. Written for, well, at one time they were written for children. You know what? Not worth explaining. Like a holodrama."

"Ah, yes. I can see that. We have holodramas on Plassek. I do not like this solution, but my love is not wrong. It is the prescribed way to move forward in this highly unusual situation."

Wei Li shook her head. "A situation which should never have arisen."

Mai Si snapped at her. "That is not helping. This was Master's wish. If you want to hold anger about it, that is your prerogative, but keep it to yourself, please."

The security chief looked ready to respond, then swallowed her words. "Fair. I shall render judgment silently from now on."

Mai Si glared at her for a moment, then broke down and laughed. "I missed you, my dear. More than you know. Your humor lit up our household. I hope you are treasured here as we treasured you."

Rohan cleared his throat. "Absolutely she is. We love Wei Li. She's the best. I have no idea where I'd be without her."

Wei Li's face tightened as if she were fighting a smile. "Do not give me too much credit for your situation, Rohan. Blame is the other side of praise, and I do not want to answer for whatever bizarre conditions you come to in the future."

"Got it." He heard a child's voice, muffled, from the hall that led to the apartment's front door. "I know that voice."

Katya's eyes opened wider. "It's your almost-son, Rohan. Amarinthalytics. Do you see? I remembered his entire name. It is so long."

Rohan nodded as he wiped his mouth on a napkin and stood. "What is Amarinthicus doing here?"

Wei Li looked at him. "I would like to know how he knew to come here at all."

"Yeah, good question."

"—speak to Rohan. I know he's in here. It's important!" Rinth's voice cracked on the final word.

"Move along, little man. We are having serious discussions here; it is no place for a boy."

"I'm not—I need Rohan's help. Let me through!"

Katya followed Rohan toward the entrance. "Is he here to save you again, Rohan? Twice in one day? Perhaps you no longer need me after all. Perhaps this boy can be your bodyguard."

"I never asked for a bodyguard, Katya. And I don't think he's here for me. I hope his mother's not in trouble. Krai Wu, let him through, he's with me."

"Are you sure?"

"Yes."

Rohan turned the corner; Krai Wu was holding Rinth back with one hand. Rinth's face was grim, not easing as he spotted the Hybrid.

"Rohan! I need to talk to you, please! It's really super important!"

"It's fine, come on in. You want some food? We have leftovers. I . . . have no idea what it is, but it's good."

"I need help, Rohan. It's not about food. This is serious. Really."

"Okay. Come on in."

Wei Li stood as they reentered the dining area. "Hello, Rinth."

"Hello, Auntie. Maybe you can help me, too."

She nodded, her face serious. "What sort of trouble are you in?"

"I'm not in trouble."

"I rather think you are, or will be, once we find out how you knew to come to this apartment to find us."

Rinth's face paled to a yellowy green as he looked up at Rohan. "Oh. That."

Rohan patted his shoulder. "Relax. I think she's kidding. Mostly. How did you find us, though?"

"Well. Um. I wanted to keep track of you, Rohan. With everything going on. You know. In case Grandpa had you kidnapped again or we had trouble with those guys who might be after Mom or something else happened. I don't like not knowing anything." His words came faster with each sentence.

"I get it, I get it. Slow down just a bit and tell me."

He gasped in a lungful of air. "So I made a tracking device out of stuff that Dad keeps lying around, and I put it on your pants before. You know, when you were tied down and I hugged you. Why did you *think* I did that?"

Rohan patted himself. "You sneaky little—is this it?" He pulled a sliver of metal out of the seam at the waistband of his pants.

"That's it! Be careful, that was hard to make."

Rohan considered twisting the bug into a ball but instead handed it back. "Take it. But that's not cool, Rinth. Surveilling people. How did you even know how to do it? That's not what they normally teach in the fourth grade, is it?"

"Fifth grade. I'm just good with these things. My dad says I get it from him, but Mom says I get it from her. I dunno."

"Okay." He looked at the others, as if inviting them to ask their own questions.

None did.

Rohan put his hands on Rinth's shoulders. "Now I know how you found me, but I'd like to know why. What's the problem?"

Rinth took a deep breath. "I know I'm not supposed to spy on people but it's really hard when you're a kid and nobody tells you anything and also you notice after a while that some people aren't good at taking care of themselves and keeping themselves safe even though they're adults and they should really know better already—"

"Stop! Breathe!"

Rinth stopped and took another breath. "Sorry. I do that when I'm anxious."

"Okay. I get it. Stick to the things I need to know. Is your mom okay?"

"As far as I know. She called and said she was with Uncle Ang and not to worry but I still did a little bit I'm sorry—"

"Breathe."

Rinth inhaled again. "Right. She's fine."

"Great. Who were you spying on, Rinth?"

The boy looked at the floor, then at Wei Li's stony face, then back at Rohan. "Well . . . lots of people, I guess. Not all the time, you know, and not too much. I know I shouldn't be."

Rohan sighed. "Let's stay on track, okay? Why are you here? I'm going to go out on a limb and say it's not just to confess. Or is it? Because it really better not be."

"No, no. Not that. I mean, yes, that too, but not that. You see, the thing is, I put a listening device on Dad."

"Dad."

"Yeah. My dad. I know you know him."

Rohan looked at Wei Li plaintively. "He's talking about Lahnegarn."

She nodded. Master Turtle watched them, a sweet smile on his face, while Mai Si and Krai Wu gathered up the dishes and brought tea around.

Rohan turned back to the boy. "What happened with your dad, Rinth?"

"Look, I know you and he aren't best friends or anything and I know he was kind of a jerk to you and he keeps calling Mom his wife and that annoys you a whole lot I'm not blind just because I'm a kid—"

"Breathe. Tell me what you heard. No, don't. Tell me specifically the thing you heard that concerned you."

The boy inhaled deeply and nodded. "I'm sorry. The thing is, Dad was really upset with you. I listened to him talk a lot. He even did it in front of me, some of the time. Talk, I mean. He never used to. He would save it for his friends. But they stopped listening to him so much, and he wanted to talk to somebody, so he'd talk to me, but then I didn't want to listen anymore and then things maybe got a little worse you know." He took another breath, this time without prompting.

"Okay. I can see that."

Katya nodded. "He needs a tribe of his own. People who will listen to him even when he makes no sense. I do this for Rohan frequently."

"Not helping, Katya."

She smiled. "I think I am. See, the boy is smiling now. Perhaps he will be calmer."

Rinth's color *was* returning. "You know he puts cameras all around, right? Like on shuttles and stuff. So he knows what's happening all around the system. It's kind of how I know how to do this stuff. From watching him."

Wei Li leaned forward and looked at Rohan. "You knew of this?"

The Hybrid shrank back from her, shrugging. "I guess. Didn't I mention that to you? I could swear I did. Huh. I must have sustained some brain trauma around the time I found out."

"Likely story."

"Besides, I don't work for you, remember? It's not my job to find the security problems on this station."

She pointed at him. "That, as inconvenient as it is at this exact moment, is quite true. You may continue, Rinth."

"So Dad was kind of sort of obsessed with you and the stuff you were doing on Toth 3 these past couple of weeks. Which he knew about because of the cameras he kept on some shuttles. They caught you going down, something about your ship's stealth technology not working in an atmosphere during daylight. Well, he figured there was no reason for you to be down there unless you had discovered some kind of secret, like a weapon or something, maybe a treasure, and he really really wanted to know what it was. Like, really really."

"I do not like where this is going."

Wei Li rubbed her head. "Neither do I."

Rinth nodded. "That's why I put the bug on him! I was worried. He was talking a lot, and some of it was sounding kind of weird. Maybe even crazy. A little. I'm sorry, I know I shouldn't say that about a grownup."

Rohan patted his shoulder. "Don't be. Tell me what you heard, Rinth."

"Dad wanted to take something from you, since you'd taken stuff from him. That's what he said, not what I said, Rohan, I don't even know what he's talking about. But to do that, he had to get to the surface, and you know nobody's allowed down there except you, because of all the kaiju and stuff. You know, eating people who go down."

"Right."

"But he figured that if you could survive on the surface for days, which you did, the last couple of weeks, without your Powers, remember, this is what he said, not me, but he said if you could do it, then so could he. So he went to steal a shuttle. With a couple of his friends."

"Steal a shuttle. Can he do that?"

Wei Li sighed. "He has clearance to work on them. If he has sufficient technical acumen to plant cameras on them without being caught, he can probably override the piloting functions."

Rohan rubbed his forehead. "You're telling me your father stole a shuttle and intends to go down to the surface?"

Rinth nodded. "Yeah. That's why I had to come here straightaway even though I know I'm not supposed to just interrupt you when you're doing stuff."

Rohan looked at Katya, then at Wei Li. "What are we supposed to do?"

Katya smiled at him. "Save him, of course! You cannot allow the father of this cute little boy to be eaten by giant monsters."

Rohan looked down into Rinth's hopeful face and wished his stomach would settle. "No. I can't. I guess it's time to mount a rescue."

"Rohan, am not for understanding reason for being here." Ursula shifted her three-hundred-plus-kilogram bulk in the reclining acceleration couch in *Void's Shadow*'s cabin.

Rohan moved his hands farther up the front wall of the cabin, where the ship had displayed a live feed of the planet's surface. He leaned close to the image, squinting to pick up any details he could spot around their landing site.

"You're here because Master Turtle isn't quite all there, so he can't give consent to helping me with a situation like this."

"Who is being this Master Turtle? Am not understanding."

"He's the guy who gave me the idea for this rescue. *Void's Shadow*, do you have an approach plotted?"

The ship's voice came from speakers hidden behind the walls. "I know where to go, Captain. I picked you up from there."

"Yeah. Same spot. That's the best place to start."

"War Chief, you are not for answering my question."

He nodded while studying the images.

He froze, thinking he spotted the metal gleam of a shuttle hull, but it turned out to be a pond reflecting the sunlight.

"You're here to help me rescue somebody who needs help. Well, probably a few somebodies, since I think he brought company along."

Ursula nodded. "Am happy to be for helping, Rohan. However, am also happy for knowing specific details of project to come."

"I'd love to give you all the specifics. The problem is, I'm making this up as I go along."

"Yet you requested help from me. Is it not Ang who is for helping with these missions to rescue the fools who are for coming to the planet?"

He sighed. "That used to work. We'd bring Ang into the upper atmosphere, and he'd project a good old dose of anger into the planet and draw all the kaiju toward him and away from whoever we needed to find."

"Yes. Was good plan."

"The problem is that the kaiju started to figure it out. They stopped responding. I'm honestly not sure what the deal was. Maybe they heard something specific in his aura that told them he wasn't really serious?

Mystery for another day. The point is, that won't work, at least not reliably. So we need a new tactic."

"Yes. Am for agreeing. What is this tactic you are thinking, Rohan?"

"Well, the kaiju respond to angry feelings. Which they can sense through auras. Presumably."

"This am knowing."

"It gets them all worked up and brings them in for a fight. Now, I managed to stay down there safely because I controlled my anger."

"Everyone very proud of you for that, Rohan."

"Thanks. Not the point. The problem is, knowing Lonnie, I'm sure whoever he brings with him is going to get annoyed, sooner than later. Might want to punch him in the face. Or maybe they'll spot a kaiju and get scared. As we all know, fear leads to anger, so . . ."

"How are all for knowing this, Rohan? Have never heard this."

"Never mind. The point is, Lonnie's not equipped to last on the surface. I can't fight off the kaiju, and since Ang's thing isn't working anymore, I can't distract them."

"So we are for going to die on planet? Not your best plan, War Chief."

"No, I don't think we're going to die. I certainly hope not. We're going to come at the kaiju from the other direction. Instead of distracting them with more anger, I think you can calm them down by doing your thing."

"Ah. My thing. By this you are for meaning projecting calm onto the, er, kaiju."

"Yep. You're like the anger antidote. The cure for fear. You just get there, open the door, and think soothing, calming thoughts at the terrifying, giant monsters. They'll relax, drop Lonnie and his friends, hopefully before eating them, and we'll be on our way."

"And we are for testing this tactic how, Rohan?"

"We don't exactly have a way to test it. Or the time. Sorry. We're just going to go in there and take our shot. How does that sound?"

She shifted nervously in the chair. "Like overcooked fish."

Void's Shadow interrupted. "Entering atmosphere now, Captain. Atmospheric conditions are within normal parameters."

"Super, thanks. Look, Ursula, you stay in the ship, okay? If things go badly, just close the door, and *Void's Shadow* will whisk you to safety."

Ursula nodded. "Is good for knowing that ship's stealth tech makes her completely invisible to kaiju."

Rohan swallowed. "That's not exactly accurate. But they don't go after her, because her aura is basically invisible. With the hatch closed, they won't sense you either, even if you happen to be angry or something. So you should be safe."

"Yes, yes. Is good for knowing that kaiju do not ever attack things without an angry aura, even if they are already for being agitated."

He turned to face her. "I know it's not a perfect plan, okay? Your sarcasm isn't helping."

"You want for helping? Help by explaining to Ursula why you are not for flying down and rescuing these mans yourself. What are for doing, War Chief?"

He sighed. "I can't."

"Can't? Or will not? Is your Power truly for gone, Rohan?"

"It's complicated."

"Do not for risking Ursula's precious life on complicated. Do better."

"Look. You're right. I'm asking a lot. The thing is . . ."

What do I tell her?

I need to stop Hyperion. He's already caused a billion deaths that I know of.

That's a lot of deaths.

I'm not sure anybody else can do it; he's too strong. Or if they can, the collateral damage will be incredible. He'll make sure of it.

This is the only path I can see that leads to me having a chance.

I have to stick to it.

"Ursula. I can't explain it all. But I need you to believe me when I tell you this: I wouldn't risk your life, risk the safety of all the people around me, if I didn't think it was really important. There are countless lives at stake. Maybe billions. I'm not sure I can save them all, but this is the only way I have a chance. I hope that's good enough."

She looked at him with her brown eyes so wide he could see the whites all around. "Billions?"

"Yeah. I'm gambling, and those are the stakes. It's the safest bet I know how to place, but it's a gamble."

"We take risks in order for saving whole planets of people."

"Yeah. You in? Because if you're not, we can turn around right now, no hard feelings. I'll try to think of another way to save Lonnie. Or let him get eaten by kaiju. Rudra knows he kind of deserves it."

She stared at the screen for a minute, eyes focused on the growing image of the landing site. She let out a sigh. "Ursula will be for helping save Rinth's father. Boy should not know loss as that."

"Good. We're almost there."

18

Nothing to Fear but Fear Itself . . . and Monsters

The ship came in low and slow; wind and noise would bring kaiju to investigate, and that was the last thing they wanted. Her hull could absorb or reflect electromagnetic radiation, and her aura was all but undetectable, but she still displaced air and still presented as a black shape against a bright sky.

Rohan took four seconds to admire the setting sun before returning his attention to the screen. Ursula stood and joined him, impressed by the resolution of the optics.

"That's the dig site. Right over here you can see the hill where Ben's students first landed and detected the ruins. And over here"—he pointed out a clearing in the forest—"you can see where I set up my camp."

"What were you for hoping to find, Rohan?"

He sighed. "I have no idea. It was more about practicing to control my own anger. I did find a door, but I couldn't open it."

She snorted. "You should be for asking Ang for helping. He loves opening of things."

"I'm sure he'd show up with a backpack full of explosives. We'll try to pick the lock before we risk blowing up the installation."

She barked, and he continued searching.

"*Void's Shadow*, can you spot the shuttle? I don't see her. Do you have any surveillance footage?"

"I checked Wistful's video feeds, Captain, but they're kind of glitchy. Almost as if someone interfered with the feeds so we wouldn't have a clear picture of what's going on."

"Almost. That bastard Lonnie. Making things difficult."

Ursula laughed. "He is for being very annoying but also little bit clever, no?"

"Yes."

"Maybe Rinth is also for being this way, too?"

"Rinth is cute. And Rinth doesn't call my girlfriend his wife. Wait, that didn't quite come out right. You know what I mean."

She barked again.

Rohan stabbed the screen with a finger. "There! *Void's Shadow*, zoom in there! Bring us a bit closer! The forest just north of the campsite."

"Yes, Captain. What do you see? Is that the shuttle? You have good eyes!"

"Not the shuttle, but there's a break in the tree canopy. I don't think that was there before. I wonder if the shuttle went down through there."

"Oh, good catch, Captain! Do you want me below the tree line?"

"Not yet. Just . . . get closer."

Ursula's hot breath wafted over him as the tip of her nose drifted over his shoulder. "If you tap here, it will brighten the image . . . magnify it a bit . . . dial this up to pick up the darker spots . . . oh boy."

"What is it, War Chief?"

"That's the shuttle. At least, it's *a* shuttle. There are only two problems."

"Two only?"

"One, it's down, and that's how they look when they crash, not when they land."

"And for the two problem?"

"Someone's poking the shuttle, and it looks a lot like Terry."

Rohan turned toward the door, then back to the front wall.

I was about to jump out the airlock and fly down.

Old instincts die hard.

"Try opening a channel! See if we can talk to them!"

"Yes, Captain. Go ahead."

"Hail the shuttle. This is Rohan, er, just Rohan, I guess. No title. Are you okay in there? Lahnegarn, is that your shuttle?"

He waited, Ursula breathing over his shoulder.

"Captain, I don't know if—oh, hold on."

Lonnie's voice erupted from the speakers. "Rohan, don't try to stop me. I know you spent the past two weeks down here; I'm going to be just fine."

"How's that shuttle holding up, Lahnegarn?"

"I'll fix it. Just go away. I'm going to find out what you were digging up here. Had trouble getting to something, did you? Maybe you don't have the brainpower to solve these kinds of mysteries. Give you a problem you can't punch your way through and watch as you fall apart."

"Lahnegarn, that's not what happened. The surface is dangerous. Are you inside that downed shuttle? There's a kaiju sniffing around outside it." He tapped the screen to mute the channel. "*Void's Shadow*, can you take us closer? But not straight in. Maybe forty or fifty meters east of it."

"Yes, Captain."

He tapped the channel open again. "Be careful, Lahnegarn. That kaiju is dangerous."

"Kaiju. What a stupid word. You think you're so clever, don't you, naming everything?"

"I have a knack."

"I don't think you do. Everyone humors you because you're the great and powerful Griffin. I'm not so impressed. This monster is barely bigger than Rak. In fact, they're going to take care of it right now."

"Rak? Rak is with you?" *Isn't that the name of one of Eldarinth's body-guards? The Quattro?*

"Rak and Ruk are here. Since they took you out without any problems, and you managed to survive here for two weeks by yourself, they should be able to handle anything that comes our way. Including that ridiculous reptile. Even if it is a few hundred kilos. Not exactly a giant monster, is it? They're supposedly hundreds of tons and a hundred meters long. Another one of your lies."

"No, Lonnie, that's not it. The kaiju are Powers, Lonnie! They'll tear apart the Quattros. Do not fight the kaiju, Lonnie. I'm dead serious. Don't do it."

"There must be something really interesting at that dig site, isn't there? Go on, guys. Open the doors. Show the Hybrid what we do to animals who act up. We'll be eating flying lizard for dinner. I have just the sauce to go on it."

One of the Quattros could be heard over the line, muted and distant. "Yes, boss. We're getting the door open now."

"Lonnie! I'm not trying to hide anything from you, I'm telling you, Terry is dangerous! Especially if you try to fight him! The only way I survived for two weeks was by *not* losing my temper! I had to focus on not wanting to fight, every second of every day!"

Lahnegarn snorted. "Sure you did. Look, I know you don't respect me, but please, come up with a better lie than that. I don't know a lot about Hybrids, but one thing I do know is that you think about fighting. All. The. Time."

"Lonnie, if that were even remotely true, I would have put my fist through your face six months ago." *I'm not sure that helped.* "Please, tell them to calm down and get back in the shuttle, we'll figure a way to get you out of there."

"Boys, have at that lizard! I'll start the fire."

One of the Quattros answered. "Door's almost open. It got jammed by the—there we go. We're headed out now. Give us five minutes, tops."

"Good. Rohan, you can take off. We'll be fine. If I need it, I know how to call down another shuttle."

"Lonnie! So help me, call them back right now or—"

"Who's starting to sound angry now, Rohan? Better work on that temper of yours."

Rohan cut the channel. "Can we get a better view of what's going on?"

"The sun is setting, Captain. I don't have instruments designed for this. I assume you don't want me shining a spotlight on the area."

"Better not."

"I thought so. I'll enhance the image."

Rohan looked at Ursula. "If those two try fighting Terry, they're going to get ripped apart."

"Who being Terry?"

"That kaiju. He's tiny for a kaiju, but still, you know. Still a monster. He kind of liked me, so he hung around the dig site whenever I was there."

"Can you for calming Terry?"

"Huh. I can try. Not sure. *Void's Shadow*, take us down low enough for me to get out without breaking a leg."

"Yes, Captain." She eased to the ground and opened a hatch.

Rohan turned his Third Eye inward; checked on the helix of esoteric energy he'd been maintaining. It was intact but vibrating erratically.

He stepped through the hatch.

Light flooded the forest as the damaged shuttle turned on all its exterior lamps.

The Hybrid shielded his eyes from the sudden illumination and noticed Ursula's head and shoulders sticking out through the hatch.

She pointed. "Looks like overcooked fish again."

Rohan blinked and looked toward the shuttle.

The two Quattros, tall and muscular men with four arms each, had emerged from the shuttle.

A pterosaur loomed over them, the top of his head-crest over three meters off the ground. Rohan could *feel* his aura: strong and simmering, anger ready to be unleashed, pushing back against every living thing in the area.

Tree branches bent; moss rolled away from him in concentric circles.

The creature raised his beak up to the sky, opened his mouth, and let out an eardrum-shattering roar.

—◆··◆—

Rohan began to run, his feet sticking in the wet moss as he struggled to cover the fifty meters between his ship and the Quattros. "Oh boy, Terry's pissed."

Ursula called out. "Am I for following you?"

He tapped on the comm behind his ear. "Don't! Hang back and get ready to project calm and peace like your life depends on it."

"Those are not being calm and peaceful words, Rohan! That is not for making me feeling either of those things!"

"Well . . . try! Other lives depend on it!"

"Even being less helpful now, War Chief!"

"Rudra save me." In the bright lights of the shuttle, he could see the open door, Lahnegarn standing just inside it, watching the Quattros face off against the tiny kaiju. "Get them inside!"

Lahnegarn pointed at the kaiju, and his head moved up and down.

Is he laughing? That . . . I'm going to rescue him so I can kill him with my own hands.

Rohan pulled his feet free of the sticky moss, one annoying boot at a time, reduced to a trudge as he wove between trees on his way to the shuttle.

Terry lifted his head and roared again.

Rak, or maybe Ruk, Rohan couldn't tell them apart, stepped forward and punched the pterosaur when his head came back down.

"Don't! Don't make him any angrier!"

The other Quattro shook his head and patted the first one's shoulder; he punched again.

Rohan shouted from twenty meters away, "Terry, stop! Don't hurt them!"

Terry stood up straighter and spread his arms wide, leather wings unfolding to dwarf the Quattros beneath.

He lifted its head, opened his mouth, and intensified his aura.

Rohan paused, the pressure of the creature's esoteric energy stopping him in his tracks.

Exactly as it paralyzed the Quattros.

Terry's head came down, snapping shut over one Quattro's head. His mouth closed, the tips of his beak reaching halfway to the man's belly.

Blood spurted from the sides as his mouth tore completely through the Quattro's torso.

Terry's head rose, the upper third of the Quattro's torso inside his mouth. The pterosaur looked up and jerked his head up and down, working the chunk of meat inside through his throat and into his belly.

The Quattro's lower torso, arms, and legs toppled over to the ground.

"Rak!" Ruk shouted.

Rohan gritted his teeth and pushed through the kaiju's pressure. "Ursula, if you can project some calm right now, we could really use it."

"I am not for feeling calm."

"Think about good things. Think about fish. Holding cubs. Your niece just had a couple, didn't she? Think about holding the cubs on your chest while they sleep."

A wave of calm, aquamarine aura wafted between the trees.

Rohan slogged forward. "Terry! Terry, it's me, Rohan! Calm down, little buddy! No more killing people!"

Ruk stepped closer to the pterosaur, pulling a knife from a sheath at his hip, and drove the blade into the reptile's chest.

The steel shaft broke on his chest.

Terry's head snapped down, engulfed the second Quattro to the waist, and bit down. He tore the Quattro almost fully in half, pulling the man's upper body free at the waist. Then the pterosaur lifted his head like a bird and shook the body back and forth, snapping at it from various angles to get the hunk of meat down his throat.

"Terry! Calm down! Stop eating people!"

The kaiju looked at him. An intense aura, stronger than that of almost any Hybrid he'd ever met, perhaps greater than Hyperion's, enveloped him.

From behind, the soft breeze of Ursula's calm washed against it.

Stay calm. Whatever you do, don't feed his anger. And don't lose the helix.

Terry's head dove toward Rohan.

He reached up with his right hand, his palm meeting the pterosaur's snout at the tip, absorbing all his momentum.

Rohan exhaled as the creature's anger swept over him.

The pressure was enormous; it was all consuming; it was . . .

It was terrifying.

Terry glared at him with his flat reptilian eyes, then lifted his head as if to strike again. The Hybrid stepped back and slid in the blood-soaked moss. He looked over and saw intestines spilling out of Rak's open lower half.

Rohan's heart raced; a thread of anger erupted from the base of his spine, poking through his soul with red-gold surges.

The Hybrid looked down at his left hand as the helix of energy shook apart, blowing the skin off his palm in a cloud of blood and shreds of skin as it discharged its collected energy.

That's not good.

"Ursula!"

"I am for trying! Tell to me something calming! Something funny!"

"It doesn't work like that! I can't just be funny on command!"

"Always you are working to being funny, no matter how annoying or how all do not want for it, all the time, and now, when I am for asking you to tell a joke, you cannot? This is my War Chief?"

"That's not how it works! Just calm him down! Wait, is it him or her? I just assumed 'him,' I'm not sure. How do you sex a pterosaur?"

"You wish to mate with it? Always you and mating with things! This is not for being the time, Rohan!"

"That's not what sexing means, Ursula! It's finding out the sex of something. Like is it a boy kaiju or a girl kaiju. Not mating!"

Ursula laughed, and the breeze of esoteric calm intensified, blowing light-blue cool over the pair as Rohan faced the pterosaur.

Huh. The sexing joke did the trick.

He exhaled and looked at his palm.

The damage seemed superficial.

He looked up at Terry and met the pterosaur's gaze.

You did not have to kill them. They were dumb but they did not deserve to die.

He spoke quietly, hoping his comm would pick it up but that Terry wouldn't react to the noise. "Lonnie, you need to get out of that shuttle.

And you need to stay really calm while you do it. Make your way over to my ship. Ursula will get you inside and you can go."

The Lukhor answered over the comm. "I'm not sure I can."

"Lonnie, that shuttle can't keep you safe. Terry can rip through it like an aluminum can if he wants to. And he will, unless you get out while Ursula is providing cover and go into *Void's Shadow*, where whatever you are feeling can be masked by my ship."

"That thing just killed Rak and Ruk."

"Yes, he did, Lonnie. Do you want to join them? Because if you do, just say the word and I'll leave you to it."

"No."

"You want Rinth to lose his father? You want Tamara to lose her ex-husband?"

"No." The Lukhor's voice was quiet.

Ursula grunted. "Rohan, hurry. I cannot be continuing forever."

"Lonnie. If you die here, you'll never know if you had a chance to win her back, will you?"

"No."

"Get moving. Get out of the shuttle. Do it now or you'll lose her forever. Lose both of them."

Terry leaned toward Rohan, slower this time, not striking, his mouth closed, large dark eyes focused on the Hybrid.

"You feeling better now, boy? You calming down?" The pterosaur's mouth moved, not opening but working on something, and he swallowed.

Probably a big hunk of Ruk stuck in his throat.

Don't think about that.

Terry pushed his snout toward Rohan; the Hybrid reached up and ran one hand up his beak, toward the nostrils, scratching the dry, scaly skin. With the other, he scratched under his chin.

"Good boy. Calm down, now. No need to fight. Nobody left to fight."

I really hope Lonnie's moving.

The kaiju shuffled forward, careful not to bump into Rohan, and squatted lower.

Rohan stepped in and started scratching his neck. "You like that, don't you, boy? I know, I know. You got all worked up. Those guys wanted a fight and you . . . you just don't know how to say no, do you? That's not how you're built. Not how you were designed, I guess."

The creature exhaled slowly and lowered his body further, not stopping until his haunches were on the ground.

Ursula's calming aura continued to lap at them like waves on a beach.

"Good boy. Good boy. It's not your fault. We know. They shouldn't have been here, I know. I know. I tried to warn them. And now, well. They won't be making that mistake again. But you. You, boy. You should not be eating people. Not okay. But I forgive you. I understand. You are what you are. It's not as if you had anybody to house-train you."

Terry sneezed, the expulsion of air nearly knocking Rohan off his feet.

"Rohan." Ursula spoke over his comm. "Lahnegarn is aboard *Void's Shadow*. You can stop."

"Give me a minute. I'm going to get him good and calm. You can stop pushing when you have to, Ursula."

"I can only keep this up for another few minutes."

"That's okay. Just let it go. Terry and I are good. Aren't we, boy? Aren't we?"

Terry leaned into Rohan's body and exhaled loudly.

Almost a purr.

19

Remember That Stadium from Turn Three?

Rohan broke the silence in *Void's Shadow*'s cabin with a huff. "You're going to have to call Grandpa and tell him you got his henchmen killed."

Lahnegarn rubbed his eyes and turned to the Hybrid. "Grandpa? You mean Eldarinth. He won't care."

"What do you mean he won't care? They're dead because of you."

The Lukhor shrugged. "They're just clones. He'll order new ones."

Ursula looked at Rohan. "What does this meaning 'order'?"

The Lukhor answered. "Quattros are all clones. They're trained from birth to fight. Rich people open contracts with the Quattro Corporation. If any die, they just send replacements."

"All clones? All the same? No females?"

Lonnie shrugged. "I don't think so. I've never heard of one."

Rohan shook his head. "They're still people, Lonnie. And they're dead. Tell Eldar."

"I don't see why you're so upset. Their only goal in life is to die in battle. They sure as hell did that today."

Ursula shook her head. "Not so glorious. Perhaps are wanting to die because no females. No future beyond selves."

"They don't care. Like I said, they live for battle. Nothing to be sorry about."

Rohan stared hard at Lahnegarn. "Ursula, tell me not to kill this guy right now."

"Rohan, do not kill this guy right now. For if you do, Rinth will for being very angry, and you do not want that."

"Thanks."

"Instead, allow Ursula great pleasure of killing this guy. Will not even consume meat; will spit out every morsel of flesh after mauling."

Lahnegarn paled slightly. "She's kidding, right? Tell me she's kidding."

Rohan shrugged. "It's hard to tell with Ursans. Different culture. They don't have typical humanoid facial structure. She might mean it. If she tries, I'd stop her, but you know, I don't think I have what it takes to pull three hundred kilos of angry Ursan off you right now."

Lahnegarn sank deeper into his seat. "I thought it was safe! I figured—"

Rohan shook his head. "Shut up, Lonnie. We know what you figured. Your problem is that you think you're so much smarter than everybody else, so you don't listen."

Lahnegarn opened his mouth, then shut it, then spoke. "I'll call Eldarinth."

"You do that. When do we dock?"

The ship answered. "Five minutes, Captain. Wistful knows I'm coming."

"Okay. Lonnie, tell Wistful you got her shuttle destroyed while you're at it."

The Lukhor squirmed in his seat as Ursula leaned closer to him, black lips parted in a snarl, sharp teeth exposed. "I will! I will!"

Rohan sighed. "Ursula, it's not worth it."

"We can for telling he died on surface. Nobody needs to know."

"Wei Li would know. Heck, for all I know, Rinth hacked his father's video feeds and watched every second of what just happened."

The anger dropped off Ursula's face as she faced him. "Are you for thinking so? Is not something child should see."

Rohan shrugged. "If he doesn't want to see traumatic things, he shouldn't spy on people."

"You are for being annoyed."

"Yes. No. A little. He saved his father's life, though, so I shouldn't be too mad."

"Yes."

The ship docked with Wistful and opened a port.

Rohan waited for Lahnegarn to exit the ship and walk out of his sight.

"Thank you, Ursula."

"Is for being my pleasure, Rohan. Am happy to be helping."

"Happy and I are not close friends at the moment. Those Quattros died for nothing."

"Is not for being your fault, Rohan. What are you for doing now?"

He cracked his neck and thought. "I just want to sleep. Can you ping Katya, please? Tell her I'm back and heading to the room. Please."

Ursula nodded. "Of course. I will also be returning to my home. Will you eat with us?"

"Not tonight. Not in the mood for company, to be honest. I'll grab something on the way."

They parted; Rohan made his way to Wistful's back alleys before turning toward the boardinghouse.

I almost feel bad for Terry.

Poor guy is just following his programming.

On the other hand, he's eating people that don't need to be eaten. He bought sandwiches, ground meat with layers of crunchy deep-fried nuts packed in, and ate in the room, alone.

◆━◆

Katya's vibrating comm woke them both the next morning. Rohan sat up and faced her, his head groggy.

He hadn't slept well; Katya had woken him when she entered the room.

She held up her comm. "It's Ang. The urgent signal."

Ang? He's guarding Tamara.

Rohan stood up in his underwear, pulse racing. "Is he in danger? What's happening?"

"He's not in danger, he is excited. He wants us both to come to the arena."

Ten minutes later, Rohan and Katya lurked behind a food stall a hundred meters from the entrance to the arena.

"I don't know, Katya. That's a lot of people. What if the Tolone'ans are there?"

"It would be nice to fight them again, wouldn't it? But they will not attack, not with this many people around. I see many fighters."

"Still. I'm not sure about this."

Katya looked at his bandaged hand. "What happened to your hand, Rohan?"

"Oh, just an accident on the surface. Fighting kaiju. You know how it goes."

Her expression did not convey agreement, but she dropped the subject. "Come, Rohan. Ang was very excited. Let us see why."

"Okay."

They sidestepped the cart and walked up the promenade. A throng had gathered in front of the arena, two hundred or so people waiting for the big double doors to open and let them in.

As they neared the crowd, Ang saw them, held up an enormous arm to wave, and approached, his limp better than it had been but still pronounced.

Katya waved back, her eyes wide as she took in the gathered horde.

"Katya! Ro—er, good friend! Come!"

Rohan sighed and pulled his hood lower over his forehead. "Nice catch."

They met in a little cluster a dozen meters from the edge of the crowd just as the doors cracked open.

"Ang, what is this? Are they selling tickets to the sector wrestling finals? Did you call us here to help you get some?"

Ang barked out a laugh. "No, Brother Ro—good friend. Is special announcement by Wei Li's home friend. Was announced over all feeds of interest to fighters."

Katya tapped delicately at her tablet. "I see it now. Krai Wu made a statement that would be of interest to all martial artists on the station. One of the big federations shared it, and all the others followed."

Rohan nodded. "You see The Consortium around?"

Ang pressed his lips together and turned his head to scan the crowd. "Yes, was at front of line. Must for being inside already. Come, people are for entering now."

Rohan shrugged and positioned himself more or less behind the Ursan, hiding from any onlookers.

I shouldn't be here, but I want to know what's happening. Curiosity already killed the cat, I guess it's my turn.

The group joined the crowd filtering into the arena.

Katya looked him over. "I did not check last night, as you were sleeping, but it is good you were not more injured. Usually, when you leave my side, you are hurt in some way."

Rohan shook his head. "I'm fine. Can't say the same for the two Quattros."

"Ah. Do they need assistance?"

"Not anymore. They're both dead."

"Is too bad, I wanted to fight them."

"They were no match for you. Come on, let's hear what Krai Wu has to say."

The arena had a square platform in the center and seating in the round for several thousand. Huge screens up near the ceiling meant to show different angles of the action on stage were full of ads for various gyms, apparel lines, and food supplements for athletes.

The friends took seats near the exit and waited.

Katya pointed. "Look, that screen is showing the stage! That's Master Turtle, Ang. He is very quiet. I don't think I'll get to fight him."

Rohan nodded. "His fighting days are over. Krai Wu is standing, like he's about to say something."

A whine filled the arena, quickly peaking and shutting off, feedback from the sound system. The Vor'karei cleared his throat.

"Friends, greetings. Thank you for coming.

"My name is Krai Wu, and I am a disciple of this man, the great Master Turtle. Behind me sits Wei Li, Security Chief of this station, and a person many of you know. If you doubt anything I am about to tell you, please remember that she is here to verify my statements."

A soft murmur rippled through the crowd.

Wei Li was well-known, especially to the station's martial community.

Krai Wu coughed softly and continued.

"Sorry, I'm not used to addressing crowds like this.

"I am here to announce a private tournament. It is open invitation, though the risk of injury is significant, so please enter only if you're prepared to accept that risk."

A voice called out from the crowd. "What do you mean 'private'?"

Krai Wu nodded. "The only people allowed in will be the competitors, judges, some security, and medical staff. There will be no media coverage, no recordings, and no publicity."

The heckler called out again. "Better be a hell of a prize, then!"

"There is. Perhaps the highest possible prize of any fighting tournament in the sector.

"You see, my people have a treasure. It is, as far as I know, unique."

Rohan snorted. When Katya turned to him, he whispered, "It's not unique. Rare, not unique."

She nodded; Krai Wu was continuing.

"This treasure, to put it simply, will make someone into a Power."

"We already have Boost!" Ripples of laughter traversed the arena.

"This treasure can make anybody with the discipline to master it into a Power permanently. No need for fresh doses, no addiction, no debilitating side effects. This man"—he pointed at Master Turtle—"was the recipient of this treasure, and he has decided it is time to hand it over. If any of you are sensitive to Powers, you will be able to sense his strength for yourself."

Wei Li stood. "You know me, you know my word is good. He speaks the truth."

A hush fell over the crowd. She sat back down.

Krai Wu nodded. "The winner will have a chance to take this treasure. There are, as you might imagine, conditions. The winner must swear to defend this station. And to pass the treasure on their own deathbed, using a ritual you will be taught."

Voices rose, first a few, then more, as people conversed with one another, some shouting incoherent questions toward the stage.

Rohan grunted. "That will get them excited."

Ang looked at him. "Is this truth? Can make anyone a Power? Like you?"

Rohan shrugged. "I guess so."

"Ang did not believe such things possible."

"It's very, very rare. Which means a lot of very tough people are going to be after it."

Krai Wu tapped his microphone. "Please. Quiet." The crowd settled. "The treasure can also make an existing Power into a stronger one. As you can imagine, it is the pride of our people, so we will only allow it to pass to someone worthy."

"What are the rules?"

Rohan spoke softly. "There are no rules."

Katya tilted her head and looked up at him. "What?"

"I just always wanted to say that."

The Vor'karei smiled, the big screen behind him showing his white teeth in an image five meters tall. "Competitors will fight one-on-one. Each fight will end when one fighter submits or is unable to continue. The judge's assessment of ability to keep fighting is final."

"Who's the judge, then?"

Krai Wu pointed to the woman standing next to him. "Wei Li."

The crowd stilled.

He smiled again. "If fighters stall or attempt delaying tactics, they will both be disqualified. Any use of weapons will result in disqualification.

"If a fighter has two more losses than victories, they are disqualified from the tournament. In other words, a fighter may lose a fight, or even several, and still win the tournament."

A new voice chimed in. "This could last forever!"

Krai Wu nodded. "We'll make sure it doesn't. The judges may disqualify any fighter at any time. In addition, no fighting is allowed outside the ring, starting . . ." He made a show of looking up at a screen that displayed the current time. "Now. That means no fighting other contestants and no violence, either threatened or acted upon, on their loved ones, hostages, etc. You must win by virtue of your actions here in the ring, under the judges' eyes and sight, not anywhere else."

A few conversations burst out. Rohan spotted the Tolone'ans in the front row, their heads glistening as they huddled together and talked.

Krai Wu waited for the noise to subside. "This is a test of spiritual character as well as of fighting ability.

"After each fight, each victor may ask a question of the loser. The loser must answer. A refusal to answer, or any attempt to lie, will result in disqualification.

"Please be reasonable. Don't ask anyone to disclose their financial codes. Questions must be personally meaningful."

"This is just martial truth or dare!"

Krai Wu shrugged. "I do not know that game, but it sounds somewhat related. We want a champion who is honest and forthright, while also being perceptive. Beat your opponents in the ring, then eliminate them by asking a question they are not willing to answer.

"Fist and Eye. These are the pillars of our order. The inheritor of our treasure must possess both qualities."

The Hybrid spotted seven Rogesh, their enormous rhinoceros horns almost clashing as they pressed their heads close together to discuss something.

The Seven Knights of Ch'Doon. He'd fought them on Wistful, a while before.

The Rogesh stood and left the arena.

The oath to protect Wistful probably interferes with their loyalty to their own thing.

Rohan looked at Ang, whose own gaze was fixed on the far wall. Then he turned to Katya.

"Tell me he's not thinking what I think he's thinking."

She looked back. "We both know what he's thinking. He is a wonderful man, but he's not complicated."

Rohan sighed. "This is going to be a huge problem. Or a huge opportunity."

Katya smiled. "There will be much fighting!"

The first heckler called out again. "Where do we sign up?"

Krai Wu smiled and pointed to the edge of the stage, where Mai Si sat between a pair of meter-diameter screens. "Please form two lines and enter your names and planet of origin.

"We will compile lists of entrants and post it outside the main doors.

"The first matches begin in"—he checked the clock again—"three hours and thirty-two minutes."

⬥ ··•·· ⬥

Ang had pushed past Rohan's seat and was at the end of their row, ready to charge down the stairs to the stage, before the last word out of Krai Wu's mouth had finished echoing.

"Ang, what are you doing?"

Ang paused and turned. "Entering! We will for meeting on the stage, Ro—good friend in hood!" Without waiting for a response, he turned and half-ran down the stairs, moving his bulk with an agility that would have surprised anybody unfamiliar with the Ursan, his limp forgotten.

Rohan turned to Katya. "What about you? Are you going to enter?"

She scratched behind her right ear. "I do not think so, Rohan. I am not prepared to swear my life to this station. I am already sworn to protect you."

Rohan grunted and looked at the fighters filing down the aisles to the sign-up area. "I mean, I'm not stopping you."

"This treasure . . . I would have to absorb another person's soul, yes?"

He nodded. "That's the basic idea. But the soul has been, I don't know the word. They say beautified. I'd say sanitized. There will be nothing left of Master Turtle but the raw Power, nothing to corrupt your psychology. It should be safe."

She crinkled her nose, her whiskers wiggling around it. "I am content with my own strength, earned through my own efforts. Leave this treasure for Ang, who was not born as blessed as I. What about you, Rohan? In the state you are in now . . ."

He looked down. "I don't know about winning the tournament, but I have to enter."

"Why 'have to'?"

He pointed at the leader of The Consortium, where she bent over the tablet on Mai Si's left and tapped at the screen. "As long as I'm a contestant, she has to leave me alone. More to the point, she has to leave Tamara and Rinth alone. I bet I can buy a few days of peace that way."

"I see. That does sound like a useful plan."

Wei Li sat at the center of the stage, talking to Krai Wu. She seemed less than pleased.

Master Turtle sat to her left, smiling at the swarm of fighters massing at the base of the stage.

Krai Wu scanned the lines, his mouth hard.

I don't think he wants to do this. I guess he doesn't really have a choice.

Rohan stood and studied the people in line, intending to wait for the crowd to thin before joining it.

He saw the surviving Quattro waiting to sign up.

What was his name? Kor?

I want to tell him I'm sorry.

Would that help, or make it worse?

Katya tugged on Rohan's arm. "That is the woman we fought! Over there! Sirc!"

"What? Oh, the Takslee enforcer! Good for her." *If she wins, is she going to get out of the Boost trade, or is she just going to be much better at it?*

A pair of Ohnians were lined up together, their large single eyes making them stand out from most of the other humanoids. *Nobody I recognize.*

Rohan nodded slowly, took his helmet out of his hood, and relinked his comms to Wistful's intranet. *If the Tolone'ans have signed up for the tournament, they won't mess with me here.*

He scanned news updates, ads, messages from Tamara, and other miscellanea while the lines dwindled.

When he'd read or cleared most of the queue, he looked up.

Krai Wu stood, bowed to Master Turtle, descended the stairs built into the side of the platform, and joined the line.

Right behind Lahnegarn.

20

Reunited and It Feels So Good

R ohan avoided eye contact with Krai Wu and with Lonnie while waiting in the line; both signed in and walked away without seeming to notice him.

When his turn came, Mai Si caught him with a wide smile.

"You have changed your mind, Hybrid?"

He shrugged. "I don't really think I'll win. But the tournament interests me."

"Then please join! I'm sure your presence will help bring out the best in our other competitors."

He shrugged and filled out the form, then turned, found Katya, and left the arena.

"You don't have to watch me anymore, I'm safe. Everyone who wants me dead is in that tournament, and they all want the Eternity Ki more than they want my head on a pike."

"I do not know the word 'pike,' but I worry about your reasoning."

"What do you mean?"

"I think you are perhaps underestimating the number of people who want you dead."

"Very funny."

"I was not trying to be."

"I'm just saying, you don't have to guard me quite so closely. Go hang out with Ang or something. I think he's going to need some support."

"Why is that, Rohan?"

"I love Ang, you know I do. But there are Powers in that tournament. He's not . . . I don't think he's going to be able to handle all of that."

"Ang is stronger than you believe. He will be fine."

"Still. He'll need a good friend."

She smiled. "I will take care of Ang. You go see your girlfriend. I believe you have much to discuss, such as the date for moving in together. What color wall hangings you will choose, who will sleep on the side of the bed closer to the toilet, what to do about the fact that her father might try to have you killed . . ."

"I didn't say I was going to see Tamara. Why would you assume that? I have lots of friends I could visit."

"As you say, Rohan. I will give you your privacy. Enjoy your time with . . . whoever you are spending it with."

He laughed and turned away, his helmet already in his hands.

First, get back to Ben. Shouldn't take long.

He placed the call; Ben picked up quickly.

"Rohan! This is a traceable channel."

"I know." He quickly explained the tournament and its implications. "It should be safe to talk."

"Good. Actually, no, I'm not so sure. I have information for you, but it's sensitive. Meet me somewhere private."

"Sure. I can come to *Insatiable*."

"Great, I'll be waiting."

Twenty minutes later, Rohan walked through the ship's main airlock and followed the colored lights inside her to a conference room.

Ben sat at one of the long tables, an open box in front of him. "Donut?" He stretched his lanky legs to either side of the metal and plastic chair.

Rohan nodded. "I'll take one. We skipped breakfast. Urgent meeting."

"Right. The tournament."

"Yeah. Anyway, what's going on? You were going to help me find out something about Boost, weren't you?"

"I was." He paused, gathering his thoughts, his hands steepled together in front of him. "I'm going to talk in English, just in case we're overheard. I've also called security protocols on this room. Even *Insatiable* can't listen in."

"Sure."

"Okay. So, I started in the usual places."

"Library."

"Yes. I have greater access than a normal civilian. You know I *am* still faculty at Academy."

"I know, Professor Stone."

Ben smiled. "So I did the normal searches, which didn't get me as far as I expected."

"What does that mean?"

"It means something is scrubbing mentions of Boost from the libraries. Actively scrubbing."

"So you can't find anything?"

"Very little. At least, not with regular searches. It's very similar to the way the il'Drach treat information about the il'Sein, except in that case the cleanup was done thousands of years ago. In this case, it's ongoing. There are laws in place—I checked a dozen worlds—that have to do with prosecuting Boost dealers, but in every case the available references are nonspecific. For all you'd know reading the text, they're chasing heroin dealers."

"Huh. Does the Empire want to pretend that Boost doesn't exist?"

"Yes and no. They definitely allocate resources to combating it. I found ships and personnel assigned to the drug trade that are clearly not going after anything *else*. You know, you find a task force here going after stimulants, there going after hallucinogens, and here's a task force going after nothing in particular, in an area where local law enforcement has been overwhelmed by drug dealers with Powers."

"Meaning those local situations are pretty obviously Boost users, and those task forces are going after Boost specifically, but you can read the brief and it doesn't say that anywhere."

"Right. I imagine those officers know what they're doing because someone takes them aside and literally tells them. Verbally. Or there's an encrypted, nonpublic set of orders. But officially . . . nothing."

Rohan sighed and ran his fingers through his hair. "That makes some sense, I guess. They think of Boost as an actual threat to Imperial security. Which I suppose it is."

"Right. And you can't say the same thing about magic mushrooms or good old meth."

"Okay. Well, that's good to know, I guess. Is that all?"

"No. Not by a long shot." The Professor leaned back in his chair, his blue eyes twinkling.

Rohan smiled. "All right, Dr. Stone. What did you do next?"

"I realized that *I* know next to nothing about Boost. And I'm a biologist, and an expert on lots of things, including Powers. Which is odd. So I figured it was time to do some real research, not just run search queries in a database."

"And?"

"I asked Wei Li for samples of the Boost she'd confiscated from the Takslees. Inside the Empire, those would have been sealed and sent straight to Drach, but here . . ."

"One advantage to living on an independent station."

"Exactly. She gave me a hefty amount. Enough to retire on, if I wanted to sell it."

"Don't get ideas."

"Of course not. I did the usual analysis." He tapped his fingers together.

"You want me to guess? What is it, dehydrated kaiju tears? Extracts from Hybrid pineal glands? Herbs that can only grow on the Ringgate?"

"I'm not sure. It's biological, with a fairly complex profile. Lots of proteins, both plant and animal. Definitely a mixture. And the proteins varied. I got a number of different samples, and they didn't have a consistent makeup. Similar, but I had a hard time finding a single protein or marker that was present in every sample."

"Okay. That doesn't sound promising."

"It isn't. And I'm not done. Another week of analysis and I'll have a better handle on that end of things. But Marion made a suggestion."

"Did she?" *She's a physicist, not a pharmacologist.*

"Do you remember the basics of shadow-walking?"

Rohan cracked his neck. "I guess. Depends what you mean by basics. I can't do it, if that's what you're asking."

"Tell me what you know."

Rohan held out his open hand, parallel to the floor. "Our world is like this, maybe a sheet of paper. But there is another world just beneath it, like a shadow cast by this one. As if there was a light above, shining down on it. And below that is another world, the shadow of that one, and so on. And so on."

"Forever."

Rohan shrugged. "I've been told there's a bottom layer, where things sort of collect. Where the shadows end. I've known a few Powers who could step into those shadow worlds, at least a layer or two down, where things aren't quite so real. The doors aren't there, the locks don't work. They can get into sealed places, bank vaults, whatever, then rise back into our world, take stuff, go back down, and leave."

"Right. And there are ways to interfere with that process. You can bet that where the Empire keeps its secrets, nobody is shadow-walking in or out of those vaults."

"What does this have to do with Boost, Ben? Does it come out of shadow?"

"No. Look, these are not three dimensions we're talking about, but our language is three-dimension oriented. If someone goes into shadow, we call it down, right? Or shadow-ward. Which is awkward to say."

"Shadow-ward. That is awkward. But I get what you mean."

"Then what do you call it when they come back? Maybe they rise out of shadow."

"Sure."

"The term we actually use is source-ward."

"Source?"

"You said it yourself. There's a . . . a light above the stack of worlds, shining being itself down onto the whole thing. Bringing it all into existence."

"And you just lost me."

"The light above, that allows for there to be a shadow. It's often called source. In the old books."

"This is starting to sound very metaphysical."

Ben nodded. "Technically, ontological. Or spiritual. And outside my area of expertise."

"Okay. Still not sure I'm following you."

"Things can move from our world shadow-ward, into shadow. Then they move source-ward, back up into our world."

"Right."

"Why stop here?"

"What?"

"If something comes up, through the stack, from deep shadow to our world, what's to say they can't rise . . . higher?"

Rohan scratched his beard. "Huh. What's up there?"

"I have no idea. But I'm pretty sure Boost comes from that side of, er, things."

"You know that bottom layer, the deepest shadow. They say that's where the Wedge come from."

"I've heard that."

"It's like hell, a realm of devouring monsters. Devils. If that's hell, and this source sounds a lot like . . ."

"I'm not a religious man, Rohan, I can't and won't entertain those metaphors too seriously."

"Okay. But you are telling me that Boost comes from those higher layers? Above us?"

"Source-ward of us. Of this plane of existence. We have instruments that can detect that sort of thing. Not too sensitive, not very accurate, not very quick, but they work. And when I put Boost into those instruments . . ."

"Okay. That's, well, that's really interesting. I'm not sure what to think. I'm trying to find the supplier. It must be someone who can . . . what do we call it? Reverse shadow-walk? Source-walk?"

Ben shrugged his wide shoulders, still solid despite carrying less muscle than they had in his prime. "I don't know if there is a word for it. But that's it. The ultimate supplier is someone who has a way to go up through the layers. Or found something that started higher up and shadow-walked down to us. You can figure out the possibilities."

Rohan bit into his donut; a bear claw analogue, the frosting had a slight hint of citrus that wasn't authentic to the original pastry.

He chewed and thought while Ben watched him.

"Got any coffee?"

Ben smiled. "Just made a pot. Hold on."

The older man stood and walked to the food table that lined the back wall, poured coffee into a paper cup, and returned. "No sugar, I used it all on the donuts, and I haven't had a chance to resupply."

"No problem, I'll take it black." He sipped it.

Good, but not as good as Pop's. How does an alien who's never been within ten thousand light years of Earth make better coffee than anybody else I've ever met?

"Can I use this to track Boost? Like, scan the station, looking for things from . . . source-ward?"

Ben shrugged. "I don't have tools that can do that. Wistful might be able to run a scan like that. And if you asked Marion, she might be able to rig something that could do the job. I honestly have no idea how long that would take or if she even has time."

"Right." His comm chimed: Tamara. "Can you do me a huge favor and ask her to look into it? Not a matter of life and death, but it could turn out to be really handy."

Ben nodded. "I'll ask her. You go take care of . . . that." The man's grin said he knew exactly why Rohan was so eager to rush off.

⬥ ⋯•⋯ ⬥

Ten minutes later, Rohan was at Tamara's apartment.

She met him at the door draped in a strategically pinned bolt of cloth, leaving one shoulder and arm exposed and offering a tantalizing look at a strip of bare waist, ending with her other calf naked and alluring. Her makeup was tasteful but limited, darkening around her eyes and lips.

She greeted him with a kiss that took his breath away in both senses of the term.

He disengaged and smiled at her in his arms. "I thought you'd be asleep by now. Otherwise I would have come straight over after signing up for the tournament."

"Not yet. I was working on . . . something."

"Ooh, a mystery project. Exciting."

Her smile widened. "Not that sort of something. Come in, Rinth is at my sister's asleep."

He followed her inside. "Look, Tamara, I'm really sorry about all this—"

She turned and put her finger on his lips, standing so close her chest touched his ribs. "Hush, Rohan. Why are you apologizing?"

"I put your life in danger."

"Did you?"

"Well, yes. I mean, I guess."

"How?"

"The Tolone'ans, remember? They came after you. Right about when they came after me."

"You are saying that your presence in my life caused a threat to my physical safety." Her smile never wavered.

He shrugged and scratched his beard. He looked down at his shirt; he was due for a change into clean clothes. *I can go back to my apartment after this and freshen up.* "Yeah, that's what I mean."

"So tell me what happened between you and my father."

He smiled back at her. "Oh yeah. Your father. He reminds me of my father, and that's not really a compliment."

She giggled. "Maybe that's what attracted me to you, Rohan. We have similar issues with our fathers. Each of ours wanted us to do things that would have made us unhappy, and neither are willing to stop interfering in our lives to make it happen."

He shrugged. "I hadn't really thought of it that way."

"Rohan, my life has been in danger . . . my entire life. I have known nothing else. My father is a very wealthy, very powerful man. There were attempts on my life, and on my safety, before I could walk or talk."

"Right. I don't know that I thought of that either."

"I do not enjoy that sort of attention, but I am not unused to it. Nor does it send me crying to the corner of the room, weeping with fear."

"No, I guess it doesn't."

"And it is my father who put your life at risk, is it not?"

"You mean the Quattros? They just roughed me up a little."

She stroked his cheek. "You poor thing. Did they hurt you badly?"

A sigh escaped him. "Nah. I'm fine. They're nowhere near as dangerous as Terry."

"Who is Terry?"

"That's a Lahnegarn thing. Did Rinth tell you about that?"

She sighed and leaned her head on the top of his chest. "I love my son, but there are days I regret the time I loved his father."

"We all make mistakes. Except me, I have excellent taste in women. Impeccable. All my exes are delightful."

She laughed and pushed him with one hand, the other snaking around his back so he didn't actually go anywhere.

"I am sorry for Lahnegarn's behavior. Did he put you in serious danger?"

"Kind of. He got those two Quattros killed for sure. And no way he would have survived if Ursula and I hadn't gotten there."

"Then thank you for saving him, though that was not your responsibility."

"Can't let Rinth's father get eaten by my pet kaiju. Wouldn't look good."

She snuggled closer to him. "I suppose not. What did my father say to you? Rinth said he was threatening, after his men kidnapped you."

"Oh, the usual. Stay away from my precious daughter, blah, blah, blah. You can't protect her without your Powers, you're not good enough for her. The same old thing."

"Ah. I am sorry."

"It's okay. He's not entirely wrong, I guess. I haven't been doing a very good job protecting you."

"Haven't you? I am uninjured."

"You had to go into hiding because of me."

"And you were beaten because of me, and nearly died on Toth 3 because of me. Indirectly. I'd say if anyone should be upset, it is you."

"Nah. Getting thrown in danger is kind of my thing. It's not yours, though."

"I am more than a simple shuttle tech, Rohan. Like it or not. I knew when I first approached you that any relationship we shared would not be simple. Or safe."

"Yeah?"

She laughed. "Of course. The first time I saw you, Ang was shooting you in the chest with that enormous gun! Then cutting you open with that chained gauntlet. That is a far cry from a normal introduction to a male."

"Right. The spiked chains that tore open my shirt."

She reached her hand up to his collar, turning it over, then slid her fingers under it to stroke his upper chest. "Tore it open and exposed all that strange hair. And all that muscle."

Rohan reached up and stroked her upper back just below her neck, bared by a cutout in her top. "Now I'm really glad Ursula managed to calm Terry down."

"You'll have to tell me more about this. Later."

"Definitely later."

—◆·•·◆—

Later.

She faced away from him, drifting in and out of sleep.

"Rohan, are you all right?"

"Why?"

"You seem . . . melancholy."

"I'm fine."

"Are you sure?"

He patted her shoulder. "I'll be fine. Just tired. Go to sleep, it's late."

21

Let The Games Begin!

Rohan left his girlfriend snoring in her bed and made the lonely walk back to his fancy apartment, stopping only to pick up food.

She put on a brave face, but she didn't come here to be a shuttle tech to have problems like Tolone'an Powers attacking her and threatening her life.

It was probably stupid of me to think I could have a normal life after everything I've done.

The tournament gives us a reprieve, but it's only going to last a few days.

I have to think about this.

I hate thinking.

The door slid open, and he waved the lights on.

"Anybody still here?" The apartment had been searched, thoroughly if not disrespectfully.

The only sounds were the echoes of his voice and the tinkling of the undisturbed waterfall.

"Music." The high tempo electronica of "Vele" started playing, rewarding the ten thousand credits he'd invested in the audio system. He checked the dishes; two were broken, the rest looked unharmed.

He sat and ate, his foot tapping to the tune.

Rohan finished and checked his injuries: all healing faster than they would for any human, but nowhere near as fast as they would with his Power in full bloom.

No surprise.

He exhaled and checked his mask: he had less than an hour to make the first test.

Ben had sent a message saying that Marion and Garren were going to look into the Boost detector, but not to keep his hopes up.

That explains where Garren's been.

He showered and brushed his bristly hair, then put on a clean outfit.

Spiral would be proud; I'm practicing his technique, and now I'm wearing his clothes. Red shirt, loose black pants, split-toed ninja boots.

If I'm not a tow chief, I might as well look the part of a disciple of the Orphan Clan.

He left for the tournament.

—◆··•··◆—

The arena was open; a private security team guarded the entrance, preventing noncompetitors from entering.

The promenade was busier than normal. A group of paparazzi and curious passersby watched the fighters come and go, some taking notes or snapping pictures.

A second huddle of friends and relatives was growing; people associated with the fighters but kept out of the arena.

Katya waved him over from the second group. "Rohan! Ang is already inside."

He nodded. "I'm sorry you can't come in. I'll ask Wei Li to make an exception."

"I already found a way in! I got a job, aren't you proud of me?"

He looked her over; nothing in her clothing seemed unusual. "What?"

"My first job! I joined the security team." She pointed a furry thumb at the nearest guards. "They did not like my idea at first, but after I tossed four of their men across the promenade, they reconsidered. It turns out that businesses such as theirs are always eager to employ Powers who enjoy a good fight!"

Rohan grunted. "That's fantastic. Wait, is it?"

"Yes! I will be working near the stage, making sure that nobody interferes with the contest and also possibly helping the fighters remember themselves if things get out of hand. I am to be a professional reminder! A memory enhancer!"

"That sounds right up your alley. But no—"

"I know, I know, no licking the fighters. Not even for luck. Not even if they ask me to."

"*Especially* if they ask you to. Don't ask me why, just trust me."

"Yes, Rohan. It is part of my contract. And no eating any of the fighters even if they die in combat."

"Is that a thing? Do they expect people to die?"

She shrugged. "So many of your species are so fragile, I always expect you to die, all the time. I cannot understand how so many of you have survived to populate all these planets." A few competitors' spouses near her made unpleasant faces at her words and pulled back, giving the il'Zkin extra space.

Rohan smiled despite himself. "I hope you never change, Katya."

"Ang says the same thing. Constantly. I told him I will eventually grow old and gray; he just laughed and said he wants to see it with his own eye."

"Speaking of eyes, I'm worried about him in the tournament. Has he talked about it at all?"

"What?"

"The cybernetic eye. It's dangerous. For him."

"He has not spoken of it to me."

"Okay. I'll do what I can to keep him safe."

"Yes. Take care. I have two hours before my work begins; I cannot enter yet."

"Okay. I better go inside so I'm not disqualified for being late."

The security at the door asked his name and sent him through.

Inside the arena, contestants took seats in the front rows, eyeing the central platform and waiting for things to start. Rohan walked a slow perimeter before spotting Ang, then hurried to sit next to the big Ursan.

"How are you, big fella?"

Ang's voice was serious. "Am ready, Rohan. Is great opportunity."

Ursans had no Powers; hadn't even known such a thing existed before traveling through a wormhole and coming to Toth.

Rohan looked at his friend and sighed.

How positive do I want to be here?

"Ang, about that—"

"Hush, Wei Li for talking now."

Wei Li stood up from the judge's chair she'd occupied and climbed onto the platform, microphone in her hand. She tapped it twice, then a third time to get everyone's attention.

The crowd quieted.

"I am Wei Li. I am the security chief for this station, but I am not here in that capacity. Instead, I am here to discuss this tournament.

"You are all aware of the prize." She paused and looked around the gathered fighters. A hush was her answer. "We expect you to be able to defend the Eternity Ki, so we will test your fighting ability. But not only that. We expect the custodian of the Ki to have character, and wisdom, and insight, so we will test those things also."

Ang coughed softly. "Am not for liking this turning of things."

Rohan snorted and put his hand on the big man's arm. Others around the room muttered; one called out, "I'm not here for another psych eval!"

Wei Li faced him. "You are free to leave. I am a Class Four Empath; you've never experienced a psychiatric evaluation even close to what you'll get spending one minute in front of me."

The man grunted but stayed.

She surveyed the crowd. "There will be other tests of your fitness. Some might disqualify you immediately; others will present rewards. You will be told the parameters only as you approach each stage."

The angry man spoke, loudly enough for everyone to hear. "Sounds like she'll be making it up as she goes."

Wei Li shrugged. "You are all free to leave at any time. Krai Wu is competing, so he will not participate in the design of the tests. That will be up to Mai Si and myself. If you have any questions, save them for someone who cares to listen."

Rohan laughed, drawing a startled look from a pair of Ohnians nearby. He shrugged. "That's just her. You learn to appreciate it."

They turned their gazes away.

Wei Li pointed at the stage. "The first test is a simple screen of physical strength. On the stage are a pair of implements. The test consists of two parts." She pointed; two metal rectangles were placed on either side of her. A pair of handles protruded from each.

"First, you must stand next to the stage and, in one motion, jump onto it. It is approximately one meter high." Rohan looked at Ang. Could the Ursan *jump* a meter off the ground from a standing start? Especially with a bad leg?

The big man showed no concern.

"After that, you must lift the two-hundred-kilogram weight off the ground and stand straight."

The Tolone'an leader, Squeya, one of the two members of The Consortium at the contest, stood. "Jump onto the stage and lift the bar?"

"That is correct."

She pulled a tentaclekerchief out of a pouch at her side and cleared her sinuses into it noisily. "Let's get this over with." She strode forward, leapt onto the stage, and approached one of the bars.

Wei Li stepped out of her way and watched her grasp the bar in her hands, brace both feet against the platform, and stand up.

Rohan could *see* lines of Power reinforcing her glutes and spinal erectors, adding force to the movement.

The Tolone'an nodded once, her tentacles quivering with the motion, and dropped the weight.

Wei Li nodded and watched the woman walk to the other side of the stage and take the steps down.

The male Tolone'an took his turn; two lines formed approaching the stage as the fighters queued for their chance.

A slender Andervarian male near Rohan shook his purple head. "I don't see what lifting a weight has to do with being able to fight."

Rohan shrugged. "It's not my call, buddy. But I bet she's doing this so people don't get broken in half during the fighting."

Ang huffed. "Is good test. Will help people for not being too badly hurt. Let the strong be fighting."

The line moved in fits and spurts. Most of the fighters cleared the jump and the lift quite easily; using his Third Eye, Rohan could see who did it *too* easily. A handful failed: two dozen out of the well over a hundred contestants who had gathered in the arena.

When Ang approached the stage, Rohan braced himself for his friend's failure.

The Ursan flexed his knees and pushed, launching his five hundred kilograms high into the air.

He landed on top of the stage with room to spare.

I should have more faith in the big guy.

Rohan casually hopped up, his il'Drach muscle fibers far more explosive than a human's, even without esoteric Powers adding force to his movements.

The fighters who had passed the test clustered in the aisles of the arena and watched their competitors, looking for an edge in the fights to come.

Ang approached the weight, leaned over, and easily snatched it overhead, slamming it down when he was done.

"Is child's toy. For Ursan child."

Rohan walked up behind him, studied the implement, then squatted, gripped the parallel handles, and stood, lifting the weight to his chest. He eyed Wei Li, who nodded, then tossed it to the ground.

He cracked his neck and surveyed the line. Only a few dozen fighters were still waiting for their turn. Near the back of the line, he spotted a familiar Lukhor.

Oh Lonnie, how are you going to manage this? You don't look like the type of guy who's picked up this kind of weight before.

He looked closer and spotted a familiar Tolone'an.

Squeya leaned on the corner of the stage and looked up at him. "We have not forgotten you, Murderer."

Rohan sighed. "No fighting during the competition, remember? Except in the competition."

"I remember. Once I win, however, I will use the Eternity Ki to destroy you. Master will be pleased with me."

Rohan shook his head. "Nurse Kraken? You're calling that guy your master? Lady, you're twice the cephalopod he is. You can do so much better."

She shook her head. "He speaks with the voice of the old gods, Hybrid. You could never understand the depth of our faith. Our gods were old when your ancestors took their first raspy breaths of air, when they first crawled out of the muck and slime."

"Oh, I'm not arguing that. They're old. But maybe that just means their time has passed? Time to move on. What have they even done for you in the past, I don't know, hundred million years?"

She hissed and turned away, then cast a final glance his way. "We will meet on the stage, Hybrid, and I will make you regret those words."

He shrugged as Ang stood by his side. They watched as the other Tolone'an joined her to walk to the back of the arena.

Ang patted Rohan's back. "You are for making the most interesting enemies, War Chief."

"I have a knack."

Lahnegarn approached the stage. The Lukhor was dressed in loose-fitting canvas pants and a sleeveless shirt; his arms and shoulders bulged with muscle that hadn't been there a year earlier.

His antennae bobbled as he approached the weight, his expression grim and focused.

Ang hopped off the stage and turned to see if Rohan was following. The Hybrid held a hand out, palm facing the Ursan, telling him to wait.

Lonnie leaned back, arching his spine, then squatted by the weight. He reached down with two green hands and gripped the handles tightly.

He turned his head to Rohan, made eye contact, and smiled.

With a little grunt, he straightened, muscles trembling in his arms.

For a moment the weight stayed motionless; the Lukhor blew out a puff of air and strained against it.

Rohan was about to step forward to stop the other man from hurting himself; two hundred kilos was enough to sprain a back or tear a knee in an untrained man.

Then he caught something.

Rohan focused through his Third Eye, checking the flow of esoteric energy in Lahnegarn.

Power flowed through the Lukhor's hips and lower back: bands of yellow-green energy.

The weight moved; hovered a few centimeters above the ground; rose to the height of Lahnegarn's hips.

Since when can he *do* that?

———◆┄◦┄◆———

One big screen showed a schedule; the other showed blanks where the matchups for the first-round fights would display. A countdown timer told them they had twenty minutes to wait.

Ang stretched out across three seats and closed his eyes; Rohan wasn't sleepy, so he walked over to the one person in the arena who drew him in.

Master Turtle.

Mai Si sat next to the older Vor'karei, watching him the way a parent watches a toddler.

Rohan sat in an empty chair across from the old master and leaned forward.

Mai Si smiled. "His presence is very calming, is it not?"

The Hybrid nodded. "Was he always like this?"

She shook her head, lines of scales catching the overhead lights when she moved. "His presence was always strong and powerful because of the Eternity Ki. Not quite as intense as an angry Hybrid, of course, but very strong."

Very few planets in the Empire had any native Powers that could match an angry Hybrid. "I can imagine."

"The peace and calm you're sensing are a result of the beautification. He's stripped away everything else, this is . . . it's like a naked soul. Unencumbered."

"It's . . . I don't know. Beautification sounded like such a silly description for it, but now I think . . . ."

"Yes. I will miss it when it's passed on."

He cocked his head. "He got rid of all his anger? All his ferocity? His fighting spirit?"

"He did."

Huh. "You mind telling me how he did that? Let's say I'm interested in a method for quelling anger. For a friend."

She laughed. "Is that friend you yourself?"

He shrugged. "Maybe. Let's just say that anger is not an asset to me right now. For some things I have to do."

She nodded. "I am familiar with the techniques he used. They are not complex, but they are difficult and take much practice."

"Can you simplify it for me? Or get me started?"

She looked around, as if checking to see whether anyone more qualified could be found to take over the conversation, then turned back to him. "It is best described as letting go."

"Okay. Maybe you could elaborate on that?"

"Yes. Here, take this exercise. Sit very still."

"I can do that."

"Breathe in. When you do, bring in everything around—your sensory experiences, your thoughts, your feelings. Draw them all into your chest and focus them there. In a knot, or a ball. Different people respond to different visualizations."

"I've done similar things before."

"Don't talk. Now exhale. Slowly, at a measured pace. I would tell you the count—I would say inhale for a count of four, exhale for eight—but wars have been fought regarding the precise times that should be used."

"Wars."

She laughed. "Skirmishes. When you exhale, blow the ball out of your chest along with your air. Cast it away."

"That's it? That will get rid of the anger?"

"Well, there is another caveat."

"Like . . ."

"Like you might have to repeat this action a thousand times. Or ten thousand. Or perhaps—"

"Let me guess. One hundred thousand. Or a million."

"Yes."

"So this isn't a short-term solution."

"Did you think we had developed a quick and easy method for ridding oneself of a fundamental component of sentience? This is not easy. It is a rare individual who can undergo this process successfully."

"But the person who inherits the Eternity Ki is going to have to do it, one day. Right?"

"Yes, they will. And that is why we have a selection process."

"I'm not sure finding the best fighter is going to get you the person who can do . . . all this."

She smiled again. "That is why the tournament is not simply about fighting. Good luck to you, Rohan. I hope you achieve the success you deserve in the coming days."

"I want to say thank you, but now I'm not sure. What I deserve? Can't you wish I get *more* than I deserve? Or *better* than I deserve?"

"That wouldn't be very fair to the others, would it?"

22

First Round's On Me

The fights were fast, brutal, and efficiently managed.

Rohan had been peripherally involved in a small-but-nonzero number of martial arts tournaments in his life. The sporting events had rules that minimized quick finishes; if sport fights all ended in seven seconds, people would stop buying tickets to watch them.

There were no such considerations in this event.

The second pair of fighters began slowly, each gauging the other's reactions with careful, long-distance jabs and soft kicks; after about forty seconds, Wei Li unceremoniously disqualified them both.

After that, the pace picked up.

Few fights lasted even a minute; when both combatants began the match swinging hard, damage was dealt quickly and conclusively.

Once one fighter was down, Wei Li gave the victor a chance to ask a question.

Very few of the victors had anything meaningful to ask, so Katya or one of the other assistants would wait for the answer, then pull the downed fighter onto a stretcher and off the stage for medical care.

Rohan was called up for the tenth fight, against an unusually tall and skinny Kratic.

Tattoos covered almost every inch of the Kratic's skin, leaving just a few square centimeters of his natural pink to be seen. Even the whites of his eyes had been dyed, giving him a menacing glare.

The Kratic snarled at Rohan, showing off teeth filed to points, and flexed, muscles writhing under paper-thin skin.

Rohan sighed. "You're trying to intimidate me?"

"I'm going to break you! You'll never forget the day you faced me in battle!" His eyes were wild and slightly unfocused; Rohan wondered if he was drugged.

"Break me? That's a lot of hostility, bro. Have we met?"

The Kratic growled and rushed forward.

Rohan sidestepped; as the Kratic passed by, he snapped his shin into the back of the man's knee.

The leg buckled; the Kratic turned to face him, catching a vicious uppercut to the chin that sent him to the ground.

Rohan closed on the tattooed fighter, but the referee stepped in and waved the fight off.

Wei Li looked at Rohan from her spot next to the platform. "Ask your question."

Rohan looked at the glassy-eyed man. "I don't really have a question."

"Then ask him anything. Be quick about it, there are many more fights to come."

"Okay, fine." He looked down at the man. "What . . . is your favorite color?"

"Blue! Wait, no, yellow! Oh no!"

"Disqualified." Wei Li signaled to Mai Si, who entered something on her tablet.

Rohan shrugged and walked off the stage.

His next opponent hadn't been chosen, but there were forty more fights to get through before the second round would begin. He took a seat near Ang and checked the schedule.

"You're up in five more fights, big guy."

"Am aware, War Chief. Am ready."

Three more fighters were disqualified before Ang's turn on the stage; two for lying and one for being too hurt to continue. A running tally of remaining contestants was available through the dedicated app.

I wonder if they made that just for this or if it's a traditional design. Maybe the Vor'karei have been conducting tournaments with dedicated apps for ten thousand years. When did they get net technology, anyway? I have no idea.

Ang stood and brushed his hands over his arms, then shook vigorously. "Am warm now. Take care, War Chief."

"Good luck, Ang."

Ang shrugged his powerful shoulders. "Will not be needing luck."

The Ursan mounted the stage.

Facing him was the Tolone'an, second-in-command of The Consortium, Squero.

——◆ ··◆·· ◆——

Squero's tentacles never stopped moving; they twitched and probed at the air, pawing at the space around him as if driven by their own curious intelligence.

He glared at Ang with his flat black eyes and grunted. "I know you. You were protecting the Hybrid."

Ang shrugged. "Were swimming together. You were for attacking us."

He shrugged, sending little ripples through the slick scarf of flesh surrounding his neck. "You are no match for me."

"Will be for seeing that, yes?"

The Ursan glanced at the judge, who nodded.

Then Ang's upper body dropped toward the ground in front of him, and he exploded toward the cephalopod, short but powerful legs driving into the ground so hard he dented the clay surface of the stage.

The Ursan made contact before Squero could react in any way other than widening his eyes and exhaling.

Ang's shoulder struck the Tolone'an's chest, his five hundred kilograms breaking through the resistance of two outstretched arms as if they weren't there. He dug both arms underneath, hands grasping at the slick upper back. With a snap, he stood, lifting and turning at the same time, and slammed Squero to the ground behind him.

The Tolone'an hit the ground and rolled, coming up to his feet behind the Ursan, shirt lightly stained by the dirt on the stage.

Rohan blinked.

What had at first looked like an impact with the ground had been anything but.

Squero had caught himself, tentacles touching the ground, pushing into an eight-limbed cartwheel instead of a collision.

Ang rushed again, a low growl coming from his chest.

Squero met the charge, thudding two powerful uppercuts into the Ursan's midsection, lifting him into an upright posture.

He growled and raked savage claws across his opponent's shoulders and upper arms.

Power flared through slick skin, which strained but didn't break.

Rohan swallowed. *Guy's got too much Power.*

Ang punched in the center of a fleshy, noseless face; Squero responded with two hooks to his belly. The sound made by those punches proved to everyone in the arena that they would have demolished any normal person; heavy layers of fur, dense fat, and even denser muscle absorbed the impact.

It was enough to force the Ursan to take a step back and reset.

The Tolone'an nodded, crouched, and slid forward, feet staying close to the ground, taking small steps, two rear tentacles reaching for the stage to support his balance.

He struck: straight punches directed into Ang's midsection, too short to hit the Ursan's face or head without jumping or forcing him to bend over.

Ang caught the blows on thick forearms.

Rohan could see from his face that he wasn't enjoying the impact.

Ang took two more punches, then burst forward, once again knocking Squero back with a hard blow from his shoulder.

The Tolone'an tumbled, spun, and reassumed his position.

"I do not know your species, your home, or what gods you worship. What are you?"

Ang panted lightly. "I am Ang of the Ursans. Wistful is my home, and my gods are my own."

"Your own or not, now is the time to call upon them for help, Ang of the Ursans. I see you have an artificial eye. Such things are rare."

Oh no. Don't.

Ang shrugged. "Came from far away. Not so rare there."

"Do you even understand why we don't use cybernetics? Do you understand the risks?"

Ang shrugged again. "Talking too much. Both will be for disqualified."

Squero held up a flat, shiny palm.

◆ ┄ ◆

Every sentient being, from puppies to sufficiently complex artificial intelligences, including Ang, possessed a soul.

Every such soul had the ability to exert force on the material world. Powers were able to exert *more* force than non-Powers, but the principles they worked under were the same.

Every soul became associated with a particular physical body; its ability to exert force on its own body was dramatically larger than its ability to affect anything else.

Most importantly, a soul's ability to *resist* forces acting on *its* body from the outside was greater still.

Those facts explained why esoteric abilities could only directly impact the living bodies of others with great difficulty. It would take an enormous amount of energy to *reach* inside another being and directly impact their physiology.

The major caveat governing those interactions was that the precise limits of what counted as part of a body was mutable. If a person put on a ring, it would not be part of them, and an external Power would be able to yank it about at will.

However, over time, the ring, if worn consistently, would be incorporated into that person's self-concept. That person's own aura would defend that ring as much as it would defend the fingers it adorned.

That was the reason people who fought as Powers wore uniforms; a particular outfit could become part of a person's informed body, but only if it was worn most of the time. Any new set of clothes would be vulnerable.

That was also the reason cybernetics were dangerous; Garren wore his powered armor, but it had become part of himself only because he designed it, understood every nanometer of its electronics, and had built it himself by hand. Very few individuals could incorporate equipment that sophisticated into themselves.

One of the first techniques most Powers learned was a simple wave of telekinesis that could be projected to disrupt any machinery or electronics nearby. That wave would deflect bullets, break cameras, and otherwise render inert any technology they faced.

That was the technique Squero employed.

Rohan stood, a terrible sour feeling in his gut, as he directed that wave of telekinesis at Ang's face, at the glowing red eye the Ursan had carried since first appearing on Wistful.

The big man growled, lowered his body, and rushed again.

What?

Squero stood, shocked, as the big man struck his upper torso, knocking him back. Tentacles reached behind and caught the ground, but the Ursan's tremendous mass still landed on top, nearly flattening him to the stage.

For several seconds, the Tolone'ans tentacles struggled to support the mass above him and were almost crushed. Then he reached a hand down, gave a little push, and managed to roll Ang off and come back to his feet.

"I don't know how—"

Ang rushed again.

Squero struck, ducking below claws that tried to take off his head. Punches landed under Ang's right arm, at the lower edge of his ribcage, and then in his liver.

The Ursan growled and spun.

The Tolone'an circled, knees bent deep so his rear tentacles could reach the ground and add to his lateral speed.

He punched again, and again, lancing fists deep into Ang's liver and kidneys.

Rohan *saw* Power flooding Squero's arms; waves of blue-green energy swept into each limb like tides, adding weight and heft to the blows.

Ang kept his arms up, absorbing what he could, but was driven backward, step by step.

His labored breaths could be heard over the hushed crowd.

Squero's Power intensified; Ang's body shook with each punch, tremors passing through so the fur on his back shuddered.

The Tolone'an established a rhythm, hitting him with wide hooks to the body, then paused.

Ang reached for the expected blows, moving his arms out of position; his opponent stepped in and drove an elbow into his solar plexus.

He staggered, stumbling back; Squero hopped forward, propelled by two rear tentacles, and kicked his legs out from underneath him.

The big man went down.

Squero leapt on top of him and used tentacles to pull his arms away where they protected his vulnerable spots; then landed punches on exposed targets: armpits, solar plexus, throat.

Ang pushed one elbow into the ground to try to roll away; two tentacles snatched the arm and lifted it.

More punches landed.

The referee stepped in. "Stop."

Squero froze.

He's disciplined, I'll give him that.

Ang looked up at the referee, who shook her head. He sighed. Squero got off him.

Once he was clear, the Ursan pushed himself up into a seated position. He probed his sides, feeling for broken bones.

Wei Li looked up at Squero. "You get one question."

The Tolone'an nodded and faced the Ursan. "Why wasn't I able to destroy your eye?"

Ang laughed. "Understood problem with eye two years ago. All was explained. Am needing eye; am for being half blind in other eye. Without seeing, being for little use to anyone.

"Every day, two hours, three hours, studying schematics. Memorizing each bend of wire in eye.

"After year of this, year and half maybe, eye as much part of Ang as claws."

Squero nodded. "That requires a remarkable level of discipline."

"Not enough, yes? Losing today."

"Still. We will destroy you, when this is over, but I will regret it. A small amount." He faced Wei Li, who nodded.

"Both advance."

———◆··•··◆———

Rohan followed Ang to the back of the stadium, where a handful of hired nurses were patching up any fighters injured enough to need help but not enough to be forced out of the tournament.

A male Kratic scanned the Ursan's skeleton.

"How do you feel, Ang?"

Ang sighed. "Badly. Losing is never being fun."

"I meant physically."

Ang winced as the nurse poked at a sore spot. "Have had worse injuries dating Katya. Will be fine."

Rohan nodded as Katya ran back to see them. "Are you okay, my love?" She ran up and hugged the big man.

He sighed. "Am fine. Am sorry to have lost."

"It's not over! Just don't lose the next one."

"Yes."

Rohan looked at her. "When is the second round?"

She shrugged. "There is only a short break between rounds, so ten or fifteen minutes after this round ends."

He stood and stretched. "Okay. Ang, I'm going back to watch the other fights. I have some questions I'd like answered."

Ang waved him away. "Go, go. Will be for joining you soon."

Katya patted her man on the shoulder. "I must return as well. This pink-skin will take good care of you."

The Kratic frowned at her but apparently thought better of responding verbally.

Rohan and Katya walked back into the arena.

She looked at him. "He cannot win."

Rohan shrugged. "I can't tell."

"I love Ang, but he cannot beat any strong Powers in a fight."

"No. But this isn't an elimination tournament. They're disqualifying people for all sorts of things. The questions. Taking too long. If it's about character, Ang has more of that than any ten people in this thing."

"You think so?"

Rohan exhaled slowly. "Let's see how the next few rounds go. Come on, let's get you back to your post before they fire you."

Katya returned to her position as Rohan walked by the Tolone'ans. They didn't look at him.

He found his seat as Lahnegarn climbed onto the stage.

Rohan focused his Third Eye, eager to get some clue regarding the Lukhor's display of Power.

His helmet vibrated on his back; he took it out and looked at his messages.

Marion Stone and Garren had something to tell him, but it wasn't urgent.

Rinth's aunt let him know the boy was safe and sound in her home.

Eldarinth Lastex requested a meeting; perhaps over dinner, station time.

Rohan sighed just as he spotted Kor, Eldar's Quattro henchman, sitting in the tenth row on the other side of the arena.

He answered Eldarinth's text; he'd eat with the man, but only if he had the time to spare from the tournament. Without a schedule, he couldn't be sure when that would be.

A big body sat in the chair next to his, a heavy arm, covered in hard scales, pressing against his shoulder. He looked up.

"Sirc." The Takslee, former and possibly current enforcer for Boost distributors, nodded her orange-scaled, snakelike head. "Hey, I was wondering. You're Takslee. Are your people related to the Vor'karei? Are you, like, Wei Li's distant cousin?"

She shrugged. "Are you related to the Ursan?" Her sibilant pronunciation dragged out the middle of the word. "I bet you are. From where I'm sitting, you look a lot alike. Lots of hair."

He looked away from her. "One of these days I might figure that out. Not today, though. Anyway, you sitting here for a purpose or just looking for someone handsome to chat with?"

She smiled. "It's nice that you think you're handsome."

"My mom told me I was the handsomest boy in my class."

"If I were your mother, I'd tell you the same thing. But no. I'm here to convey a message."

He held up his helmet. "People can't just text? I have a comm. Why all the drama? Sending people with messages. It's like I'm an extra in a bad mafia movie."

"None of this was my idea. I don't even know what the message means. If that helps."

"That does not help. Wait, does it? Now I'm not sure. I don't have the bandwidth for this question. Just tell me the message."

"The message is simple. Watch Lahnegarn; everything that happens with him from now on is a warning. To you."

"A warning? From whom?"

She shrugged, powerful shoulders about to burst out of her shirt. "I'm not supposed to tell you. But they said you'll be able to figure it out."

"No, I really won't. Why does everyone keep overestimating me? I'm not that bright. I need clear instructions at all times to understand anything. Even then, I'm lost half the time."

"Ssh. Watch." She pointed at the stage.

Lahnegarn faced off against a Rogesh. Rohan recognized the man; he worked for Wei Li as part of ship's security and had a history as a decorated wrestler. Rohan had sparred with him once, years earlier.

Tamtam.

The Rogesh loomed over the Lukhor, carrying more than twice his mass, the single large horn jutting out of the end of his snout polished and gleaming in the arena's bright lights.

Lahnegarn pulled off his shirt and tossed it to the side.

A year had turned the man's office-worker physique into something very different. He carried significantly more muscle; so much so that Rohan doubted the transformation was natural.

The Lukhor assumed a boxing stance, bounced on his toes a few times, and took practice steps. Forward; back; slip left; slip right; pivot. Pivot again.

Rohan straightened in his seat. Those were not the movements of an untrained person.

Lonnie's been practicing. But why? Does he think Tamara cares if he suddenly knows how to fight?

Maybe he does. Being good at electronics doesn't mean you're smart about people.

Sirc patted his arm, as if answering his unverbalized question. "You'll see."

The referee gave the signal.

The Rogesh charged, arms wide to capture the smaller man in a tackle.

Lonnie let him.

They collided; bands of esoteric energy anchored Lonnie to the floor. When the Rogesh attempted to throw the smaller man to the ground, nothing happened.

Lonnie smiled and lifted his arms, tossing away the Rogesh's hold.

He struck, landing hard punches on the security officer's chin, knocking the bigger man's huge head to the side with each shot.

The Rogesh's knees buckled on the third punch. He bent forward, reaching for a fresh grip, but Lahnegarn stiff-armed his hands away.

He's just brute-forcing through the grappling exchanges. Not a lot of technique, just plenty of . . . Power.

Another flurry of punches and Tamtam went down.

Rohan was on his feet, his heart beating fast in his chest.

This shouldn't be happening. He's using a lot of Power.

That means Boost. A lot of Boost. That can't be good for you.
Oh, Lonnie, what kind of trouble are you in this time?

23

Sirc the Whole Way

R ohan looked back at Sirc. "You knew."

She shrugged. "I don't really know *anything*. It's not profitable, you understand. I get paid for not knowing anything. For not noticing."

He nodded slowly and turned back to Lahnegarn.

The Lukhor faced him and smiled, then turned and walked off the other side of the square stage.

Rohan cracked his neck and took his seat. "Have you fought yet?"

"No. I'm up after two more fights."

"How will you do it?"

She crinkled her nostril slits at him. "What do you mean?"

"What if you're facing a Power?"

She grinned. "I've faced Powers before. Just the other day, remember? I held my own against your friend, and she's nothing to line the creche with."

"Line the . . . that's a great phrase. Can I borrow that?"

She shrugged. "Why wouldn't you? You think I'll sue you for cultural appropriation?"

"I guess not. I don't think it's illegal here."

"Anyway, I can take on Powers. I have skills." She slapped her right fist into her left palm, flexing as she did it. It was an imposing sight.

"Come on, it's not just about skills."

"I have Boost, too."

"That's what I was getting at. You won't try to fight without it?"

"Would I have a chance without it?"

"Probably not."

"There's your answer. I'm a gambler, that doesn't mean I enjoy taking unnecessary risks. Or that I'm stupid."

A pair of Andervarians came by pushing a metal cart; they handed out drinks and snacks in plastic bottles and paper wrappers. Three other pairs worked the other sections of the stadium.

"What if you run out?"

"I have a stash. If I run out, then that's what happens. What else am I supposed to do?"

"I don't know. Kick the habit?"

"After this long? I can't just stop on my own. I don't know if it would definitely kill me, but I'm not taking the chance. Now if I win, and have the Eternity Ki . . ."

"You hope it will kill the craving."

"Replace it. Why crave Boost if my own ki is enhanced like the old man's?" She pointed a thumb at the chair where Master Turtle sat. "I don't know why you're in this, but that's my endgame."

"I get it. Good luck, I guess."

"Thanks. You too, I guess. I have to go, I'm fighting next. Care to wager on my match? Five thousand credits says I'll win."

He paused. "Not this round. Catch me later."

She nodded and cracked her knuckles. "Will do."

He looked up and saw her name flashing two rows down from the current fight. "I meant it. Good luck."

"You're a strange one, but I'll take it."

Rohan ate his snack—a wrap stuffed with chunks of fish, pickled seaweed, and sliced egg—then drank. He got up to throw out the trash, walking around and in between other fighters.

On the way back to his seat, he lost track of where he was for a moment, his mind on Lahnegarn, Boost, and the situation with Tamara.

When he looked up, he was facing Master Turtle.

The reptile caught Rohan's gaze with his vertically slit pupils, nictating membranes closing from the sides, then top and bottom, the double-blink of the Vor'karei.

"Are you looking at me, old man? Is anybody in there?"

Mai Si disengaged from the Andervarian she'd been talking to and shook her head at Rohan. "Do not disrespect the master, please."

"I didn't—sorry. I didn't mean it that way."

"I know. Still."

"He looked right at me."

She sighed. "It is tempting to think that, isn't it? The fact is that he was staring at nothing in the exact direction of your face. If you can derive any meaning or understanding from that interaction, that is lovely, but it comes completely from you, not from the master."

"You're a little bit of a killjoy."

She smiled warmly. "I am a realist. Someone needs to stay grounded around here. I keep Krai Wu's idealism in check. As I used to keep Wei Li's."

He nodded. "Hey listen, I have a question for you. Since you're the realist. And the grounded one. Do you have any thoughts on the prophecies? Do you agree with Wei Li's interpretation?"

She shrugged. "I am no scholar, Rohan. I can only say that I understand why Wei Li does what she does. I don't blame her for it, even if it's proven inconvenient."

"I get that. If not for her, this whole tournament wouldn't be happening, the Eternity Ki would be safely ensconced in a new host, and everything would be . . . not good, because Master Turtle would be dead, but the way that maybe you think it should be."

"Exactly. Instead we have . . . this." She waved a hand, her gesture encompassing the entire arena.

Sirc was called up onto the stage.

She stretched her thick arms over and behind her head, cracked her neck, and faced down a hairless humanoid of a species Rohan didn't recognize.

"Why is it that I can't stop staring at him?"

Mai Si laughed. "You know why. It's the calm. The tranquility. It's intoxicating, in a very soft and subtle way."

"It feels like it means something. For me."

"Rohan, I will tell you a secret."

"Yeah?"

"Everybody feels that way in his presence. It's an illusion. The master's way is not your way."

The Hybrid shrugged. "I don't know what you mean."

"Give it time. Oh, that was quick."

Sirc stood over the unconscious body of her opponent. Wei Li called up. "Wake him up to answer his question. Sirc advances."

Mai Si smiled. "He didn't calm her down much, did he?"

"I guess he didn't."

<hr />

As the last question of the last fight of the first round was asked and answered, Wei Li climbed onto the stage and tapped her microphone.

"Fifteen minutes until the second round. Watch the boards or your comms for matchups." She tapped the microphone off and turned to return to her seat.

A voice called out from the crowd. "Aren't you going to wish us luck?"

She looked up and smiled. "If you need luck, you won't win," then continued on her way.

Rohan met her by the judges' table. "Hey."

She rubbed her eyes, then looked at him, double-blinking. "This is tiring."

"Tiring enough for you to take the Eternity Ki for yourself and call this whole thing off?"

She glared at him with hardened eyes. "You aren't funny."

"People disagree. I mean, some people. All right, just a few people, but they mean it."

"Can I do something for you, Rohan? I am quite busy."

"I was just curious. How are the matches picked? It's not random, is it?"

"Not quite. Each round has a theme."

"Care to elaborate?"

"The first round was elimination. Put a first loss on the weaker half of fighters. I deliberately made mismatches."

"I get it. What will the second round be?"

"The round of friends. You'll see."

"I don't like the sound of that."

"You're not supposed to."

He looked at her, waiting for an elaboration.

None came.

"Well, I guess I'll go back to my seat and wait for my next fight."

"Good plan."

He sat and checked his helmet for messages.

Reminders that he owed people responses.

Receipts for bills paid, including the rent on his fancy apartment.

Sirc settled her bulk into the seat next to him.

He looked up at the Takslee enforcer. "We haven't actually been introduced. It feels awkward now, since we've talked a few times."

She reached over with a big, scale-covered hand. "Call me Sirc."

"I'm Rohan. Are we friends now?"

She shrugged. "How do you feel about friends who are willing to take a paycheck to beat the snot out of you?"

"I'm okay with that."

"Then sure, we can be friends. Also, if we're matched in this tournament, I'll crush you."

"You drive a hard bargain, but . . . deal."

Katya walked over, nodded to Sirc, and sat on the other side of Rohan.

The Hybrid pointed to Sirc. "Katya, this is Sirc. Sirc, Katya. Katya, no licking."

Sirc cocked her head, curiously. "What?"

Rohan shrugged. "She likes new things."

Katya huffed. "I don't lick *everybody*. I'm learning. Don't make fun of me."

"Fair."

The names for the first few matches appeared on the big scoreboard.

Rohan read through them but didn't recognize any.

The two Ohnians, single eyes darting back and forth nervously as they navigated the crowd, came to the stage.

"Oh boy. That's what she meant."

Katya looked at him. "What who meant?"

He sighed. "Something about this round being about friends fighting. Those two came together from Ohn to try to get the Eternity Ki. Let me check their records . . . yeah, I think at least one of them is going home."

Katya frowned. "So one will receive his second loss and exit the tournament at the hands of his own friend?"

Sirc snorted. "If they both intended to win, they would have had to face one another eventually. Better to get it out of the way early."

Rohan shrugged. "I guess. Let's see what they've got. Ohn isn't a very martial culture."

Sirc shook her head. "They're the ones who lived on Wistful a few months ago? In tents on the promenade, right?"

"Yeah."

The Ohnians bowed to one another, assumed stances, and began exchanging techniques: swift, proficient combinations of punches and kicks, back and forth.

Sirc grunted. "Funny."

Rohan looked at her. "Why? What's funny?"

She pointed. "They fight like beginners. Well-trained beginners, but still. But they're using ki."

Katya hopped up, bringing her feet up under her hips so she sat higher in the chair, and patted Rohan's shoulder enthusiastically. "They are! They are!"

Rohan focused through his Third Eye.

The Ohnians were channeling esoteric energy into their fists and feet, enhancing the impact of their strikes.

It wasn't a lot of energy, and it wasn't done very efficiently, but it was more than most martial artists could accomplish without years of training.

"It kind of makes sense. They're a very spiritual culture. They learn to meditate before they can walk. They just don't use the energy they cultivate in a martial way. Except, I guess that now they do."

Rohan watched the pair continue to fight.

One of the Ohnians was slightly taller and carried a bit more muscle; otherwise they could have been brothers.

Maybe they are brothers.

The taller Ohnian had more spiritual energy to use; his blows were having a greater effect as time went on, despite landing mostly on the other fighter's forearms and hands.

Sirc pointed. "They're like sparring partners. Taking turns. Look, that one throws two punches and a leg kick, then the other one responds."

Katya nodded. "You're right! What does that mean?"

Rohan held up his hands to frame the fighters. "It means they were taught how to fight recently. They know the techniques, you see? The punches look good, they're not awkward. They're moving fluidly, shifting their weight, all of that."

Sirc pointed. "There, see that? The short one covers up with his arms, takes the punches, then punches himself, while the other one covers up. Neither is moving laterally or trying to really create any openings. And they're cycling through the same combinations. I think the one wearing green has an edge. Five thousand credits says he wins the fight."

Rohan nodded. "No bet, I think you're right. The tall one is about to jab and hook with the left, then right straight and—there it is, the right knee."

Katya bounced on her heels. "I see it! I do. Why do they fight this way?"

The Hybrid sighed. "I have a pretty good guess."

Sirc looked at him. "They're young?"

"Not just that. They come from a race of pacificists, more or less."

Sirc flinched as the taller Ohnian, the one in green, landed a hard uppercut to the other's midsection, following with a knee that folded the shorter fighter in half. "Don't look like pacificists to me."

"The il'Drach wiped out ninety-five percent of their species six months ago. I'm going to guess a few of the younger ones decided to learn how to fight after that."

"Six months? They're not bad if that's all the training they had."

"Yeah. And since they've been manipulating esoteric energy their whole lives, incorporating that into their fighting will come easily to them. Compared to, say, anyone else, anywhere else in the sector."

Katya nodded. "That is very interesting. I believe this fight is soon to be over."

Rohan nodded. "The short one's done. Ref is about to call it."

The taller fighter asked his question, and the two were cleared from the stage.

Katya nudged Rohan. "Look."

"What? Oh." His name was on the big screen, four fights away.

Across from Ang's.

———◆◆◆———

Sirc looked down at Rohan. "Is that your friend?"

"Yeah."

Katya nodded. "Also mine. Well, more than friend."

"How did he do in the first round?"

Rohan sighed. "He lost."

Sirc nodded slowly. "Finish it. Save him some suffering."

"I don't know if I can."

"It's better for him in the long run. He's big and tough, but he won't stand up to any of the Powers here, not without a huge dose of luck. And, frankly, I don't believe in luck."

Katya crinkled her nose at the bigger woman. "I believe in luck! My Ang can do great things in this tournament. He has an enormous . . . heart."

Rohan shook his head. "I'm not sure this is a contest of heart. Then again, I'm not sure it *isn't*. I hope he makes it out in time for the fight to start; he was getting medical care in the back."

Katya bounced on her heels again. "Here he comes! I don't have to go back to work for a bit. I can sit with you all!"

Sirc provided running technical commentary on the next few matches; Rohan couldn't think of much to add.

The Takslee knew a lot about fighting.

By the time Ang ambled toward them from the back room, he owed her ten thousand credits.

Ang spotted the group; he waved as he approached.

Rohan waved back, heart sinking a bit as he did it.

This is a guy I don't want to fight. Did you have to line this up, Wei Li? I guess you did.

Ang slowed as he recognized Sirc. "Friends now?"

She stood and reached a hand to shake his. "My name is Sirc. We'll be friends until I get paid to fight you again."

Ang paused, then nodded and shook her hand. With his other, he caught Katya as she launched herself onto him. "Ang! My sweet! Are you hurt?"

Rohan looked at her. "Maybe if he's hurt you shouldn't be jumping on the guy? He took a beating."

Ang shook his bearlike head. "Day cannot hold up Katya-le is day you are for burning my body and sending soul to Great Stream."

Sirc laughed. "I like you!"

Ang shrugged and made his way to the empty chair next to Katya's. He eyed Rohan as he passed. "You saw board?"

Rohan nodded. "We're up in . . . two more fights."

Ang nodded and settled down.

Katya leaned on him and stroked the fur on his cheek. "Are you ready?"

Ang nodded. "Am ready. Soon."

Sirc looked at the board. "Ooh, I see my name. There, three below you."

One of the fighters on stage got behind the other, snaked an arm around his neck, and rendered his opponent unconscious.

The next pair climbed up.

Rohan cracked his neck. "I am not looking forward to this."

24

Friends All A-Round

Ang rolled his shoulders, powerful muscles bulging out from under his fur, and planted his feet heavily into the surface of the stage.

Rohan set his own feet, taking his usual stance: left foot forward, left fist next to his belly button, right fist by his chin.

"Brings back memories, doesn't it, Ang?"

Ang grinned, showing a set of ferocious teeth.

He stood between two and two-and-a-half meters tall and weighed close to five hundred kilograms. He wasn't a Power, but his aura had a unique quality that made it . . . loud.

That pressure squeezed Rohan, filling the stage with an almost palpable battle rage.

"Is different today, War Chief. No guns. No war gauntlet. And you, no Powers."

Rohan grunted and focused inward.

The esoteric spiral he formed within his soul was intact, anchored to both palms, ready to absorb and release whatever the big Ursan was going to throw at him.

"Have I ever mentioned just how *big* you are, Ang? Like, really big. And I know from big. I've fought some big things. Have I told you?"

"Yes, Rohan. Have heard. Big bugs. Toothy fish."

"Sharks. They were sharks. With legs. Really big. One hundred fifty meters long. Ten thousand tons. I think. I don't know, I didn't get one on a scale or anything; I just did a back-of-the-envelope calculation. I might be off by a zero or two."

"Much meat. Earthlings must have all become very fat after battle."

"You know what? I don't remember anybody chowing down on shark meat. The first couple were nuked, I think. Nobody wants a shark steak that glows in the dark. And the last one we left alive and sent him back home. But before that was one we just killed. Somebody might have eaten him."

Wei Li cleared her throat. "Stalling."

"Of course I'm stalling, Wei Li, I don't want—"

Ang slammed into him like a bus hitting a texting pedestrian.

Rohan went down, the five hundred kilos striking his chest too much to resist, and was instantly choking on hot fur.

He rolled from side to side, pushing against Ang's mass. He couldn't get a good grip; the Ursan's fat was heavy and thick. As big as he was, his skin was stretched tight by his enormous body, and it was all over Rohan. Suffocating him.

The Hybrid pushed, using just his arms, straining to create space he could work with; he managed a few centimeters, but Ang used it to drive a heavy elbow into his belly.

I could have absorbed that with the helix if I'd been able to anticipate it. This close, though...

Ang spread his feet wide, solidifying his base, and lifted himself up for a moment.

Rohan tried to move.

Ang dropped back down, crushing the Hybrid into the platform.

Rohan felt a ping of anxiety; he couldn't breathe properly, and he didn't know how to get out from under the Ursan.

Ang lifted one shoulder up, then dropped it onto Rohan's face. The heavy knob of bone inside it struck him like a fist.

"Son of a—" He barely forced the words out through a mouthful of damp fur.

He inhaled, filling his nose with Ang's musky scent, then twisted his hips back and forth, cranking with his knees against the big bear's bulk.

Ang lifted his shoulder again; rammed it into Rohan's face. Again.

The Hybrid saw sparks. His heart raced; his lungs burned, and he couldn't move.

He couldn't move.

Panic spiked inside him, the tip penetrating deep into his psyche, opening like a blooming flower and spraying a pollen cloud of anger through his mind.

This lump of meat doesn't remember what I did to him last time.

He thinks he can stand up to me? Has he forgotten what I am? What I'm capable of?

He's seen me fight kaiju. Seen his bullets bounce off my chest.

If I cut loose . . .

Fresh, hot energy surged through him; coursing through his body and also through the esoteric spiral anchored to his palms.

He *felt* the helix of energy buck as its structure lost coherence; it jerked and lost a coil. Then a second.

Rohan relaxed, loosening first his hands, fists unclenching, then his shoulders, letting Ang press him flat to the floor.

He stopped twisting his hips; let his legs hang loose and floppy.

Rohan exhaled slowly, forcing back the air hunger that filled his chest. He turned his head to the side and inhaled through his nose; slowly, slowly, slowly, ignoring the urgent need in his lungs.

Calm down.

Ang hit him again; he let a spark of irritation wash over and through him, imagining himself breathing it out the way Mai Si had suggested.

Let go of it.

He absorbed another heavy blow; felt the floor under his cheek grow slick with his blood.

The helix of energy inside him stabilized with two full turns, down from the four it had held.

Still a coil; still a spring.

But barely.

The world was a sliver of light between Ang's body and the stage; he saw feet slap the ground near him, and something happened above.

Ang rolled off, cautiously at first, then faster.

Rohan blinked at the bright lights and saw the referee pushing between him and the Ursan.

"It's over."

Rohan nodded and inhaled deeply, exhaling slowly once again, fighting his anger.

The ref looked at Ang, making sure the Ursan was backing away, then back at Rohan. "You hurt? You need a medic?"

Rohan lifted his hands in the air, then patted his own chest. He inhaled again and coughed lightly. "I'm good." He curled up into a seated position. Ang towered over him.

The ref looked them both over, then stepped away. Ang was panting; he'd worked hard to keep his body on top of Rohan's.

Rohan looked down at Wei Li as he gathered his feet under himself and stood.

She pointed at Ang. "You get one question."

Ang nodded and turned to his friend. "Were you for letting me win, War Chief?"

Rohan inhaled again; let it out slowly.

How do I answer that?

Wei Li cleared her throat. "You are close to disqualification."

Rohan nodded. "I used every . . . ability I have available for this tournament." He looked over at Wei Li.

Does obfuscation count as lying?

Ang nodded. "Was good fight, War Chief. Feeling lucky today."

Rohan shook his head. "I'm lucky you didn't smother me."

Wei Li looked at them. "Both advance."

The pair of friends descended to the floor of the stadium.

◆ ･･◆･･ ◆

"Not for feeling badly, Rohan. You are very small."

"I don't think that's making me feel better." They walked up the aisle toward their waiting seats.

"Also, are much diminished. Meaning ability. Not half as strong as you were for being in the past. Not one-quarter. One-tenth!"

"Still not helping."

"Old Rohan would have been for winning in seconds only. Very fast. Would have been marvel for all to see!"

"You're not even trying, Ang."

"Is not your fault are so small. And lacking hair."

"I have plenty of hair. An above average amount, thank you very much. For my species. You're the abnormal one with all that fur."

"Is too much? Katya likes."

Rohan sighed. "I'm sure she does. Do you know her people kept thinking I'd been shaven? I had to keep explaining—"

Ang lifted his head and barked three times, loud enough to echo clearly off the far walls of the arena. "Shaven! Oh, is funny. Too funny. Like shaven cub, you are. After accident. With, what is word, gum!"

"How do you even know what gum is, Ang? Who gave you gum? Who looked at a bunch of Ursans drinking and eating raw fish and thought, what these guys need is chewing gum?"

Ang shrugged as he turned to sit in Katya's empty seat. "Cubs are liking gum. Is fun to chew. So they saying."

Rohan sighed and took his own seat, dwarfed between Ang and Sirc.

He touched his face; his hand came away bloody. "I wonder if I should get this looked at." *I'm still used to these things healing on their own.*

Nobody responded.

The next fight ended when one of the fighters choked the other unconscious; Sirc stood and looked over her shoulder with her snakelike head. "I'll be back. Or not."

Ang nodded. "Being careful."

"I will."

Ang looked down at Rohan. "She is Power."

Rohan sighed. "She uses Boost. So she's a Power, I guess, for as long as she uses it."

Ang nodded slowly. "Why do not Ursans also for using Boost?"

"You know why. If she runs out of the stuff, she'll . . . she might die. And to prevent that, she'll do almost anything to get it."

"Like Ursans bitten by ar'Tahul. Other ar'Tahul, not you. Only worse."

"Only worse."

Ang paused. "Rohan. In back room." The big man hesitated.

"What?"

"Was next to one-eyed person. With big . . ." He put his palm over his face.

"You were with the Ohnian."

"Yes. Ohnian. Other man came, talked to us. Offered us some Boost."

Rohan's heart quickened. "Did he."

"Yes. Was not for saying so with Sirc here. But now . . ."

"Yeah. Makes sense. Who would actually need the stuff? Maybe someone desperate to win this tournament."

"Yes."

"And that might be a person I could use to get to Granny."

"Not knowing who is Granny. But knowing you for looking for Boost dealers to questioning."

"Yeah. Yeah, I am. Thanks, Ang." He paused, thinking. "Hey, who did they match up with Sirc?"

Ang looked up. "Man naming Kor. You know?"

Rohan sighed. "Funnily enough, I do. I'm not sure they qualify as friends, but I assume Wei Li knows what she's doing."

Sirc and Kor faced off on stage; matched in height, he had two more arms, and her limbs were each twice the mass of any of his.

Sirc cleared her throat. "You seem like a nice fellow, but I need to move on in this contest."

He shrugged. "You will try. My need is just as great."

She shook her head. "I doubt it. Without that weapon, I'm a slave to certain people who don't have my best interests at heart."

He grinned. "You think I'm not? I lost two brothers yesterday because the man who bought us sent them into senseless danger. Without that weapon, I'm just as much a slave."

Rohan winced. *They're not wrong.*

The referee gave the start signal, and they began to fight.

Kor was faster; his limbs moved in a blur, blitzing combinations up and down Sirc's body as he circled, moving side to side to find odd angles from which to punch.

Sirc covered up, fists to her face, and blocked with forearms and elbows, letting about a third of the punches land on her lower abdomen but keeping her head protected.

Kor stepped back and took a few breaths, waiting for the Takslee to close, but she waited patiently.

He attacked again.

Rohan straightened in his seat. "She knows what she's doing."

Ang nodded. "Appearing so."

Kor took another break, then closed with a fresh onslaught.

Sirc waited patiently, taking the shots, taking small steps to shift her body a dozen centimeters at a time, just enough to force him to adjust.

The Quattro was slowing.

"He cannot for being this fast for much longer."

Rohan shook his head. "I wonder if it's too—"

Sirc lifted her left leg and covered the distance between them in one huge step, her right fist shooting out just as the foot landed.

Kor crossed his two lower arms in an *X* shape in front of his chest; the punch still launched him across the arena.

Ang sighed. "She being Power; he being not Power. Is hard."

Rohan nodded. "Really hard." *I've only seen a few people overcome that kind of gap in ability.*

Spiral, for one.

He caught a punch thrown by a god.

But he did it with this esoteric technique that nobody else uses and is damned hard to master.

Sirc crossed the stage quickly, her speed belying her bulk, and finished the henchman with two more massive punches.

The tournament paused while Kor recovered consciousness, then Sirc was given permission to ask her question.

"Who owns you?"

He sighed. "Anyone with the credits to pay. Right now, it's the First Citizen of Lukhor. Next week, it could be anybody in the sector."

Sirc returned to her seat; Kor was helped to the back for a medical evaluation.

The two Tolone'ans, members of The Consortium, mounted the stage.

Rohan cracked his neck and prepared to watch more carefully. *Chances are good I'll be fighting these two eventually. Whether inside or outside the tournament.*

Squeya, the female and leader of the group, was taller and thicker than Squero, but not by much.

Did they say they were siblings?

The ref told them to begin; Squero stepped back and took a knee. "I forfeit."

Wei Li looked at him. "Are you sure?"

"I cannot fight my sister."

"Those are the conditions of the tournament."

"Nevertheless."

She nodded. "Squeya advances. Squero is disqualified."

Squeya looked at her. "He won his first-round match; this loss makes him even. Why is he disqualified?"

Wei Li shook her head. "Forfeiting violates the spirit of the tournament."

"But—"

The security chief's eyes hardened. "As does arguing with the judges."

Squeya exhaled loudly, moist membranes in her airway flapping to make a very rude noise, and turned away.

Rohan took another snack from a passing vendor and watched a pair of black-feathered avians fight.

They weren't fliers, strictly speaking, but they had feathered flaps under their arms that generated enough lift to make legitimately impressive jumps and change direction midair.

Their fighting style wasn't something the Hybrid had ever seen before.

Ang was watching carefully. "Interesting they are."

"I was thinking the same thing. You think they'd be tough to fight?"

The Ursan shrugged. "With weapons am thinking yes. Fighting one of those, with a bow, in the open? Very tough for being. Here? Unarmed? Meh."

Rohan nodded.

One of the avians cracked the other's arm with a looping kick and an audible snap; the fight ended.

The Hybrid checked the board; the next fight was Krai Wu.

Against Lahnegarn.

Rohan sputtered. "They're not friends. Are they? Do they even know each other?"

Ang shrugged. "Krai Wu is not for having friends in tournament. Who is the Lukhor?"

Rohan sighed. "That, my friend, is Lahnegarn."

Ang tapped his furry chin with one massive paw. "Lahnegarn. Lahnegarn. Am not—wait, father to Rinth?"

"That's the one."

"He looks not too bad."

The Ursan was correct.

If anything, the Lukhor had gained confidence after the first round. His movements were more even, more relaxed; the bands of esoteric energy that flowed along his limbs were more stable, more . . . solid.

Krai Wu, on the other hand, moved like a master.

The Vor'karei's feet slid so smoothly over the ground it was as if he floated; he seemed to be in perfect balance at every moment, every one of his joints moving precisely the right amount to get his body where he wanted it.

And that was just getting onto the stage and bowing to his opponent.

They took fight positions, Lahnegarn's posture higher up, the Vor'karei deeper, his hips closer to the ground.

Ang snorted. "The male is for moving like Wei Li."

Rohan nodded. "Makes sense, right? They trained together."

Sirc shook her head. "He is a more skilled fighter than she. Not by much, but . . ."

The Hybrid shrugged. "Maybe."

Lahnegarn struck first, leaping in with a vicious left hook, following quickly with a right straight aimed at the place Krai Wu had escaped to.

The reptile easily parried the straight and leaned away from the following kick.

He turned again, put a hand on Lahnegarn's chest, and pushed him over.

If not for the band of magical energy holding him upright, the Lukhor would have fallen to his back; instead he stayed upright and spun away.

Both men reset.

Lahnegarn sneered. "You'll need more than that to stop me."

Krai Wu shrugged. "Then let us see how much more I have to offer."

The Vor'karei embodied the physical ideals of a warrior monk. He maintained perfect control of his emotions; demonstrated exceptional strength, flexibility, and conditioning; had a master of technical fighting, tactics, and martial strategy that was worthy of a professional warrior.

For about ninety seconds, Rohan thought that would be enough for him to win the fight.

Lahnegarn, for all his bluster, for all his annoying habits, clearly embodied a few traits that served him well in his fight.

He had evidently trained with a maniacal fervor in the martial arts over the previous year.

This dude channeled his obsession over Tamara into a ridiculously intense practice regime.

Whether through luck or planning, he had emphasized the skills that would do him the most good in the shortest period of time, when enhanced with Boost.

I wonder if he hired amazing coaches or if he's so smart he figured this all out himself.

His body responded to Boost exceptionally well; the amount of esoteric energy he could manifest was high.

Bastard just got lucky with that.

It took another thirty seconds for Krai Wu to realize he couldn't overcome the difference in Power between them; couldn't negate the fact that Lahnegarn was moving faster, hitting harder, and reinforcing his body in ways that weren't physiologically possible, allowing him to escape traps and joint locks that would have ended the fight with any non-Power.

Forty-five seconds later, the Vor'karei was on the ground, the Lukhor holding onto him from behind, applying a clumsy chokehold that the warrior simply could not escape.

This might be harder than I thought.

25

Back In The Shell

The remainder of the second round took up the rest of the afternoon and the early part of evening.

After the last fight, Wei Li stood and told the fighters they were free to leave but to return the following morning at half past nine.

Rohan set an alarm on his helmet and stood, stretching his neck and shoulders. "Ang, you have plans?"

Ang nodded. "Am for eating with Katya. Will you for joining us?"

Rohan paused. "I would, but I should check on Tamara first. And if she's busy, I have an invitation I think I should accept."

"Not sounding very certain, War Chief."

"Oh, I'm certain. That I don't want to do this. But, you know, want and should aren't always the same thing."

"You are for truth as volcano, War Chief, erupting always with sayings of wisdom."

"I . . . I'm going to take that as a compliment and move along. Here comes Katya. You kids have fun."

Ang grunted. "Am not cub, Brother Rohan. Nor is Katya-le."

"Just an expression, big guy. See you in the morning."

Rohan called Tamara.

He got an auto-reply saying she was busy with a project but would try to contact him the following morning.

What the heck is she working on? She would have said if it was related to her job.

If she wants me to know, she'll tell me.

Maybe she's planning a surprise party. For my birthday.

When is my birthday, anyway?

He left the arena and walked across the promenade, enjoying the smell of grass as he looked for a bench to sit on. He found one, about halfway across the field, and sat.

He scrolled through contacts on the display inside his helmet, rolling up and down past the one he knew he'd have to use.

Damnit.

The Hybrid sent a simple query to Eldarinth Lastex, First Citizen of Lukhor: "Where should I meet you?"

⬤┄•┄⬤

The Ton'ga Shell wasn't the sort of place most people ate at casually; there had to be a reason. Impressing a client, celebrating a special occasion, proposing marriage, apologizing for ruining a marriage. It also wasn't the sort of place one came to dressed in clothes that had survived two fights, complete with bloodstains and a slight air of sweaty fur.

Rohan entered and made his way directly to the host's podium; he'd been there before, though he didn't think they'd recognize him without a uniform and long hair.

The host, a slender Kratic, stepped around and approached him, arms spread wide as if ready to usher him out before he could exhale and contaminate the atmosphere with working-class breath.

Rohan smiled. "Here to see Eldar."

The host froze. "You mean . . ."

"You know who I mean. I'm expected. Back room?" The restaurant had a private room, very exclusive, with privacy security that rivaled any other spot on Wistful. Conversations could be held there that even the station herself wouldn't be able to hear.

The host looked Rohan up and down, then opened his eyes wide, finally recognizing the Hybrid.

Also recognizing that Rohan hadn't offered his name. "Of course, sir. Of course. I apologize for any delay, right this way. Right this way." He ushered Rohan past well-appointed tables and to an unmarked door in the back wall, opposite the kitchen.

Rohan touched his cheek, then checked his hand for fresh blood.

It was dry.

A conversation from inside the room cut out when the door opened, so the host led Rohan into silence.

Eldarinth Lastex sat at the head of a table for ten that was covered by a spotless white tablecloth. He made eye contact with the host, nodding quickly.

The Kratic turned and left, closing the door behind him.

A second Lukhor sat next to Eldarinth, a younger man wearing a Lukhor business suit: long tunic with slits up both sides that draped to his knees, made from an embroidery-rich fabric that probably cost more than Rohan's monthly rent.

Eldarinth waved at the man. "Boruscant, Rohan. Rohan, Boruscant."

Rohan looked down at the man, who stared into his tablet, tapping at the screen.

The Hybrid sighed. "Pleasure to meet you, Boruscant." He changed the pitch of his voice. "You too, Rohan, I've heard so much about you!" And again. "All lies, I'm sure, I'm really quite charming." Once more. "Yes, that's what they said! I kid, I kid. Please, have a seat. Can we order you some wine?" His own voice. "Sounds great! You don't mind if I call you Borus, do you?" Change. "Not at all, not at all. All my friends do."

Eldar laughed, a single harsh note right on the border of humor and scorn, and waved Rohan to the seat at his left. "Boruscant is my aide. He manages a great deal of my affairs. As you can imagine, he's very busy."

Rohan shrugged and sat. "My mother runs a planet. She has time to be polite, and so does her aide."

The older Lukhor frowned at him. "Does she? I had no idea. What planet? I might know her."

Rohan waved his hand dismissively. "Tiny place, off the grid. Not even in the Empire. Anyway, you asked me to come, here I am."

Eldarinth nodded and sipped his wine. "Excuse me, that was rude. Hold on." He tapped a small button on the table that seemed to have only one purpose. "Someone will bring something for you straightaway."

"Sounds great. I'm parched." *Did he just admit he was rude?*

The old man cleared his throat. "We can fix that. This place was recommended to me. It's not Lukhorian cuisine, but it's not terrible. Better than I usually find off-world."

Rohan forced a smile onto his lips. "It's on the list of fifty finest restaurants in the sector. I actually think it outranks any of the places on Lukhor."

The Lukhor shook his head. "I'm sure it doesn't. Anyway, we're not here to be food critics." The door opened, and a uniformed server entered. Eldarinth pointed at Rohan, and the woman nodded once and exited. "Have you eaten? We just had appetizers." He pointed at the empty plates.

"I could eat." *Is he being . . . polite?*

"Good, good. Have you been here?"

Rohan's smile felt tight enough to split the wound on his cheek. "Funny story. I have eaten here, a few times. The second time was with a particularly attractive shuttle tech, who I was desperately trying to impress. It worked, I think. She seemed to enjoy it."

"The second time?"

"Yeah. The first time, I sat in this very room across from a Shayjh Adjudicator who asked me to do the silliest thing. You want to hear the story? It's crazy. The girl's father had actually hired the Shayjh, probably the third most deadly species in the sector, to make sure nobody inadequate tried to socialize with his daughter."

Eldarinth grimaced and sighed. "I find managing my daughter a . . . trying experience."

"You should try to do a better job of it, maybe. I'd start with a change in perspective. Like, don't think of it as managing anything and just try to be her father."

Boruscant looked up from his tablet and opened his mouth; Eldarinth silenced him with a single upheld finger.

The older Lukhor nodded. "You might be right, Rohan. I am not too stubborn to admit when I have acted incorrectly."

Rohan leaned back in the plush padded chair. "That's not exactly your reputation, but I'm listening."

The door opened again, and their server brought in a tray with a clean glass, napkin, handcrafted china and flatware, and a small plate of food. She poured wine into the glass and arranged everything in front of the Hybrid.

He muttered a thank you and leaned over the dish: tender round morsels of meat, something like a snail or a mollusk, drizzled with a dark savory sauce, surrounded by an herbaceous foam that exploded in his mouth with a grassy flavor.

He sipped the wine: a red with a half dozen layers of complexity before the taste and another dozen in the aftertaste.

Rohan sat back into his chair and let the flavors wash over him.

"This dish is new."

Eldarinth shrugged. "Tasting menu. If my wife were here, she'd pick something specific, but . . ."

Rohan nodded. "Sounds great. So, you wanted to see me?"

Boruscant looked up. "Sir."

Rohan met his gaze. "Yes?"

The younger man sneered. "No, you're supposed to call him 'sir.'"

Eldarinth waved his hand. "Never mind the formalities."

Rohan grunted and glared at the aide. "I'm not from your culture, but where I'm from we reserve that term for people we respect. Not, for example, people who have threatened to torture or kill you for absolutely no reason. So, no, *you* can certainly call *me* 'sir,' but you don't want to start telling me what to say unless and until you want to find out why the Shayjh decided to abandon Eldar's contract the hard way." He leaned back in his chair and exhaled slowly.

Boruscant looked ready to stand up and continue arguing, but another glare from Eldar shut him down. The older Lukhor turned to Rohan.

"We got off on the wrong foot, Rohan. Should I call you something else? Any titles?"

The Hybrid held his lungs empty for a count of four, willing himself to relax. "Rohan is fine. I have plenty of titles if we need any later."

"I'm sure. I know a handful of them. You've had a colorful career. Er, military career."

He's trying to be nice. That's actually aggravating me more. "I've been around." Rohan lifted another snail-thing to his mouth with the small dedicated spoon that rested on the plate; the foam, sauce, and slightly rubbery meat contrasted and complemented perfectly.

"Yes. Well, we're not here to talk about that."

"What, then?" *Be nice, Rohan. He's trying, you can try.* "No rush to answer that, not if you keep feeding me like this. You can take your sweet time; I'll just keep eating and drinking."

Eldarinth sighed and sipped his wine, smacking his lips before continuing. "I do have a tendency to be, let's say, overly aggressive in the way I solve my problems."

Rohan nodded. "I may have noticed that." He ate the last snail-thing and sighed, melting a bit into his chair.

"I hope you can give me a chance for a . . . call it a fresh start."

Rohan rubbed his forehead. "That's a big ask, Eldarinth. Fresh? Like, totally fresh? After the way things went the other day? I'm not much of a grudge-bearer, but I don't know. How about a start that's past the sell-by date, but before the use-by date? Not fresh, but not spoiled either."

Eldarinth traded a look with Boruscant, who shrugged helplessly. "You don't speak Drachna like a native."

Rohan laughed. "It's not the Drachna, I'm just weird. You'll get used to it." *Or not.*

"I understand where you're coming from. I suppose you have no reason to trust me, particularly. But it's in your best interest to get along with me better."

"Is that a threat? Because it's hard to tell, and I know a lot about threats."

"I didn't mean it as a threat. At least not this time. I meant, if you want a relationship with my daughter, you should try to get along with me. We may not be as close as I'd like, but I am still her father. Family. That means something."

Rohan nodded and exhaled slowly. "You want us to get along better. Which, to me, implies you want something from me, right? Get along means do something you want. What did you have in mind? I assume you're not looking for a tow chief."

Boruscant snorted. "Not like you could—"

Eldarinth interrupted. "Button it." He turned to Rohan. "Not quite. I'd like your help with something else."

"My help? Mine?"

"Yes. I'm worried about my daughter, you see. She's the jewel of my life. My most prized achievement."

"Yeah, that's a little weird, Eldarinth. You should try talking about her as if she's, I don't know, an actual sentient being, not a science experiment you conducted."

"I'll admit I'm not good at this. But she's my pride and joy."

Rohan nodded vigorously. "There you go, that's much better. You're already getting better. Just put a little effort into it."

"And, as I said, I'm worried about her. About what she's been doing."

"Doing . . . as in, what?" *Me? No, that's not what he means.*

"I restored some of her inheritance. I . . . reconsidered the wisdom of cutting her off from her financial resources. And she's been spending that money. Do you have any idea where it's going?"

This is about money?

"Her money? Spending? I don't know. Wait, maybe I do. I don't think it's a secret. She bought me a present."

Eldarinth's eyes narrowed. "What kind of present?"

"I bought an apartment, and she had a waterfall installed. In the bedroom. Wait, is that too much information? Bedroom stuff? No, I think it's fine. You know, I like water, the sound is very relaxing."

Eldarinth traded a glance with Boruscant, who shook his head. "My daughter has drained over a billion credits from her accounts. What kind of waterfall are you talking about, exactly?"

Rohan swallowed and reached for his wine. He took a sip, letting the flavors wash through him, then shook his head. "I didn't see the work order, but I don't think it was a billion credit project. Five thousand, maybe. Ten?"

"I hope you can understand why I'm concerned. That's a very significant sum. It's an amount that will be noticed."

Rohan swirled the wine in his glass and watched the liquid coat the sides. He had never understood what qualities he was supposed to check for while doing that. Should the wine drain quickly? Slowly? Form a thin layer? Thick?

The door opened, and their server, accompanied by two assistants, brought in fresh plates of food.

The men sat in silence as their glasses were refilled and flatware replaced.

The server faced them. "We have slices of smoked tawntawn rib over a bed of greens imported from Drach itself, sauteed in tawntawn tallow and seasoned with Tolone'an salt. Over it you'll find twiggs, a delicacy from Kratic, fried in whale oil. Please enjoy."

Eldar took the first bite, Boruscant waiting for his employer to swallow before trying the dish.

Rohan had never had the twiggs before; crunchy and delicate, their flavor reminded him of Korean white sweet potato.

The Hybrid looked the older man in the eye. "I have no idea what she's doing with that kind of money. But I can probably find out."

Eldarinth sighed in relief. "You would do that? Tell me what she's up to?"

"That's not what I said. I said I could find out. Maybe. And if I do, I can figure out if it's any of your business, or mine, what she spends her money on."

"That's not what I asked for."

"That's okay, rejection is good for you. Builds character. Something tells me you have the bad habit of getting what you want way more often than you should."

Eldarinth shook his head softly and took another bite of his food.

Rohan tapped his fork against the expensive plate. "I tell you what, though, maybe we can trade. Assuming Tamara is okay with it."

A glint snuck into the older man's eye. "What kind of trade?"

Rohan smiled broadly. "How about you tell me something? Like, I don't know, why the hell you sent three of your goons to Toth 3 to help out Lonnie?"

The old man blinked once; twice.

"Lonnie? Oh, Lahnegarn. The Quattros."

"Yeah, the Quattros. First of all, terrible move, throwing their lives away over nothing. Second of all, what the hell, Eldar? You don't like Lonnie any more than I do. Maybe less. Why help him like that? And don't try to tell me he hired them behind your back or anything. I know how men like you treat henchmen. You're not going to let someone else hench them out on the side."

Eldarinth sagged a bit in his seat. "Rohan, you know how things are. Lahnegarn is . . . he's an unsuitable mate for Tamara, but he is my grandson's father. I can't just stand by and watch him die on the surface of some credit-forsaken planet, food for beasts."

"You have a bunch of goons available. He wants to go on a suicide mission so you send them *along*? You didn't even think for a second that they could just as easily—no, a lot *more* easily—tie him up and stop him from going in the first place?"

"He's a slippery bastard. He always finds a way. And with those damned cameras of his, he always manages to collect some information that you don't want exposed. You don't know how annoying he is."

"I really do. I really do."

"You did not do me any favors, scaring off the Shayjh. It's your fault Lahnegarn—what did you call him?"

"Lonnie. It's funny if you're from my home planet. Which you aren't."

"You couldn't have told the Shayjh to keep him away from Tamara?"

Rohan sighed.

You think I haven't had that same thought about a thousand times since then?

"Doesn't matter now. Are you behind his recent acquisition of Powers, too?"

Eldarinth choked on his mouthful of wine and coughed violently. Once he'd caught his breath, he stared at the Hybrid with wide eyes.

"What?"

26

Justifying Unjustifiables

Rohan sipped his wine. "Lonnie. Powers. He entered the tournament."

Eldarinth looked at his aide Boruscant, who looked back and shrugged.

The older Lukhor sighed. "He's using Boost now? Is that going to be an issue? I've heard other fighting drugs cause rage issues."

"I don't think so. Not exactly. You're thinking of other stuff. Androgens. But it's pretty addictive. And it isn't cheap."

Eldarinth sighed and rubbed his eyes. For just a moment he looked very old and very tired.

He picked up a bite of the tawntawn ribs and popped it into his mouth.

Rohan matched the older man bite for bite, finishing another glass of wine as he went.

The Hybrid swallowed. "Any idea where he got the Boost?"

The old man shrugged. "You think he got it from me? He doesn't need me for something like that. The way he has cameras everywhere, all fed through his personal systems? You think he needs contacts from halfway across the sector to find a drug dealer?"

Rohan grunted. "Okay. Are you going to keep supplying him with muscle?"

"I'm experiencing a rather serious shortage of local manpower at the moment, aren't I, Rohan? Kor is staying in the tournament. It's too big of a coup if he wins for me to risk it."

"So that's it? You just want me to find out where Tamara's money is going?"

"That, and I want you to stay away from her. Oh, I know you're not tied down anymore, and I'm all out of Quattros to force you to do anything. But if you really care about my girl, you'll cooperate."

"Because you think I can't protect her."

"Damn right that's why. Leave her alone, for her own good. You've proven I can't make you do it, but you say you love her, so . . ."

"I'll think about it." To his own surprise, he wasn't lying.

"Good. And while you're at it, find that billion credits. She might be getting in over her head."

"I'll figure it out. Just don't assume you're going to be part of that process."

"I'll take those terms."

Rohan nodded.

Servers brought in dessert, a bird's nest formed out of strands of sugar sprayed with different fruit juices, some sour, some sweet.

The structure crunched under Rohan's fork.

I really don't have good memories of this place. But the food is fantastic.

◆┈◦┈◆

The Hybrid patted his stomach as he left the Ton'ga Shell and walked to his apartment.

The promenade was dark; not pitch black, but like an open field on a clear night on most inhabited planets. Wistful dimmed the diamond plate roof to restrict the sunlight that passed through and lowered the interior lights to simulate nighttime.

Most species on the station required a day-night cycle to keep biological rhythms in place.

He considered finding Tamara, but she'd asked for time to work. *Maybe her project is connected to that billion credits.*

He mused as he walked.

Tamara might be better off without me. If I'm going to take on Hyperion and his followers, then work on the Assessors, who knows what kind of trouble I'll stir up?

What right do I have dragging her into that?

Why wasn't I thinking about that before?

I didn't plan to get involved in this sort of thing, on this scale. It crept up on me.

That's a crappy excuse.

I should have known better.

He passed a couple out on a romantic walk; they exchanged silent nods in the dim starlight.

That's assuming I manage to beat Hyperion.

I need the spiral for that.

And that technique needs a name. Something cool, like it came from an anime.

Power Spring!

That's dumb.

Magic Helix!

Worse.

It returns damage to the person who tried to cause it. It's like Karma.

Karmic Fist!

Fist of Karma!

I almost like those.

He passed through Wistful's central hub, the corridors mostly empty at that time. He nodded to a pair of security officers and walked close to Wei Li's office.

For a moment he thought about seeing if she was there, but he continued on instead.

Leave her alone. She has enough on her plate with this tournament.

Which I could win if I could keep Spiral's technique going more reliably.

For which I would need to control my anger.

I might manage that if I could get to the source. Where does anger come from?

Fear, I guess. How do I get rid of my fear?

Master Turtle seems pretty fearless.

Gotta learn to let go of it the way he did.

He continued onto the southern promenade and made his way to his apartment building. It didn't quite feel like home; he'd only moved out of his place on Wistful's central hub a few months prior and had spent a lot of that time away from the station.

He made his way inside and took the elevator to his penthouse apartment.

Everything was clean and orderly again; the building staff had straightened up inside. He showered, put a little ointment on his scraped cheek, and changed into fresh clothes.

Sleep? Maybe not yet. I should sit by the pool.

What else do I need to figure out? Maybe getting rid of the Boost supplier on Wistful.

Maybe I can fight Sirc; when I get a question, I can ask her for someone higher up the food chain.

Maybe Marion Stone and Garren can get me a Boost detector. I can wear it on my belt like Batman. I'll call it a Bat-Boost detector; nobody within ten thousand light years will appreciate the joke.

Nobody other than Ben, I guess. He'll laugh.

He'll probably be patronizing me, but he'll laugh.

Rohan passed through the big glass doors that led onto the pool area. It was the most peaceful place in the building.

Toth 3 caught his gaze, hanging white and blue overhead, dim in the artificial night sky.

Rohan made his way to one of the poolside chairs and got ready to sit.

Before he could, sprays struck him as three forms lifted out of the water.

Squeya landed at the edge of the pool, just a meter from Rohan's toes, and glared at him.

"Rohan."

The Hybrid leapt to his feet as he experienced a brief flash of panic; he felt his esoteric spiral unwind two coils before he could exhale, blowing out the fear, and relax it into stability.

Breathe. Stay calm.

"Oh hey, Squeya. Nice to see you. I didn't know you lived around here. Did you move? It's a great building, have you seen the vending machines? Fourth floor. You can get these little—"

"Stop your prattling."

Her brother blew water out of his airways. "He's nervous. It's what he does. You've seen the reports."

Reports? They have reports?

"You have reports? Who filled those out? I almost feel sorry for them, I'm a really boring guy. Whoever was spying on me, oof, that's not fun. Tedious work."

Squeya shook her head, lines of spray flying off her tentacles as they swung. "Dr. Kraken told us all about you, Hybrid. You made quite an impression on him."

"Oh, that. Impression? More of an excision, am I right? Because I ripped off his tentacle. Not really like a dent."

Her head shook in anger, her tentacles quivering. "We will never forgive you for what you've done, Hybrid."

Rohan sighed. "Which is what, exactly? You're pissed I fought your precious Dr. Kraken? He's not exactly innocent in that situation, you know. Guy kidnapped and tortured me. When I saw him last, he had kidnapped another Hybrid. It's not like I just dropped in on his chiropractor practice and attacked him out of nowhere."

Squeya shook in place, and the male stepped forward.

"My sister is not talking about Dr. Kraken. We don't need him as an excuse for hating you."

Rohan looked from one to the other as an unpleasant feeling settled in his gut. "Oh."

The Tolone'ans stood in place, staring him down with their flat cephalopod eyes.

Rohan shifted from foot to foot. "Are you guys going to attack me, or what? I'm not really sure what's happening here."

Squeya shook her head. "I . . . I can't. Squero, tell him."

The male to her left nodded. "We want you to understand, Hybrid. We won't attack you now. Or any of your people. We understand what's at stake. If we step out of line, your friend the judge will disqualify us. And that weapon is too much of a prize to risk."

Rohan shrugged. "Yeah. That's kind of why I signed up. So what are you doing here?"

Squero huffed, little spitting noises coming from the folds of his fleshy head. "Are you stupid? I told you already. We want you to *understand*."

Rohan looked from one to the other. "I'm listening. I can't promise much more than that."

Squero nodded. "We will leave you alone for the tournament. But when it is over, regardless of outcome, we will destroy you, Griffin. You and everything and everyone you love."

Rohan swallowed. "I guess I understand that. Except I don't. Not really. What's going on here?"

Squeya balled her hands into fists. "We remember you, Griffin. From Tolone'a."

"Ah." He exhaled slowly, willing away the ball of anxiety growing in his belly.

Squero put a soothing tentacle on his sister's shoulder and addressed the Hybrid. "We weren't religious caste, we were warrior caste. Our parents were tasked with guarding the Temple at Cthulhu's Crucible. We lived there, in the temple, alongside the religious caste."

Rohan exhaled slowly and sat down on the lounge chair. "Ah."

Squeya nodded. "We were barely more than children when you came. You know the name they gave you? The il'Drach call you Conqueror. Because you ended our freedom, ended our power, our ability to control our own destiny.

"But to the Tolone'ans, you are now, and always will be, Murderer. Because we know that what you did put you hip-deep in the blood of our kin. Our families. Our parents."

Squero stepped forward, fists formed at his sides. "You slew our parents with your own hands, Slayer. They knew you were coming, you see. They could have fled. Could have taken us to safety, perhaps. But they wouldn't abandon their posts. Their duties. So they hid us."

Squeya shook her great head. "We were adolescents, too young to fight. They shoved us into a food storage unit. It was so cold. So cold."

Squero squeezed her arm. "We almost died there. Maybe we should have. Maybe we were meant to. All I know is that we could see out. You see, the units have a glass panel on the front so you can see what they contain without opening them and releasing the cold. We could see out, so we did. And we watched you murder our parents.

"You killed them, and their colleagues, then you went through the temple and slew every priest, every man, woman, and even child of the religious caste.

"When you finished, you turned around and walked back out. And we saw you, from our frozen little hiding place. We saw you walk by, the white wings on your back stained red with our blood."

His hand was shaking, as were those of the other two Tolone'ans.

Rohan ran his hands over his stubbly hair. "Okay. So you're here to give me fair warning. I guess."

Squeya spat. "We are here to make you afraid, Hybrid. Not to give warning, not to be fair. We are here so you know that while you are safe for the next few days, now that we've found you, we will never stop hunting you.

"You will die by our hands. And as I said, so will everyone you love."

Rohan exhaled slowly, then held his lungs empty for a count of four. *I should have some kind of comeback for this.*

"I understand."

Squero shook in place, his rage as palpable as his sister's. "Is that all you have to say for yourself?"

Rohan sighed. "What could I possibly say that would make any difference? Look, talking my way out of things is sort of my brand. It's why Nurse Kraken hates me so much. Well, that and the fact that I maimed him and almost killed him."

Squeya shook her head. "You owe us better than that."

You owe them your best shot. And then some.

"Do I? I mean, yes, sure I do. I guess. But look at what you've been saying. I mean, really think about it. What do I owe you? Based on what you said, I think I owe you a lot. Way, way more than I could ever repay. Right? So what's the point?"

"Tell us . . . something."

"I can tell you all sorts of things. They're all going to sound like excuses. Will that make you feel better? I really, seriously doubt it. But, sure, I'll give it a try, since you asked so pleasantly.

"The fact is, the il'Drach are your enemy, not me. I was a bullet. They pointed the gun, metaphorically, and pulled the trigger. I had no choice but to do what I did. They wanted your rebellion stopped. The priests were churning out Powers just like you guys at a rate the Hybrids couldn't handle. And the il'Drach are not in the business of losing wars.

"So they sent me in. Why me, you ask? That's a terrible question, don't ask that, you won't like the answer.

"Anyway, I'm there, and it doesn't take long to realize that we can't win the way we normally do. Like I said, the priests could make new Powers as fast as we could kill them. I lost three Hybrids in the early days. Friends. Well, not friends, two of them were okay, Earl was kind of a jerk. Forget about Earl.

"I had to cut off the supply of new Powers at the source." He looked into Squeya's eyes, then into Squero's, then into those of the third Tolone'an who had yet to speak. "Do you know what 'source' means in this context? I had exactly three choices.

"I could kill every single Tolone'an child.

"Or every single Tolone'an priest.

"Or I could fail. I could let you kill or capture me and let the il'Drach decide there was no way to defeat the Tolone'ans."

Squero nodded. "Yes. Yes. That is what an honorable man would have done. A man with a conscience. A man with a soul."

Rohan shrugged. "If you say so. But if I had done that, you guys wouldn't have been around to enjoy the outcome."

"What do you mean?"

"I mean that the il'Drach would have destroyed your world from space. Killed every last member of your species. Obliterated Tolone'a and every Tolone'an from the sector. Fifty years from now, the word would be gone from the language, your system unvisited. That was the third choice.

"You see, the only reason you're here, alive, able to threaten to kill all my friends and destroy everything I love is *because* I killed your parents with my bare hands."

Squeya and Squero faced each other, their faces inscrutable as they stared into one another's eyes.

The third Tolone'an put her tentacles on their shoulders.

After a long pause, Squeya turned to Rohan. "I cannot believe what you are saying. It is too convenient. You left our world to the full glory of the il'Drach. Your name was lauded; your praises sung in every corner of the sector. The Conqueror, they called you. Parades were thrown for you."

"I remember. I don't think I enjoyed them very much."

"That isn't good enough!" She was shouting, leaning forward, her tentacles snaking in front of her, reaching for Rohan.

Squero pulled her back. "Not now. We need the weapon to fight the Empire."

Rohan sighed. "I told you it wouldn't help. You don't want to believe me? Go talk to some Ohnians. One is still in the tournament. Ask him how he feels about the capriciousness of the il'Drach."

Squeya shook her head. "You lie to save yourself and your friends. You lie for your own conscience, so you can claim to be other than a monster."

Rohan held his hands up. "Whoa, hold on there. I never said I wasn't a monster. I just said I had *reasons* for my . . . monstrosity. No, wait. That didn't come out right."

Squero pulled his sister back. "We should go. This isn't helping. He's been warned. He will live his last days knowing our vengeance is coming. Knowing that we will come for his people, that their suffering will go on long after he is gone."

Rohan shook his head at them. "You don't want to do this. You really don't. See, I feel guilty about what happened on your world. I do. Even though, like I said, I had reasons.

"And maybe, just maybe, I feel guilty enough that I'd roll over and let you kill me. Or hurt me a lot. Sometimes I'm dumb like that.

"But there is no way, absolutely none, that I will lie down and let you walk over me to get to the people I care about.

"So if you make this about them, and you stick to that, you're going to put me in a place where I ignore my better side. Where I stop listening to my conscience.

"And when that happens? You *think* you've seen a monster. You haven't.

"Not yet.

"But you will."

Squeya stepped forward, but Squero pulled her back again. "Come. Let's go. This accomplishes nothing."

She pointed at Rohan. "This conversation isn't over."

He shrugged and pointed to her tentacles. "You know where I live. Once you unpucker your suckers, stop by for another chat."

The curtain of flesh around her neck flapped as she huffed angrily, giving off a raspberry sound.

She turned and stormed away.

27

And That's Why People Have Kids

R ohan slept poorly; he woke damp with sweat, the echoes of violent dreams bouncing around inside his skull in time with the alarm.

He showered, wishing the water would do more to soothe the injuries he'd accumulated in the previous few days.

I miss healing fast. These bruises just seem to be getting worse.

The Hybrid exhaled, relaxed his shoulders, and built his magical construct.

Drew a line of energy.

Anchored the ends.

Twisted it into the shape of a spring.

Watched to ensure it retained its form.

Structure is intact. Now I just have to keep it that way while going about my daily business. It doesn't help me if I lose it every time I experience any strong feelings.

Or even if I lose it every time I feel any fear.

He checked his messages and news feeds.

Ben Stone invited him to breakfast to discuss the Boost detector; he checked the start time for round three of the tournament and clicked that he would attend.

Ohj and Vade of Con-Conspiracy spent eleven minutes discussing Rohan's participation in the tournament.

Ohj thought it was proof that Rohan had lost his Power; after all, why else would he even be in the tournament?

Vade argued that it proved he still had them; after all, without Powers, how would the Hybrid have any chance at victory?

Rohan sighed and tabbed away from the discussion. Before he could close the feed, he spotted another news story.

A reporter from Shayjh reported that Hyperion and his associates had attacked and stolen a stealth-equipped battleship.

That's not good.

Rohan sat on his bed and tapped at his mask, searching for other sources verifying the story or reporting on the efficacy of stealth technology on a ship that size.

Nothing reliable popped up, and after ten minutes his comm beeped, warning him that he was going to be late to meet Ben; he closed the app and headed out the door.

Turning onto the promenade, he nearly collided with a double stroller pushed by a stern-faced Purkatan, her tail twitching upward in irritation.

Rohan froze.

Does she recognize me? Have the Tolone'ans been spreading stories?

The woman angled the stroller away from him and stormed off.

Or is she just annoyed that I almost ran over her kids?

He moved closer to the wide open center of the promenade and made his way to *Insatiable*.

———•———

A savory smell greeted Rohan before any of *Insatiable*'s biological inhabitants had a chance to; the kind of smell that made his mouth water and permeated his clothes and skin to an extent that he was sure he'd exude it for days after leaving.

He entered the cafeteria room, smiling as he watched Ben Stone, white apron tied around his jumpsuit, tending to a griddle with a spatula in one hand and long tongs in the other.

Garren stood next to the Professor, and two other students stood and left as Rohan entered, nodding and smiling to the Hybrid.

Ben waved him over. "Come, come! I need you to try something. Well, some things."

Rohan swallowed. "What fresh devilry is this, Dr. Stone? I was expecting donuts."

Ben laughed. "I think I got the donuts down pretty well, don't you? Time for a new challenge! Besides, well, you can say that you can never have too many donuts, but in fact . . ." He patted his belly, still trim at his advanced age, and smiled.

Rohan shrugged. "Fair enough. Though if you're worried about your waistline, I'm not sure this is going to be an improvement. Assuming that's what it smells like."

"It is. Well, almost. I haven't gone so far as importing actual Earth swine, but we have six different cuts, from four different planets, that are all very promising candidates."

Garren pointed at the griddle. "He's cooking from three of the samples, but there are some ready right over there."

Rohan walked over and pointed at the plate where long, skinny strips of meat were resting on absorbent towels. "May I?"

"That's what you're here for!"

The Hybrid picked up one strip and bit into it; the outside was cooked just shy of blackening; crispy and caramelized and carrying a subtle hint of grease.

Ben studied his face as he bit into it.

Rohan's eyes widened. "If you're telling me that's not real bacon, I'm calling you a liar."

Ben smiled and nodded. "Pretty good, isn't it? That particular cut is from . . . let me see . . . Garren?"

The Powered Tolone'an, dressed in a simple student uniform instead of his gravity-controlling armor, checked a tablet resting on a table several meters away from the griddle. "That's Andervarian, Professor."

"Ah, yes. We have two from Andervar, one from a heritage domesticated animal, another from a wild game they still hunt."

Rohan wolfed down the strip. "I'll never understand how there are any skinny Andervarians. Everything on that planet is delicious."

"Don't you own a chain of distilleries there, Rohan? I think that claim is a bit self-serving."

The Hybrid shrugged. "Maybe. Doesn't mean it's not true. But seriously, I assume you didn't invite me here to test bacon strips."

Ben turned to Garren. "Not entirely. Garren, can you call Marion in?"

The Tolone'an's tentacles waved in the air as he nodded. "I'll do it." He tapped at the tablet while Rohan ate another strip of bacon.

Ben moved the cooking strips to a clean plate and motioned the Hybrid to a table. "We can sit and wait for her. I have coffee."

Two minutes later, his wife stepped through the door.

Almost as tall as Rohan, Marion Stone still had the striking bone structure that had led to a brief career as a pinup model in her sidekick days.

She joined the men at the table and pointed at the plate. "Worth trying?"

Ben nodded to his wife. "You tell me. But I think it is."

She picked up a piece and leaned back into the chair. "Now I remember why I married you."

"Only now?"

She shrugged. "How about, especially now?"

"I'll take it!"

Rohan sipped his coffee. "What's going on, guys?"

Marion sighed. "We've been working on the Boost detector. I have good news and bad news."

"Can we skip the bad news? Not a fan."

Garren snorted through moist slits near his neck. "It's not terrible."

Marion shook her head. "We can build a Boost detector. Knowing its origin gives us the hook."

Rohan looked from her to Garren and back. "What does that mean?"

Garren made gestures in the air with his hands and tentacles that didn't make any sense to Rohan. "The math is . . . complicated. To simplify, the mass of objects that come from source-ward of our plane of existence doesn't behave like the mass of native objects."

Rohan sighed. "You lost me at 'math.' What do you mean 'doesn't behave'?"

Marion swallowed her bite of bacon. "Dear, this is delicious. Rohan, the thing is, mass means an object's resistance to acceleration, right? The more mass, the more force it takes to change something's velocity."

"Yes. I mean, sure. I think. I took that class. In high school. Fifteen years ago."

"Mass also determines the strength of an object's gravitational pull. The more mass, the higher the force of gravity."

Rohan rubbed his forehead. "I knew that. Except when we generate an artificial gravity source, right? Like in a bootstrap drive."

Garren nodded. "Exactly. We can create artificial gravity sources that have no mass."

Marion shook her head. "Not no mass, just very little."

Garren sighed. "Yes, Professor. That's what I meant. Very little."

Marion looked at Rohan. "It's almost zero, really. Might as well be none."

Rohan swallowed. "Then why did you correct him?"

"He's still my student, Rohan. Can't have him using sloppy language. For your sake, though, you can think of them as massless."

Rohan smiled at her. "Got it. What does this have to do with Boost?"

Marion nodded for Garren to continue; he did. "Objects from other planes often have a discrepancy. When something is here from source-ward, it has a smaller gravitational field than is warranted by its inertial mass. The values diverge."

Rohan cracked his neck and pondered. "Diverge how much?"

"Very little, unfortunately. Or fortunately. If you could get a big enough lump of something that behaved differently relative to inertia than to gravity, you might see some unusual effects. But never mind that. It's a very small difference, almost immeasurable."

Marion nodded. "'Almost' is the key word in that sentence."

Rohan tapped the table. "Can someone bottom line this for me? Do we have a working detector?"

Marion shrugged. "Yes and no. I assume you were hoping for something like a Geiger counter."

Rohan swallowed. "That thing that counts horror artists?"

Ben patted Rohan's shoulder. "Geiger. E-I. Not H.R. Giger. The boxes that detect radiation."

"Right. I knew that. Just testing you guys."

Marion sighed. "I wish you were as funny as you thought you were."

"Me too."

"Anyway, you wanted something you could carry around the station, correct? Well, we can't do that."

Garren nodded. "You see, we can only detect this variance by surrounding an object with a gravity nullification field, measuring its own gravitational force inside that field, then applying an external force. It can be done in a very subtle way, but only in space."

"So . . . no, I don't follow. How would that work?"

Ben pointed at Marion. "My wife has a device you could use in space. Suppose a ship is coming to the station, powered down. We have a device you could use to determine whether that ship had any source-ward materials on board."

"So not detecting Boost specifically, but . . ."

Garren nodded furiously and waved his hands in the air. "It's actually really wonderful engineering. To calibrate the fields to detect such a small variance without applying a large external force, Professor Stone had to—"

Marion put her hand over his and forced it to the table. "Garren, Rohan doesn't care about the details. He would also never understand the details. But yes, Rohan, it's actually a detector for source-ward materials, but they are quite rare, so it should in effect tell us which ships are carrying Boost."

Rohan nodded slowly. "We're assuming that it's coming from somewhere else."

Ben looked at him. "You suspect otherwise?"

"Not exactly. I just want to be clear on the assumptions. This thing is subtle enough to use on ships without them noticing?"

Garren shook his head. "Probably not. But we can pass it off as an innocuous scan. They'll know we're pinging them but not exactly why or for what purpose."

The Hybrid ran his fingers through his hair. "This is great. Not exactly what I wanted, but a lot more than I had a few days ago. Thanks."

Ben nodded. "It won't really do anything on the station, though, Rohan. We know there's Boost somewhere on Wistful. The detector won't narrow it down any further than that. It won't tell us where on the station we can find the drug."

"Then I'll have to figure out something else for that." He picked up another slice of bacon and bit into it.

⬥ ⋯⬥

Rohan found Rinth Lastex on the promenade, playing a game that involved hitting heavy wooden balls with a long-handled mallet. More croquet than golf. The boy had set up a small course on the grass and was diligently practicing tricky shots.

"Hey, Rinth."

"Oh hey, Uncle Rohan."

The Hybrid stood and watched as the young Lukhor took several more shots.

Rinth sighed and looked up. "Why are you watching me, Uncle Rohan? Is something going on?"

The Hybrid sighed. "You ever want to ask someone for something, but you weren't sure you *should*?"

Rinth shrugged shoulders just starting to bud with muscle. "No. Adults are the ones who make things complicated. If you want something, ask for it. If the other person doesn't want to give it to you, they can say no. Then it's your job not to whine about it or make a fuss. That's it."

"But what if the other person might say yes, but you're not sure they should?"

"Why not? Maybe this would be easier for you to explain if I knew what you were talking about, Uncle Rohan."

Rohan sighed. "I need . . . no, I guess I want a favor. From you. And I'm not sure I should ask."

"Is it going to get me in trouble?"

Rohan bent over and picked up one of the croquet balls, tossing it in the air to get a feel for its heft. "I don't think so. But maybe. Part of the favor is me asking you to help me figure that out."

Rinth exhaled loudly. "Mom said you always overthink things, but I wasn't really paying attention. She wasn't kidding!"

"Your mom said that?"

"Oh yeah. A bunch of times. I'm not sure I was supposed to tell you, though. Let's keep that between us. She always says it with a big huff and a huge sigh, and I have to give her a hug to make her feel better after."

"Right. Sure. Huh." *Do I?*

Who am I kidding, of course I do.

Rinth nodded sagely and pointed at Rohan. "You might as well tell me what you're thinking about. We've all seen this before, and once you get started on a topic, there's no way you're ever just going to realize you shouldn't have said anything and walk away. Right? So spill it."

"You think? I guess you're right."

"You don't have to feel bad. We all know you thought long and hard about this before talking to me, weighing all your options, considering every alternative. You don't have to go through all of it with me. Just go ahead and ask me for the favor. You want me to say something to Mom? Maybe about us moving in with you? Tell her I don't want to, so she stops pressuring you?"

"What? No. Nothing like that."

Rinth turned to face the Hybrid. "Really? Nothing like that?"

"No. Nothing to do with your mom. And how did you even know about that, anyway? You weren't supposed to know yet."

"Try to keep up, Uncle Rohan. I always know this stuff. It's my . . . what do you call it?"

"Your brand?"

Rinth snapped his fingers. "Yes! My brand. I don't know what that means, but I like it. If it's not about Mom, then what? Is it about Grandpa? You want me to get him to leave you alone? More alone?"

"Not him either."

"Dad, then?"

Rohan sighed. "No." He exhaled and held up a finger. "Wait. Let me explain."

"Finally."

"Nobody likes a smartass."

Rinth wrinkled his nose at the older man. "Then how do you have any—"

"Don't say it! Is this what I sound like to other people?"

"Pretty much, yeah."

Rohan took a deep breath, let it out. Rinth watched him with calm eyes. "Okay. Here's the thing. You know how to hack your father's camera system, right?"

"Sure, that's easy. The tricky part isn't breaking into the camera streams, it's the storage and the algorithms that let you process all that data. I mean, if you want to find somebody, unless they're sitting in one room all the time, one camera won't do, so you have to hijack part of the processing array—"

"Okay, okay, I get it. Just . . . spare me the details, okay? I'm sure you know what you're doing. The question I have is, how risky is that for you? Let's say I ask you to follow someone."

"You mean through the camera system or in person?"

"Cameras only. I want to know where someone goes. What's the risk profile? How dangerous is that for you?"

Rinth rubbed his chin. "Do you mean what are the chances my dad finds out, or what are the chances these other people can trace it back to me?"

"The second one. I'm not worried about your dad; he might get annoyed, but he's not going to hurt you. Right?"

"Right. The chance that someone else will catch me is basically zero. They'd have to be smarter than me, and, well, how would that even be possible? Maybe if it was Mom. She's wicked smart. Don't tell her I said that."

"It stays between us. Okay, that's a good start. Second question. Would you do me a favor and track someone for me?"

"Who? And why?"

Rohan sighed. "They're selling Boost. I'm trying to stop them, or at least find out where they're getting it from, and I need some help."

Rinth nodded. "Is this about Dad using that stuff?"

"Actually, no. I mean yes, but also no. I was going after the Boost dealers before Lahnegarn got involved."

"Okay. What do you want me to do?"

"You back in school yet?"

"No, I'm on vacation. All week."

"Great. I'm going to give you a description. This dealer has been poking around the back rooms at the tournament. I want you to see if you can figure out where he goes, who he talks to. Track him to his supplier. Do you think you can do that?"

Rinth paused and tapped his chin again. "Pretty sure I can. What's in it for me?"

Rohan smiled. "What do you want?"

"You never got me those Ursan war gauntlets."

The Hybrid sighed. "Really? You still want those? Your mother will never let you keep them. And you'll get me in trouble."

"You let me worry about hiding the gauntlets. Now, do you want the Boost dealer followed, or not?"

"I do."

"Then you know what to do."

"Can we negotiate? Isn't there anything else you want? Money? A ride on a starship?"

Rinth paused. "Nah. Just the gauntlets."

"Okay. I'll see what I can do."

"It's almost bedtime, Uncle Rohan. I'll do it when I get up."

"Deal. Thanks, buddy."

28

The Bloodless Round

The crowd around the arena had grown as the one inside had shrunk.

Word of the tournament had spread through a variety of media, and interest had grown to the point where journalists and would-be tough people of all genders and species hovered near the entrance, eager for any interaction with the competitors.

Once inside, Rohan realized the number of fighters had thinned considerably. Wei Li had remained true to her promise to eliminate contestants liberally, and only a third of those who had started were still eligible.

Ang limped over to the Hybrid and put a heavy paw on his shoulder. "War Chief. Is good seeing you."

"Ang. I have a favor to ask."

"Of course."

"Do your gauntlets come in smaller sizes? Like, a training version? For cubs?"

"War gauntlets? Being with chains, blades, guns, and many spikes?"

"Yeah, those."

"Of course is for cubs! Is how Ang lost eye." The big Ursan pointed to his prosthesis.

Rohan swallowed. "Really?"

Ang leaned his head back and barked three times. "No, that is longer story. Is for young Rinth?"

"Yeah. I promised him and I don't think I'm getting out of it this time."

"Will see what can be done. Come, now is time for fighting."

Katya sauntered over and stroked Ang's chest. "It is lucky the contest is not one of handsomeness, Rohan, or you would surely lose, and my Ang would be the victor over all."

The Hybrid sighed. "I don't think a beauty contest was ever on the table. Besides, do you really think I'm uglier than all these other people? Even the hairless mammals? I thought this was a fur-no-fur thing with you."

"Oh, Rohan, it is sad how you attempt to make excuses for your short-comings. I do think you might be the ugliest one here. But it is fine, Tamara loves you for some other reason I cannot quite fathom, and she is a more than adequate mate for one such as you."

"Thanks. Very kind."

Ang patted Katya's furry shoulder. "Be more nicely to War Chief, Katya. Is sensitive being."

"I am sorry, Rohan. Of course. I am too honest for my own good."

"I think it's *my* own good that's at risk here. Anyway, what's the first round?"

Katya looked at the boards. "Still blank."

Wei Li took the stage and held up the microphone. The crowd quieted as they awaited instructions.

Rohan stepped closer, drawn to Master Turtle's calming presence.

I wish I could absorb whatever secret he has to being so calm.

Wei Li tapped the microphone and spoke. "Thank you for your attention. As you know, round three is about to commence." She paused and surveyed the room. "After two rounds, all fighters with two losses are gone. No fighters can be eliminated in this round by their record. However, should any of you violate the spirit of this contest, you will be declared ineligible to continue."

A voice rang out from the crowd. "Violate it how?"

"By giving it anything less than your best. And before you ask, yes, that is completely at my discretion. I would ask whether you understand, but, to put it simply, I do not care.

"After the round, there will be a short rest break, then a brief elimination test before the fourth round commences.

"Next to me you see a pair of jars. They are sealed, and made of single-facet diamond. Inside each jar is a bell.

"Each contestant will have to ring the bell without touching the jar. Any who fail to do so within a sixty-second window will be eliminated.

"Check the boards for your assignments. We begin the bloodless round in five minutes." The large boards above the back row of seats began to light up.

Rohan looked at the big Ursan next to him. Ang nodded his massive head.

"How do you feel about this one, big guy?"

Ang shrugged his massive shoulders. "Have never managed such a feat before, War Chief. Never. So now thinking, today will be first time."

"It's a test of esoteric Power, Ang."

Ang reached out and squeezed the Hybrid's shoulder. "Worry less and ready yourself more, War Chief."

"Okay, then."

Rohan looked up at the boards and searched for his name.

Ang grunted. "War Chief, are fighting Krai Wu."

Rohan sighed. "Am I? I guess I am. And we're fourth."

Ang grunted again. "Am first. Surprised."

"So you are. Good luck, big guy."

Ang stood and stretched his arm, joints popping and crackling as he moved, loud enough to startle fighters seated nearby. "Wish luck on opponent, War Chief."

Rohan checked the board; Ang was fighting the remaining Ohnian.

Oh boy.

Rohan felt restless, so he stood to watch the fight. With only forty or so fighters left, they were all in the first two rows, so he wasn't blocking anybody's view.

Ang dwarfed the Ohnian, who didn't seem to have the training or experience to handle an opponent so much larger and stronger than himself.

The referee pointed at them and commanded, "Begin."

Ang set his eyes on the Ohnian, lowered his hips, and launched his body forward.

The smaller man tried to sidestep the charge, obviously imagining the Ursan would be slower on the move.

He was wrong.

Ang caught the Ohnian with one flat palm dead center on the chest; the blow sent the man stumbling back.

Ang turned, his right leg buckling slightly with the strain, and roared as he charged after the falling man.

The Ohnian caught himself and threw a low kick at Ang's injured leg.

That's actually a smart move. He's paying attention. I'm not sure it's going to be enough.

Ang roared again with the impact, but the leg held despite the esoteric energy the Ohnian had poured into his shin.

Ang managed to place his massive paws over the man's shoulders and grab on, locking the Ohnian in his grip.

The Ursan bared his teeth and gave his opponent one violent shake back and forth; just as the man's eyes rolled up, Ang leaned forward and fell over onto him.

The Ohnian hit the ground with a slap like a bag of rice falling off the top shelf of a warehouse.

The Ursan landed on top of him.

He caught his weight on his elbows and knees.

If he hadn't, he might have killed that guy.

Good for you, Ang.

The referee waited a moment to see if the Ohnian was struggling against the Ursan's bulk; he was not.

"Ang is the winner."

Ang huffed and pushed himself to a kneeling position, lifting his weight off the Ohnian.

Wei Li called up from her seat at the side of the platform. "You may ask your question."

Ang cocked his head for a moment, then shrugged. "Will you be for ringing of bell?"

The Ohnian sat up, his single eye wide open as he stared at the five-hundred-kilogram behemoth who had just smothered him. "You mean will I be able to?"

"Yes."

The Ohnian breathed deeply. "It will be easy. I have been training in this sort of thing for my entire life."

Ang nodded and offered a hand to the smaller man. The Ohnian took it, and Ang effortlessly hauled him to his feet.

Katya came close to the pair. Ang looked at her. "Will be needing some help, Katya-le. Leg is not being so good."

She frowned and rushed in to offer him a shoulder. The Ohnian stepped back, surprised, and watched her help her man away.

Wei Li looked at him. "Clear the stage, please. It's time for the next fight."

The Ohnian nodded. "I'll see if I can help him."

"As long as you leave the platform."

━━━ ··•·· ━━━

Rohan began walking toward the stage during the third fight when a wall of scales appeared, blocking his path.

"Sirc! When are you fighting?"

She grinned. "Tenth round. I see you're fighting the Vor'karei?"

He shrugged. "I guess I am."

"Isn't he close to your friend, the security chief?"

Rohan coughed. "Pretty close. At least, he used to be."

Her grin widened, scaly lips parting to reveal a glimpse of a forked tongue and sharp teeth. "The question I have is whether she matched you up to punish him or to punish you."

Rohan paused. "That's an excellent question. You going to give me a chance to win back what I owe you? A bet?"

She hissed, a sound he was beginning to associate with Takslee laughter. "Always. Ten thousand on the Vor'karei. He's too smooth for you."

Rohan sighed. "It wouldn't be reasonable for me to bet against myself, would it?"

She shrugged. "You can't throw the fight without being kicked out of the tournament, so it's not a crazy idea. Are you looking to do that?"

"Nah. Ten thousand on me." He held out a hand; she shook it. "If I win, how will you pay? You don't have any cash."

"How do you know?"

He cocked his head. "You don't seem the type to ever hold on to credits. Tell me I'm wrong."

She hissed again. "You're not wrong. What's your point?"

"Once you owe me thirty thousand, I'll have to take another form of payment."

"Are you sexually harassing me, mammal?"

"No! Not *that* kind of payment. Why do people always think that?"

She shrugged. "What was it you said? You seem the type."

"I'm not! Really! I have a girlfriend."

"Sure you do. On your home planet, right? And she sends you tachyon bursts every day. Real love letters."

"No—we're getting off track. I meant information. I want information."

"I'll answer whatever you want. Once I owe you *fifty* thousand."

"Done."

They shook, and Rohan walked around her wide body and approached the judges' area.

Mai Si had her notebook out as she traced the writing inside with a fingertip. Master Turtle stared right at Rohan, his lips parted slightly.

Rohan looked at the woman. "I'm about to fight your partner."

She nodded. "So you will understand if I don't wish you good luck."

"I just . . . you know I don't really want to fight him."

"I understand tournaments and fights, Rohan. Do your best. I know you will, because you cannot risk elimination, can you?"

"I really can't." Rohan stepped closer to Master Turtle, leaning toward the old man and soaking in the peaceful aura he exuded. "That still amazes me."

"Me as well. Now go, don't make Wei Li impatient."

"No." He looked at the writing one last time, wishing he could decipher the clusters of alien symbols, then leapt up onto the stage.

Krai Wu stood ready for their fight. Katya had returned and was acting as backup to the referee.

Rohan cracked his neck and rolled his shoulders to loosen them. He squatted down, touching glutes to heels, and pushed his knees out to the side to stretch his hips.

The Hybrid bounced on his toes and breathed deeply, pulling a bit of warmth into his system.

Krai Wu watched him with vertically slit eyes, double-blinking as he studied Rohan's motions.

"She trained you."

"Why, hello to you too, Krai Wu. Nice to see you again. How am I? Fine, fine. How are you? How are the kids? Do you have kids, Krai Wu? I never got all the details on your little situationship."

The Vor'karei snorted. "Is this your way of distracting your opponents?"

Rohan shrugged. "Actually, yeah. You'd be surprised at how often it works, too. I'm very annoying. Wei Li says it's my greatest talent."

"If she says it, then it must be true. I will do my best to resist the urge to anger."

"Oh, come on. You can get a *little* angry. What's the worst that can happen?"

The Vor'karei stepped back with his right leg and extended his left hand straight out from the shoulder, fingers pointing up at Toth 3, palm facing Rohan. "I am ready."

Rohan looked at the referee, who nodded. "Begin."

The Hybrid flung himself at the martial arts master.

He led with Wei Li's favorite combinations.

Left jab, right straight, right head kick. Bring the foot down into a right-foot-forward stance.

Right double jab, right hook, spinning sweep with the right leg.

Krai Wu anticipated the moves, blocking and sidestepping as appropriate. If he was shaken by the Hybrid's speed or strength, he didn't show it.

He finished the sequence with a palm strike that landed on Rohan's chest just as the Hybrid finished his spin.

Rohan stumbled back two steps and caught his balance as the other man closed with a sequence of hooks—left, right, then left, followed immediately by two round kicks and a final flying knee straight up the center.

Rohan blocked them all, absorbing the impact of the knee with his esoteric spring.

Krai Wu's eyes widened with the last move.

He senses something is strange but . . . I don't think he knows what it is.

"I'm faster and stronger than you, Krai Wu."

"You do not yet know the extent of my physical abilities, Hybrid. But I will admit that you are impressive."

Rohan rushed him again.

The reptile stood his ground through three, five, eight, ten moves; he blocked and pivoted but refused to retreat.

What he didn't have time for, however, was to counter.

Rohan's breath came faster and faster through his dry throat. At fifteen techniques, he had to step back and reset.

Krai Wu came for him; he was slowed, however, the edge of his speed shaved off by the effort it had taken to survive Rohan's attacks.

Rohan pivoted and stepped away, avoiding damage but unable to deliver any of his own.

The men reset their stances and faced each other.

Krai Wu pointed at Rohan's feet. "Your moves are predictable, Hybrid. This will be over soon."

Rohan shrugged. "I've lost track of the number of people who have told me that. I've also lost count of how many of them are resting in their graves right now."

"You take pride in the murders you've committed?"

"Not pride exactly. Just warning you. And, you know, catching my breath. People just don't—"

He leapt forward mid-sentence.

This might take him by surprise. Nobody expects—oh. That didn't work.

Krai Wu sidestepped Rohan's attack and responded with a knife hand strike to the back of the Hybrid's head that put a ringing in his ears.

Rohan twisted into a hook to the body that threw the reptile to one side, then a wide round kick that caught him from the other.

The Vor'karei grunted at the impact; a drop of blood crawled down out of the corner of his mouth.

Rohan pointed. "Almost over."

"We shall see."

Krai Wu attacked.

He slid in, footwork so smooth his feet seemed to glide along the floor. His fists snapped out, almost no motion at his shoulders giving away the direction or speed of his punches.

One foot flicked up from the floor, effortlessly, the tip of his toes cracking into Rohan's temple like the tip of a bullwhip.

The Hybrid resisted the instinct to retreat.

Time to make this ugly.

He stepped in, close to the Vor'karei, and rammed his forehead into the man's slit nose.

Krai Wu stumbled back, off balance, not having expected Rohan to be so close.

The Hybrid stepped with him, sticking almost chest-to-chest, and swung his right elbow across the Vor'karei's chin.

Krai Wu's head twisted to the side.

Another elbow, this one landing on the man's neck, stunning him.

Krai Wu reached out and grabbed Rohan's waist with one hand, setting his feet and readying for a throw.

Rohan grabbed him back, widening his stance and resisting the twist that would have sent a less stable fighter to the ground.

He shoved with one hand and pulled with the other, turning Krai Wu around, and slapped the back of the man's neck with an open palm.

Krai Wu bent forward at the waist.

Rohan stayed behind him, dropping an elbow into the reptilian's kidney.

Then the other kidney.

The Vor'karei's knees buckled.

Rohan lifted one knee to his chest and stomped into the bend in Krai Wu's leg.

The man went down.

Rohan shoved as he went, adding momentum so the reptilian's chest hit the ground.

The Hybrid landed on the taller man's back, completely flattening him out, facedown in the clay surface of the arena.

He looked at the referee, ready to do more damage if she refused to stop the fight, but she stepped forward.

"Winner: Rohan."

29

Fair Play

R ohan met Wei Li's eyes.

Her flat expression didn't show surprise or disappointment or sadness. They also didn't show any joy.

"Ask your question, Rohan."

The Hybrid cleared his throat and watched as Krai Wu gingerly rose to his feet, Katya right behind him, waiting for an untoward move.

The Vor'karei nodded. "Ask your question, savage."

Rohan laughed at the insult. "You're a martial artist. I'm a warrior. Different things. Unfortunately, the rules for this thing are in my favor. Don't blame me for playing by them."

Krai Wu nodded. "As you say. Ask your question."

Rohan exhaled slowly. "What do you really think the prophecy means?"

The taller man shook his hairless head. "Which one?"

"When open eyes become The Shield. What do you really think it means?"

"I meant what I said before, Hybrid. When the eyes—the wormholes—open, then eyes—meaning the Watchers—become The Shield. The Guardians of this station, and the planet above, and all the designs the Lifters left behind to save us from the terrors between the stars."

"But you're no Watcher. Why are you even doing this? If you win the tournament, you'll get the Eternity Ki. But you don't believe you're supposed to have it."

Wei Li cleared her throat. "You answered the question, Krai Wu. You have satisfied the rules of the tournament."

He shook his head. "I don't mind. You see, Hybrid, I know where the Eternity Ki is supposed to be. I will win this tournament and be a host for as long as I need to be. Until The Watcher accepts her role and takes it from me."

"Which will kill you."

"Better me than someone else. And better me than someone who would refuse to give it up."

Rohan sighed. "Well, you're a true believer, I guess. I have to respect that. At least a little."

"And you are as much a warrior as Wei Li said. A true Guardian."

The Hybrid shook his head. "I'm not sure of all that. But, you know, who do you want protecting the station, after all? You want the warrior. The rough and tumble guy. Don't you?"

The Vor'karei nodded. "I suppose so. If any were to beat me, I am glad it is you."

Wei Li cleared her throat. "Off the stage. We have more fights to come."

Krai Wu unwound to his feet and walked off the other side of the stage as Rohan turned and went back to his seat.

He approached Sirc. "Any sign of Ang?"

The big reptile shrugged her heavy shoulders. "I think he's getting medical attention. I should join him."

"You're hurt?"

"Only my pride and my credit. I owe you twenty thousand now."

"I told you, I'll cancel the debt for—"

"I know, I know. And I told you, wait until I owe you fifty. I mean if. If I should owe you fifty. Which I won't, because I'm winning the next round."

"Who are we betting on?"

"I'm betting on myself. I'm up against that Lukhor you don't like."

"I don't—okay, fine. I don't like him. You're betting against him?"

"He's not a fighter, he's just enhanced. I can take him in my sleep."

"I'm not so sure. He's smart. And better trained than he has any right to be."

"You sound pretty sure of yourself. I assume that means you're taking the bet. Care to make it twenty thousand?"

Rohan considered.

"Done. Twenty thousand says Lonnie beats you. It's a sadness hedge."

She grinned. "Does that mean what I think it does?"

"Yeah. I want him to lose. This way, I get something either way. You win, I'm happy. He wins, at least I get the credits."

"Fair enough." They shook on it, his hand almost disappearing inside her scaly fist.

They took their seats to watch the next fights.

Squeya, leader of The Consortium, strongest of the Tolone'ans, faced off against a Kratic Power.

The pink-skinned Kratic, a female, *reached* to a water bucket by the side of the stage and *pulled* the water out into a jet that split in midair and froze into an array of seven spikes that hurtled toward the Tolone'an.

Squeya spread her tentacles and blew air across the skirt around her neck, vibrating the flesh in a rude noise that Rohan assumed was derogatory.

"You use water against me? Your ancestors crawled out of the water millions of years ago, exiting her warm embrace for the cold rewards of dead air. Mine stayed, and the water nurtured us ever since. It remembers us, not you."

She waved her arms, forming small circles in the air, and the ice spears splintered as if they had collided with a shield.

She stepped forward and waved her arms again.

The shards of ice rose from the stage and re-formed, then turned, their pointy ends facing the Kratic.

Squeya stamped her foot; the spikes flew toward the other Power, who covered her face with her arms and curled into a ball.

"Stop!"

The spikes fell to the ground before impaling the pink-skinned woman.

The referee pointed to Squeya. "Winner."

Wei Li stood. "Ask your question."

Squeya faced the Kratic. "Did you think you could defeat me with water? Me, a Tolone'an? A child of the seas?"

The Kratic shrugged. "I've seen you use your fists. I thought the water was my best chance."

"It was no chance at all, child."

She shrugged again. "Then that's what it was."

Squeya looked over at Rohan. "This will be your fate soon enough."

Rohan smiled at her but said nothing.

Sirc looked down at him as the two water wielders climbed off the stage. "I'm surprised you resisted the urge to banter with her."

He sighed. "I've lost my appetite for it. At least with her. She has good reasons to be angry with me. Tormenting her about it just seems . . . wrong."

"She seems to really hate you. Do you think being kind will win her over?"

"Not really."

"Oh well. I was going to see if you'd lay a wager on it."

"Not this one. Hey, the Quattro is fighting."

"Let's watch."

Sirc's turn came shortly after.

Lonnie ascended the stairs to the stage with a confident walk that looked nothing like the man Rohan had first met a year earlier.

He's moving differently even from yesterday. How is that possible?

Sirc stood across from the Lukhor and swung her fists in tight hooks through the air, twisting at the waist as she did it, warming up her body.

Lahnegarn pushed his head to either side with his palms, to stretch his neck, and dropped into a half-squat to loosen his hips.

Rohan opened his Third Eye; colorful bolts of energy cycling through the Lukhor's aura told him that the man was using Boost.

A lot of Boost.

He's going to burn out. But if he wins the contest, he'll get the Eternity Ki. So he's risking everything for this.

Why?

Just to one-up me?

Sirc towered over the man, but he didn't seem fazed in the slightest.

She nodded to him. "You're taking a gamble, with the things you're doing. And I should know, I'm a gambler."

He shrugged. "It's only a gamble if you don't understand the odds. I know exactly what I'm doing."

"Do you? I see you, boy. You think you're the first one to discover Boost? The first one to use forced hypno-training to get an edge?"

Rohan stiffened. *Is that what he's doing? That's dangerous.*

Lahnegarn shrugged. "Not everyone is born with the same . . . advantages. If there are ways to catch up, I'm going to take them. And I'll prove they work."

"That stuff will mess with your mind, boy. Mess up your personality. I've seen it. I used to compete, yeah?"

"Compete at what? Wasting time talking?"

She chuckled. "I was this close to the championship. This close."

"And now you're here, fighting me. No cameras, no prize money, no audience. And you're giving me advice on how to live my life?"

She shrugged. "You want advice from the successful? That's a waste. Take advice from the losers, they'll point out all the big pitfalls. And I might be the biggest loser in this arena."

He laughed. "I like your attitude. That won't stop me from beating you senseless."

"Maybe. Care to make a wager on that?"

"It's not a fair wager when I know the outcome."

"I never asked for fair. Ten thousand credits says you're going to be crying my name when this is over."

Lahnegarn shook his head. "I'm not here for your money. Let's go."

She swarmed the smaller man, launching a volley of punches in combinations that would have confused even a more experienced fighter.

Double hooks alternating with left-right straights; soft jabs followed by thunderous crosses high and low, aimed over and under his guard.

As soon as he picked up the rhythm, she lifted a knee into his midsection, putting her considerable mass behind the blow.

Rohan blew out the breath he'd been holding and settled back from the edge of his seat. *This is intense.*

The Lukhor survived.

More than survived; he took very little damage from the blows and began to pepper his own jabs in between Sirc's strikes, sticking his left fist out, popping it into her chest or dead center on her face—a quick, snappy motion.

Each time, her head rocked back despite the thick muscles bunched around her neck.

There's more to those jabs than there should be:
He's putting Power behind them.

Sirc stepped back, inhaled deeply, and began rocking her head left and right, dipping her hips from side to side to make herself more of a moving target.

With a broken rhythm, she moved forward, her head and upper body bobbing randomly, and started popping little punches out at her shorter opponent.

Rohan found himself leaning from side to side in his seat, adopting her rhythm unconsciously.

Lahnegarn split his lips apart and gave her a fierce grin.

"Not bad."

She panted and nodded. "Not bad yourself. Where did you learn to box?"

He tapped the side of his head. "I have the best instructors from two dozen worlds right here."

She grunted. "That's cheating."

"Is it? I don't remember any rules against it."

"It's cheating in every sporting association in the sector."

"None of which are sanctioning this tournament. Come on, let's finish this."

Rohan's mask pinged.

He pulled it out and screened the message.

Tamara had sent it on a timer; as a nocturnal, it was the middle of her sleep cycle.

The message stated that she was still working on her project and wouldn't be able to see him that evening, but all was well.

Huh.

I guess as long as she's okay . . .

Unless 'working on a project' is code for 'is annoyed at me about that whole moving-in-together thing' . . .

Sirc moved forward again and tried to use her size and reach to push Lahnegarn into making a mistake. She threw heavier, slower punches, intended to keep him moving, unable to set his feet and throw back.

It might have worked, but with his Power enhancing his footwork, he could get traction and launch his own strikes with hardly any setup. As soon as his foot touched the stage, it might as well have been glued in place, and he could put his full body into return strikes.

The big Takslee started to wear down.

Rohan swallowed.

Lonnie is looking good. Too good. Way better than he should.

Sirc seemed to agree.

"That's not just Boost you're using."

Lahnegarn laughed. "I'm using everything I can find. I told you, there are no rules here. I'm no athlete, not a natural fighter, but I'm smart. I've spent a year looking for every possible advantage I can get for a fight. If it weren't enough to beat the likes of you, I'd have been completely wasting my time."

"What were you getting ready for? You're doing dangerous things, man. Dangerous things. Who did you think you were going to have to fight? A Hybrid?" She laughed.

Lonnie's eyes hardened.

He stepped forward and began his own attack.

Jab, jab, right cross.

He hammered her left leg with low kicks, putting his hip behind each one, delivering thudding blows that reverberated through the stadium.

Sirc continued to wilt.

She had clearly prepared for the kicking game, but not well.

Boxers didn't spend years learning to deal with low kicks.

Lonnie's lips parted as he continued his assault.

"I. Will. Do. Whatever. It. Takes."

Sirc gave up defending the kicks; she stepped in with each one and punched him in the face as his shin impacted the meaty side of her thigh.

They traded blows: her fists thudding into his face, his instep into her knee.

He kicked; she punched twice.

He kicked again; she landed a jab and a hook that twisted his head to the side.

He growled and kicked her one more time; when she punched, he caught it in his palm.

With a shout, he pushed into her straightened arm and sent her stumbling backward.

He followed, kicking her leg just as her weight settled on it.

The knee buckled, and she went down.

He stepped around her as she twisted, rolling onto her stomach, then up onto hands and knees, on her way to standing back up.

He planted his left leg and swung the right up into her jaw just as she pushed herself up into a crawl.

The Takslee's head snapped back; Rohan saw her eyes double-blink, and again, and she fell to her side.

Lonnie planted his left foot again and swung his right back, eyes on her head as it rolled back and forth on the ground.

The referee jumped in and waved her arms before he could launch the kick. "Winner: Lahnegarn of Lukhor."

Lonnie turned to Rohan and smirked.

Ang came ambling out of the back while the referee waited for Sirc to re-gain consciousness. His knee was wrapped in a brace, his limp pronounced but not as bad as Rohan had expected.

The Ursan settled heavily into the chair next to Rohan's. "Sirc is for losing?"

The Hybrid shrugged. "Badly."

Ang exhaled harshly. "Surprising. Sirc having skill."

"Looks like Lonnie is doing more than just training."

"How means War Chief?"

"There are systems to teach skills really quickly. Machines that immerse you in an artificial world where your nervous system can practice contin-uously in a way you could never do with your actual body. Almost like studying in your dreams. You can add to that drugs that make your nervous system extra malleable, so those skills imprint even faster."

"Sounds as very good thing, then. All schools should be for having this."

"It's great, except that when your nervous system is extra malleable, it can change in all sorts of ways, not all of them good. Your personality can alter. Really fast. It turns out that nature gave us a certain amount of neuroplasticity and no more for some pretty darn good reasons."

Ang paused. "Ah. So, not good?"

"It's a big risk, big reward kind of thing." The Hybrid paused. "It only make sense if you're desperate. If the stakes are really high. I guess that's how he sees things right now."

"Why is Lonnie for so eager to fighting?"

"He thinks he can beat me. Or, I guess I should say, he wants to beat me, and he'll do anything to be able to do it."

"Is possible?"

Rohan shook his head. "Not without a lot more drugs and a lot more training."

Ang shrugged. "But is very smart man, yes? Smarter than War Chief?"

Rohan scratched along his jaw, under his beard. "They say that. Well, he says it. And his kid. I guess everyone says it."

Ang put an arm around the Hybrid. "Am sure all are exaggerating. Certain War Chief is safe, is much better fighter, no matter drugs or special training."

"Thanks, Ang."

"Yes. Am sure. Remembering, however, this is same Ang who attacked War Chief with gun inside space station. Perhaps listening to Ang not best idea."

"You've been a tremendous help. How's the leg?"

"Ohnian for helping with healing. Feels good. No, not good, maybe, better than before."

"The Ohnian you fought helped you?"

Ang shrugged. "Yes. Also helped with learning how to ring bell. For later."

"Huh. He's giving advice to you? When you're competing in the tournament against him?"

"Yes. He was for saying . . . not sure. Something universe doing good and returning. Stopped paying attention."

Rohan nodded. "Good for him. He was never going to win this thing anyway. Might as well make some friends."

Ang nodded. "Always good to be for having friends."

30

On The Origins of Humanoids and Also Lunch

When Sirc returned, she left with Ang and Katya to eat and rest before the fourth round.

Rohan considered going with them but stayed behind; he wanted to stay close to Master Turtle, as if by osmosis he could absorb some of the other man's spiritual discipline.

Or, perhaps, just to stay close to that wellspring of calm.

The round ended with a surprising streak of injuries; three fighters were hurt too badly to be able to continue, with two of them possibly maimed. Permanently.

Rohan sat rubbing his shoulder, thinking about the damage that had been done to the last fighter before the referee could step in and stop the match.

He looked up when a shadow fell across his face.

Wei Li looked down at him with hard eyes. "Rohan."

He looked over both shoulders. "Did I do something wrong?"

She scowled. "Do *you* think you did something wrong?"

He looked around again. "Now I really don't know. What are we talking about?"

The reptilian exhaled and shook her head. "I am teasing. I am not upset with you."

"Oh. Okay good. I mean, not good, because you're clearly upset about something. But I'm really glad it's not me. Not glad you're upset."

"You can stop now. I know what you meant. Remember? I always know."

"Of course. Class Four Empath. Can I help, though? Not like I have anything on my plate. A little criminal investigation. An angry ex-husband. Not mine, of my girlfriend. A possibly angry girlfriend. An angry future father-in-law. My own anger issues. There's a lot of anger going around."

She paused before answering. "Yes. Come to lunch. I will . . . how do you say it? Bounce ideas off your skull?"

"That is not how I say it. But I know what you mean. At least, I hope I know what you mean, because what you said is definitely not that."

She turned away. "Come. I will buy. You will listen."

Rohan followed her out of the arena. "You're being very assertive. Is that your thing? Were you the top person in your throuple? Did you just tell Krai Wu and Mai Si to come along, and they followed you around like puppies?"

Her hairless head glistened as it shook back and forth. "I will not speak of that relationship, Rohan. If you have questions, ask Mai Si. She is the open one."

"Maybe I will. Maybe I'll ask her a bunch of questions and maybe she'll answer them and then maybe I'll know things. Stuff. How would you feel then?"

"I would not care. Where should we eat?"

"I don't know. Someplace where they won't recognize me. I still have enemies, you know, and with the rumors about my de-Powerment spreading, I don't want to ask for trouble."

She nodded and turned out onto the promenade. "Come. I know a place."

He pulled his hood low over his forehead, tugging the sides to cover most of his face, and followed his friend down the promenade, away from Wistful's core and the busier areas of the station.

Rohan jogged a few steps to catch up. "You're worrying me now. This isn't like you."

She continued walking. "We can talk at the restaurant. Come, you'll enjoy the food."

"It's good?"

"No. It's Chandian. They have terrible taste, so everything is over-cooked, but they mask the lack of flavor with copious amounts of grease and spices that are nearly intolerable to anyone outside their racial group."

"Spicy *and* greasy? Sign me up."

"As I suspected."

They walked for a while in silence, Rohan following Wei Li's lead as she took him down a side corridor and up some stairs to a quiet restaurant out of view of the promenade.

The tables were clean but bare, plastic and metal surfaces all around. The staff were short, heavily built mammals, apparently from a high-gravity planet, covered in sandy fur.

Wei Li took a menu and a seat at a back table.

Rohan sat across from her. "Any recommendations?"

"No. Nothing here is good. But it won't kill you, and nobody you know would be caught dead in here."

The Hybrid cleared his throat. "Well, okay, then. Good thing the menu is in Drachna. I guess I'll have these ribs."

Wei Li nodded and put down her menu as the server approached. "Two orders of the ribs and a pitcher of klaver juice."

The server nodded and left. Rohan sank a bit into his chair and looked over his friend. "You okay?"

"I already said I am not. I do not like this tournament. It feels like senseless violence."

Rohan sighed. "It's not exactly senseless. There's a very particular sense to it, right? You need a home for the Eternity Ki. You guys said this is the best way to find it."

"I do not need you to explain that to me. I am not senile."

"No. My point is, do you disagree with the reason for it? I thought you agreed to the tournament."

"I did. I don't . . . I don't know. I have doubts, Rohan. I am usually more confident than this."

"I noticed."

"Do not mock me. I am an empath. Where others live lives of uncertainty, never truly knowing what is in the hearts of those around them, I have never had that."

"I guess you haven't."

"So I am used to acting from a more certain perspective. Now, however . . ."

"Now you're basing your decisions on things you're not sure of, and you don't like it."

She sighed. "That is accurate."

The server came by with a small pitcher of a green juice and two glasses. Rohan poured for both of them while Wei Li tapped the table.

Once the server was out of earshot, she continued. "If I am wrong about these prophecies, Rohan, then I am causing a great deal of harm by not taking the Eternity Ki for myself."

"If you're wrong. But you don't think you are, do you?"

"I do not. But I can't be sure. My belief is based on the knowledge passed down through my family for a very, very long time. What if one of my ancestors made a mistake?"

Rohan sipped his juice: tart and strongly flavored. "That's a big responsibility. And I get what you're saying, it sounds really difficult. I'm not sure how I can help with that."

She tapped the table faster. "You are fluent in Fire Speech."

He coughed. "Pretty much. I can understand spoken language. Any spoken language. You've known that for years. Why?"

"You have said that you learned spoken Fire Speech but not how to read it."

"I think I see where this is going."

"You've looked at the words of the prophecy, haven't you? In Mai Si's notebook?"

"Yes. But—"

"But since you can't read Fire Speech, you don't understand the meta language behind all other languages."

"Right. I can only make sense of it when it's spoken."

"If she were to read it aloud . . ."

"I would know exactly what *she* meant when she read it. Which doesn't necessarily tell you anything about what the original writers thought."

Wei Li nodded. "That matches my understanding. I wanted to verify."

Rohan sat back in his chair and realized his foot was tapping along to the beat of the house music, a drum-heavy arrangement that he felt through his bones as much as heard. "Food's coming. Smells . . ."

"I warned you."

He smiled. "I'm sure I've eaten worse. You should try il'Zkin food. I mean, you shouldn't. It's awful. Boiled auroch meat. They don't even garnish it with anything. I think Katya cried the first time she tried a sweet."

The server brought over a tray and set down matching plates of food: ribs covered in a dark orange sauce.

The pair ate; the meat didn't quite fall off the bone, but it didn't crack Rohan's teeth either. He grimaced at the puddle of grease left on his plate by the meal but continued eating.

Wei Li paused about halfway through her rack. "I have a follow-up question."

Rohan put down a half-finished rib. "Of course you do. I'm pretty sure I know what you're going to ask, but go ahead."

"Who taught you Fire Speech?"

"Lyst. She's—"

"I remember her. She came here from Earth. When they needed you. When was it, two years ago?"

"Yeah. Almost exactly two years."

"What is she? Is she a Lifter? I knew she was one of the older races, but I didn't think . . ."

"I'm not sure. She's really, really old. I know she looks humanoid, you know, two arms, two legs, upright, barely any tail, but she wasn't born that way. Her species . . . I think they looked a lot more like velociraptors. And as I say that, I realize you have no idea what that is. Dinosaurs."

Wei Li stared at him. "I do not know these words."

"Hold on a sec." He pulled his mask out of his hood and tapped at the screen inside, looking for imagery of Earth dinosaurs. "I don't know if I have anything on here that will do the job. I can ask Ben for some help."

"I don't think it matters."

He nodded as he continued scrolling. "The point is, she made herself humanoid to fit in with the younger species. Modified her own body. She predates any of us."

"And she taught you Fire Speech."

"She did. Though she never really explained why, and she doesn't teach very many people. Come to think of it, I don't know if she's taught anybody else."

"It seems like a useful ability. Understanding it."

"I guess. Maybe I asked her, I don't remember. She's not big on explaining herself to people."

"The older ones rarely are."

"Yeah. Anyway, she never taught me to read it, and I'll be honest, I'm not sure she can read in Fire Speech herself."

"No?"

He squirmed a bit before answering. "I don't even know if that exists. Reading and understanding any text like that."

"But you—"

"I say a lot of things! They're jokes! I never actually said, hey, look, let's go learn to read Fire Speech this summer! Let's get the premium version of that phone app that teaches you to read Fire Speech! I didn't think anybody would take me seriously!"

Wei Li sighed. "It did seem implausible."

"Right! You should pay attention to your instincts. If I say something, and it seems wrong somehow, it probably is."

"Who else could actually read those prophecies?"

Rohan shrugged. "I assume your Lifters were the il'Sein. Have you tried Wistful? They built her, too, only she remembers it."

"I have. When I learned Master Turtle was beautifying himself, I searched for a way to translate the prophecies with greater certainty." She bent to tear the meat off another rib.

"And? What did she say? You're leaving me hanging." He waved for the server; the pitcher of juice was empty. The ribs were *hot*.

"She said she couldn't read that writing."

"She said that. Was she lying?"

Wei Li locked her vertically slit eyes on his. "Not exactly. Nor was she telling the truth. Not the whole truth."

"It can't just be her orders. We freed her from the il'Sein governor. She doesn't *have* to do what they told her to."

"It might be that she does not want to interpret. Or that she can, but isn't confident in her reading. Or, really, any number of things. The end result is that she will not help me determine the truth of the matter, so I have to direct my efforts elsewhere."

"Right. Right. So Wistful won't help. And I have to tell you, I can't imagine Lyst reading those lines for you even if she could. She's not big on interfering in things like that. I can try to find her and ask, but even that's not so easy. She tends to find you when she wants you, not the other way around. It's not like she has a big old brownstone in Greenwich Village where you can just go knock on the door when there's a problem. Any other il'Sein you can ask? What about Tollan?"

She shook her head. "I tried that. He said the writing belongs to a different caste, that he doesn't know it well enough to interpret it accurately. This is one of many ways his people seem to have over-compartmentalized their society."

"And he was telling the truth, I take it."

"He was." Wei Li frowned as she sucked the meat off another rib. "It is . . . puzzling. How we are left with crumbs of information, open to interpretation, instead of clear instructions."

The server brought over a fresh pitcher. "How about when you and I set up systems to save the universe twenty thousand years from now, we make it super transparent? Like, on September 6, 22025, connect the red wire to the blue wire while wearing a radiation suit, and make sure to have seven Tic Tacs in your pocket."

Wei Li smiled. "You and I? Is that going to be our legacy?"

He smiled back. "I was kidding. But also kind of not kidding. I'm supposed to start building something, right? Black gold. Become the kind of leader who makes connections, builds alliances, recruits help to face the dangers that are coming."

"And have you been?"

Rohan sighed. "You know what I've been doing. Trying to master this technique. Which still needs a name, by the way. I don't know what to call it, and Spiral never told me. Just gave me the pattern for it."

"You have used it. Several times. You have not mastered it?"

He sighed. "It goes away when I get angry. I'm considering Master Turtle's method. Maybe get rid of the anger."

"His methods have . . . consequences. What else have you done to build a coalition? Or have you?"

Rohan finished his last rib and placed the bone carefully on top of the others. "I wish it didn't, but it all comes down to Hyperion. Man, I wish I hadn't saved his sorry behind when the Drexians were trying to kill him."

"You couldn't have known."

"That . . . that actually does help, but only a little."

"I understand. You believe you can defeat him with Spiral's technique? Didn't you know it before the last fight?"

"I have to master it. Or master me. It's the anger, it destroys the technique. So all I've been doing is trying to control the anger."

She nodded and filled their glasses. "You have been very . . . focused."

He sipped his drink. "He's a danger. You know what happened on Ohn. He basically forced the il'Drach to wipe out the planet, kill a billion people. A billion. That's a really big number, Wei Li. A lot of zeros."

"I am no mathematician, but I am aware of the relative sizes of numbers."

"Also, I made promises. And I try to take that seriously. And lastly, if I do get rid of—I mean kill—Hyperion, that opens certain other doors. Other people will owe me favors. The Empire. It gives me leverage. I can start to make some things happen."

She sipped her juice, then exhaled harshly, as someone does when they need to cool their mouth. "The ribs were far too spicy."

Rohan snorted. "Better than tasting the flavor."

"Was it that bad?"

"Maybe. I'm starting to think it's a high-g issue. Something about the air density. Maybe it affects taste?"

"I'm sure someone has studied the issue at length. That somebody, however, is not me."

He laughed. "Not important. Anyway, I'm sorry I can't help you with the prophecy, Wei Li."

"To be completely honest—"

"No need."

She smiled. "To be honest, I didn't expect you to be able to help. It was a stretch, is the phrase I believe you use."

"Yeah."

"We should head back to the tournament."

"You're going to let it continue?"

"I have no choice. I am sincere in my belief regarding the meaning of the prophecy, Rohan. If I take the Eternity Ki, disaster is said to follow. I cannot allow that."

"Then I guess we go back and fight it out. I just hope Lonnie doesn't win the whole thing."

"I wish Lonnie didn't appear, so far, to be one of the more promising candidates. I wish any of them were to my taste."

31

Bears and Bells

The bell test was common, in some form or another, in high level martial arts training schools across the sector.

Every ambitious martial artist sought, eventually, to use esoteric energy to reinforce their physical bodies. A magically enhanced muscle could transcend the limitations of simple physical meat, no matter how well-trained that meat might be.

Most individuals could only exert a small amount of force using their spiritual abilities alone, and it was often difficult to sense that force if it was added to a bodily movement.

A hundred grams of force added to a trained punch wouldn't even be noticed, and there would be no way for the practitioner to know they'd successfully done anything at all.

Put the target away from the body, and the results became much more obvious.

The Rogesh were known to place a lit candle behind a screen and let students attempt to snuff the candle without touching the screen.

Sid, Spiral's teacher, placed an iron fist inside a glass container alongside a ribbon. His students fasted, meditated, and prayed until they were able to wrap the ribbon around the fist without touching it.

Rohan's first teacher of esoteric ability, his father, had used no such method:

Once a Hybrid's Power awakened, there was never any doubt that they were managing to utilize it.

More than half the fighters, familiar with the basic idea of the test, simply strolled up to the stage and, with a wave of their hands or a moment of concentration, rang the bell.

Squeya, Lonnie, Kor the Quattro assassin, Sirc, and Krai Wu all passed effortlessly.

Rohan returned to his seat; Katya took the seat next to his, squatting with both feet on the cushion.

She gripped Rohan's left hand tight in hers.

"I am nervous, Rohan."

He sighed. "Do you really think breaking my hand will help you feel better? It's definitely not making me feel better. Maybe ease up a little?"

She dropped her head and loosened her grip but did not let go. "I am afraid for my Ang."

"He'll . . ." *I almost said 'he'll be fine.' Will he?* "There's nobody tougher than Ang."

"I know. But his heart is set so much on being a Power." Her eyes were damp, her nose dripping.

Rohan sighed. "He's had his heart broken before. That sounds awful, maybe, but he knows how to stitch it back together."

Katya smiled. "With a tremendous quantity of alcohol, I would guess."

Rohan smiled. "You know how Ursans mourn? It takes seven days. Let me tell you a story . . ."

Ang ascended the stage.

The crowd didn't hush or focus their attention on the Ursan; to most of the fighters there, he was just another person, just another competitor. The largest, perhaps, but nobody special.

The Ohnian that Ang had defeated in the previous round walked up to Rohan. He pressed his palms together in front of his chest and bowed.

"Hello, Guru Rohan. May I join you?"

"Oh. Sure. Just Rohan, please."

The Ohnian smiled, his single large eye flashing to the seat to Rohan's right, then back to the Hybrid. "Thank you. Can I tell you a funny story? You said the same thing to some of the others, and they believed you were instructing them to call you—"

"Please don't say it."

"Just Rohan. As if the word 'just'—"

"I asked you not to say it. Stop there or you're going to find out just how unjust I can be."

The Ohnian smiled. "I apologize, Guru Rohan. I mean . . . Rohan. It is a funny story."

Katya elbowed the Hybrid. "Good news, Rohan! Someone who finds you funny! I mean, someone other than yourself. It is a glorious day to be you. Of course, you are still hideous, but it is good to have a sense of humor if one is cursed to be as unattractive as you."

"Thanks, Katya. Let's watch Ang give this a try."

The Ursan crossed the stage, splayed his legs far out to the side, and crouched in front of the diamond cylinder.

He inhaled slowly as he brought his fists to his hips, palms facing up.

With a long, slow exhalation, he pushed his hands forward, opening them as he turned them over so his palms now faced the single-facet diamond.

Rohan held his breath waiting for the sound of the bell.

Nothing happened.

Katya gripped Rohan's shoulder; her claws dug into his flesh with enough force to break the skin. "He is not doing it."

The Ohnian stood and shouted. "Calm your spirit, Ang! Just like when you studied the schematics! Focus on the images and stay calm!"

Katya shook Rohan's shoulder back and forth. "Is he trying to help or to get my Ang eliminated?"

Rohan pushed futilely at her fingers, wincing at the pain of her claws. "I think he's trying to help."

"It is not the same thing at all."

"You don't have a better idea, do you? Let him try. And let go of my shoulder before you send me to Medical."

She pulled her claws out of his skin. "Sorry. He will be sad."

"I know, believe me. But he'll recover. And who knows . . ."

Ang stood up and stepped away from the lantern.

The referee called out. "Thirty seconds."

Ang nodded and reset himself, then tried again.

Rohan leaned forward, Third Eye wide open as he checked the air for any hint of esoteric energy extending from the Ursan.

Nothing.

A pair of fighters two rows behind Rohan started arguing with Sirc, disputing the results of some bet or other they had placed on the total number who would pass the bell test.

The Ohnian shouted again. "Calm your spirit!"

Ang pressed his hands forward a third time, exhaling.

Rohan swallowed.

The bell held still inside the diamond container.

"Ten seconds."

Ang stepped back and shook his massive head.

He turned to the Ohnian, anger in his biological eye, and shook it again.

His lips pulled back from his teeth; he lifted his snout to the ceiling and let out a roar that shook the far corners of the stadium.

The Ursan's aura, the color of fresh magma, permeated the space.

The crowd fell into a hush, momentarily cowed by the Ursan's rage.

By his fighting spirit.

Master Turtle turned to face the Ursan.

Ang shook his head one last time, raised his fists high in the air, roared, and brought them down onto the packed-clay surface of the platform.

Through the sudden hush that fell over the stadium like a weighted blanket, Rohan heard a single, tinkling sound.

The bell had rung.

◆ ⋯ ◆

Ten minutes later, the Ursan was with his friends, Katya draped over his back, her hands wrapped around his neck, her head next to his where she could repeatedly lick his cheek without interference.

The big bear was smiling.

"Am thinking I for sure cheated, Rohan. Hitting the ground . . ."

Rohan shook his head. "I don't think so, big guy. You're big and strong, but not enough to shake that stage. It's made out of tons of clay. I think you really did it."

Ang shook his head ruefully. "Maybe, War Chief. Maybe."

"Should you even be calling me that anymore? You beat me in the contest. I think it's time for you to take that title back."

Ang scratched his jaw. "Not for thinking such, War Chief Rohan. Fight in competition not same as true fight, as were having on shuttle deck."

Rohan sighed. "Okay, buddy. Whatever you say."

The Ohnian shook his head. "I thought my advice would help, but it didn't."

Rohan laughed and patted his shoulder. "You meant well. You just don't understand Ursans. What's happening now? Fourth round?"

Katya took one last lick, then slid off of Ang's back. "I must return to my duties. The round will start in a few minutes."

Rohan cracked his neck, laced his fingers together, and stretched his arms overhead. He looked up at the big screens; they weren't showing the fourth-round matchups yet. He turned to the Ohnian. "You ready for your next fight?"

The Ohnian shrugged, his eye focused on the ground. "I do not think much of my chances, Guru Rohan."

"You've been training seriously for, what, six months?"

"About."

"Then cheer up. You're doing incredibly well. Most of these other guys have been fighting for ten times as long. Twenty. Heck, I've been training seriously for more than twenty years, and for half of that I was elbow-deep in actual life-and-death combat."

"Thank you, Guru. Still, this was perhaps a once-in-a-lifetime opportunity, and I am not ready."

"Yeah. Oh, look, the pairings are up."

The Ohnian sighed. "I am fighting the man you fought last, Guru."

"Krai Wu?" Rohan paused to think. "Try to overwhelm him. He's skilled but cautious. If you let it drag on, he'll pick you apart."

"Thank you, Guru."

Rohan checked the board, looking for his own name.

His breath caught in his throat as he saw his opponent.

Lahnegarn of Lukhor.

Damnit.

Ang sighed heavily.

Rohan looked over at his friend. "Who do you have?"

Ang lifted one massive paw. "Squeya. Leader of The Consortium. Already lost to second-in-command. Is not good day for being myself."

Rohan reached up to pat his friend's shoulder. "Sorry, big guy. That's a rough draw."

Ang nodded. "Perhaps victory in tournament was never for being."

Rohan didn't have an answer.

——— ···•··· ———

The Ohnian fought first.

Rohan's assessment had been accurate; Krai Wu had too much skill for the youngster, and the Ohnian's greater ability to use esoteric energy wasn't enough to overcome that advantage.

The Vor'karei hammered the Ohnian on the feet and, once he had the younger man stunned and stumbling, took him to the ground, grabbed an arm, and forced a submission.

The master stood calmly after his victory, no joy on his face, and returned to Wei Li's side.

Two more fights went by; Rohan barely watched, distracted by random thoughts.

What am I going to do about Tamara? Am I in any position to move in with anybody?

How do I fight Hyperion when I can't even beat a non-Powered Ursan?

Even if Rinth tells me where to find a Boost dealer higher in the hierarchy, what am I going to do about it? How do I get to their distributor when they have empaths who will know that's what I'm trying to do?

How can I get that prophecy translated so Wei Li doesn't make a colossal mistake?

I haven't checked in on Void's Shadow *in a while. I hope she's okay.*

Ang's name was next on the screen. The big Ursan stood; Rohan stood with him, too nervous to stay down, and fidgeted while Ang strode up the walkway to the stage, head up, aura projecting nothing short of confidence.

Squeya waited for him on the platform, her eyes fixed on Rohan.

The Hybrid glared back.

The ref waved. "Begin."

Squeya's hand had yet to reach her hip when Ang barreled across the space between himself and the Tolone'an, head down and arms spread wide, five hundred kilograms launched by his powerful legs as if shot from a missile launcher.

Squeya locked her hourglass-pupil octopus eyes on Rohan, then lazily turned to the charging Ursan.

She dropped her hips, her two rear tentacles extending to touch the clay behind her, and raised her hands to meet his charge.

Ang collided with her like a car being crash-tested into a concrete pillar.

Rohan could see flesh rolling and shaking as the Tolone'an absorbed the full impact of Ang's charge, his fat and muscle wrapping around his skeleton, his shoulders caught and frozen in place instantly by the Tolone'an's Power-reinforced hands.

Squeya's front tentacles reached down and snaked around Ang's knees. With a shake of her head, she pulled, yanking his feet off the ground and to the side, sending the big man crashing to the clay.

"You have no chance against me, mammal."

Ang growled and rolled back to his feet. He spat blood onto the ground and charged again.

Rohan could not imagine any path to victory for his friend. If he charged with less than full speed, he'd take less damage, but also have even less chance of hurting The Consortium's leader.

Squeya set her rear tentacles and waited for him to come.

If she'd expected Ang to reduce the ferocity of his charge, she was disappointed. He drove himself forward with abandon, his feet digging ruts into the clay as they accelerated his massive body.

They collided.

Squeya didn't move back by even a centimeter.

Ang shuddered with the impact, his body quivering. He grabbed under the Tolone'ans arms and tried to lift her off the ground, perhaps a first step in tossing her to the side so he could grapple her.

Her front tentacles wrapped up over his elbows from underneath and pulled his hands down and away from her armpits. She reached forward and grabbed fistfuls of his fur by his chest, digging hard fingers into his flesh.

Her tentacles reached for the ground again, all four anchoring her body in place, and with a powerful heave, she tossed him to the ground.

The big bear hit the clay rolling and came back to his feet.

Before Rohan could blink, Ang had charged again.

The Hybrid stood and ran his fingers up into his hair, then held them in place as he watched, mouth open.

Ang collided with the Tolone'an again; like hitting a wall.

She swiped at his legs with her front tentacles; he stepped back, avoiding them, and slashed at her with his claws.

Squeya blocked with her hands, gripped his paws in her fingers, and tossed him to the side again.

The Ursan hit the ground hard but rolled over his hip and came back to his feet.

He coughed, spitting more blood onto the ground, gave his body a massive shake, and launched himself at his opponent.

You don't have to do this, Ang. Just give up.

Katya watched from the edge of the platform, her eyes wide.

Wei Li stood up out of her chair as her friend was battered.

Rohan cracked his neck.

Squeya's punishing him.

Because he's my friend.

His knuckles whitened.

Squeya met Ang's charge by leaning forward at the waist and driving her forearms up into his ribs, standing the Ursan up straight.

He coughed blood in a spray over the Tolone'an.

She straightened her arms, lifting the Ursan higher, reaching around to grab him with her front tentacles as his feet left the ground.

The massive bear was helpless, suspended above the platform in the woman's hands; she released him and stepped back, then shook her head slowly as he thudded into the clay.

He climbed to his feet again, slower than previous times. He coughed and rubbed his arms across his ribs.

Something's broken in there. He needs to stop this.

Squeya paused, as if expecting the Ursan to quit.

Instead he set his feet and threw his body into hers once again.

She met the charge, the impact loud enough to echo off the back walls of the stadium. Her two front tentacles swept his feet out from under him, and he crashed to the floor.

He was back on his feet before she could capitalize.

He charged again.

Don't do it.

She met the charge with another double forearm blow, standing him up again. She stepped close, her front tentacles wrapping behind his knees, and she shoved him over, sending him to his back.

He tried to roll, but she got on top and used all four tentacles along with her arms and legs to stay on top of him as he rolled from side to side, trying to buck her off.

Once she caught his rhythm, she started dropping heavy punches onto the Ursan.

Tap out, Ang. Tap out.

Blood sprayed from his mouth as she landed a hook flush on his jaw.

Katya stepped onto the stage, then stepped back, her eyes cold and furious.

Ang ran his claws along Squeya's side; her Power reinforced her skin, and he didn't even draw blood.

He reached a leg up and tried to hook it over her hip, but she slapped it down with one foot and a hand.

He slapped at her head, but she blocked the blows with her hands and reached around his neck with a tentacle.

That tentacle began to squeeze.

Ang thrashed back and forth, slapping at the tentacle with both hands, but he couldn't break its hold or her skin, not with the quantity of esoteric energy she poured into the limb.

She punched him again, solidly on the other side of his jaw, and his eyes glazed over.

His arms slapped at her sides, more feebly than before.

Katya glared at Rohan.

I know. I don't like it either.

This was his choice.

Ang swiped again, with even less force.

His arm fell limply to his side.

The referee stepped in.

"Done! It's over. It's over."

Squeya looked at her and unwrapped her tentacle from his neck.

The Ursan lay stretched out on the clay.

"Winner: Squeya of Tolone'a. Competitor Ang, with three losses and one victory, is eliminated."

The Tolone'an stood, straddling the much bigger man, and lifted her leg high to clear his massive torso. She turned to face Rohan, the unconscious body of the Hybrid's friend directly behind her.

She pointed at him. "Just the start."

Rohan met her glare with ice cold eyes that had once paralyzed enemies on a hundred worlds.

It didn't seem to faze her at all.

32

You May Now Punch the Ex

Katya rushed to Ang's side and squatted next to him, one hand on his big chest, the other stroking his cheek.

She stole a glance at Squeya, to ensure the Tolone'an wasn't considering any continuation of the fight, then looked at Wei Li.

The security chief nodded. "Take him to get help. He's eliminated because of his record, so there's no need for him to answer any questions."

Katya eyed the Tolone'an again, perhaps wishing the woman would try something, but Squeya had eyes only for Rohan. The il'Zkin effortlessly scooped up Ang's massive body and ran to the back of the arena, her legs and core strong enough to move quickly without jarring the Ursan.

Rohan pressed his hands together, prying open his clenched fists, and exhaled slowly.

Fully emptied his lungs, then held them empty until the burning was almost too much to take.

Inhaled sharply, filling his belly, then exhaled slowly.

He turned his Third Eye inward and checked on the esoteric construct he maintained. He'd built it up to five coils that morning; it was down to three.

Squeya climbed down from the stage and approached him. "It's a terrible feeling, isn't it? Seeing the ones you care about be hurt. Or die. And not being able to do anything about it."

Rohan exhaled and looked down, away from her angry face. "Squeya, I respect your anger. Your reasons for being angry. But you don't want to do this."

"Are you threatening me? It's what you do, isn't it? Not so much lately, though. Not in your current state."

"I wasn't threatening you. I'm telling you, you don't want to do this. It's wrong, and you're going to figure that out at some point. Hopefully before it's too late. Before you do something you can't come back from.

"And it's a place you do not want to visit. Never mind me, it's living with yourself that's going to be the big problem."

"Who are you to talk to me about conscience, Hybrid?"

He looked up and met her gaze. "I'm the most qualified person you've ever met when it comes to that particular conversation, Squeya. I'm telling you, turning into me is not a good strategy for nurturing your own long-term mental health."

She blew air across the moist membranes in her neck, spun, and strode away.

Rohan exhaled again; held his empty lungs again.

Let it go. Relax and let the anger fall away.

You don't need it. The anger isn't you; it's just a thing that you don't have room for in your life.

Let it fall away.

Exhale. Hold.

Inhale.

Drop the anger.

He felt a presence; when he looked up, Mai Si stood in front of him.

He swallowed. "Hey."

Her lips tightened into a smile. "It is your turn to fight, Rohan. Unless you desire to forfeit the tournament?"

"What? No. No, that's not . . . really? Already?"

The Vor'karei turned and pointed to the scoreboard. Rohan and Lahnegarn were printed just below Ang and Squeya. "You are next. If you take much longer, you will be dismissed from the competition."

He rubbed his face. "No, that's not what I was trying to do. Just . . . it's Ang."

"I understand. And Wei Li will understand if you choose not to continue. You are obviously in distress."

My friend is hurt.

Because of me.

Maybe I am in some distress.

"No, I'll continue. I'm coming."

"Now, Rohan. Right now."

"Yeah, I got it. Coming."

He cracked his neck, slapped first one cheek, then the other, and looked up at the stage.

The Lukhor was already in place, smiling down at him.

Here we go.

—◆··•·◆—

Rohan stepped toward the stage.

Focus on the fight at hand, Rohan.

Assess the fight.

Lahnegarn bounced up and down on his toes a few times, then shook his arms to the sides, fingers relaxed, getting blood into the muscles and joints.

His antennae bobbed gently with the motion.

He's skilled. Normally he'd be no match for me physically, but now . . .

But I have way more fighting experience.

But he might be some kind of genius when it comes to learning tactics.

Rohan climbed the shallow steps built into the edge of the platform, eyes on his opponent.

He doesn't stick to rote combinations the way the Ohnians did. He's not afraid to get hit. His Power isn't natural, it comes from Boost, but he's still got a really solid knack for using it.

On the other hand, I . . . have a better beard.

And one trick he's probably never seen before. Spiral's final technique.

The referee locked eyes with first Lahnegarn, then with Rohan.

"Follow my instructions at all times. If you disobey my instructions, you will be disqualified. The fight continues until one of you submits or until either a judge or I decides you can't continue.

"Any weapons or outside interference will result in immediate disqualification."

Lahnegarn grinned. "I'm not going to need any outside help."

Rohan sighed. "Who are you posturing for, Lonnie? You trying to scare me? You have to know that's not going to work. You trying to pump yourself up?"

"You're accusing me of talking too much? Have you ever listened to yourself?"

Rohan paused. "You might have a point."

"I've been looking forward to this for a long time, Rohan. I wasn't sure I'd ever get the chance to really do this. Not before Hyperion . . ."

"Don't get too excited, Lonnie." Rohan stepped back with his right leg and lifted his right fist to the side of his jaw; left fist across his belly, near his liver. "You're about to find out the difference between school and a real fight."

Lahnegarn took his own fighting position, left foot back, both fists up near his face, elbows tucked tight to his sides. "Ready when you are, Hybrid."

The referee looked them over, nodded as she verified that they were prepared to fight, and chopped her hand through the air between them. "Begin."

Lahnegarn launched his body through the air, knee rising in a savage opening strike.

He's going for the quick kill.

Rohan pivoted on his back foot, spinning to the side and away from the knee, and snapped a straight punch with his right hand at the Lukhor's head.

Lahnegarn blocked it as he landed in his stance, unperturbed by missing with the knee, and threw three quick punches at Rohan.

The Hybrid absorbed the force for two of them, forcing a flash of confusion across the Lukhor's face.

Having a punch absorbed like that doesn't feel the same as having it blocked. Or having it land.

They traded blows, Lahnegarn staying mostly in his left-handed stance: left foot back, right hand forward. It was an awkward matchup; across the sector, most people were right-handed, and throughout his life most of Rohan's sparring partners had fought accordingly.

Is this just one trick in his arsenal or did he do it specifically to fight me?

Rohan reached with his left hand to paw at Lahnegarn's right, pushing it up, down, swatting it away, occasionally shooting a jab straight at the Lukhor's face.

The less experienced man reacted by moving side to side, his quick feet searching for a position from which he'd have a clear angle to land punches on the Hybrid.

Rohan landed a jab square on Lonnie's jaw, then absorbed the return left straight with his esoteric technique.

Lahnegarn followed with a high kick that Rohan barely caught on his right forearm; the impact sent him stumbling several meters.

Lonnie didn't let up; he chased Rohan and landed a jab to the nose and two hooks to the belly before the Hybrid managed to set his feet and drive him back with a return hook of his own.

Blood leaked down Rohan's face.

The Lukhor smiled.

"You have no idea how much I've been wanting to do that."

Rohan fought his own breath; the last punch he'd taken was making it difficult to exhale. "You'd be surprised."

Lahnegarn laughed. "You think *you* hate *me*? Everything that's gone wrong here, everything that led to this, is your fault, Hybrid."

"Hey, if not for me, you'd still be cowering off somewhere, too afraid to even talk to your own kid. Remember?"

Lonnie's eyes narrowed; his antennae stiffened. "Well, I learned my lesson. I'm not going to be afraid anymore. I'm not going to be intimidated. I'm going to do what it takes to handle things myself. No more hiding."

Rohan nodded as he wiped blood from his mouth. "You're going to stand up for yourself. Good for you. Sounds like you owe me a favor, Lonnie. Why all the hostility?"

"You stole my family from me, Rohan. I'm going to make you pay, and I'm going to get them back."

Rohan laughed. "There's an old saying about two wolves that I can't quite remember. You might manage the first one, Lonnie, but if you do, you'll never get the second. You really can't see that?"

A green leg swept up toward Rohan's face; he ducked and passed underneath, landing a hook to Lahnegarn's lower back.

The Lukhor spun and faced him, kicking again.

Rohan absorbed the force with his right palm, sending the energy directly into his esoteric spring. It stiffened, tightening, the surface shimmering to Rohan's Third Eye in a familiar way.

It's storing more and more of the energy. A couple more kicks and I'll be able to use it to actually hurt him. Even with all that Boost running through his system.

"That's a neat trick. Some kind of internal art?"

Rohan grunted as he took a heavy punch on his upper arm. "Just being like water, my friend."

Another Bruce Lee reference wasted on someone who's never been within fifty star systems of Earth.

Lahnegarn shook his head and threw another combination: right jab, right hook, left body kick; attacking one side, then quickly switching to the other.

Rohan parried the jabs, his arms stinging with the contact; the amount of Power the Lukhor was able to put into his limbs made every touch painful.

He absorbed the kick, continuing to prime his esoteric structure.

Lahnegarn snarled at him. "I understand what you meant. About revenge. And you're right. If I just punish you myself, that won't look good. To either Tamara or Rinth."

Rohan grunted. "I'm glad you're starting to see things my way."

"That's why I'm not going to do it myself. I'm going to let you punish yourself. I mean, maybe I'll help things along, just a bit, but it will be all you, Rohan. I'll just be the innocent bystander, there to console both of them in the end."

Rohan stepped in and threw a double jab, his left fist pumping, followed by a brutal low kick that Lahnegarn simply stood and absorbed.

"What are you talking about, Lonnie? Tamara's smart, you don't think she'll see through your lies?"

The Lukhor feinted, twitching his left shoulder, then his right, then landing a right straight that broke Rohan's nose with a wet crunch. "What lies? I'm going to show them the truth, Rohan. Unfiltered. I know how smart my wife is; believe me, I wouldn't dare try to trick her with some kind of fakery."

Rohan stumbled back, pinching his nose to straighten the cartilage. "Truth?" A burnt orange spear of irritation rose up in his soul, poking its way out of the source of Rohan's Power.

"Yes, Rohan, the truth. I'm going to show it to her. Get it? It's a joke. Like the ones you try to tell, only mine is funny." He giggled.

"It's not funny, you're delusional. What do you even mean?"

"It's funny because it's video. It's all on video, Rohan. Don't you remember? Nobody is better at digging through the streams and finding old records than I am. Nobody. Well, not when I'm properly motivated. And thanks to you, I was very motivated. Very."

Rohan growled. "What did you dig up, Lonnie?"

"So many things! You really shouldn't have made me an enemy, Rohan. Typical of a Hybrid. You see a normal guy, a guy without Powers, a guy who's not special the way you're special, and you just dismiss him. No threat. You see me as someone you can do anything to without consequence. But I'll tell you something, you were wrong, there are going to be consequences. Nothing you don't deserve, nothing you didn't earn. But still."

Rohan slid in with a four-punch combination, finishing with two sweeping kicks.

Lonnie parried them all.

"What did you dig up, Lonnie? Don't make me ask a third time."

"There are cameras everywhere, Rohan. Did you know the Shayjh had cameras in Zahad? Maybe you didn't notice that while you were, let me try to remember, committing genocide? Wiping out an entire star system?"

The tendril of irritation grew and swelled inside him. "You don't want to do that, Lonnie. Distribute video from Zahad and the il'Drach are going to come after you."

"Oh, don't worry. Only Tamara will ever see it. As good as I am at finding things, I'm even better at hiding them after." He skipped close to Rohan and drove his knee up toward his midsection; the Hybrid leaned down to block it, but Lahnegarn cut the movement short, planted the foot, and dug a punch into Rohan's side.

The Hybrid pivoted away, coughing, pain lancing through his ribs and across his lower back.

That actually hurt. I need to finish this guy.

Is the spiral loaded up yet?

Not enough. He's tough.

"You're playing with fire, Lonnie."

"And yet I'm not the one who's going to burn for it, am I? You remember another situation you were in, around the time you first met my wife?"

"Ex-wife."

Lonnie shook his head sharply, antennae twisting with the motion, hair swirling a halo around his head. "You fought those Ursans, didn't you? On the shuttle deck. Tamara loved that. You stopped them without hurting them. Well, not much. But those weren't the last Ursans you fought, was it?"

Rohan stepped back, creating distance between them. *I need him to throw something big so I can absorb it and counter. End this.*

Lahnegarn continued. "There were those other ships you fought a few days later, remember? Came right through the wormhole. They were broadcasting their last moments, did you know that? Sending the data back through the wormhole to their homeworld. Really old tech, too. Electromagnetic waves. The funny thing about that is those waves move at the speed of light. The fight happened, what, two and a half years ago?

You know how easy it is to hire a ship to jump two and a half light years out into space and record those transmissions? Took a bit to decode and turn it into something useful, but, oh boy, the shots of those poor Ursans begging for their lives while you rip through them with your bare hands, covered head to toe in blood and gore . . . totally worth it."

"Those Ursans had just killed thousands of defenseless refugees."

"Oh sure. I mean, I don't blame you for any of it. But what will my wife think of that scene? Or my son?"

"She knows what I am, Lonnie."

"I know you say that. Maybe you even say it to yourself. But I think what she knows and feels, and what she has actually seen with her own eyes, are different."

Rohan's anger swelled. "If you upset Tamara, I'm going to make you wish you'd never been born. I'm going to—"

"Oh, stop doing that. It's pathetic. You can't make me wish anything, other than wishing you were gone from my life. And I'm not just wishing for that, I'm going to make it happen. Because I have another lovely little morsel that I dug up, thanks to our friends in The Consortium." He stepped in with two punches and another knee; Rohan managed to absorb the knee, but one of the punches cracked a rib.

"What?" His breathing was fast; too fast.

"There were cameras there, too, Rohan. In Cthulhu's Crucible. Did you know that? All over the place. In the halls. In the creche. They caught everything, Rohan."

Lahnegarn stepped at angles: to his left, then his right, each time closing on the Hybrid. With the final step, he feinted a jab, digging an uppercut under Rohan's raised hand, driving the air out of the Hybrid. He followed with a left kick that Rohan managed to absorb.

"Lonnie . . ." His voice was guttural. Harsh. Barely human.

Lahnegarn closed and attacked.

And attacked.

He slipped from side to side, never slowing his barrage of punches, his kicks with either leg. He varied his targets: punching high, then low, always aiming for the spots Rohan wasn't covering.

The damage mounted; after two shots landed solidly on his temples, Rohan's thoughts grew fuzzy.

"They're cephalopods, but the kids are still cute. Heck, my son has a plushie of one, doesn't he? The way you slaughtered those cute little creatures, well. You should see the look on your face when you did it, Rohan. Or maybe you shouldn't. It wasn't a nice face."

Anger took hold at the back of Rohan's soul as he stumbled, knees shaking, legs barely able to support his weight.

Lahnegarn spread his arms wide. "You're pathetic, Hybrid. You're about to lose everything you care about, and this is the best you can do?"

Rohan half-stepped and half-fell forward, his left arm extended, palm out, as if to catch his weight.

But it wasn't to catch his weight.

He made contact with the Lukhor's sternum and *looked* inside, willing the esoteric spiral within to release the energy he'd stored there.

It was gone; blown away by his anger like ashes in the wind.

Lahnegarn twisted his body to the left, pulled his left fist behind himself, and unwound, driving that fist into, and through, Rohan's jaw.

Darkness fell.

33

Just One Question

Rohan blinked against the harsh lights illuminating the stage. He didn't realize where he was at first, only felt the hard packed clay under his back, heard the hushed murmur of fifty people talking quietly, waiting for something to happen on the stage.

He lifted his head.

Losing a fistfight to Lonnie wasn't printed in any fortune cookie I've opened in the last ten years.

I can't see any way to recover from this one gracefully.

The referee crouched by his side, mild concern showing through her eyes. "Do you know where you are?"

"Mom? Mom, is that you?"

She looked away from him, toward Wei Li, and shook her head. "You think I'm your mother?"

"Mom, I'm so sorry. I swear I didn't know I wasn't supposed to have those cookies."

She stood and waved for help.

Wei Li stood. "He's fine."

"But, ma'am—"

"No, you are correct, he is not fine. He has a rather severe neurological divergence which results in an inability to discern social situations where his bizarre sense of humor is appropriate. He is not, however, concussed or seriously injured. At least not more than usual. He does get punched in the head with alarming frequency."

The ref looked down at Rohan. "Humor?"

He sat up and shrugged. "Sorry. She's right, I can't help myself. If it's any consolation, most people find it somewhat irritating."

The referee shrugged. Rohan took a breath, then leaned over to the side and set his hands on the ground to help himself stand.

Wei Li stood near the edge of the platform. She looked up at Lahnegarn. "He is alert. You may ask your question."

I forgot about that. Maybe I am concussed.

Lahnegarn looked down at the Hybrid, a sheen of sweat coating his hairless chest and arms. His lips were tight, his brow bunched between his antennae.

Rohan cleared his throat. "You should be happier, Lonnie."

The Lukhor nodded. "I should." He shook his head. "Anyway, my question."

The Hybrid shrugged. "Hard to imagine what you'll ask. After all, you already know everything, right? What with the cameras everywhere. Unless you want to know something . . . intimate? That would be really awkward, considering who my current partner is. Might be a way for you to get me out of the contest, though." *I really should not be giving him ideas. What is wrong with me?*

Lahnegarn shook his head again. "I don't care if you continue in the contest, Rohan. You're no threat to me, not here. No, I have a real question."

"Shoot."

Lahnegarn looked over at Wei Li, who nodded acquiescence. He turned back to Rohan. "What did Hyperion do to you?"

Rohan swallowed. "What do you mean?" He cast a quick glance at Wei Li. "I'm not refusing to answer! I'm really not. I just don't understand the question. I've known Hyperion a long time; he's done a ton of things."

Lahnegarn nodded. "What did Hyperion do to you when you fought three months ago?"

"I thought you saw the video? Weren't you bragging that you verified it?"

"I want to know what he *did*. Why you ended up . . . like this. It's not on video."

Rohan nodded and looked at Wei Li, who tapped the table in front of her impatiently. "Err on the side of overexplaining, Rohan. Respond to the spirit of the question, not the letter."

He cleared his throat.

She's asking me to overexplain? That's, like, my superpower.

One of them, at least.

Can I just tell him to jump out an airlock?

No.

I have to answer. If I don't, I'm out of the competition, and there's nothing protecting Tamara and Rinth from The Consortium.

Might as well give him what he asked for. Even if it's not what he wants.

"You want to know what he did. I'll tell you."

He took a deep breath and continued.

"He beat me.

"I can't tell you all of it, you know. There are secrets involved, things you're better off not knowing, and to be honest I'm glad you didn't ask for any of those specifics, because then I'd be in a real bind figuring out what to do. But you asked what he did to *me*, and that I can answer. He beat me.

"You see, I knew him, the old Hyperion. Back in the day. He was sort of my mentor. Or more my idol? We fought side by side, over a decade ago, and he got me through some of the toughest spots I've ever been in. I'd be dead if not for him. The old him.

"Then he . . . returned. I can't explain that to you, that's another one of those things I'm glad you didn't ask. Because, well . . .

"That's not the point. The point is, this guy, the one who came back, he's bad news. He does . . . bad things. I can't explain how, or why, but he's responsible for the deaths of at least a billion people.

"That's a lot of people.

"And I saved his life. One more sin, right, Lonnie? One more thing on my conscience. This guy is out there wreaking havoc on the sector, and it's my fault. I could have stopped him, or at the very least let other people stop him, back when stopping him was easy. Easier. And I didn't do it. I couldn't. He had been my mentor, like I said. My idol. Like I said. And I couldn't see past that, I couldn't just admit that this guy was something different, that I didn't owe him. All I could see was the potential for good in him, the potential to be someone who could maybe someday come close to being what Hyperion had been, what he had meant to so many of us.

"I was blind, you know. Or nearsighted.

"I wanted him to be something great. So I kept him going, propped him up. Protected him. Saved him.

"And now . . . I realize my mistake.

"I'd really like to leave him to other people. You have no idea. I want nothing more than to stay here, do my job, mess around with your ex-wife . . . sorry, that wasn't relevant. Just couldn't help it.

"I'd love to leave the Hyperion problem to other people. I really would. But, Rudra save me, I might be the only one who *can* stop him now. At least, that's what I thought.

"So I figured out where he was going to be. And no, I'm not going to tell you all of that, because that's not what you asked. And I took my ship and I went out there and I fought him."

Rohan stumbled; his legs were weak. He held out his hand; the referee handed him a metal flask of water. He drank and swallowed.

Do I tell him about the others? How I made my way to Hyperion's side?
Nah. He didn't ask about them.

"I attacked. I could give you a blow-by-blow, I guess, but you've seen the video.

"I had a trick to use, but to do it, I needed to stay calm. And that was probably my downfall.

"Because once we started fighting, he started talking.

"He talked about all sorts of things. The guy loves the sound of his own voice. I have to be honest, in that way he isn't that different from the old Hyperion.

"And he's strong. Stronger than he has any right to be. Maybe as strong as he used to be. Before. I'm not sure, it's hard to say.

"Don't forget, he was the strongest Hybrid the Empire had seen in generations.

"I shouldn't have had a chance, but this guy is a little like the old guy in some other ways. He's strong, overwhelmingly so, but he's not the most skilled fighter. He just doesn't have to be. Why hook off the jab or learn to feint when your most straightforward attacks can just plow through somebody's defenses? There's no point to it.

"That gave me a chance. I used tactics on him. Fought defensively. Moved around. It frustrated him, I could see it. I thought I had a chance.

"But like I said, he started talking. About my homeworld. About people I cared for. Started talking about his plans for the sector. About ending the Empire. Admitted there were some casualties incurred along the way; he called it 'necessary evil.' After all, they were 'just' Ohnians. Nobody important.

"Do you have any idea how much I hate that term? 'Necessary evil'? Like, with every fiber of my being, hate it?

"And the way he said it, so smug. So callous. Yeah, a billion people died, but it was all for the greater good, in the end, right?

"And that's about where I lost it.

"I don't know if I would have gotten so mad if anybody else had said it. Like, if you said it to me, right now, I'd just shrug it off. Right? Because you're just Lonnie. No offense. Well, a little bit of offense. You can take it.

"I don't expect more of you. And I shouldn't have expected more of Hyperion.

"But to hear him spew that stuff. To hear him just dismiss all those lives as unimportant.

"See, my Hyperion, the old guy, that's what he didn't do. He was the most important person around, pretty much all the time, but he never minimized anybody else's value.

"If you were the second toughest fighter in the Fleet? Great, you mattered. If you were the guy who washed his uniforms after a battle? Great, you also mattered. Casualties happened, sure, but they were never acceptable. Never.

"Then I had this guy speaking through those same lips in that same face and saying such horrific dreck . . . I couldn't." Rohan swallowed; anger raged inside him, sparked by the memory.

"I couldn't handle it.

"I lost it.

"And the trick I'd been saving, the one edge I thought I had, the one thing that I'd been depending on when I faced him, failed me.

"After that, he just beat the tar out of me.

"He didn't do anything special or clever. Just flew faster than me, hit harder than me, tossed punch after punch so hard and so quick that even though I blocked ten in a row, the eleventh came through and knocked the wind out of me.

"Then the eighteenth cracked me in the temple and knocked me silly. And the twenty-fifth nearly left me unconscious.

"After that, I lost count.

"What did he do to me? He beat me, Lonnie. Fair and square. A straight up butt-kicking. Which is an expression; I don't remember him actually kicking me in the rear. Though he might have, I lost track of what was going on. Check the video if you're curious.

"He beat me. Stone-cold. That's it, that's the answer."

Lonnie looked at Rohan, then at Wei Li, who stared back, impassive. "But that's not it. That can't be it."

Rohan shrugged. "Ask Wei Li if I'm lying."

"I'm not saying you're lying. Well, yes, you are. By omission. You're leaving something out."

"What am I leaving out, Lonnie? What else do you think I need to say to answer your question? Be specific; you might get what you're looking for after all."

"You've been beaten before. Not a lot, not as often as I expected. But I've done my research. I've looked at a lot of footage, spoken to a lot of people. Or at least watched a lot of interviews. You've been beaten before, and badly. Hurt enough to lose months of your life recovering. Which you definitely didn't need this time.

"But those fights didn't change you, Rohan. They didn't take anything away from you. Not for this long. So, no, you didn't really answer my question.

"What I want to know is, how did he get rid of your Power? What did he do to turn you into . . . this?"

Rohan looked at Wei Li, hoping she'd tell him he could avoid the question.

She didn't.

He sighed and looked around.

"Wei Li, he gets to ask, and I have to answer. I get that. Does everyone have to *hear* the answer? Can I tell just him?"

She nodded. "I'll throw a privacy screen over the stage. You have one minute."

The referee turned and left the two men alone on the platform. Rohan waited for the sounds of the arena to mute and fall away.

He stepped forward, close to Lahnegarn, and leaned in, his lips close to the Lukhor's cheek, so nobody with a camera could capture them and read his words.

"The answer is simple, Lahnegarn.

"I can't tell you *how* Hyperion got rid of my Power because he *didn't*.

"I still have my curse. *All* of it. Every last drop, every erg. Enough to tear you into your component atoms, Lonnie. All that rage, all that Power, just simmering inside."

He exhaled slowly, breathing down the Lukhor's neck.

"The thing is, and you can't imagine how hard this is, I've been holding it back.

"For now."

Then he collapsed.

Krai Wu and the Ohnian rushed the stage and helped Rohan to the back of the arena where medical staff were on hand.

"I'm okay, I'm okay."

The Vor'karei laughed. "I'm not an empath like Wei Li, but even I can see that you are not okay."

The Ohnian nodded from his spot under Rohan's other shoulder. "I'm a paramedic, Guru Rohan. You need some help. You've been concussed, have a badly broken nose, and there is significant damage to your left knee."

"The first two I believe. Not the knee, though. I don't remember getting hit in the leg at all. Not once."

Krai Wu shook his head. "I do not think that claim actually supports your position, Rohan."

The Hybrid considered. "I believe I see your point. It's hard to tell with the clouds in my brain obscuring all the thinking I'm trying to do."

The Ohnian paused as they worked to maneuver around a corner without dropping the Hybrid, whose feet barely skimmed the floor as they moved. "We'll need imaging to know for sure, but nothing seems too serious. You might even be ready to fight in time for the next round."

"Oh, good. That's absolutely what I was worried about."

They found Katya alone in the changing area. Her eyes were sad as she faced the trio. "What happened?"

Krai Wu shrugged, adjusting his grip on Rohan's arm. "He was beaten by a Lukhor. He was having trouble walking, so . . ."

The Ohnian nodded. "Help us lay him down. I think I can fix his knee."

Katya stepped closer and picked Rohan up like a child, then carried him to an elevated cot obviously designed for that purpose. A Kratic in station uniform, diagnostic tablet in hand, hurried over and began scanning the Hybrid.

Good thing I'm keeping my Power suppressed or that wouldn't be working on me.

Katya licked his cheek as the Vor'karei waved goodbye to return to the competition.

Rohan turned to look at her face. "How's Ang?"

She sighed. "He'll be fine, but they took him to Medical. Broken ribs."

It was Rohan's turn to sigh. "How's his mood?"

"He was very upset when the doctors told him to restrict his alcohol intake during the early stages of recovery."

Rohan laughed. "Guess he'll be fine." A chime rang from inside his hood. "Oh, good, a message for me. Can you help me reach that?"

The Ohnian put his hands over Rohan's knee and concentrated. "Hold still."

Warmth flooded into the Hybrid's limb: a charge of esoteric energy.

His own Power rose to combat the intrusion; Rohan snuffed it away.

That's getting easier. All that practice is paying off.

Rohan relaxed as the discomfort in his limb dissipated. "Can you fix my head while you're at it?"

Katya reached into his hood and pulled his helmet out from where he'd been lying on it. The doctor ran his scanner over Rohan's forehead.

The Ohnian didn't respond for several breaths. Then he lifted his hands, opened his eyes, and smiled. "It only works on the simplest injuries, Guru. Two tendons were damaged; I pressed them together in a noninvasive way. With a brain . . ."

"No, don't explain it. It's a neat trick. I've heard of it before but never seen it."

"A specialty of my people. I should go back to the competition, Guru. Heal quickly."

"Thanks."

Katya handed him the helmet. "I should return to my duties. Will you manage?" She looked up at the doctor as she said it.

The Kratic nodded. "He'll be fine. Head injury is minor, and his lungs are clear. As long as he doesn't—"

Rohan interrupted. "If you say I need to stay away from alcohol, I'm going to be very—"

The doctor humphed and continued, "—drink alcohol or incur further physical damage in the near future, he'll recover."

Rohan sighed. "—be very sad. Sad. I could really use a drink. Doc, are you sure?"

The Kratic typed on his pad. "I'm sending you a referral for alcoholism treatment as well. You and your big hairy friend might want to attend meetings together."

"Thanks, Doc. I appreciate it." He looked inside his helmet.

Text message.

An address.

Rinth had found the Boost distributor.

34

Finding Strength In Weakness

R ohan's knee held up surprisingly well as he left the arena and turned up the promenade.

I need to get that Ohnian's contact info. He might come in handy.

The address Rinth had provided was way out on Wistful's western arm.

Once, Rohan would have flown there.

Earlier that week, he might have walked.

That day, he took a transport pod.

He climbed the stairs to the station's main residential level, coming out onto a promenade empty as far as he could see. He found an address marker and started walking.

I had a plan. I really did.

First, master Spiral's technique, then use it on Hyperion.

With the influence that gets me with the Assessors, start changing the way they do business.

Save some lives and keep my friends safe all at the same time.

It all hinged on that first step.

But every time my curse kicks in, every time that angry Power floods through me, I lose the spiral.

So mastering that technique means mastering my anger.

And I thought I was really making progress on that front, but I can't even keep my cool fighting a loser like Lahnegarn.

Is it time for plan B?

That question would be easier to answer if I had a plan B.

He reached his destination: an apparently unused doorway. He pushed through.

Something rang as the door opened, alerting the inhabitants to his presence. He entered a dimly lit lobby.

Probably a camera on me. Time to say hello.

Just have to talk my way into a meeting.

And I can't lie.

He looked around and waved. "I'm here to talk about Granny."

A door opened, and four humanoids with gray skin and flat yellow eyes stepped into the lobby.

They wore outfits of reinforced dark leather, somewhere between motorcycle gear and full-on body armor, and carried stun batons that sparked lightly when they moved.

They formed a semicircle around the Hybrid, faces grim.

"Hey, guys. Just here for a chat."

One of the goons nodded and pressed his ear. "Is the street clear?" He waited for an answer.

Rohan kept his hands open and spread to his sides. "Really no need to fight here. Just want to talk."

Another goon looked at him. "You came alone?"

"I did. But you don't need me to tell you that, do you? I'm sure you have eyes on the promenade."

The first goon nodded. "Come with us." Then he turned, waved open a second door, and stepped through.

Rohan looked at the others, who watched him. He shrugged. "Coming!"

The door led to a hallway; ten meters down, it opened into a spacious office with an executive desk of polished red wood, two visitors' chairs, and a pair of plush couches lining the sides.

Seated at the desk, in front of a very large abstract oil painting, was a male of the same race, dressed in a business suit. To his left sat another suited male, also gray-skinned with the same dark-yellow eyes.

Riegellians, maybe?

Rohan stood in front of the desk.

The boss pointed at the empty chair; Rohan sat.

"How did you find this place?"

Rohan shrugged. "Trade secret, can't tell you. But . . . that guy's an empath, right? He'll know if I'm lying?"

The boss nodded.

Rohan continued. "You don't have a leak, and nobody else can use the method I used. You're safe."

The boss checked with the empath, who nodded. "Fine. Call me Grell. And I don't know who this Granny is, so I think you're wasting my time."

Rohan sighed. "See, I should have brought my own empath. I know one, you know. I mean, she's busy, but we're pals. I bet if I had my own empath, they'd be all up in my ear right about now, whispering something that we both know just means that they think you're lying."

The empath to the boss's left smiled fleetingly.

Grell cleared his throat. "What do you want?"

"I told you, I want a meeting with Granny."

"Assuming I know who that is, and further assuming I could get you that meeting, why? And why would that person wish to meet with you?"

"Look at my face. Notice anything unusual?"

Grell looked at his empath, who shrugged. "You're bleeding a bit. Looks like you've been roughed up. Was it my people? Are you looking to complain?"

"No, not at all. I lost a fight, nothing to do with you guys. Except I think you can help me make sure I don't lose any more."

Grell swallowed. "You're looking to score? You don't need Granny for that. Uh, assuming I know who that is."

"I can already get Boost. What I need is something a little more substantial."

"Like what?"

"Like a real connection. A supply. I'm facing some . . . challenges. I'll be honest here, I'm struggling. In some ways, more than I ever have. I don't see a way clear. Not really. And I'm grasping at straws. You don't know what that means, do you?"

The boss shrugged, the shoulders of his full-canvas suit jacket moving unnaturally with the motion. "I understand enough. You're telling me you're desperate. I'm not sure that's smart."

"If I were smart, I wouldn't be here. I need a bigger connection. I have enemies. A pinch of Boost I can use today, when tomorrow maybe my dealer is off the station and people are coming for me, just isn't going to cut it."

"Why would Granny be interested in doing that for you?"

"Do you know who I am?"

"I know who you were. I also know you're a guy desperate enough to come to me for a favor. So what I'm wondering is what the guy in front of me has to offer to someone like Granny. Assuming that's even a real person."

Rohan leaned forward in his chair; the empath flinched and stood, putting his body in front of his boss's.

The Hybrid smiled humorlessly. "I'm still who I am, Grell. My name is still whispered on a thousand worlds. If Boost helps me return to that, Granny will have me owing her a favor. A big favor. And if it doesn't, what have you lost? Not much of anything."

He relaxed his face and settled back in the chair.

The empath sat back down.

Grell nodded. "I hear what you're saying. Leave your comm ID; we'll be in touch."

"I thought you'd say that."

⬤ ··•·· ◆

Rohan's legs shook a bit as he left the building. He leaned against the outside wall, took deep breaths, and waited for the tremor in his thigh to subside.

Five minutes later, he pushed away from the wall and headed for the transport level.

When he exited, he stopped at a sidewalk vendor for food: a fat sandwich, with fried slices of a mashed blue tuber instead of bread and the meat of a flightless Drexian bird as the filling.

As he walked away, the Hybrid paused to record the name of the shop; the spicy dressing they'd layered over the meat was something he knew he'd have to try again.

Fighters were walking away from the arena, turning up or down the promenade.

He entered and found the stage clear, the fighters muddling about, engaged in conversation, or heading for the exits.

The Hybrid approached the judges' area near the stage; Wei Li sat back in her chair, hands behind her head, and stared at the far wall.

He saw Mai Si. "Is the round over?"

She nodded. "Wei Li considered running round five tonight, but many of the fighters are injured or exhausted. It can wait for morning."

Master Turtle looked right through the Hybrid, a soft smile on his scaly lips.

"Speaking of Wei Li. Is she okay? She looks tired."

"I'm sure she is. It's a strain. Strong emotions all around, and she can't escape them. Are *you* all right, Rohan? You look . . . less than well."

"It's just my face. And my leg. And my head. You know, nothing important."

She shook her head. "I'm not sure what you think you gain by such self-deprecation, but I assure you it is unnecessary."

He sighed. "Forgive me, force of habit. I'm going to go over and distract Wei Li from her problems."

"How do you intend to do that?"

"By bothering her with mine. Works every time."

She laughed. "Best of luck."

"You too." He crossed the few meters separating her from Wei Li and sat next to his friend. "How are you doing?"

She shook her head, breaking her gaze from the distance, and turned to him. "I am unchanged. Which is more than I can say about your nose."

"It will heal. I think. Anyway, the nose is the least of my problems."

She stared at him for a few seconds, then double-blinked her vertically slit eyes and exhaled. "Is there any way I can prevent you from telling me what's troubling you? Short of disemboweling myself right this minute, spilling my still hot entrails over your feet, to demonstrate just how much I don't want to have this conversation?"

"Oh, come on, Wei Li. You live for this."

"I most certainly do not."

"Mai Si was just saying what a kind and generous person you are, always eager to help other people in their times of need. She even encouraged me to come to you for help. I wasn't going to, you know. I was totally going to figure things out for myself. But then, Mai Si—"

Wei Li snorted loudly, impressive given the narrowness of her nostril slits. "I do not need to be an empath to know that's not true." A smile broke through her words.

"Fine. You caught me. Let me buy you a drink. Tea, maybe. Or I'll buy you whatever you want; I'll have tea, because the stupid doctor told me I can't drink because of this stupid concussion. I don't even like tea."

"You like tea just fine when nobody is preventing you from having something stronger. But fine, I will come. Just a drink; I promised to dine with Krai Wu and Mai Si and the master."

"Great. I won't need long. You have a place in mind?"

"There is a Rogesh tea house up the block. Come."

She checked in with Mai Si, relaying her plans, then led the Hybrid out of the arena and toward the tea house.

The decor did not agree with Rohan's appearance—it was far too elegant for a man with that quantity of blood on his shirt—but they let him in after a whispered word from the security chief.

A Rogesh, massive horn jutting up from the end of his snout, led them to a black lacquered table in the back. Wei Li ordered for them both without asking Rohan what he wanted. Music played: a soft, jazzy flute array that felt like a temple soundtrack.

She leaned forward and breathed in from a hole in the table; Rohan did the same. A compartment under the surface held burning incense.

He leaned back in his chair as some of the tension wound out of his neck; the combination of sensory experiences was taking the edge off.

Wei Li looked at him. "You made me laugh, which I sorely needed, and gave me an excuse to come here, which I also probably needed. So I will let you tell me what ails you. If I am feeling generous, I will also advise you. But do not count on it."

"I knew I could count on you, Wei Li."

"I said—"

"Joke! Joke! Look, it worked, you're smiling. You can't help it, I'm adorable."

"That was a significant stretch of the truth."

"Fine." He leaned back as a waiter placed two steaming earthenware mugs between them. The Hybrid picked his up and took a gentle sip. "This is delicious."

"Yes."

He played with the mug as he gathered his thoughts, then took another sip.

She raised an eyebrow of red and green scales. "Your mood is getting worse."

"That's because I was distracted by the idea of talking to you, and now I'm thinking about what I have to say. If it wasn't frustrating, I wouldn't need help."

"Tell me."

He sighed. "I thought I knew what I needed to do. I can't just . . . turn off my anger. It doesn't work like that; it's too essential a part of who I am."

"As a Hybrid."

"Yeah. It's our curse. But I thought I could take away the triggers. You know, eliminate the things that *make* me angry. The things that spark it."

"You want to eliminate everything that angers you? That would probably amount to half the sentient beings in the sector, Rohan. Perhaps an extreme measure to solve this particular problem."

"That's not what I meant. I was trying to let go of my fear."

"Your fear."

"Yeah. To stop the cascade. The dominoes. The chain of events that lead to my rage." She stared at him blankly. "You know, because of what they say."

She sipped her tea. "What do they say, Rohan? Tell me, for I am uncertain."

"Well. Fear leads to anger, anger leads to hate, and hate leads to—"

"Who says this, Rohan? From whom did you garner this bit of wisdom? Was it Spiral, your instructor? His master, whose name I cannot remember at the moment?"

"Sid. No, they didn't say it. It was . . . a puppet."

"A puppet. I see."

"In a movie. It was a character, in a movie. Played by a puppet. Or by a guy with his hand inside a puppet. I don't know. It's, what do you call it, conventional wisdom. Anger comes from fear. Right?"

She sipped her tea again. "Rohan, I will offer some advice."

"That's exactly what I'm here for."

"Any aphorisms that reduce human emotion to a simple causal statement are false."

He scratched his beard. "I don't like where this is going."

"What was your plan, Rohan? The plan inspired by this statement about fear?"

"Like I said, I thought I could let go of my fear. Exhale it away. Like when you meditate. The way you let go of intrusive thoughts. I thought for sure that would do the trick. But then I fought Lonnie, and that bastard—excuse my language—that bastard got me so angry. But I wasn't afraid, Wei Li. I mean, he's tough, but he's just such a loser. I couldn't be scared of him if I tried. Even though he was threatening to do some stuff that would be really inconvenient."

"You're not afraid of Lahnegarn."

"I'm really not. There's something about him I just can't take seriously that way."

"Yet he aroused your anger."

"Oh yeah. And I lost control of Spiral's technique, and that's the short explanation of how I got my butt kicked. Which you saw."

"I did. It sounds to me as though you have reached your own epiphany. Congratulations, Rohan, well done."

"Wait, no I haven't!"

"You now realize that your anger does not, in fact, necessarily come from fear. Well done."

"But that just sends me back to square one! What am I supposed to do now? I can't just breathe out my anger, it's not working."

"That technique will work if you give it sufficient time."

"I don't have years to spare, Wei Li. I'm not sure anybody does. There's a timeline here."

She tapped the table and sipped her tea again.

He watched her. "If you'd prefer, we could talk about the bind I'm in with Tamara."

She covered her eyes with one hand. "I really wouldn't, Rohan."

"Because I'm starting to think that it's unfair of me to be a part of her life, the way I complicate things—"

"Please stop. That's too much for me today. I'll tell you what your problem is."

He nodded and leaned back in his chair. "Please."

"Rohan, you are trying to let go of your anger. To let it fall away, the way a romantic partner might stop calling if you simply ignore her messages often enough."

"Sure. I guess. You're saying I'm trying to ghost my own feelings? Accurate. A weird analogy, but accurate."

"Tell me, has this process ever worked for you? Have you ever been able to still your thoughts by simply relaxing and, as you said, exhaling them out of your mind? Have you ever attained peace with this method?"

"I don't . . . I don't know."

"I will tell you: you haven't. That is why I had you meditate to a mantra. You moved your mind away from negative thoughts by focusing on something else, on a saying of yours. You combated a line of consciousness by grasping harder onto a different thread, not by simply willing it to fall away."

"Be nice."

"I am being nice."

"No, I meant, that was my mantra."

She waved her hand in the air. "It doesn't matter. You're a warrior, Rohan."

"What does that mean? I should embrace my anger?"

"Not at all. It means you can only combat your rage by opposing it with a countering emotion."

"Combat the rage. With another feeling."

"Yes. You could learn the other way, if you had a decade or two to spare, but you say you do not. So you must learn to balance your anger with its opposite."

"Its opposite. You can't be serious. Its *opposite*."

"I am, sadly, all too serious."

"That's a terrible cliché, though. Terrible. Like, the worst. You can't ask me to do that."

"I'm not asking you to do anything. I am explaining the most direct path to the emotional state you seek."

"That can't be the answer. I'll never hear the end of it. My friends will mock me."

"And yet."

"Rudra save me. I have to fight my anger . . ."

"Yes. You see it."

"With the power of love. I'm going to be sick."

35

Hey, What About . . .

R ohan sipped his tea; it was still hot, but no longer scalding.

He tipped the three-quarters-full mug into his mouth, swallowing as quickly as the liquid filled his throat, and held it there until the mug was completely drained.

Wei Li cleared her throat. "You are being dramatic."

"Am not."

"Yes, you are. And a tad childish. If you find the word 'love' so problematic, say 'compassion' instead. Perhaps try, 'understanding.'"

He lowered the mug and wiped his mouth. "I just—" His comm began to ding.

Not with the usual 'incoming call' signal, and not quite the emergency sound one of his close friends could activate with the right calling code.

It was a sound he'd never heard from his unit before.

He met Wei Li's quizzical glance, shrugged, and tapped the screen. "Hello?"

"Rohan!" Rinth's voice cracked as it erupted over the speaker. "Rohan, it's me! I'm Rinth! I mean, it's Rinth! I have to talk to you it's super important and I know we talked about hacking the video feeds and seeing stuff but really it's your fault because you—"

Rohan smiled at Wei Li and tapped the screen to shunt the audio to the comm behind his ear. "I need to take this, sorry!"

He slipped the mask over his face and listened.

"—so that's when I realized he was missing and I don't know what to do but I figured you would definitely know!"

Rohan coughed. "Rinth, slow down. You're right, I asked you to look through video feeds. Slow down and tell me what you saw."

"It's not what I saw, Rohan! That's the problem! He's not there! He didn't come through the airlock when you guys came back! I mean, I know Rak and Ruk were, well, they got killed, right? By the monsters on the planet? So I wasn't expecting them to come back when your ship docked at Wistful. I didn't have any video from inside *Void's Shadow*, because even I can't hack her internals, though you know I've tried, it's kind of a fun challenge—"

"Don't tell me, I need plausible deniability if you piss off my ship. So this isn't about Rak or Ruk? Or your father? Who is 'he,' Rinth?"

"That's what I'm trying to tell you! You have to let me talk."

The Hybrid held up a finger as Wei Li began to stand. He looked at her and mouthed, "One second." Then he spoke into the mask. "Who is it, Rinth?"

"It's Tracker, Rohan! He went down in Dad's shuttle, but you didn't bring him back!"

Rohan sighed. "Tracker? Wait, the dog? The Quattros' dog?"

"Yes! Tracker! Is this a bad connection? He went down with the group. He always travels with the Quattros. But you didn't bring him back."

I didn't even know he was there. "Are you sure he went down with them?"

"Of course I'm sure! Well, just in case, I checked other surveillance records. Like the place where the Quattros were staying, Grandpa's place, stuff like that. And he's not there, Rohan! You don't think . . ."

Think he got eaten by a monster on the monster planet where we left him for . . . two entire days? Yeah, that's what I think. "Of course he's fine. He's a smart dog, right?"

"I guess he's smart. I don't know if that's going to be enough, though. I mean, the Quattros got eaten, right? What chance does Tracker have?"

"Why do you care about Tracker so much, Rinth? I mean, we hope all animals are safe, I guess, but . . ."

"I used to play with him all the time, Rohan. Whenever we were around Grandpa, you know. I've known him since he was a pup. Please, you have to help him!"

Help him . . . what? Bring him back to life? "I'd like to, I really would. But . . . what are you suggesting? Because I'm not sure what you want me to do here."

"Go to the planet, Rohan! You have a ship. Please, just go down there and see if you can find him! We can't just leave him down there."

"Rinth, buddy, I hate to say this, but it might be too late."

"I know! I know, I'm not stupid. But we have to try! Please please please!"

"Okay. How am I supposed to find him, though? It's a big planet and he's a pretty small dog."

"It's not a whole world, Rohan! He went down with the shuttle. You know where it landed, right? If you don't, I can send you the coordinates. I have that footage. He can't be that far from the crash site, can he? I mean, he's just a little dog. It's not like he would have been running for two straight days. I don't think he could."

"No. No, you're right. It's not a whole world." Rohan locked eyes with Wei Li as she put down her tea. He took off his helmet and tapped the audio back to the speaker. "I have an idea. I'm not going to promise anything, but I'm going to try, okay?"

"Okay, Rohan. Thank you thank you thank you. Please find him and bring him back."

"I'll do my best, kid. You just . . . I don't know. Stay out of trouble for a few hours, okay?" *Fat chance of that.* "Or hack some satellites and see if you can get any video imagery of the area."

"Okay, I'll do that. I mean I'll try. Thanks, Rohan. Thank you."

"Thank me if I bring him home." He looked at Wei Li, who groaned. "Rinth, I'm hanging up. I have work to do." He tapped off the call.

Wei Li shook her head. "Whatever it is you want from me, this is not the time. I shouldn't have even come here to have tea with you."

"But wait, you haven't heard my crazy idea."

"I don't want to know your crazy idea."

"Of course you do. This will make a great story, and we both know how you love telling cool stories about all the cool hijinks I get you into."

"I have never, and will never, do that."

"Well, I'll tell the story for both of us. Deal?"

"What? No. What is it you even want me to do?"

"Come down to Toth 3 and help me find a dog."

Thirty minutes later, they were onboard *Void's Shadow* and on their way to Toth 3.

"Captain, I don't think this is a good idea. The sun is setting at the crash site. I don't see how you're going to find this animal."

Rohan rubbed his forehead. "I don't know. I don't even think the dog is still alive, to be honest. But we have to try."

Wei Li sighed. "No, we do not. Dogs die, Rohan. Especially Quattro assassin tracking dogs. In fact, they die quite frequently."

"Well, we might be able to save this one."

"At the risk of our own lives."

"Sure. Some risk. But not much! No, listen, I'm serious. I hung out there for days at a time. You know how to restrain your own angry tendencies. At least for a while, right? The kaiju don't attack for no reason."

"It is highly unlikely that the dog has survived."

"I know. I know! But I'd like to try. I need some wins. I've been taking a lot of losses lately. I feel like . . . I was about to make a sport analogy that would have made no sense to you."

"I'm used to that. I'm here, I said I would help."

"I was trying to convince *Void's Shadow*. And myself."

The ship responded. "Captain, I've decided to take you down and help as much as I can. Not that I can do much more than take you there and wait. But if we can save this dog, we will."

"That's my girl." He took out his mask and checked messages.

One from Tamara.

Oh crap. I should have called her before.

But I didn't want to.

Maybe because her ex-husband just broke my nose.

He braced himself, then opened the message.

She was finishing up her project and would be busy most of her day, his night. She'd try to see him for breakfast the following morning.

He relaxed.

She's not mad.

Unless she is *mad and she's hiding it.*

Nah, that's never been her style.

Still, I should cover my bases.

He messaged back, explaining his mission.

Running an errand to help her desperate son has to be the best possible excuse for not calling.

Right?

He went through the rest of his news feeds, specifically looking for mentions of Hyperion.

Or dying worlds.

Stories of Hyperion stealing a Shayjh battleship were gone from the net. For a moment he thought it was because they had been false; then he reconsidered.

Somebody's making sure that story doesn't spread.

He sighed.

The Hybrid turned his attention inward, or perhaps sideways, to the world of ethereal substance. He had rebuilt his esoteric spiral, broken during the fight with Lahnegarn; it was holding its shape.

Holding its shape for now. As long as I stay calm.

Either let go of the anger or fight it with something more ... positive. What a ridiculous life I lead. Am I leading it, though? More like following.

"Captain, we're arriving."

He checked the screen; it was dark. "Switch to UV."

The image brightened as the ship switched frequencies and enhanced the results.

Wei Li stood and stretched. "No sign of the dog, I assume."

"As expected. It's a small dog and a big forest. Our best chance is if you can sense it."

"You realize my empathy has limited range. If it's a kilometer away, I'll never *see* it, unless it's a very unusual dog."

"I know. It's not a great plan, okay? I admit it. Let's just try."

"I said I would. Let me set up my mask." She pulled out a mask similar to Rohan's: roughly oval shaped so it could seal to her face, with a single-facet diamond front to see through. The air supply and electronics were built into the foam edge between the diamond and the rubbery sealing material.

Rohan tapped his own, setting up the ultraviolet cameras; the electronics would superimpose an image of what was in front of him over the inside of the mask. It would enable him to see in the dark.

Void's Shadow landed with a soft bump. "We're by the crash site, Captain."

A few meters from the clearing around the dig. "Thanks. You ready?"

Wei Li nodded. "I didn't plan on becoming kaiju food when I woke up this morning, but if I'm eaten in this godsforsaken place, at least I won't have to go back and watch Master Turtle die."

"That's the spirit. Come on." The hatch opened, and they exited.

Rohan pointed into the woods. "We should split up, cover more ground. I'll check around the crashed shuttle, see if there are any tracks left. You want to check out the dig site? There was stuff there. A tent, food. Maybe Tracker is hanging around it."

Wei Li nodded, her face glowing behind her mask, lit by the interior projections. "Good." She turned toward the clearing and began trudging over, working hard to pull her feet free of the moss with every step.

Rohan made his way to the shuttle.

Wish I were flying.

But if I turn my Power loose now, I might as well be giving up on Spiral's technique.

What should I call it? Something with reflection, since it returns energy? Palm of Reflection?

That sounds like a salad at a fancy restaurant.

Vines were already creeping up the shuttle's landing gear, the forest eager to reclaim the few square meters of territory it had lost. Rohan walked a slow, deliberate circle around the ship, eyes focused on the ground, searching for some trace of the missing dog.

He completed two loops and sighed.

"Wei Li, you find anything?"

"I'm at the site now. Nothing yet."

"I'm going to try a wider circle."

A branch cracked nearby.

Void's Shadow spoke in his ear. "I think your pet is here, Captain."

Rohan froze.

"Wei Li, that wasn't you, was it?"

"I don't know what you're talking about, Rohan. I'm at the site. Is this the door you were studying?"

Another branch cracked, louder. A heavy breathing sound came from the trees.

"Yeah. Now might not be the time for that."

"What is wrong, Rohan?"

He swallowed as the trees moved, branches rustling.

A head emerged from the forest: reptilian, with a long, pointed snout, two flat black eyes above.

Rohan exhaled. "It's Terry."

"Is that a problem, Rohan?"

He thought. "Maybe? Just don't get mad. Don't think about fighting him. Or anything. But especially don't get mad."

"I shall try."

"There is no try. Do, or do not."

"Is that more so-called wisdom from your puppet?"

"How on Earth did you guess that? Especially since you've never even been to Earth?"

"You repeat yourself, Rohan. And I, sadly for me, tend to actually listen to what you say and to remember it. So, after a while . . ."

"I don't know whether to apologize or bow to you in amazement. Right now, I'm going to see if I can keep Terry calm. I'll never be able to get people down here to study those ruins if he keeps hanging around, waiting to eat them."

The pterosaur approached on thick legs, his talons digging wide ruts in the moss with each step, his wings folded close to his body to keep clear of the trees.

The ship spoke again. "He doesn't seem agitated, Captain. But be careful anyway."

"I will."

Fresh scars lined his left shoulder.

"Have you been fighting, boy? What happened?"

The pterosaur raised his head as if to unleash a massive roar but paused, and instead exhaled loudly, more than a sigh but less than a bark.

He doesn't look like he wants a fight.

Rohan stepped toward the kaiju, hands up. He hurriedly pushed his mask up onto the top of his head, rendering himself all but blind.

Let's make sure he recognizes me. Does he even know my face? Or is it smell? I have no idea. Ben Stone would know.

Terry lowered his head as Rohan approached.

Wei Li's voice emerged from the speakers in the helmet, tinny as it passed through his hair instead of directly into his ear. "Rohan!" There was something in her voice. Surprise? More than that? Panic?

What's going on?

Terry raised his head, muscles around his neck and chest tightening suddenly.

"No, no, boy. Stay calm. Stay calm. Here, let me look at that shoulder. Stay calm."

Rohan stepped closer, his mouth drying and his heart rate increasing as he pushed into the kaiju's potent aura.

Terry looked down again as Rohan reached up and put a hand on his clavicle.

Wei Li's voice came again, louder. "Rohan! The door! Did you see the door?" Her voice was edged with something he'd never heard from her before: a tint of hysteria.

Crap.

Terry straightened, eyes turned toward the clearing, then settled a bit as Rohan rubbed trembling fingers over the skin of the kaiju's upper chest. "Shh. Shh. It's all right, boy, just Wei Li. Something scared her. Wonder what, right, boy? I wonder if she opened that door. Wouldn't that be a thing? I spent days with it. Maybe she just spun the dials and hit the right combination on the first try."

Terry lowered his chin over the Hybrid's back and relaxed further as Rohan stroked his neck.

The gashes in the kaiju's shoulder were pink lines of rapidly healing tissue.

Meaning they were fresh.

"What hurt you, Terry? Not much on this planet that can put a scratch on you. Were you fighting other kaiju? Why would you be doing that, boy? It's not smart. You're just a little one. The others will eat you alive."

Wei Li was shouting. "Rohan! The door! The letters! I recognize them!"

Rudra save me, this is going to be one of those days.

He used both hands to scratch Terry's neck, hoping he could counter the effect of Wei Li's shouting on the kaiju.

He swiped at his mask, knocking it back down over his face so she would hear him. "Wei Li, listen very carefully. Unless you're about to die, you have got to stop shouting. I am scratching this kaiju's neck as if my life depends on calming him down because it absolutely does. You understand? If he gets angry, he'll swallow me in one bite, and you're going to feel really guilty."

She answered, her voice lowered but still filled with a panicky energy he'd never heard from her. "Rohan, these markings . . . these letters. I know them. It's the language of the Lifters, Rohan."

He sighed. "That makes sense. I guess."

Her voice rose again. "It's not just that! I know these words, Rohan. Each dial . . . the letters . . . they form a word. Look, I can spell it out."

"Maybe now is not the time to do that."

She mumbled something he only vaguely understood: names of letters, but letters he didn't know. "'When'! The first word is 'when'! It clicked, Rohan, it clicked! That's the combination for the first dial!"

Terry settled a bit more, resting his chin on Rohan's back, the weight pressing the Hybrid's feet deeper into the moss. "That's amazing, Wei Li. Let's come back tomorrow and open the thing." His knees buckled slightly with the pressure, and his head started to hurt.

"You don't understand. O-P-E-N. By the Twelve, you don't understand. Are you listening? Do you know what this is? By every last one of the Lifter-damned Twelve. Oh, by the Gods, there are vowels here. And diagrams. There are diagrams. The order, Rohan. Arrows showing the order."

"What arrows, Wei Li? I spent a week staring at that door, what are you talking about?"

Terry stiffened and straightened, head tilted so he kept his eyes on Rohan.

Oh no. Is he about to go off?

Terry exhaled loudly, blowing air that rustled Rohan's short hair, then stepped back from the Hybrid's embrace.

"Where are you going, boy? What's up?" He was about to tilt his helmet back so the kaiju could hear his words, then remembered that it was just an animal.

It wouldn't matter.

Terry lowered his face and dug a small hole right in front of Rohan's feet. Then he hopped back three meters, pointed his snout at the hole, and hopped back another three.

"You want me to stay, boy? Right here? I can do that. I've got nowhere else to go. Not as long as you stay calm." The Hybrid pointed at the hole, nodded, and knelt over it. He pointed at the ground. "I'm staying right here."

The kaiju hopped back again, watching the Hybrid.

Rohan stayed in place, swaying slightly but not daring to take a step.

The kaiju spun and leapt up into the air.

Wei Li shouted again. "Eyes become The Shield! It's the prophecy, Rohan! The dials spell out the prophecy!"

36

The Importance of Proper Grammar

R ohan remained frozen in place.

Priority one: do not anger the person-eating kaiju.

"What did you say, Wei Li? I think I misheard you."

Her response was duller. "This can't be right. It can't be. It doesn't make sense."

"I mean, it might. If the Lifters were il'Sein. Or if the il'Sein didn't put the kaiju here. Maybe they're just connected in some way. We're talking about tens of thousands of years of history; they could have splintered into a hundred different groups and we'd have no idea."

"It can't be. Why here?"

"Well, the Lifters specifically tasked your order with watching Wistful, right? It would make sense that they had connections to this place. Wouldn't it?"

"It would. It would. But, Rohan . . . the arrows. The diagrams."

"I still don't understand, Wei Li. What arrows?"

"Hold on." Her voice faded away, then came back. "This can't be. It can't."

Rohan exhaled slowly, emptying his lungs. "What arrows, Wei Li?"

"You haven't seen them. They aren't visible under normal light, Rohan. Only UV. I slipped my mask off and shined a regular light on the door, and they're invisible. They only show up through the mask's camera."

He exhaled again.

Okay, that's weird. But it make sense. It's like a puzzle. They hid the markings. In plain sight.

"What do the arrows show, Wei Li? I don't understand what they do."

"It's a sentence diagram, Rohan. The . . . the language of the Lifters isn't straightforward. You don't always read it left to right or top to bottom. The words are usually presented in more of a cluster. This cluster, on this door, has arrows showing the order. Orders."

Void's Shadow interrupted. "Captain, I'm going to just fly over there and take some pictures. With UV this time."

"Great. Go for it." He exhaled. "Wei Li, what do you mean 'orders'?"

"I don't know. I don't know. I have to think."

"Okay. Calm down, okay? It's really important that you stay calm. Terry's coming back now, I hear something through the trees."

"Terry? The kaiju?"

"Yes. You haven't been listening. You were just saying something about how I repeat myself and you notice because—"

"Never mind that. Is the kaiju attacking?"

"No. He left."

"Left?"

"Yeah. He flew away and . . . and now he's back. Hello there, Terry."

"Are you in danger?"

He watched Terry approach; evaluated the kaiju's body language.

After weeks together, he had an idea when the animal was agitated. He knew the signs: lowered chin, extra tension across the shoulders and neck.

He didn't see it.

There was, however, something in the kaiju's mouth.

"I don't think so, Wei Li. But stay back just in case."

What is that?

"Hey, *Void's Shadow*, can you scan for other kaiju? I see Terry, but are more coming? Or are we safe? I can't quite figure out how everybody's auras are projecting. A lot of strong emotions."

The ship answered. "I'm monitoring the area via satellite and none of the larger kaiju are moving near us, Captain. Would you like me to do a scouting run?"

"No, I'll trust the sats for now. You be careful flying around Terry, though. I don't want him to take a bite out of you."

"Will do, Captain."

Terry folded his wings and walked toward Rohan. He stopped a few meters away and lowered his head to the ground, then carefully dropped the item he'd been carrying to the moss in front of the Hybrid.

The ball of fur yelped as it touched the moss and leapt up in a frenzy of movement. It jumped into Rohan's arms, hard enough for him to have to lean back and put a hand out behind himself to catch his weight.

"Whoa, there. Tracker?" The dog squirmed and pawed at Rohan's chest and arms, claws digging lightly into him, trembling violently. The Hybrid wrapped his free arm around the animal and rubbed its back vigorously. "Hey there, boy, it's okay. You're safe, boy. You're safe."

How the hell is he safe?

Terry woofed and locked his eyes on Rohan's.

"Did you save him, Terry? Did you . . . you did. You saw this poor little guy running around, and, somehow, you knew to save him."

The dog's trembling slowed as he snuggled deeper into Rohan's arms, his cold wet nose buried in his neck.

Wei Li spoke. "I have to get back to the station. I have to show these pictures to the others. This changes . . . everything, Rohan. It changes everything. You have no idea . . . I was so wrong."

"That's fine, Wei Li. We can go back. And fix things. Our work here is done."

"What do you mean? What about the dog?"

"Terry had him. The whole time. I think he put Tracker somewhere safe. And he's hurt. I mean he was hurt. I wonder if he protected the dog."

"Your pet kaiju saved a dog and then fought to defend it?"

Rohan shrugged, though he knew she couldn't see it. "It's just a guess, but it tracks. The kaiju don't fight each other often, so what are the chances Terry got into a scrap during these two days completely by chance?"

"Rohan, this is too much to think about. We need to get back. I need to show these pictures to Mai Si. And Krai Wu."

"Yeah. You said the other dials were the other words of the prophecy? Did you put the words in?"

She paused before answering.

He scratched the dog's back, then stepped in to Terry and ran his fingers along the underside of the kaiju's neck.

"I did, Rohan. I put them all in. I followed the diagram. You have to run the sentence twice, you see. You wouldn't know without the arrows."

"What happened?"

"The door opened."

◆ ┄ ◆

Tracker wouldn't leave the Hybrid's arms.

Wei Li sighed. "That dog is terrified."

"Of course he is. Two days alone on a strange jungle planet while huge monsters fight for the right to eat you? I'm scared just thinking about it."

"Yet here we are, watching you scratch that monster's neck."

"You're right, it's silly. Come here and help."

"You want me to scratch its neck?"

"I'll show you the spots to scratch. He really likes when you get the back of his head." Terry lowered his chest to the moss as Rohan spoke, bringing more of his body in reach of the smaller humanoids.

Wei Li sighed and got to work. "I hope Terry isn't like dogs in other ways. If he tries to hump my leg, he's going to rip me in half."

"So far he hasn't tried that. Don't give him ideas, though."

"You think he can understand our words? Or do you think he's empathic?"

"He's at least a little empathic, right? Anyway, better safe than sorry. If you're feeling too casual with him, just ask *Void's Shadow* to show you the video of him eating two Quattro assassins in two bites."

"I will remember that. I would also like to get back to Wistful. I really do need to discuss these findings with the others."

"Five more minutes. Terry deserves it. He's been a very good boy." *Also I really don't feel like walking anywhere. My legs are shaky.*

She sighed. "He has. Five more minutes, Rohan. But then we go back. Directly back."

Void's Shadow piped in. "I'll bring you back, Wei Li. If he won't come, we can always leave the captain behind."

"Hey, whose side are you on?"

"I'm just trying to be a good host, Captain. Your guest wants to leave. We can't just keep her here."

Rohan grumbled.

Wei Li took out her tablet and tabbed through a set of photos she'd taken, her yellow skin bunched between scale eyebrows.

Never seen her like this.

I hope things work out.

—◆·••·◆—

Reuniting Tracker with Rinth proved uneventful; the most difficult part for Rohan was trying to determine who was more excited to see whom.

That and his growing headache.

"Is your mom around?"

Rinth scrunched up his face. "She's locked away in her room, says she's busy. She's been super busy the last few nights. All I know is that it isn't work, because she doesn't do that from the house."

"Do you think I can stop in and say hello?"

"Are you sure you want to interrupt her while she's busy? I'll take you to her if you want, but I wouldn't dare, and I'm her kid. You're just some guy she likes."

Rohan scratched his beard. "I see your point."

"Thanks for rescuing Tracker! I don't know what to do with him, though. You think I should give him back to Grandpa?"

The Hybrid shrugged. "Honestly? I don't know. I say keep him. But, you know, I'm not in charge, so . . ."

"I get it. I'll ask Mom. Or Grandpa." He giggled as the dog licked his face. "I should feed him and give him some water, I think. If he's been all alone for two days."

"Sounds like a good idea." *I should have thought of that.* "I'm going now, I have things to do. Okay?"

"Okay. And thanks again, Rohan. I'm really glad you saved him."

"Don't thank me, thank Terry. No, don't thank Terry, he might eat you. Go ahead and thank me, I'll convey the sentiment to Terry myself. Next time I see him."

The boy walked away halfway through Rohan's statement.

The Hybrid shrugged and headed for the Vor'karei's apartment.

Ten minutes later, he sat at their dining table.

Wei Li leaned over it, running her fingers along the printouts Mai Si had made of the photos.

"See? Follow the arrows. It says, 'When eyes become open, eyes become the shield.' Two passes through these words, clear as daylight."

Mai Si nodded. "Also, see these vowels? I've never seen an official set. There are at least four reconstructions of the vowels, but if we believe these, the repeated words have some differences on each pass-through. The word 'eyes' isn't the same."

Krai Wu grunted from his seat; Master Turtle said nothing. Rohan looked between the women. "What does that mean?"

Wei Li grunted. "I can tell you what it seems to mean."

Mai Si glared at her. "You still have doubts? How is that possible?"

Wei Li slapped the table. "Of course I do! You know what this means! What has to happen if it's true!"

Rohan cleared his throat. "I don't. Can you explain it?"

Mai Si pointed at the words. "The first 'eyes' is passive. A noun, but one that can't be the subject of a sentence. Can't be an actor. The grammar doesn't exactly match Drachna, so it is hard to explain."

"Meaning that it's . . . what? An inanimate object? Objects?"

"Yes. Wormholes. They don't open of their own agency, they *are* opened. But the second 'eyes' is a noun with agency. A proper subject, so to speak."

Rohan looked at Wei Li. "So this is saying . . ."

She turned her glare on him. "I know! I know what it seems to say! By the Twelve—"

Mai Si shook her finger at the taller woman. "Language! Do not swear on them in vain, Wei Li."

"My love, this is not the time or place for you to scold me. I will swear on them, for this is exactly the right time. I am not taking their name in vain in the slightest."

Rohan looked at Krai Wu. "Do you get this?"

The man nodded, double-blinking twice in rapid succession. "This reading affirms the classical interpretation. When the wormholes open, The Watcher is to become The Shield. If we'd been able to maintain these writings with the proper annotation, perhaps the schism within our sect could have been avoided. Perhaps Wei Li would have seen things differently these past years."

Rohan swallowed. "Wei Li, does this mean you have to—"

She stood out of her chair and slapped the table. "No! This means nothing of the sort. At least not right now."

Mai Si stood to match her. "What do you mean? This is clear, Wei Li. I know you—"

"I said no! I will not make a hasty decision. I am shaken. *My world* is shaken, and I am upset beyond easy description. I will not be making any kind of permanent decision in this state. I will eat, and sleep, and study these words again in the morning. I will take my time to make any decisions I have to make. If, and I do mean *if*, not when, if I change my mind about anything that matters, I will do it after giving matters due consideration. Is that understood?"

Mai Si stared at her but didn't respond.

Rohan nodded. "Seems fair to me . . ."

The pain in his head intensified; the room spun.

The ground tilted under his feet, and he collapsed to the floor.

37

You Thought He Was the Dangerous One?

Rohan woke in a strange bed. He sat up; he was naked, his clothes folded on a chair next to the bed.

The furniture was familiar: Wistful's infirmary.

He ran a quick inventory of his body.

Then he stopped, realizing it would be faster to search for something that *didn't* hurt.

I think my head is the worst. What happened?

As if on cue, a Drexian female ducked through the doorway and entered the room, her twin horns barely clearing the top of the entrance.

"Rohan. It's been too long."

"Hey, Dr. Simivar. Are you wishing more head trauma on me?"

She smiled, showing off wickedly sharp teeth. "You don't need a reason to visit, Rohan. We're friends. I've seen bits of you that even your girlfriend hasn't seen. Inside bits."

He smiled. "Yeah, sorry about that. I lead a tumultuous life. Believe me, I tried to avoid it. Didn't take."

"I understand. The good news is, patching you up this time was easier than normal. Mild concussion, which, given your biology, should be mostly healed by now."

"I thought you weren't supposed to let people sleep with concussions?"

She pointed at the wall behind his head. "We were monitoring you for brain hemorrhaging, Rohan. You're fine. And, like I said, different biology."

"But the concussion is why I passed out?"

"Yes. And accumulated other traumatic injuries. By the way, you're welcome; I straightened the pieces of your nose while you were out. Try not to get punched in the face for a couple of days, and it will be good as new."

He grunted. "Do you have any idea how hard it is for me to avoid getting punched in the face?"

She smiled and gave an exaggerated sigh, her red scaly skin crinkling around her eyes. "Just try. That's all I ask."

"I will. How long have I been here, anyway?"

"Ten hours. It's . . . right after nine. In the morning."

"Oh man. That's a long time." He rubbed his forehead. "There are a ton of things going on. I can't even keep track of what I'm supposed to be worried about."

"Your vitals are stable, heart rate normal. Normal for you, at least, though if you were fully human, I'm sure you'd be dead."

He scratched his beard. He didn't *feel* worried. "Doc, you ever realize something in a dream? Find a solution to a problem?"

"I have. The subconscious continues to process information while we sleep, it's well-documented. The difficulty lies in distinguishing a genuine fresh understanding from, well, something that's just a dream."

"I feel like that just happened. That's why I'm so calm. But I know I shouldn't be. Can I see my helmet?"

"I'm ready to discharge you. You can have all your things back. I'll step out. Get dressed and you're free to go and do whatever it is you do that leads to you coming back here."

"Will do. I mean, I won't do that, I'll be careful. Thanks." He tapped open the apps in his helmet. "Messages . . . messages . . . here we go."

Rinth thanking him, again, for saving Tracker.

A video of Tracker licking a camera, presumably thanks coming from the dog himself. The return address wasn't Rinth's, meaning the boy had hacked the comm system to send it.

If that's the most mischief he gets into today, I'll be happy.

A report of Hyperion spotted leaving a planet Rohan had never heard of; he flagged the text and saved it to peruse later.

A group message sent to the participants in Wei Li's tournament.

Oh no. I think I'm late for the fifth round.

Rohan tapped it open.

The fifth round was canceled.

Rohan swallowed hard.

Canceled? Not even postponed? Why would she . . .

The prophecy.

If she believes the other interpretation, then she's the one who has to become the shield. She's the eye that becomes the shield.

She's going to take the Eternity Ki.

Master Turtle is going to die, and she's taking his soul.

He read on.

Not just the round: the tournament was canceled. Deepest apologies to all the contestants. Financial compensation would be offered to anyone who had entered.

Of course. There's no point to it now, is there?

Wait. Wait. Wait.

The tournament was the only thing keeping Squeya and The Consortium from going after Tamara.

He closed the message, frantically searching for the timestamp.

Seven minutes.

It had been sent seven minutes earlier.

He panted, his heart racing; hopped out of the bed; grabbed his undergarments and pulled them on, the fabric tearing with the force of his movements.

Tamara.

He was out the door before he could get his left arm through its shirt-sleeve, his helmet up against his face as it placed a call to his girlfriend.

"Pick up, pick up, pick up."

As soon as his arms and legs were sorted, he took off at a sprint. He stopped short of running through an Andervarian nurse, spun around him, and took off up the hallway.

"Hello? Rohan?"

"Hey, look I know you're working on a thing and you asked me not to bother you but this is important."

"Rohan, are you all right? I heard you collapsed, but Dr. Simivar said you just needed some rest."

"I'm fine. Mostly. Look, this isn't about me. We have a much bigger problem. You have to get out of the apartment. Go back to the Ursan neighborhood, hide somewhere. Take Rinth too. Do it now. Don't even pack."

"Rohan, why? What is going on?"

"Just trust me, get out now."

Her tone hardened. "No. Dear, I know you are trying to protect me, but no. You tell me what is going on, and then I will decide what I should be doing. I am not just going to follow orders. Not from my father, not from my ex-husband, and not even from you."

He rubbed his forehead and nearly ran into a food cart as he exited onto the promenade.

"Seriously?"

"I am completely serious. Stop treating me this way. Tell me what is happening."

"Wei Li canceled the tournament."

"So what? Oh, wait. Oh. Never mind, I see what."

"Yeah. So I need you to get out of the apartment and somewhere safe before Squeya finds you. For all I know, she figured out where you live sometime during the tournament and just postponed going after you because she knew Wei Li would kick her out."

"No."

"No, she didn't find out where you live? How do you know that?"

Tamara huffed over the channel. "That is not what I meant. What I meant is no, I will not be running."

"What the heck are you talking about? You can't fight Squeya. I can't fight Squeya. She just put Ang in the hospital, like, I don't know, yesterday. Was that yesterday?"

"I will not fight Squeya. But I do have a plan, and you are going to take direction from me this time."

"What are you talking about? What do you want me to do? I mean, I'll do it, just tell me. Anything."

"I need you to trust me."

He stopped in place, mask in hand, and thought.

Do I?

"I'll trust you."

"Then go to Pop's. Be there in . . . ten minutes. And set your social media location public."

"If I do that, anybody can find me."

"Exactly."

———◆··•··◆———

Pop's House of Breakfast had the best coffee and the best eggs on Wistful. As coffee was hard to find anywhere else that wasn't Earth, it probably had the best coffee in the entirety of the Empire.

The café was more of a serving counter—set into the side of a building that faced the promenade—and an open area covered with mismatched tables and chairs that everyone knew were to be used only by Pop's customers.

Pop himself approached Rohan's table carefully, his two frontmost eyes focused on the Hybrid while the two other eyes on each side of his head pointed out in other directions.

Toth's light gleamed off the man's yellow and blue diamond-patterned scales. "Tow Chief. It's been a while."

"Hey, Pop. The usual, if you don't mind. Tamara's meeting me here any minute."

"Sure. Special occasion?"

The Hybrid shrugged. "I have no idea. Might be some extracurricular activity going on. You'll have to ask my better half when she gets here. If it goes down, I'll try to keep the damage minimal."

"Appreciate that."

Rohan set his location as Tamara had asked and called Katya.

"Rohan? I thought you were in the hospital."

"I was. I left. How's Ang?"

"He is resting comfortably. Are you safe?"

He sighed and explained the situation. "Tamara should be here any minute. Can you get over to Pop's?"

"I will be there very soon, Rohan." She clicked off the call before he could add anything.

He tapped the table and thought.

A Power approached from behind. Rohan turned his head and saw a Tolone'an figure.

He twisted in his chair to get a better look.

"Garren. Hey. Wasn't expecting you."

The Tolone'an, dressed in his full gravity-controlling armored suit, nodded and took a spot next to the Hybrid. "Rohan. Your significant other asked if I might stop by. She said there was a possibility of some unpleasantness, though she also suggested it would not last long."

"Is that what happened? If you meant that as a question for me, I'm going to disappoint you. I have no idea what's going on."

"Well, have a seat."

Garren shook his massive head. "These chairs are flimsy, and with the armor I am fairly heavy. I will stand. I'm not here for coffee, anyway. Or eggs."

"Fair enough."

Garren's helmet faced the Hybrid as the Tolone'an gathered his thoughts.

"Rohan, one thing."

"Sure. I owe you big time, Garren. You've been a huge help. And this isn't the first time."

Garren waved his armored tentacles in the air. "Rohan, The Consortium represents a way of thinking I find . . . reprehensible. They are locked into the past of our planet."

"Yeah, I get that."

"Dr. Kraken encourages the worst of this ideology. Hatred for outsiders. Revenge. Things I despise."

"I get that too."

"And at every turn, I see you fighting for the opposite of those positions. I see you seeking a better future. Not for Tolone'a, specifically, but for everybody."

Rohan sighed. "I mean, I'm trying."

"Well, if I can, I'd like to help."

"You've already helped."

"What I'm saying is, you can count on me. If you call, I will come. If you need me, I will be there."

Rohan swallowed. "I appreciate that, Garren. Maybe more than you know. Especially coming from a . . ."

"I understand."

Pop approached one side of the table as Tamara emerged from the crowd up the promenade. Garren stepped to the side and began surveying the crowd.

The Lukhor was outfitted in a high-quality dress: a bolt of red cloth embroidered in gold thread and heavily bejeweled—diamonds and jade and a half dozen other stones Rohan couldn't identify.

Her makeup was on point, slightly heavier than he would have seen in an Earth executive suite; wings by her eyes and subtle gradations along her cheeks emphasized bone structure that might have otherwise gone unnoticed.

As usual, she took his breath away.

Behind her, walking in lockstep, were three heavily armored Rogesh, each with an artificial right hand and intricately painted horns.

Rohan looked at Garren. "Those are Knights of Ch'doon."

Garren nodded. "I've heard of them. I didn't realize any were on Wistful."

"I saw them at the tournament." *Was that her project? Hiring the Knights? I'm not sure they're going to be enough.*

Tamara smiled when she spotted Rohan and turned to come his way; the Knights followed closely, their eyes scanning the passersby for threats.

Rohan stood and let her come into his arms. He kissed her lips, briefly so as not to disturb her carefully applied lipstick, and smiled. "You look beautiful."

She laughed. "And you, my dear, look worse for wear. I hope your nose returns to its former size or we may have to discuss our relationship."

He tsked and pulled out a chair for her to take. "You're so superficial. If you really loved me, a little nose damage wouldn't interfere with your feelings."

"A little damage would not. That is more than a little damage." She sat as he pushed the chair in.

As if by magic, Pop appeared with a tray and put coffees and two plates of eggs on the table. He looked over the assorted bodyguards, shook his head, and walked away.

Katya came running up the walkway. "I am here! Do not start the fighting without me!"

Rohan waved her over. "Dear, should I get food and drinks for the Knights?"

"I'm paying them to guard me, not to join us for dinner. I mean breakfast."

"Fair. Look, I don't want to criticize, but the Knights aren't going to—"

She put a hand over his arm. "I asked you to trust me. The Knights are here as insurance. That is all."

"Okay."

Garren squeezed Rohan's shoulder with a gauntleted hand. "They're here. The Consortium."

Rohan sighed and turned his head. Within seconds, he could *feel* their auras: potent and cool and wet, pressing down over the area like a heavy fog.

He swallowed and watched his love take a bite of her eggs and sip her coffee.

She smiled at him, her eyes gleaming mischievously.

If she was afraid, it didn't show.

He scratched his beard. "You know how dangerous they are."

"I know everything I need to know, Rohan. Now trust me. And watch."

"You're not on any new medications, are you?"

"I said trust me. Now hush."

Squeya walked in the center, the other four fanning back from her in a tight formation. They locked eyes on the Knights, on Garren, and on Katya.

Garren and the Knights turned to face The Consortium, forming a wall between them and Rohan's table. Katya walked up behind Garren, peeking over his shoulder at the enemy Tolone'ans.

She turned back to Rohan. "Do we fight now? This looks like fun."

The Hybrid opened his Third Eye and let the part of his brain that was devoted to analyzing combat situations work through all the permutations of the fight to come.

He checked his esoteric weapon; the spiral was intact, four loops holding their shape. He wasn't particularly angry yet, and his fear was manageable.

So far.

The Knights were Powers, but barely. They were tough and well-trained and wouldn't give up; he would know, he'd fought them before. But together they were, at best, a match for one of The Consortium, not more.

Katya could match another. She would probably win, but it would take time, and she wouldn't be able to hold off the others.

Garren was a match for Squeya, but he wouldn't be able to finish her quickly. If Squeya had help, they would likely overwhelm him.

That meant that unless Rohan fought, at least one Tolone'an would be free to attack Tamara.

If Rohan *did* fight, he had three paths.

He could let his anger out and use his Power on them. With that, he could tip the scales and beat them all, with the help of his friends. But he'd lose control of the esoteric weapon; whatever new understanding he had about controlling his rage, he wouldn't yet be able to use it in a fight where

Tamara's life was at stake. Which could set him back weeks, or more, in his path to mastering the weapon.

Or he could keep his anger under control and use Spiral's technique, and only the smallest portion of his Hybrid Power, against Squeya's group. That might work, but the odds were against him.

Or he could fight without the technique *or* his rage. In which case he would be all but useless. And Tamara would die.

He swallowed.

Tamara took another bite of eggs and washed it down with coffee. "This is truly growing on me, Rohan. You know I don't love bitter tastes, but I need less and less sugar in this to enjoy it every time I come here."

"That's great. Really."

Squeya stepped to within two meters of Garren; the promenade traffic routed itself farther away from the group, sensing the hostility in the ether.

The leader of The Consortium cleared her throat. "Is this it? Is this your plan? Because it's not going to suffice. We are going to destroy the five of you and then kill the female. Whether we kill the Hybrid today or not I have yet to decide."

Garren blew a rude noise. "You're not killing anyone today, Squeya. I'm going to stop you."

She laughed. "You won't be enough—"

Tamara raised her hand.

The Tolone'an stopped talking; she turned to the Lukhor.

Tamara looked up from her seat and smiled. "I think we can cut short all this posturing, yes?"

Squeya snorted. "You sound very confident. Were you concussed as well? Or are you drunk?"

Tamara let a heavy measure of steel slip into her voice. "Neither. You, however, are missing some key information."

Squero, the second-in-command, laughed. "What are you talking about?"

Tamara looked down at the small tablet she held in her hand. "You haven't looked at your comms, have you? Now is the time. Check your messages."

Squeya let out an obviously forced laugh. "What do you mean?"

Tamara locked eyes on her. "I said, check your messages. I won't say it again."

38

She Said, Check Your Messages

Squero tried to shove past his leader. "She's bluffing."

Squeya reached an arm out and shoved him back. "Maybe. It can't hurt to check, can it? Do it. If she's bluffing, we peel her skin from her body."

"But we were going to do that anyway."

"If she's bluffing, we do it slowly."

Pop walked over and opened his mouth as if to argue. Rohan stood and caught his attention, shaking his head.

Pop paused, nodded, and headed back to the counter.

Squeya looked between two of the Knights to glare at Tamara. "And I do mean slowly, mammal."

The Lukhor sipped her coffee and met the woman's gaze.

Squero shook his sister's shoulder, tablet in hand, concern puckering the rubbery skin of his face. "Uh . . . this must be some mistake, Squeya."

She turned to him. "What is it?"

"She must have hacked our comms. Or something."

The leader of The Consortium reached out with one hand and one tentacle and snatched the tablet from his hand. "What is it?" She brought it up to her face and scanned the message. "This isn't possible."

Another member of her crew piped up. "I see it too, Squeya. I'm replying; with the tachyon net, we should have a verifying response within minutes."

Rohan looked to Tamara, who smiled softly, and back to the Tolone'ans. "What's going on?"

Squeya snorted wetly. "She's trying to trick us, but it isn't going to work."

Tamara sighed and put down her coffee. "It's not a trick. Those are real messages. I'm happy to wait here while you verify their contents in any way you see fit. If you'd like, I'll pay the surcharges for an emergency short-term transmission so you can get a faster answer."

A fourth Tolone'an cleared his throat. "There are identifiers in these messages that would be very difficult to falsify, Squeya. Some personal details from home that a regular hacker would not be able to obtain. Certainly not on short notice."

The Consortium leader looked at him, then at the others, her tentacles spreading wide in confusion, then lowering to touch the ground, to anchor her. "How is this possible? Why would our leaders be telling us to withdraw?"

Squero shook his head. "Not *telling*. Demanding. In the strongest possible terms."

The third Tolone'an shook her head as well. "Ma'am, we're being told to do anything the mammal tells us to. Anything. It's very specific. It says . . . sorry, ma'am, this is verbatim . . . if she asks us to space ourselves, we should be sure to find the nearest airlock to use."

Rohan stared at his lover; she ate another bite of eggs.

Squeya shook her head, bits of spittle flying wide in a fine spray. "How is this possible?"

Tamara looked up at her. "Are you asking me? I'd be happy to explain."

The Consortium, all of them, focused on her.

Squeya clenched and unclenched her fists. "You—"

Squero put a hand on her shoulder. "Sister. Calmly. We are to treat her with all possible respect. The messages are very clear. *All* possible respect."

"I am calm!"

"You're shouting."

She exhaled, nodded, and turned back to the Lukhor. "Please, explain. I find this situation . . . confusing."

Tamara nodded. "I am actually glad you asked. It is, as my lovely Rohan would say, an interesting story. Though to be honest, when he begins with that, it very rarely is. Interesting.

"It all started when you mentioned Cthulhu's Crucible. You remember, when you and your friends attacked us in the pool and tried to kill us? For no reason?"

The Tolone'an snarled. "There was definitely a—" Her brother clamped a tentacle around her mouth.

He nodded. "Please continue, ma'am."

Tamara smiled at him.

"As I was saying, you mentioned this place, and it seemed very important to you. Now, you might not know this, but I come from a mercantile family. An early lesson in my life was that when other people value something greatly, there is often an opportunity for profit.

"After your attack, I could not go to work, or even go outside, because you were threatening my life, and I had little else to do. So I began to research.

"I discovered the most interesting things.

"Your holy sites happen to coincide with deposits of some very rare materials. Crystals that are especially useful in the creation of soulgems. Metals that can be infused with esoteric energy and given . . . I do not know what to call them. Magical properties? I know very little about such matters. What I do know is that those materials are extremely rare and quite valuable.

"So I wondered, if such valuable items are abundant in the rocks around Cthulhu's Crucible, why is nobody mining for them? Because another thing that I learned at my father's knee is that where there is profit to be made, there are always profit-seekers.

"Your people have obviously had similar thoughts, because the mining rights to those holy sites were owned and secured by a series of small companies that had absolutely no interest in exploiting them."

Squeya frowned. "What does this—"

Her brother wrapped a hand around her mouth. "Do not interrupt. All possible respect, Squeya."

She shook him off but remained silent.

Tamara nodded. "These companies seem to exist for the sole purpose of holding onto those rights and not using them. Which is quite odd. I thought to myself, perhaps if I could buy one of these companies, I could properly exploit those mining rights."

Squero's tentacles spasmed. "You would mine underneath Cthulhu's Crucible? The birthplace of a god?"

Tamara shrugged. "It's not *my* god.

"This next part is interesting. Those companies are restricted to local ownership, so I couldn't just go and buy them. I doubted I could find a Tolone'an intermediary who would buy them for me. But then I remembered something.

"You see, those kinds of restrictions are only legal, under Imperial law, for companies with smaller evaluations. Once a legal entity reaches a certain cash value, its ownership has to be publicly accessible. You can argue whether such rules are fair or just, of course, and I might even agree that you would be in the right, but the fact is that those laws are in place. Which I know, because I studied them, in my younger years.

"Those companies had been carefully established to fall under those valuation thresholds. So there was not much I could do.

"Then I had an idea! I divested myself of some of my own holdings, freeing up several hundred million credits in cash, and entered some very aggressive purchase orders for the minerals in question.

"If you understand basic economics, and forgive me if I am not sure you do, you will expect what happened next. The market value of those minerals rose precipitously. Which drove up the value of the companies holding rights to mine them. Well above that threshold.

"Normally it would take weeks or months for the relevant Imperial laws to be recognized. Weeks or months before shares in those companies would be made available.

"But I happen to know the Commerce Director for Tolone'a. You see, he is a Lukhor. I went to school with him. In fact, we dated. Briefly, but still. And he was most eager to do anything within the law that would possibly gain him favor from the Lastex family.

"And, perhaps, he was also eager to gain favor with me, personally. Poor dear never did get over me." She turned to Rohan. "Don't worry, my love, I did not actually offer him anything substantial."

Rohan shrugged. "I take it you also didn't mention being involved with me."

"I did not. Lahnegarn might have come up as a topic of conversation. And the fact that we are no longer together." She shrugged. "Anyway. You can imagine the rest. You are now looking at the owner of mineral rights to the caverns above, below, and around Cthulhu's Crucible. Among a variety of other locations."

Squeya sputtered some more.

Squero gripped her hand in his and faced Tamara. "With all due respect, this is an empty threat . . . ma'am. No Tolone'an would ever touch even a chisel to those rocks. Not even an unbeliever."

Tamara shrugged. "I realize that."

"So while you might own the rights to destroy those caverns, you will never find anyone to do the work."

"Not any Tolone'an, no."

Squero looked at his sister, who shrugged her thick shoulders in helpless confusion.

The Consortium leader breathed out slowly and spoke. "Would you be able to explain, then, the panic from home? It's not as if you could find a crew of air breathers to mine deep inside Tolone'a. The cost would be prohibitive. Unless you hire a team of Hybrids to do it. They don't usually do such base work."

Rohan grinned. "Actually, I know a Hybrid who's been known to dig a tunnel or two. Tow a ship. I'd be willing—"

Tamara put her hand over his arm. "Not necessary, my dear. Besides, that would just give these fine folk incentive to kill you right here and right now, which is not the outcome I was working toward.

"No, Squeya, I was not going to use Hybrids."

Squeya snorted. "No cephalopods in the sector would interfere with Cthulhu's birthplace."

"I suspect you are correct, though I did not test that hypothesis by contacting *every* cephalopod species. Instead, I remembered something very interesting that my dear Rohan had told me. Yes, I know I said his stories are not usually interesting, but there are exceptions.

"Most of the sentient aquatic species we know today are cephalopods. Your kind, or your cousins. Most, but not all.

"In the time when your gods were born, there were two great families of intelligent creatures. The cephalopods and the megalodons.

"That, in itself, is not important. What *is* important is the fact that these civilizations were at war for, as far as I can tell, their entire history. Sometimes directly, sometimes through proxies.

"Have you heard of the Shakaton?"

Squeya shook her head.

Tamara tapped at her tablet, bringing up an image. She turned it around to show.

At first, Rohan thought he was looking at a picture of a great white shark. At a second glance he realized that only the head matched. Below it was a wide, powerful body with a humanoid template: two arms and two legs.

He swallowed. "Is that a real thing?"

"Indeed. In fact, there is an entire planet of Shakaton. At least one. They are extremely insular, to the point that few in the Empire are aware of their existence. They do very little trade with other worlds.

"The interesting part is that the Shakaton are keenly aware of their heritage, and of the ancient animosity between their people and the cephalopods. When I made contact, which I might add was no easy feat, you could not imagine how eager they were to take on this very unusual mining contract."

Squeya sputtered. "You wouldn't dare. They wouldn't dare."

"They not only would dare, they are *desperate* to. The thought of desecrating a Tolone'an holy site filled them with glee. They were even willing to work at a fraction of their usual fee. I admit that discount is somewhat ambiguous, morally, but in the end I accepted it. I am, after all, still my father's daughter. Money is money."

The Consortium traded looks among themselves. They whispered together, furiously and quickly. Squeya faced the Lukhor again.

"You can't do this. Desecrate a site holy to all Tolone'ans. Those sites are the key to the preservation of our culture. We need them to quicken new Powers. We need those places to worship our gods properly."

Garren coughed. "Not all of us need them. Most Tolone'ans don't worship in the old ways. Not anymore."

Tamara shook her head. "You misunderstand the situation. I've already begun the destruction. Not at Cthulhu's Crucible, but at a lesser place. The Bridal Chamber of Idh-yaa. You know the place?"

"Of course. All of us have made pilgrimage to the Bridal Chamber."

"I imagine you'd be upset, perhaps even horrified, to learn that it had been reduced to gravel?"

Squeya staggered backward; two of the others caught her, their own tentacles touching the ground for added support.

Tamara stood. "You shouldn't have threatened me. And you really shouldn't have threatened my child."

"But . . . you're a shuttle tech. How is this possible?"

Her antennae stiffened; her eyes hardened. "I am a very good shuttle tech. I also happen to have a very particular set of skills, one that I developed in the past, that most shuttle techs wouldn't share." She exhaled and relaxed her face. "To be fair, I also have a substantial inheritance I was able to use to fund this little operation. On my shuttle tech salary, it would take me approximately . . . one hundred thousand years to amass the funding I needed."

Squeya stared at her, speechless.

Rohan swallowed. "I take it that's the project you've been working on."

She nodded at him. "It was more work than you'd think. Moving that amount of currency around the sector in this short a timeframe is quite difficult. I doubt there are a dozen people in il'Drach space who could have managed it."

"That's amazing. I mean, you're amazing."

She flashed a smile. "I agree. But it's nice to hear. Don't flatter me too much until we see if this works."

Squeya straightened herself. "You're going to destroy them all?"

The Lukhor shrugged. "That depends entirely on you, and on what you agree to right here. The leaders of your cult have already offered very generous terms to lease the rights back from me. Almost criminally generous, though not technically illegal."

"So the destruction will stop?"

"I haven't accepted their offer. Yet. And if I do, it will be a very unfavorable lease. One I may terminate at any time, with no notice whatsoever. And my Shakaton mining crew can spend as much time as they like near or on the sites in question."

"What do you want?"

Tamara nodded. "I want you to leave us alone. No member of your cult is to harm, or even approach, my son. Or myself. Or Rohan. Or any of Rohan's friends, no matter the species, no matter where they live. Not on Wistful, not on his homeworld, not on Tolone'a." She looked at the armored Tolone'an who had come to her aid. "And no retribution against Garren for protecting us."

Squeya's tentacles stiffened; her eyes bulged out on their stalks. "This is—"

Squero gripped her shoulder. "Careful."

She shook in place, ripples passing through her blue-gray flesh like waves. After a long minute, she continued. "We cannot let The Murderer of the Crucible go free. We cannot. I cannot. He slew my parents before my eyes."

Tamara stepped forward, still keeping two Rogesh Powers between herself and the Tolone'an. "Is that your final offer? Let me know so I can make the call I need to make. I'll be a very rich woman by tomorrow, and Cthulhu's Crucible will be a distant memory."

Squeya glared at her. "We waited so long to find him. Planned for so long. It is all we wanted. We cannot simply let him go."

"Then you'll be letting go of the Crucible and of"—she checked her tablet—"seventeen other religious sites."

Rohan shook his head. "No, Tamara. This isn't right."

She turned to him. "What are you saying?"

He swallowed. "I . . . let's compromise. Can we compromise here? How about, I don't know. Squeya. Take the deal, but leave me out of it. Just me. You don't hurt any of my friends, any relatives, anyone I know. Not one hair on the head of one person is harmed because of anything to do with me. But you can come for me, directly. How does that sound?"

Tamara shook her head. "But why?"

He sighed. "I destroyed so much of their culture, their people, their life, Tamara. I can't live with the idea that more of it is destroyed to keep me safe. To keep you safe, sure. To keep Ang and Wei Li and Pop . . . yes, that's fine. But not for me."

"Are you sure?"

He nodded. "I can take care of myself. I figured something out."

"Did you?"

"Yeah. I care about them. The Tolone'ans. You could say I love them, in a weird, abstract way.

"And I think that means they'll never be able to hurt me."

39

Dripping Bucket Number Two. Er, Part Two

The Consortium walked away, dejected, Squeya tentacle-slapping her subordinates every few steps.

Garren went back to *Insatiable* to finish up his work.

Tamara dismissed the Knights of Ch'doon after reminding them that they were on retainer to remain on Wistful for the next four days.

Katya licked Tamara's cheek, then knocked her empty coffee cup off the table.

Rohan groaned. "Katya . . ."

"I am sorry! I could not help myself! It was just sitting there. Empty."

Tamara hugged the il'Zkin. "It's fine. It did not even break. And if it had broken, we could replace it. It is just a cup."

Katya nodded. "Why are you crying?"

Tamara stepped back and wiped her face. "I'm not crying."

"Your eyes are leaking." She leaned in and licked Tamara's cheek. "Salty leaks."

"I am . . . relieved. That was very stressful. I was worried that they would be unreasonable."

Rohan swallowed. "Are you sure you're okay? Your hands are shaking."

She sniffled. "Of course. It's only adrenaline. Give me a few minutes."

He stepped close and wrapped her in his arms. "You really were amazing. I can't believe you did that."

"I'm not some helpless female, Rohan, waiting for your rescue. I can take care of myself. And mine."

"I know. I never thought that."

She squeezed him tight, then released. "Let me sit."

"Of course." He let go, hands out to steady her if needed. She sat back down.

Rohan waved to Pop for more coffee.

Katya sat with them. "I would have liked to fight Squeya again. I suppose we can't get everything we want."

Tamara laughed. "I'm glad you didn't fight her again. She's tough."

"Still."

Rohan's comm chimed. "Oh for . . . oh, hey."

Tamara looked over. "Who is it? Your other lover?"

"No, I don't—I think I should take this."

"So, take it."

He looked at her, then at Katya. "Will you stay with her? I have to do a thing."

Katya nodded. "I will make sure she is safe. Though I doubt she needs my protection."

The Lukhor looked up as he stood. "Tell me about it. Later."

"I will. I promise. I'm sorry, I just . . . I have to go."

"So, go." She smiled as she said it.

He leaned in and kissed the top of her head, where dark-green hair met skin, just above the tops of her antennae.

Then he left to meet with Granny.

———◆···◆———

She asked him to meet her at the Dripping Bucket, which surprised him but absolutely shouldn't have.

He entered the bar and an unusually attentive waiter led him to the rear, slid a floor-to-ceiling fish tank to the side, and waved Rohan into a secret back room.

The Hybrid could *feel* a Power inside, but he hadn't really expected anything different. He set his shoulders and walked past the open-mouthed fish.

A large table dominated the room, with seats for twelve, of a higher quality than the rough benches in the main area of the bar. Only two people waited for him.

One, a heavyset snake-headed pugilist he knew well, nodded. "Rohan."

"Sirc. I didn't realize you knew Granny."

The graying Andervarian female next to her chuckled. "She didn't. I figured this was some sort of trap, and I wanted someone expendable to have by my side while I sprang it." As soon as she spoke, Rohan remembered her; she and her nephews had attempted to kidnap Ben and Marion Stone, on Wistful, almost a year earlier.

Rohan smiled. "We've met before, but we weren't introduced. I'm Rohan."

She grinned, her white teeth gleaming against bright-purple lips. "The Griffin. I haven't forgotten you. I'm old enough to be your grandmother, but that didn't stop you from punching me in the face. Sit."

He took a seat across from her. "You were trying to stab me at the time, so I won't apologize."

"You want a drink?"

He shook his head. "Too early for me to start. And I have other business later."

She nodded. "Fine. I invited you here because you wanted to talk, and certain associates of mine thought I should hear you out. I think they were wrong, and this will end poorly for me, but, well, I'm an old woman, I don't have a lot to lose."

He put his hands flat on the table and stretched his neck. "I want to know who supplies you with Boost. Or how you get it."

She cackled, the kind of witchy laugh only an older woman trying very deliberately to sound witchy can reproduce. "I want to be sixteen again.

And I want my husbands back by my side. And I want the Empire to have never conquered Andervar. Are we trading empty wishes, Rohan?"

He sighed. "Come on, Granny. Boost is a bad thing. It kills people. Makes addicts of its users."

"I thought you were so desperate for Power that you wanted some for yourself. Isn't that what you convinced Grell?"

The Hybrid shrugged. "I may have . . . misled him. Don't blame them, I have a lot of practice lying to empaths."

"So this *is* a trap. Go on, then. Take me in. You'll have to fight Sirc first." The big Takslee pounded a heavy fist into her palm and smiled. "And don't think I'll talk easy. I have a very high tolerance for pain and very little to live for."

"Granny, I don't want to torture you. But, come on. Selling Boost to kids? You can't be that hard up for cash. You know what? If you are, I'll give you a job."

"At one of your famous distilleries? It's a kind offer, but no thank you. I don't sell Boost for credits, Hybrid. I sell it for a dream."

"What does that even mean?"

"It means that Boost is one of the best chances we have of ever throwing off the yoke of the il'Drach. It can turn regular folk into a match for a Hybrid. No, not one-on-one, maybe, but it gives us a chance. When the revolution comes, it will be Boost that fuels it."

"It kills its users, Granny. There will be no revolution if all your fighters are dead."

She leaned forward over the table. "They tell you that, Rohan, but it's a lie. I've been using Boost for over forty years."

He turned to Sirc. "Is that true? Is that possible?"

Sirc shrugged, her shoulders almost touching her ears. "Not everyone reacts to Boost the same way. Some can tolerate it for a long time. Others die young."

Granny nodded. "And some, like that Lukhor that hates you so much, thrive on it. He might burn out sooner than later, but in the meantime he's quite magnificent. I hear he broke your nose."

Rohan scratched his beard.

Have I been looking at this wrong?

"I might not be as well-informed as I'd like. That still doesn't excuse selling it to kids."

Granny nodded. "That was a mistake, and one I won't tolerate. But the flow of Boost must continue. We need to find the strong candidates, the ones we can turn into weapons against the il'Drach. It's very nice for you, a Hybrid, to face them, but unless you know a way we can recruit another thousand of you, we need alternatives."

"You can't fight the Empire."

She shook her head. "We can't sit back and let every planet in the sector become another Ohn. You know this is true as well as I do."

"I could have you put in jail."

She cackled again. "Won't do you any good. Someone else will take my place within hours. If I weren't easily replaceable, I wouldn't be here."

He grunted and ran his hands over the wooden table, touching the thin ridges that ran with the grain. "I really need to know where Boost comes from, Granny."

"You won't get that out of me. And Sirc has no idea. If you don't believe me, go ahead and do what you have to do."

"Granny, if you didn't think I was sincere in asking to talk to you, why did you agree to meet?"

She grinned. "I like you. I think you're smart. I think I can talk you over to our side."

"Your side? You want me to sell Boost."

She leaned back into the chair. "Not sell. But help us. Help the rebels. Be there when we need you."

"Why would I do that?"

"It was your idea, Hybrid. You came to us, looking for our help finding a home for the Ohnian refugees. Remember?"

"I remember it not working."

She shook her head. "That wasn't our fault. You asked for something we could not give. Resources beyond our means. But it showed how you think of us. You want a relationship with us. You want our help, on occasion, and we both know that means you're willing to help us. On occasion."

"You're proposing an alliance."

"On Andervar we call it a soft alliance. Occasional mutual aid. No hard commitments."

He ran his hands through his hair and muttered to himself.

"What was that?"

"Black gold. It's . . . never mind. Did you need something in particular from me?"

"No. Not a thing. And I have nothing to offer either."

"Except stopping the sale of Boost to minors."

"I was going to do that anyway, not as a favor to you."

He nodded. "I like you too, Granny."

She patted the big Takslee with her wrinkled purple hand. "I'm going to keep Sirc here on payroll. When I want something from you, I'll send her directly."

"I'm not promising anything."

"I know you aren't. And I'm not promising anything either. But if you want our help, find Sirc. If we can do something for you, we will."

"This is not what I was expecting from this meeting."

"You sound like my nephews. They always come over for tea and cake and they always wind up painting my fence and they never know how it happened."

Rohan rubbed his forehead. "I can't decide if I should be happy or devastated at how this turned out."

She laughed. "My nephews say the same thing. But they always come back."

"I should go. It was interesting talking to you. And I'm sorry about your husbands."

The old woman shrugged. "They were right to leave me. One cannot have a normal life while trying to change the world, Hybrid. I chose changing the world."

"How's that working out?"

"So far? The world is much the same. But I am better for the struggle, as odd as that might seem to you."

He stood and rested his hands on the table. "It doesn't seem that odd."

Sirc looked at her employer. "I know it's early for you, but can I order a drink?"

Rohan turned as they began to argue.

Time to test a theory.

40

For Love Or Honey

"Captain, I don't like repeating myself."

"Come on, *Void's Shadow*, that's not true. You love repeating yourself."

A sigh escaped the ship's speakers; she'd been practicing the sound. "I only repeat myself to you. Have you considered that maybe you're the problem, not me?"

Rohan checked the screen that covered the front wall of the ship's bridge; Toth 3 was growing steadily as she approached it. "I'm sure that's not it. I'm delightful."

He turned his attention inward, or perhaps sideways; opened his Third Eye and checked on the esoteric structure within him.

Steady.

He exhaled slowly.

"Captain, you're risking your life to test what seems like a very tenuous theory."

"I'm not sure it's a theory, really. More of a hypothesis."

"This test could kill you."

Rohan sighed. "I'm aware. If I thought there was a better way, I'd take it."

"I know a better way. Don't do it. Let me take you back to Wistful. Tell Tamara you want to move in with her. Spend your days making margaritas and sitting by the pool. I'll visit every day, hang out just on the other side of the roof."

"You'll block the sunlight."

"I'll move to the side. Please, Captain. You've made promises to people. If you're dead . . ."

He scratched his beard. "I don't want to die. And I don't want to leave my friends behind. But . . . I can't stand the world we live in. I can't. And I can't just sit by and drink margaritas by the pool when there's a chance I can make things better."

"How is getting eaten by a kaiju going to make anything better?"

"It wouldn't. But if I don't get eaten, it will mean I've got a chance against Hyperion. And stopping him is the first step. Besides, I want to know what's behind that door that Wei Li just opened. There's no way to get people who know what they're doing down here to do that work while Terry is standing by, ready to eat them."

The ship sighed again. "If I told you there has to be a better way, I'd be repeating myself, wouldn't I?"

"Yeah. And I don't think there is. I've kept my Power suppressed for months. When I get angry, it just trickles back in, enough to tear apart Spiral's technique. I can't just simulate the anger, *Void's Shadow*. I have to be in a real situation."

"You could fight Lonnie again."

Rohan laughed. "I'm not sure he'd survive that."

"I'd rather you risk his life than yours."

The Hybrid cracked his neck. "Part of me agrees with you. It's not the part that should be making my decisions."

The ship entered Toth 3's upper atmosphere.

"Very well, Captain. Where should I drop you?"

"Same place. Let me out, then head off and do your thing."

"You won't need me to take you back to Wistful?"

"You can hang out in orbit or something if you'd like, in case I do. But the most likely outcome is that either I can use my Power again and fly back myself or I'll be dead."

"That's very comforting."

"Sorry. Look, if anything happens to me, do me a favor and take care of Repentant and *Vyrhicant*, would you?"

"I will try."

"Thanks. They need friends."

"I know. I've been working on it."

"You're a good ship. I'm proud of you."

"Thank you, Captain."

She landed next to the dig site and opened her hatch.

$$\blacktriangleleft\!\!-\!\cdot\!\cdot\!-\!\blacktriangleright$$

Rohan stepped out onto the soft mossy ground. The air was wet with humidity and the musk of rotting vegetation.

He squatted to the ground, working his knees out the sides to loosen his hips, then sprang up.

The Hybrid opened his Third Eye and turned it inward.

Spiral's technique is intact and holding.

As expected.

The question is, can I keep it stable with my father's Power flowing through me? Can I keep it intact while my curse is flooding me with rage?

Wei Li thought I had a chance.

He exhaled slowly.

No sign of the kaiju.

That's a problem easily solved.

He reached down inside himself with ethereal hands and relaxed the tight seal he'd placed over his Power almost three months earlier.

Like a neglected child, it extended tiny fingers, angry yet hesitant, into his psyche.

There you go.

He exhaled quickly, then inhaled.

"Come on out, Terry." He shook his head and hardened his voice. "Come on out. I know you meant well, but you killed two people here who didn't have to die. People under my watch. Right in front of my face."

The volume of his voice rose until he shouted.

"You killed them right here, Terry! Come on out, it's time for punishment. You know you deserve it. Those Quattros were no threat to you."

The streams of Power thickened and darkened; deep pulses passed through them, balls of energy that grew heavier with every breath he took.

"There can only be one king here, Terry. Only one master. It's not you, and it's not the other fliers, and it's not the decipede. There's one ruler on Toth 3 and it's me, Terry. And I'm standing here to tell you that you're not going to kill people anymore."

He exhaled fast, then inhaled deep and slow, filling his chest with air. Exhaled again.

Felt snakes of Power flood through his limbs.

"Coward! Come and face me! You're so tough, come out here and show me, Terry! We'll see who's the boss!"

The Power, the curse, the legacy of the il'Drach, answered his call, building and swirling through his body.

Spiral's technique shimmered and shook, losing a coil before Rohan could stabilize its shape through brute force of will.

A growl came from the trees.

"Come out, I said! It's time you acknowledge me as your master, Terry! It's time!"

The pterosaur pushed his snout through the edge of the trees, chin lowered, flat black eyes focused on the Hybrid.

"You heard me, Terry! Come out and face me! Pick on somebody who's a match for you."

Terry growled and stepped into the clearing.

The top of his head-crest was over three meters from the ground. His upper arms were as thick as Rohan's chest, his shoulders almost as broad as the Hybrid was tall.

Wicked talons extended from hands halfway up his wingspan; a matching set sprouted from long, lean feet.

The creature sprang forward, mouth ajar, a roar that shook the tree line.

"That's it! Come for me!" Rohan *rose* into the air, his feet dangling, fists together in front of his face.

The spiral twanged as it lost another loop.

Rohan grunted and willed the esoteric structure to bend and flex, keeping the last three loops.

Still there.

Time to fight.

Twin strands of energy spiraled through his spine, meeting with little bangs of ethereal starburst, then looping around again; meeting again.

When they met at the base of Rohan's skull, a sizzling, sparking arc of Power surged through his body like a lightning strike.

Terry was prey: an animal, a lower being, who had dared to defy his authority.

Who had dared to test his patience, his rules.

Rohan wouldn't let him get away with it. Should never have let it happen to begin with.

He surged forward, arms in front of his face, cracking the air like a jet breaking the sound barrier, sending ripples through the moss and dirt of the clearing.

He struck Terry on the snout with a collision that knocked them both back a dozen meters.

He noticed another loop disappearing from the helix, but didn't care.

The Power blew through Rohan's ligaments, tendons, and muscle bellies. It lit his nerves on fire, tempering each strand, lighting up the connections across his body like a power grid. Detonated his senses.

He could hear branches shaking half a kilometer away; a creek flowing a kilometer away. He could hear Terry's breath, the soft scratch of his eyelids as they slid over alien corneas.

He saw individual spores rising into the air wherever they had touched the moss. Every line and crease in Terry's leathery skin.

The raw pink lines on his shoulder where he'd been scarred, days earlier.

Rohan flew in again, forearms landing on Terry's chest.

The pterosaur roared and threw an uppercut that caught Rohan's chest and sent him to the other side of the clearing.

His spring lost another coil.

The Hybrid smelled Terry's dry skin; leftovers from his own meals at the campsite; traces of Tracker.

The dog.

Who had run off into the jungle and been saved by the pterosaur. Protected by the pterosaur. Returned, unharmed, by the savage kaiju he now faced in combat.

Terry's not a monster.

Not just *a monster.*

He's programmed to come for anyone who wants to fight, but that's not why he hung around my camp.

He's curious. He wanted to know what I was doing.

He likes scritches and neck rubs.

He knows how to play.

Rohan rose a few more meters off the ground; out of reach of the pterosaur.

Terry kept me company when I was here by myself, week after week, wasting time.

He was there for me when I was lonely.

All he wanted was some company.

Must be hard, being the smallest kaiju on Toth 3.

It's not his fault he ate the Quattros. He was designed to do it.

Not his fault he's fighting me, right now.

Rohan reached inside his soul, focusing with all he had on the feelings that welled up within as he thought about scratching the kaiju's neck.

Thought about the monster bringing a helpless dog back to him, safe.

The scars on its shoulder.

His Power continued to flow, tempered, softer, not calm but less chaotic than before.

He focused on Terry's scars, and on the helix he had built: the spiral of esoteric energy that connected the core of his Power to each of his palms.

The spiral that was reduced to two coils; two turns.

Terry extended his three-meter lower fingers, unfolding his wings. He gave one tentative flap, then leapt into the air, fully extending both arms, and flapped them again, propelling himself toward the Hybrid.

Rohan lifted, then dropped, then reached out with his palm.

Where it met the tip of Terry's nose, all the kaiju's forward momentum transferred to the spring.

He's just a big baby. A big puppy. It's not his fault he overreacts and . . . eats people sometimes.

Rohan's Power began to wane; the helix softened slightly.

One coil remained.

He inhaled sharply.

I get it.

I see it now.

I know what I have to do.

I have to fight him and love him at the same time.

"Terry." His voice was firm; not angry, but not kind. The monster ignored him.

The pterosaur launched himself forward again, mouth spread wide, rows of jagged teeth exposed to the air.

Rohan flew to intercept and caught the front teeth in his right palm.

His skin split as he absorbed Terry's forward momentum again; the kaiju tumbled three times through the air before righting himself and turning a wide circle.

"My neighbors had a dog, you know. It was a good dog, but it needed training. Needed to be disciplined. I always thought they were too mean to that dog, but it was happy, Terry. It loved them. And when they had kids around, or left food on the counter that would have made him sick, he wouldn't touch it. You need training, Terry. That's all this is."

He flew in to intercept the kaiju, his right hand out in front.

Just before impact, he pulled that hand back and spun, extending his left hand, palm out, fingers pointed up.

His left palm struck the tip of Terry's snout as he released the energy of the spiral.

The sound of the strike echoed off distant trees as the kaiju flew back, tumbling wildly, breaking the trunk of a thirty-meter-tall tree as he fell.

He's my dog.

I love him, my brave, stupid dog.

But he's not trained. We can't have him eating any more assassins.

I wish I could train him using treats, or gentle guidance, but that's never going to work on a kaiju. I'm not even sure he really eats.

There's no other way and nobody else who can do it.

Terry stood up out of the ruins of the tree, shook off the shards of wood and branches that had fallen over him, and lifted off into the air. Rohan's face tightened as he flew up, higher, creating a bit of distance between himself and the kaiju.

He *reached* inside, grabbed the rod of esoteric energy inside him by both ends, and gave it a twist.

Another.

Three coils now.

With his own warmer feelings tempering the rage of his curse, the energy was pliable enough to bend yet steady enough to hold a shape.

Terry reached the Hybrid, snaked an arm out faster than Rohan expected, and grabbed an ankle.

With an effortless toss, he threw the Hybrid hard enough to take down three trees.

Rohan grunted with the pain but steadied himself.

Just an animal, acting out. Doing what his instincts tell him to do.

It's my job to train him out of those instincts, and that's what I'm going to do.

The Hybrid landed in the middle of the largest clear area he could find and took a fighting stance: left foot forward, hips angled to the right; right hand open by his chin; left fist across his belly.

Terry gathered himself up and dove toward the Hybrid like a falling meteor, accelerating further with every millisecond he had, the kaiju's immense Power driving him into a frenzy.

He struck Rohan's palm and fell to the ground in a cloud of spores and dead moss.

He screamed, turned, and launched himself into the air.

Flew a wide circle, gaining speed with every meter, and dove again.

Rohan absorbed the shock again.

And a third time.

The pterosaur hopped back, lifted his head, and screamed defiance.

He hopped forward and drove a massive fist toward Rohan's face, fighting almost like a humanoid.

The Hybrid absorbed the impact on his palm, stepped forward, and lifted his left palm up into the pterosaur's exposed chin.

He drove that palm upward with all the strength in his legs and hips, all the tension of unwinding his upper back and shoulder, all the Power that streamed through his ethereal body, and, finally, all the kinetic energy stored in the helix inside him.

The crack of the strike echoed off the distant trees like a peal of thunder. The kaiju flipped onto his back, the long, thin crest at the back of his head driving a meter into the ground, pinning him in place.

The creature's aura softened.

Rohan walked over and stepped onto Terry's pelvis, then his belly, and finally stood on the creature's chest.

"You're a good boy. But you were bad. Next time you try to eat a person, we're going to do this again. Not because I want to, but because I have to.

"Understand, Terry?

"I didn't beat you because I'm angry with you, or because I hate you. I did it because it was necessary, because I care about you."

He rose and fell with the kaiju's noisy breaths.

Rohan waited there, balanced on the creature's chest, until Terry opened his eyes.

The Hybrid wrapped his arms around the kaiju's snout and looked over it.

"You have enough?"

The creature snorted.

"Good boy."

I don't know if it's love I needed, but something like it.

Is it compassion?

Caring?

Something almost . . .

"Hey, Terry. I know what to call Spiral's technique.

"I just introduced you to Buddha's Palm."

41

The Price of Power

Rohan spent ten minutes with the subdued monster before rising through the air, penetrating the clouds, and entering the cold void of space.

As Rohan approached Wistful, a humanoid figure intercepted him. His helmet beeped as she opened a channel.

"Rohan!"

"Wildeye! How are you?"

She came close enough for him to see her eyes, twice the size of a human's, glowing against her coal-black skin. "This towing business is harder than it looks!"

He laughed. "It really is. Hybrids who just fight all the time would always sneer at me for being 'just' a tow chief. I was like . . . it's way harder than punching people."

She giggled. "I thought you couldn't fly on your own anymore."

"I had to work through something. Consider it worked."

"Does that mean you'll be coming back?"

"Maybe. Is there enough for me to do? I don't want to interfere with your gig here."

She laughed again. "Please, interfere all you want. Any way you want."

He sighed.

She continued, "I hear I missed some excitement on Wistful. A bunch of fights."

He turned to face the station, an oversized cross twinkling in the starlight.

Nothing quite like a diamond coating to make a station really sparkle.

"Yeah, some."

"You know you can always call me if you need a hand."

He sighed. "I appreciate that, Wildeye."

"But you don't want to."

He thought for a moment. "I will. I will call on you. Just not yet. I want you to have every chance to get settled. Let go of the war mentality, the training. Have a chance to be your own person. But someday, when I really need a hand, I'll call on you to fight with me. If you're willing."

She nodded. "I'll be ready. I have to go, though. *Love Boat* is waiting for a tow out to the beacon line."

"Say hello to her from me. I'll see you later, Wildeye."

He flew to the station and approached one of the man-sized airlocks.

It cycled open as he got close.

"Thank you, Wistful." She didn't answer.

He slipped his mask into his hood and landed on the promenade.

Tamara is probably asleep. She looked exhausted after that confrontation with The Consortium. And doing I don't know how much work over the past few days.

Whose fault is that?

My fault.

Not fair to wake her.

He visited Ang.

The Ursan was recovering; Katya was helping.

Neither needed anything from Rohan.

He returned to his apartment, showered, and stopped in front of his closet.

New clothes or my old uniform?

Maybe wait to talk to Wistful before I make any changes.

He put on his red shirt and baggy black trousers and opened the door to the recreation area.

The Hybrid stretched out on the low reclining chair and stared at the water lapping at the edges of the pool for the next six hours.

Definitely not wallowing in the hollow pit in his gut.

———••———

He met Tamara at her favorite breakfast restaurant, a soup house that served dishes from half a dozen different worlds.

She came wearing minimal makeup and a simple jumpsuit, but smiled warmly when she saw him.

She stood on tiptoes and kissed him, then let him lead her to a table in the back.

"You look beautiful."

She snorted. "You are clearly smitten. I look terrible. I have not slept properly in days."

He tightened his lips. "I know. I'm so sorry."

Her antennae wobbled as she shook her head. "Do not be silly. I am just glad I was able to remember how to conduct a hostile takeover on an alien planet. Once I started, it was like riding a giant worm."

"You mean bike?"

"What is a bike?"

"Never mind. Hey, what's going on with your father?"

She smiled. "My father has decided he has pressing concerns on Lukhor and left to address them."

Rohan grunted. "He just decided that?"

"I may have encouraged him by pointing out that if he overstayed his welcome, I might take it on myself to make sure he does, in fact, have pressing concerns on Lukhor. Very serious ones."

The Hybrid chuckled. "You're just throwing your weight around, aren't you?"

"You shouldn't be making comments about my weight, should you?"

Rohan held his hands up in surrender, then waited while she studied the menu.

She always studied the menu, despite having memorized it years earlier.

She looked at him. "Am I in the mood for spicy today?"

He grinned. "You want the noodles with the egg, not the spicy broth. You need to eat a proper meal. You're looking malnourished."

"You're not wrong. I haven't eaten properly in days. Once I set to a project, I forget everything else."

He grunted. "I know. Listen, I need to talk to you about that."

"Oh, Rohan, what is that tone? I know that tone. I hate it. It is the tone of a man about to do something both regretful and stupid."

He sighed. "Those are my middle names."

She tapped her order on the screen built into the table. "Let me guess. You are going to say something negative about us moving in together. That you cannot go forward with it."

"Tamara . . ."

Her voice turned harsh. "What, Rohan? Should I be delighted by the fact that you remain so eager to end this relationship? Or am I misreading your intentions?"

"I almost got you killed, Tamara. And it's going to get worse."

She paused. "What does that mean?"

He rubbed his eyes. "When we started dating, I had every intention of living a quiet life here. Forever."

"I am aware."

"Since then, I haven't exactly managed it, have I?"

"Others have forced your hand, Rohan. You saved your world. Saved many lives here."

"Yeah, I did. And . . . maybe I had no choice in any of that. I couldn't just sit by and let people suffer. Hell, I didn't ask The Consortium to come here and try to get revenge on me for things I did half a decade ago."

"You did not. And I do not blame you for it. You have suffered for the sake of my past as well. I know my father had you beaten. Recently. For no fault of yours."

He nodded. "Yeah. My past, your family, things happen, right? Eventually, I would probably run out of old enemies."

"What is your point? You say that as if it is only half a thought."

"It is only half. The other half is what I'm going to do now. I said, when we first started dating, I had every intention of living a quiet life.

"That's not true anymore."

———— •··• ————

They sat in tense silence while the server brought them soup and ice water.

Rohan wasn't in the mood for alcohol; Tamara followed suit.

She ate a third of her bowl without saying anything.

Rohan looked down and realized he'd finished half of his own; he hadn't tasted any of it.

This has happened to me before.

"I can't just react to things that happen anymore, Tamara. It worked out okay here, and on Earth, but with Hyperion . . . I didn't have a plan, I just did what seemed right at the time, and it cost a billion lives. That's . . . a billion."

"It wasn't your fault. You don't control the Empire. You're not in charge of what other people do."

"I know I'm not."

He spun noodles onto his fork, swirling them around in the cloudy broth. *What did I even order?*

She stared at him. "That was a very emotionally charged tone, Rohan."

"I'm not in charge of what other people do. Maybe it's time I change that."

She laughed. "What does that mean? Are you going to take over the Empire?"

He locked his eyes on hers. "Can you think of any other way to prevent another Ohn? Another Tolone'a? Another Zahad?"

The Lukhor swallowed. "You're serious."

"Absolutely. If I were joking, this would be funny, and it's not funny at all."

"You overestimate your sense of humor."

He smiled. "Touché. Look, I need to handle Hyperion. I have to. He's my responsibility."

"I do not agree, but I do understand."

"The Empire *wants* me to handle him. They think it's a way for them to get control over me, to bring me back into the fold."

"They think that."

"Yes."

"Implying that *you* think differently."

"I'm not going to be their tool again, Tamara. I'm going to make them mine."

She sipped her ice water, her eyes locked on his face, her expression calm.

He realized that her voice had lost the overtones of anger.

She bent to her soup and slurped up another mouthful.

She's thinking.

Maybe she's deciding whether I'm insane.

I hope she figures it out, I'd love to know.

She swallowed the soup, took another sip of water, and met his gaze. "You will make the Empire yours."

"If I have to. And I very much think that I have to. I can't . . . I slaughtered millions in their name, Tamara. I thought I could find redemption by coming here and stopping. Just . . . not do it anymore. Be a good person.

"But it's not enough. I can't stay here safe and warm and happy and let the atrocities continue. It's not enough. I wish it were, Rudra save me I wish it were, but it's not. I can't stand it. I have to make them change."

"You don't say *try* to make them change. You don't say you will *attempt* to influence the Empire. You say you will."

"Am I crazy?"

Please don't answer that.

Please answer that.

"I . . . yes, probably. Those words, I believe, objectively speaking, are the words of a lunatic. Of a broken man. Yet you do not sound insane. You do not look broken. You seem quite rational and coherent."

"I spent the last three months mastering a technique which should be enough for me to kill Hyperion. That's the first step."

"What's the second step?"

"I'm not sure exactly, but I'll have some time to think it over. I'm going to probably just make this up as I go along."

"Then what is the final step?"

He put his fork down and leaned back in his chair. "I don't know exactly. I don't have all the details. But I have . . . an idea of it. I can tell you a few things. No more Tolone'as. No more Zahads. No more Ohns."

"I feel as if our discussion has gotten off track."

"No, we are exactly on track, Tamara. I'm embarking on . . . a thing. I don't know what to call it. I'm not going to be the guy you agreed to be with. I'm not going to live the life you agreed to share. I'm so very sorry, but I can't live up to those promises."

"You never promised me a peaceful life."

"It was implied. We both know that. You never wanted an ambitious man, did you? You always said that. You were with Lahnegarn *because* he wasn't ambitious."

She snorted. "He is now, and he thinks that will win back my heart."

"That's a discussion for another day. The point is, I know this isn't what you wanted. I can't give you what you asked for. As much as I care for you, as much as I'd love to just hunker down in a cabin with you and live the rest of my life on a quiet mountain somewhere, I can't do it. Not now. Not knowing I have the power to change things."

"I do not like mountains."

"Don't be silly. Everybody likes mountains. Really? You don't? That's so weird."

She shook her head. "You are a complex man, Rohan, with a number of lovely traits, and also a number of less lovely ones. And right now you are embodying the worst of yourself."

He swallowed. "Sorry."

"You do not even realize what you're sorry for, do you?"

"Nope. I might figure it out eventually."

"You are making decisions for me instead of treating me as an adult. You are making assumptions about my aims and desires based on your own preconceptions of what a woman like me might want. You are taking responsibility for my safety when I have amply demonstrated that I am more than capable of handling that myself."

"Yeah." *What is she saying?* "What are you saying?"

"Rohan, I did not want to live a greedy life. I did not want to live a life of ambition for its own sake. I did not want to be my father, or to be with a man who was like my father. Who saw life as a game and accumulated wealth and power as a way to win."

"I can see that."

"Two and a half years ago, I carefully directed my son to toss a ball at you when you walked your regular path up the promenade by our apartment."

"You did? I thought it was chance."

"You intrigued me. Do not let it inflate your ego. Then I met you, and one thing led to the next. I did not choose you because you lacked ambition. I chose you because you were kind, and because you lacked greed."

Rohan swallowed. "I don't . . . I don't . . ."

"I am happy to live an ambitious life, so long as that life has a purpose, Rohan. And, from what you say, your goals have that."

"I certainly don't want influence or power for its own sake."

"There, you see? We are on the same screen. Unless what you really mean to say, when you speak to me thus, is that you do not want to be with me.

"I will not force myself on you, Rohan. I have my pride. If you do not want to be with me, I will leave, and I will be sad, and I will then be fine. That's not the outcome I prefer, but I will accept it.

"However, you should consider something before you toss me aside. For the second time, something no other man has ever done.

"Rohan, think. It took me less than three days to subdue all of Tolone'a. If you are truly to subvert the entirety of the Empire, can you really afford to attempt it without me at your side?"

He wiped his eyes and looked down at the table.

I didn't even let myself hope she'd say that.

Except maybe I did.

"Well, then. That's that." He smiled. "So, about my apartment. When's a good time to help you move your stuff in?"

Epilogue: No Answer, Just More Questions

O ne week later.

Rohan sat in Wei Li's office in his tow chief uniform: golden yellow and a shade of metallic purple that had been known to cause seizures in mammals who stared at it too long.

She templed her fingers together as she studied him.

He broke the silence. "So, no funeral."

"Krai Wu and Mai Si will take him home where he can be honored by our people. It would make no sense to have a ceremony here."

"Are you going?"

She exhaled very slowly and double-blinked, horizontal membranes closing, then the more opaque top and bottom lids, then opening in reverse order.

"I am not."

He waited for her to elaborate.

In vain.

He cleared his throat. "How does it feel? The Eternity Ki?"

She shook her head slowly. "I do not have the words. But if anyone could understand, it is probably you."

"Yeah, but when I Power up, it comes with all that ancient rage. Yours . . ."

"Yes, it is different." She blinked again. "I understand you took my advice."

"To control my technique? I did. It worked, as you expected."

"As I expected."

"Instead of letting go of the anger or willing it away, I just brought up a whole shipload of caring to put alongside it. Worked much better."

"That fits your nature, Rohan."

"Yeah. Now I think I have a handle on the Buddha's Palm."

She smiled. "Interesting name."

"Spiral will love it. Long story. Anyway, what are you going to do now? Do you stay as security chief? I never understood your prophecy. You became The Shield, right? What does The Shield do?"

"Nobody really knows. Nor do we know what the finale is, though apparently it is now at hand."

"So you get to make it up as you go along."

"Is that not true of everything in life, Rohan?"

He scratched his beard. "Can you use all that Power?"

"Not yet. There is . . . a process. I expect to be able to. In time."

"It's strange. My good friend Wei Li is a magical superhero now."

She snorted. "I always was, Rohan. You just liked to pretend otherwise."

"Fair. Are you going to miss your friends?"

"I never stopped missing them. I loved them and love them still. However, I have a calling I cannot deny. There is no use reflecting on the difficulty therein."

"No, I guess not. Hey, it turns out Tamara is okay with my, er, calling. I thought she wouldn't want to be with me if I was all, like, starting stuff. But she said it was okay."

"That is good. I imagine it will reduce the amount of pointless complaining you engage in, which I count as a victory for me and all of your friends and acquaintances."

"Yeah."

Wei Li's eyes flickered to a screen on her desk, then back to Rohan. "If that is all, I have work to catch up on. I have done very little of it this week. For obvious reasons."

"Yeah. One thing."

"What is it, Rohan?"

"Since you're a superhero now—"

"Always was."

"Yeah, but since you're a Power now."

"Yes?"

"Want to help me change the world?"

She stared at him for two long breaths.

"I am beholden to Wistful, Rohan."

"What does that mean?"

"I am to be her Shield."

"Ah." He sighed and sagged back into the chair. "That sounds like a no. You need to protect the station, while I . . ."

She shook her head. "It is not that simple. The word 'shield' is not passive in the Lifter language the way it is in Drachna. Especially the form of the word that is actually in the full prophecy."

"I see. No, actually, I don't."

"A better metaphorical translation of 'shield' might be 'hand.' The word is active. The subject of a sentence."

"So your role isn't to protect Wistful exactly. It's to be her . . . her tool."

"Yes."

"To do what she asks you to do."

"Yes."

He cleared his throat. "Then I'm not asking the right person, am I?"

"I do not think so."

He sat up and projected his voice. "Hey, Wistful. Want to help me change the world?"

He and Wei Li watched each other while they waited for a response.

Rohan was about to stand when the station interrupted him.

"That sounds interesting."

THE END

The *Hybrid Helix* continues in *Shield of The Mothership*

What's Next

The adventures of Rohan and company will continue in the next turn of the Hybrid Helix, Return of The Griffin.

If you enjoyed this book, please review it on Amazon and/or Goodreads and tell your friends about it! They'll enjoy it, and you'll seem cool and smart to have done so.

Please also go to jcmberne.com and sign up for the Book Berne-ing newsletter, read JCM's blog, and find other amusing things. Follow JCM on the social media platform of your choice! Links at his website.

The Hybrid Helix:
Arc One: Platinum
Wistful Ascending
Return of The Griffin
Blood Reunion
Shadow of Hyperion
Eyes of Empire
Arc Two:
Suppression of Powers

Also by JCM Berne:
Partial Function

www.ingramcontent.com/pod-product-compliance
Lightning Source LLC
Chambersburg PA
CBHW050023030726
47506CB00001B/89

9 781961 805064